The
Sun City
Cannabis
Club

The Metamorphosis of a Mature Woman

Amentine Duryea

OKEY
DOKEY
PRESS

Sun City, Arizona
www.okeydokeypress.com

Okey Dokey Press, LLC
13618 N. 99th Ave. #570
Sun City, AZ 85351
www.okeydokeypress.com

This book is a work of fiction. All names, characters, businesses, organizations and events are either the product of the author's imagination or are used fictitiously, unless reference is made to a person or event in actual historical context.

This book does not dispense medical advice or prescribe the use of any techniques, medicines or psychoactive plants as a form of treatment for physical, mental or medical problems without the advice of a physician either directly or indirectly. In the event you use any of the information in this book for yourself, the author and publisher assume no responsibility for your actions.

ISBN 0-9766111-9-8
First Edition

Cover and book design: 1106 Design

Dedicated to
the curiosity in exploration

Acknowledgements

The publisher would like to thank
four wonderful ladies
for their assistance
and support ...
Marcia Schafer of Beyond Zebra
(beyondzebra.com),
Michele DeFilippo of 1106 Design
(1106design.com),
Kate von Seeburg of K8 and Company

and Diane.

When one smokes marijuana,
one's eyes become bloodshot,
one's appetite increases,
one's mouth becomes dry,
and one becomes mildly euphoric.
To eliminate the redness,
use eye drops.
To eliminate the increase in appetite,
have a healthy, nutritious snack.
To eliminate the dryness of the mouth,
drink some pure, cool water.
To eliminate the mild euphoria,
scrutinize the government.

— Marian Higgins,
at Max Yasger's Farm, Bethel, NY,
August 16, 1969

Foundation

• • • • • • • •

Arrival In Sun City

Thursday, June 12, 1997

Picture yourself in a car on a highway. Imagine that it's 1959 and you're motoring in an easterly direction on U.S. Route 60, twenty-five miles west of Phoenix. You are about to pass through the town of Marinette, home to a community of migrant workers who tend the local fields and orange groves. It consists of two general stores and a gas station. Here it comes—don't blink! There it goes.

But thirtysomething years later, Marinette was the geographic center of Sun City, Arizona, the most successful retirement community in the world, according to the brochure she was reading, and boasting of a population of 46,000 retirees…soon to be 46,002.

Her name was McRae. She called herself Faye, but everyone knew her as "Nancy." She and her husband, Edwin, were on the same U.S. Route 60, enroute from San Diego and approaching Sun City.

The day glared at them through the windshield like a solid wall of bright. The air conditioner labored to keep them cool in their prize, customized, "chopped and channeled" 1940 Ford coupe. Edwin had always said the Ford was the finest customized car ever to emerge from McRae's Custom Car Garage. *Why, oh why,* she thought, *did we have to move in June, when it was already so hot?* The heat would only be something else Edwin could complain about.

"Here's something interesting," she said, referring to an Arizona booklet she had purchased before they left. "It says here there are over 60,000 abandoned mines in Arizona, some of them as much as a mile deep. Gold, copper, my—all kinds of things mined in this state."

"Great," he growled. "Something for you to fall into. I'm warning you, Nancy, you break a hip and it's the nursing home for you. I am not taking care of a crippled old lady."

She sighed, but so quietly he wouldn't hear. How long had it been since they shared an actual conversation? Now, everything she said, no matter how innocuous, seemed to be another excuse for him to aim a barb at her.

"Here's our turn coming up," she warned him.

They turned left and she watched Edwin squint as he threaded his way down the thoroughfare filled with an eclectic assortment of cars intermixed with golf carts. "Look at all these old geezers," he snorted. "No wonder your uncle moved here...so he could be with his own kind!"

Faye wasn't sure if she was glad Edwin had started talking. Between the monotonous desert landscape, and Edwin's habit of driving in silence, the ride from San Diego had been a long one. He didn't even allow the radio, which he said distracted him. She had occupied herself with the brochures that the Sun City Home-owners' Association had sent them, and the map showing the location of the house her Uncle Fred had bequeathed them. The clusters of hot-air balloons that drifted through the clear desert sky provided her only out-of-car entertainment.

She jumped as the car horn blasted, and Edwin abruptly changed lanes to dart past one of the golf carts. It was odd seeing them on the street, with license plates and all, just as if they were real cars. The heavyset woman driving it glared at them as they passed. "Slow the hell down!" she yelled, loud enough to be heard through the closed windows.

"Lose weight!" Edwin yelled back, cutting in front of her and continuing east. "Nancy, cigarettes."

She retrieved the package from the glove compartment, extracted two, pushed in the cigarette lighter, placed one in her mouth and handed one to Edwin in a smooth, practiced motion. "Faye," she sighed to herself, for the millionth time. She had coined the name, Faye, as a child, hating the way her overbearing mother ordered her around with "Nancy, this" and "Nancy, that." Nevertheless, Edwin had always insisted on calling her Nancy.

The cigarette lighter popped out and Edwin lit up, then replaced it, pushing it back in for his wife. He inhaled deeply, emitting blue smoke as he said, "Son-of-a-bitch. Why the hell did he leave us this place, anyway? No one else wanted it, that's why!"

"He had no other family," Faye pointed out.

"Maybe we can sell it."

"They have good doctors here," she said. "They helped Uncle Fred a lot, and you do need to get your liver looked at. Here, this is Del Webb Boulevard coming up. Turn right, here."

"Fat lot of good they did him. He's dead." But Faye knew the grumbling was just for show. Edwin had decided to make this move months before they left San Diego.

The road was wide, four lanes divided by a row of palm trees. It was named, so the brochure said, after the visionary who had thought to create a retirement community here. "What a wonderful contribution," she added.

"Are you kidding?" Edwin snarled. "He found a way to fill a whole town with a single demographic just so he could play them like a fiddle. Look at this! Churches, doctors offices, more doctors offices, dentists, banks. How convenient! Get all the old farts in one place so you can milk their last dollars from them!"

"It would be convenient to be able to walk to the doctor's office," she pointed out. "Healthier, too."

"In one-hundred-ten degrees? *You* walk. I'll drive in my nice, air conditioned car."

She pointed to one of the homes on the right. "Here," she said. "This is the one."

"I *know* which one it is," Edwin snarled, pulling into the driveway. He turned off the engine and, opening the doors, they got out into a blast furnace of a day. It was so hot he seemed to stagger.

"Are you all right, dear?" she asked solicitously.

He grunted in response. "Just give me the damn keys so we can get inside."

It wasn't much cooler inside, but they found the thermostat and turned on the air conditioning, and shortly the temperature approached bearable.

The house seemed odd. Fred was gone, and yet he wasn't. Uncle Fred had been her favorite relative, and this had been his house for twenty years. She had visited only a few times, but it had been fun to sit in the front room with its green, overstuffed furniture and listen to her uncle's tales of being in the Merchant Marines. True, the visits became sadder in the later years, as Fred complained of failing health and the loss of his friends, one by one, to old age. It was as though he had gone to the store and would soon be back. Everything was in its place, perfectly neat, "ship-shape" as he had called it. No doubt he had tidied up before leaving for the hospital, on what was to be his last visit. Even his refrigerator seemed ready for visitors, only the milk having soured in the weeks since his death.

The liquor cabinet was well stocked, and Edwin drank a toast or two to their deceased benefactor, and even though he referred to her uncle as "that sonofabitch," she hoped his heart was in the right place.

That night, in Uncle Fred's double bed, she found herself listening for his return, but all she heard was the incessant hum of the air conditioning, and the gentle *whoosh-whoosh-whoosh* of the ceiling fan.

At Uncle Fred's House

Friday, June 13, 1997

After a breakfast of frozen waffles and coffee, they began the job of going through Fred's personal effects. In addition to the furniture, which they decided to keep ("It's crap, but why pay good money to ship our stuff, which is also crap?" as Edwin put it), there were souvenirs from around the world, and nearly twenty albums of photographs. While Edwin criticized the knick-knacks, she sipped a gin-and-tonic and went through the albums. Most of the photos were yellowed, black-and-white prints that curled away from the page, the dried glue of the ancient corner tabs insufficient to keep them in place. They were pictures of men, mostly, in uniform, arms draped around each other's shoulders, daffy expressions on their faces, cigarettes hanging from their grins, standing in front of the Eiffel Tower or some arch, somewhere, or palm trees, or exotic stores with unreadable signs in strange letters.

Very few of them included Uncle Fred, who had, presumably, operated the camera. None of them included her, or anyone else she knew. As she closed the cover of the final album, she realized she held the sum of a man's life…a life enjoyed, perhaps, but that now had come to nothing, like tears in the rain. Uncle Fred's memories meant nothing to her, nothing to anyone. The albums were just so much landfill.

Meanwhile, Edwin, moistening his dry throat with one Scotch after another, had taken the exotic decorations that annoyed him the most into the garage, where he tossed them noisily into the large, wheeled, garbage receptacle. He scooped Fred's clothes out of his closet and dresser and threw them away. And so, by the end of their first full day, the house had been stripped to mere furniture, and it no longer seemed as if Uncle Fred, her favorite and only remaining relative, would ever return.

A few days were spent finding the nearest grocery store with a well-stocked liquor section, the nearest video rental shop, and the nearest discount department store. Faye had a list of activities suitable for people their age, from one of the brochures the Homeowners' Association had sent; but Edwin wasn't interested in any of them. "I had to go to the damn garage every damn day till I sold it," he said. "My plan now is to sit right here on my ass."

UPS delivered the trunks from San Diego, and while she organized their clothes and personal items, Edwin listened to

Rush Limbaugh on the radio. Uncle Fred had had two dressers, a highboy and a lowboy, just as they had owned back in San Diego. She put her foldable clothes into the lowboy and Edwin's into the highboy, everything right where he would be able to find it.

That included the ghastly knee-high argyle socks he had never worn, but purchased and saved because he planned to dress as the golfer Payne Stewart, in case they were ever invited to a masquerade party. They were placed carefully near the back of the top drawer where they served as a cover for the Smith & Wesson .44 magnum pistol Edwin had purchased after watching *Dirty Harry*. There'd been a robbery at Edwin's garage, and all the cash had been stolen from one of his clerks; after firing the hapless employee, Edwin kept the weapon behind the counter. After he sold the garage, Edwin took the gun home and kept it under his argyle socks. And so, there it was, loaded, even now that they were in Sun City and not San Diego.

Faye tried to ignore it.

First Day Out

Monday, June 23, 1997

Edwin developed a fever, and Faye forced him to see a doctor. He complained the whole time they sat in the waiting room. He did not allow her to go in with him. Afterwards, when she asked what the doctor had said, he growled. "Goddamn it, Nancy!" he said. "They want tests. Always, tests. It's just a way to surgically separate us from our money."

"Did he give you a prescription?" she asked. Edwin begrudgingly held out a slip.

He complained again, loudly, when they picked up the medicine at the pharmacy in Smith's at Grand and 107th Avenue. "*How much?*" he repeatedly asked the pharmacist. But she paid the money and made him take the pills, and, in a few days, his temperature returned to normal, although there was still a yellowish cast to his eyes that she didn't like.

His temperature having returned to normal, Edwin decided it was now time to go exploring. There was a restaurant not far from Uncle Fred's—their—house that always seemed to be busy. "Look at all the old farts," Edwin had said. "Place can't be expensive if those cheap sons-of-bitches always want to eat there." So, now he decided they would visit for lunch.

It was called Tivoli Gardens, for no obvious reason, and was dark and cool inside. Edwin took no time at all to locate the bar, and they sat at a small table adjacent to it; he with his first Scotch, she with her first gin-and-tonic, smoking and waiting for their food to arrive.

There were others in the room, and everyone seemed to know each other. "Just like I figured," Edwin groused. "They're all in cliques, and we'll have a devil of a time fitting in." However, the couple at the table next to theirs smiled, and the man extended his hand.

"Hi," the husband said. "I'm Steve Beehler, and this is my wife, Doris. We're betting you're new to Sun City."

They shook hands. Edwin introduced himself, "Edwin McRae. This is my wife, Nancy."

My name is Faye, she reminded herself again. But she smiled and said, "Nice to meet you."

"So, how do you know we're new here?" Edwin asked.

"Easy," Steve chuckled. "No tan. Here, you wind up with a tan just going for groceries. You're from back East?"

"No, we moved here from San Diego."

"Really!" Doris Beehler responded, surprised. "Didn't you spend time at the beach?"

"Filthy water," Edwin snorted.

"We just don't care for the sun," Nancy explained.

"We like the sun just fine," Edwin contradicted. "It's the outside air that's disgusting." He ground his cigarette butt into the ashtray, and lit another. "The pollution'll kill you. That's why we moved here."

"The air isn't always so clean here, either, I'm afraid," Steve grimaced. "It was, ten years ago, but there's been so much development here in the Valley and there's too many cars, and the smog and dust can get pretty bad."

"Valley?" Faye asked.

"That's what we call the greater Phoenix area," Doris explained. "There are mountains on all four sides of us, so we call it the Valley."

"*That's* not a valley," Edwin declared, now on his third Scotch. "A valley lies between two mountains in the same range. *Everybody* knows that."

"That may be," Steve said, "but we call it the Valley, anyway."

"Well, that's just stupid," Edwin frowned.

There was a pause, then Steve laughed. "Well," he said. "It was nice meeting you," and his wife echoed the sentiment with, "Very nice. We hope you enjoy Sun City."

Then they turned back to their drinks, and Edwin stage whispered, "See? What did I tell you? Cliques! And stupid cliques, at that!"

At The Shooting Range

Thursday, July 10, 1997

Other than her shopping, it was another two weeks before they attempted another foray into the outside world. Edwin abruptly decided it was time that "Nancy" learn to fire his Smith & Wesson.

"But I don't want to!" she protested.

"It's not like you need to *use* it," he told her, "but you should know how. Suppose, someday, you decide you need it. Maybe someone breaks into the house. Maybe they kill me, and are going to rape you! You'd be mighty glad to know how to handle the thing."

And so Edwin called for directions to the shooting range, wrapped the Smith & Wesson in a towel and placed it and three boxes of cartridges in the trunk of the car. "Shake it, Nancy!" he called as she closed the house. "I want to get there before it hits a hundred and fucking ten degrees!"

A half hour later they found themselves parking at the Ben Avery Shooting Range, the air filled with the cracks and pops of firing guns and the dust kicked up by their arrival. "They call this the 'Valley of the Sun,'" Edwin grouched as he opened the trunk of the car. "They should've called it the Valley of the Dust!" He chuckled at his own joke.

Edwin paid their fee, they watched the obligatory safety film, they were given protective earpieces and assigned a slot on the firing line.

"Now, pay attention, Nancy—"

Faye!

"—while I show how this is done." He loaded the massive revolver and assumed the combat position she had seen in countless movies, crouched over, knees slightly bent, arms extended forward and both hands supporting the weapon. Then he pulled the trigger.

The *boom!* went through her bones. The intensity was so unexpected because the other guns on the range just went *bang* in a way that her earpieces made tolerable. But now, she saw the other shooters on the range leaning back and looking around to see who had the cannon.

The first shot was followed by five more thunderous reports and Edwin retrieved the target. All six shots were in or near the bull's-eye.

"Here ya go, Nancy," said Edwin as he handed her the weapon.

Her hands sagged under the unexpected weight of the thing. She had never before held it, or any gun, for that matter, yet it felt alive, like holding a mad cat that might bite at any second. Under Edwin's guidance, she held it out as he had, in both hands, holding herself as steady as possible yet unable to keep her arms from trembling. She pointed it at the target, which seemed to dance crazily beyond the front sight of the wobbling gun. Heart pounding, she jerked the trigger, and staggered backward from the violent kick and roar of the weapon.

The target hung there, fifty feet away, untouched.

She wanted to stop then, but Edwin insisted; her next five shots produced the same result.

Edwin scowled, yet somehow seemed satisfied.

The Swimming Suit

Tuesday, July 22, 1997

On her shopping trips, she often passed one of the larger recreation centers. She knew it had a pool, and facilities for exercise, pottery making, and other crafts. The place was always busy, and she found herself wondering what it would be like to go there and have a swim.

One Tuesday, on her way to do her grocery shopping, she took a detour to Wal-Mart and bought a swimming suit. The purchase seemed so daring to her that she could scarcely catch her breath. When she came home, Edwin demanded to know what had taken her so long, and she quickly hid the suit in the dishwasher before putting away the food. It was days later before she had a chance to try it on. She looked at herself in the full-length mirror Uncle Fred had fastened to the back of the bedroom door. It fit, though she wasn't happy with what she saw. The years had not been good to her. A hundred pounds overweight, hair more gray than brown, gray eyes more watery than lustrous. She took off the suit and poured herself another gin-and-tonic, and sipped it while wondering where her youth had gone.

Sunday, July 27, 1997

A few days later, when she had managed to get Edwin into the car with her, she daringly pulled into the parking lot of the Lakeview Recreation Center. "What are we doing here?" he growled, suspiciously.

"I heard there's a cute little bar here," she said. "I'm hot. Wouldn't you like a drink?"

That got him out of the car, and they walked up the ramp to an outdoor mezzanine overlooking the pool. Rooms surrounding the mezzanine offered Yoga classes, aerobics, and more. "I don't see any bar," Edwin said.

"The woman at the grocery store said there was one," she fibbed. "But look at that pool! Isn't it wonderful?" She pointed past the railing, to the enormous blue where people swam, and even seemed to frolic.

"Looks like an elephant graveyard," Edwin snorted. "Look at them! Thank God *you* don't try to put on a swim suit. We'd be the laughing stock of Sun City."

The next day she returned the swimsuit to Wal-Mart.

Suicide

Monday, July 28, 1997

And the day after that, Edwin shot himself.

She was in the kitchen, pouring the Scotch Edwin asked for. Looking back, that seemed odd, because Edwin normally made his own drinks—one of the few things he did for himself, other than lighting his cigarettes. But she was pouring the drink when she heard the *boom* of the Smith & Wesson, just as it had sounded at the shooting range, except louder and deadlier and more awful than any noise she had ever heard. She stood there, frozen, in the echoes of that awful noise, holding the glass in her left hand and the bottle in her right, knowing in her heart what had happened but not willing to admit it.

"Edwin?" she quavered. "Are you all right?"

There was no answer, and dread welled up in her, starting at her stomach and clutching at her heart and ripping at her throat. She put the glass on the counter, screwed the cap back on the bottle, and put it back in the liquor cabinet. She walked slowly, placing one foot in front of the other, into the living room where Edwin had been. He wasn't there. Heart pounding, lips quivering, she lurched into the bedroom.

He was on the floor, face up. His eyes were open. His mouth was an angry chasm of red. Bloody tissue surrounded his head like a halo.

The wall behind where he must have been standing was splattered with blood and brains and riddled with bone.

The grip of the Smith & Wesson protruded from under him.

Clutching at her stomach, she returned to the kitchen. Every step was a nightmare, as if she were walking through quicksand up to her knees. She retrieved the bottle from the cabinet, doubled Edwin's Scotch, and then drank it, although she detested Scotch. When she was through, she picked up the phone and dialed 911.

The next days were a blur of ambulances, policemen, and funeral directors. She saw them parade past her through a haze composed of equal parts grief and gin. She tried to cry but couldn't. Waves of pain cramped through her and she spent hours doubled up on the bed.

She had no relatives and Edwin had only a sister, Karen, in Indiana. She hazily remembered calling, but Karen could offer no more than sympathy and an excuse for not being able to make it to Arizona for the funeral.

And so, the new Widow McRae found herself at the Sunland Funeral Home, alone with Edwin's body. The casket was closed; there had been too much damage to make him presentable. Faye sat, staring at the coffin, until it became unbearable; she returned home and finished the bottle of gin, then the bottle of Scotch. She wasn't present when Edwin's casket was lowered into the ground at the cemetery. Since no one else was there, she imagined it as an efficient procedure, like disposing of nuclear waste.

Weeks passed, weeks of blackness and despair. Among the things shipped from San Diego had been their photo albums; now she found herself, once again, perusing the images of days gone by, days that had meant something to Edwin and her, but now only meant something to her, and soon would mean nothing to anyone. Not even Edwin's sister would be interested in the photos of the places they had visited or the people they had known.

Like Uncle Fred's photos, they, too, were no more than landfill.

Like Edwin was, now. Landfill.

Like she would be, too, someday.

One day, a police officer arrived with a box. "The investigation is over," the officer said. "We don't need your husband's gun anymore. Would you like it back? We can dispose of it for you, if you like."

She opened the box and stared at the dull gleam of metal. "It's Edwin's." She led the policeman to the bedroom. "It goes in his top drawer, under these awful argyle socks..." And she found herself telling the officer about the proposed masquerade costume, and that Edwin had never actually worn it, and then she found herself sinking to the floor, sobbing so hard she couldn't breathe; the officer caught her and carried her back to the sofa, held her hand and comforted her.

When the officer left, the widow was alone, facing the blankness of her soul, and the blackness of her life, alone in the house with her cigarettes and her liquor and Edwin's Smith & Wesson.

And in the morning, when she arose from the floor next to the sofa, head pounding, stomach churning, still drunk, she ricocheted against the walls of the long hallway as she walked to the bedroom.

She took the Smith & Wesson from the sock drawer, sat on the edge of the bed with the gun in her lap, and stared at it. She imagined the last instant of Edwin's life. Was he despairing? Did he feel as hollow as she now did? Were his hands shaking?

The Smith & Wesson had been returned unloaded, but she knew where Edwin kept the bullets. She selected one, hesitated, inserted it, and spun the cylinder. Then, hands shaking, she put the barrel in her mouth, as Edwin had done. *Will I see a flash?* She wondered. She pulled the trigger, but the hammer slammed down on an empty chamber.

Reaching back with difficulty, she poked the barrel under her chin. *Maybe I'll hear that* boom *before my brain explodes?* Her finger tightened on the trigger, but again, all she heard was the snap of the hammer.

Somehow, she knew the chamber with the bullet was now in position. The next pull of the trigger would be her last.

She held the Smith & Wesson to her temple. Tears flowing down her cheeks, she pulled the trigger one final time.

Snap! And…nothing.

She had been married for all those years, and now had nothing! How fair was that? And now, *nothing* was what she wanted. Anything but this terrible pain in her gut, this agony of living, the terror of having to go on without the man who did everything for her. Who even *thought* for her.

She continued sobbing, dropped the revolver, fell onto the bed and began to wail.

Death of a Princess

Sunday, August 31, 1997

For weeks after Edwin's death, weeks of black days and blacker nights, Faye did little but stare at the blank screen of her uncle's TV set. It was an older model, probably one of the first color sets manufactured. It had a fine wooden cabinet and a round picture tube. Faye's uncle had never had much time for the "boob tube" as he called it. But Faye decided that, today, maybe the sound of human voices would cheer her a little. At least, it would *sound* as though there were life in the house. And so, she turned the TV on.

It took a few minutes to warm up. She was so unused to this phenomenon, that at first she thought the set was broken. But then, with a flash, it warmed up. On display was a female news anchor.

"—the tragic news," she was reporting. "All we know for certain is that Diana, Princess of Wales, has been killed in a car accident in a Paris tunnel. Our Paris correspondent is ready with a report. Jacques, what can you tell us?"

Faye was stunned. What *else* had been going on in the world while she'd been in shock, in mourning?

And Princess Di! Her marriage to Prince Charles had been one of the highpoints of Faye's life. She had been terribly disappointed by Charles' affair with that Camilla woman. Deprived of a meaningful life of her own, Faye realized, she had become involved in the life of a celebrity. Diana had been so beautiful, so vibrant! To be a kindergarten teacher who marries a prince, well, it was just a fairy tale come true!

But now, to have it all end in tragedy...Faye followed the story, rapt, as the commentator brought on reporter after reporter to share the details of Diana's last ride. It seemed there was no shortage of sordid little details. Diana had been riding with a boyfriend, some Egyptian man. Seeing pictures of the two of them together, his dark skin against her pale skin, didn't seem right, somehow. And, even if she was divorced, she shouldn't be unfaithful to her ex-husband! It was a matter of being a good example to her children, and to the millions of children around the world who loved her.

Somehow, allowing herself deeper tears for the princess than she had felt for Edwin helped purge her of the last of her grief. She knew some tears remained, but somehow felt that the worst was over.

"...chased down by paparazzi," the anchorwoman said, mournfully. "A tragic end to a fairy tale life. This is Audrey Flowers, Channel 2 News."

Recreation Center

Sunday, August 31, 1997

A month after Edwin's non-funeral, she realized she hadn't cried out loud for a day, and needed to get out of the house. Grant, the nice police detective who had returned Edwin's revolver, had come by to make sure she was all right, and had brought some groceries. But now, they were gone. Besides, the liquor bottles were empty and she had smoked the last cigarette in the house.

The car was still in the driveway where she had left it when she returned from the funeral home. She stepped out the front door, and locked it. That seemed strange. Not having been out for so long, she wasn't even sure whether the door had been locked all this time or not. She felt as if she were stepping out of a mausoleum.

Everything looked surreal. The day was so bright, her eyes hurt.

She drove to the supermarket, bought cigarettes and gin, and returned to her car. Hands trembling, she lit up and took a couple of swigs of gin directly from the bottle. As the warmth penetrated her gut, she relaxed a bit, capped the bottle, and started up the car.

She found herself at the Lakeview Recreation Center.

She found herself at the second floor railing, overlooking the pool.

Ten or fifteen women were in the pool, doing some sort of water ballet. At first, she thought they were doing water aerobics, but this was more graceful, more like something from an Esther Williams movie. She watched, fascinated. They looked like angels, like they were flying.

There were tables placed here and there on the upper terrace, serviced by a waiter from a small café located on that floor. She realized she recognized one of the women sitting with two others, though she couldn't quite recall where they might have met. Maybe the grocery store? She smiled and approached the woman she recognized, who smiled back.

"Hello, I'm sorry, I can't quite remember where we've met," she said. "I'm Faye McRae."

"Doris Beehler," the woman said. "We met at Tivoli Gardens months ago. You were with your husband...but I thought your name was Nancy?"

"No," she said, firmly, surprised at her own audacity. "My name is *Faye*. My husband...passed away."

The other ladies murmured their condolences. Doris said, "I read about it in the paper. It must have been so awful for you."

Faye, flushing slightly, said, "I'd rather not talk about it."

"So sad," one of the women smiled sympathetically. "My husband passed away five years ago. It never really goes away, either." The woman extended her hand. "I'm Alice, Alice Martin. Formerly Mrs. Martin, now one of the man hungry widows of Sun City."

The third woman put down her knitting and also offered a hand. Faye forced herself to refocus from the woman's enormous breasts to accept it. "Vera Daye," the woman said. "Also widowed. But it *does* go away," she added, "if you keep yourself busy. Find things to do. And there's plenty of things to do around here!"

Doris grimaced. "Vera is a joiner. If I was as busy as her, I'd have collapsed *years* ago!"

Vera continued, "You can take pottery classes, aerobics, we have literary clubs, foreign film clubs—any interest you have, there's a class or a club for it!"

Faye thought, and realized she had no interests...except maybe, for—

"How about those ladies swimming down there? Who are they?"

"Those are the AquaBabes," Alice laughed. "They live to swim and perform. They put on a show now and again. They're rehearsing, now."

A sudden *sproing* sound caught everyone's attention. The pool was large, and at the far end was a three-meter diving board. In mid-air, suspended above it, a woman bent, touched hands to toes, snapped straight, then slipped into the water without the smallest splash. A perfect dive.

"That's the first young person I've seen here," Faye commented.

"Her? She's not young!" Doris snorted. "Watch her come out of the water!"

Sure enough, when the dark shadow of the diver emerged at the side of the pool, the face belonged to an older woman, much older than Faye, but possessed of a much younger body. She was lithe, slim, with tight muscles. She walked like a dancer, with grace and deliberation.

She returned to the diving board, climbed the ladder effortlessly, strode to the end of the diving board, and flew into the air like a bird. She balled up, rolled once, and straightened a bare instant before entering the water, in another perfect dive.

Faye found her spirits lifted just by watching her.

If only she could do such a thing! To break the bonds of gravity, to soar like a bird into the sky and then to plunge into the cool water!

The last time she, a shy teenager, dove into the water seemed so distant as to have happened on some other planet.

And she had gotten heavier and more fearful ever since.

"Who is she?" Faye asked. "Do you know? Is she someone famous?"

Doris and Alice both looked at Vera. "She's *your* friend," Doris said.

Vera smiled. "Her name is Marian Higgins. She's not famous, but she's the most *alive* person I've ever met."

Doris snorted. "The most *annoying* person, I think. Never content, always wanting to *change* things."

Vera grinned. "Wanting to change things that need changing."

And, a few moments later, Marian herself, now wearing a T-shirt over her swim suit and drying her hair with a towel, approached the table with a white bundle in one hand. "Hello, Marian," Vera said.

"Hello, darling!" the older woman said, her voice strong, yet musical. "Here's your T-shirt."

"Marian makes homemade T-shirts," Doris whispered to Faye. "She airbrushes them herself."

The older woman held up the shirt. On it was written, "In a democracy, it's your responsibility to think for yourself!"

"That's perfect!" said Vera. "My nephew will *love* it!" When Marian handed the shirt to Vera, Faye read the lettering on the shirt Marian was wearing: "Question Authority".

Doris read it, too. "Marian, some of us think authority should be *respected,* not questioned. Or do you want the sixties back again? Riots, hippies, that rock music…ugh!"

"Darling, if we don't question authority, we'll wind up in a world where seventy percent of the assets belong to one percent of the people," Marian stated, gazing steadily into Doris's eyes.

"Well, that's the way it *is*, isn't it!" Vera exclaimed.

Doris snorted again, but Faye barely noticed. Marian had looked at her, and Faye found herself falling into the woman's eyes. Bloodshot from the chlorine, they were, nevertheless, a brilliant blue that reflected the sky and the pool and seemed to reach into her soul. It seemed as if Faye *knew* her, somehow, although she was certain they had never met.

It was almost as if Faye recognized in Marian another version of herself, one who might have blossomed but had instead been squelched.

Then, with a smile for Vera and a knowing grin for Faye, Marian nodded curtly to Doris and Alice, turned on her heel and sashayed away.

Acknowledgement

Accident

That night, as Faye lay beneath the ceiling fan on the bed in what had been Uncle Fred's bedroom, and then hers and Edwin's, and now hers alone, she smiled, thinking of what had happened, her first good day since Edwin's death.

It was a turning point. She no longer thought of herself as a non-person, someone struggling to *not* be Nancy. Now she could be herself. She could be Faye.

She had introduced herself to people as Faye, and been accepted. Accepted!

As she fell asleep, an odd thought seemed to leach from some-where beneath her consciousness. This had been her first good day since her *marriage* to Edwin...

Sunday, September 7, 1997

In the morning, she awoke with an odd, hollow feeling in her stomach. It wasn't the dull sense of grief that had lived there since Edwin's death; she knew what that was. This was something else.

She had some gin to make it go away. When that didn't work, she decided to drive to the rec center, in hopes her new friends were there. She got into her car, backed out of the garage and into the street. Almost instantly there was a screech of tires and a horn blast, and a sharp jolt as something hit the rear of her car.

Shaking, she turned off the engine and jumped out to apologize to the driver of the other car, an older man with a thundercloud of an expression. "What the hell do you think you're doing?" he cried angrily. "Didn't it even occur to you to look before backing out?"

"I'm—I'm so sorry!" she said. "I—my husband just died, and I—"

"I don't care if you just died," the man growled. "Who's going to fix my headlight? I hope you have insurance!"

"I do," Faye said, hoping she did. That was the sort of thing that Edwin had managed.

"Well, let me see your license and insurance information," he said. "I've got paper and a pen."

It took a moment to find the insurance card in the glove compartment of the Ford. Her license was handy, but as she handed it to the man, she realized the car was registered to Edwin and *Nancy* McRae.

When he was gone, she pulled back into the driveway. Her right rear fender, one Edwin had polished with passion, was caved in, and the rear bumper was badly bent.

If Edwin were alive, he would have killed her.

She returned to the cool of her house, and had another gin…and then, another. The sense of triumph was gone, and that odd, hollow feeling was stronger than ever.

When the shaking stopped, she realized that if she were to succeed in *being* Faye, she would have to make it official, on her license and everything else.

It took a few moments, in her alcoholic fog, to locate the phone number of Gary Minors, her late uncle's lawyer and executor of his will. She explained drunkenly what she wanted and he offered to draw up the papers. "It will be about three months before the hearing can take place," he explained, "but people change their names all the time; it's routine and there won't be any problem."

Hanging up, Faye smiled to herself. That hollow feeling had eased She had *chased* it away by doing something for herself—and that was a first!

At the Courthouse

Monday, September 22, 1997

Two weeks later, the Ford repaired and humming nicely, Faye drove to the county courthouse to meet with Gary Minors and file the papers. The sun was bright, as always; it was hot, but not unbearably so—perhaps Faye was acclimating to the climate. She felt wonderfully independent. She was doing something for herself!

The courthouse parking lot was packed, and a Channel 2 news truck was there. Approaching the entrance, Faye saw a crowd gathered around a TV reporter and a man in a suit. She realized she hadn't seen anyone in a suit since moving to Sun City—the heat, presumably, made them impractical. Nevertheless, this man, who had a great, booming voice, wore one.

"…is the *center* of this immoral and dangerous behavior," he was saying.

"But many doctors advocate the medicinal use of marijuana, in cases like glaucoma, AIDS, and cancer," the reporter responded.

"The drug pushers are *everywhere*," the man claimed, darkly. "Wherever you find some seemingly innocent person suggesting that marijuana use might be all right, there you find one of Satan's lackeys, trying his best to corrupt our children and, yes, even our senior citizens…"

Faye threaded herself through the edges of the crowd, finally making her way to the door, and entered the courthouse. Inside, it was cool and dark, a large room with stairways and artwork, like the lobby of a grand, old hotel. Near a window, she saw her attorney sitting on a bench next to a statue of a Hopi Indian. Spotting her, he rose and waved.

"What's that going on outside?" she asked, after shaking hands.

"That's Representative Meany," he responded.

"Meany?" Faye asked.

"Yes, one of our congressmen in Washington," he explained. "Surely you've heard of him; they say he will be running for president next year."

"No, I hadn't," Faye replied. "But it sounds like he's against drugs, and that's good."

"His first campaign was based almost entirely on keeping marijuana illegal," the attorney agreed. "It looks like he's going to continue with that approach for his re-election."

"Well, good for him!" Faye applauded. "I can't think of anything that makes me more upset than the idea of people trying to escape reality."

Looking at his watch, Minors said, "Maybe we should get on with the filing. The department we want is just upstairs."

Volunteer

That night, she turned the TV on to Channel 2 and, sure enough, the reporter's interview with the representative was the opening story.

"Carvel Meany," the reporter intoned. "Running for re-election to the House of Representatives. But will he serve his whole term...or start campaigning for president in the middle? That's the question that has his whole district abuzz..."

The picture changed to that of a couple being interviewed. "We like him," the man said. "He worked for us the last four years, and if we only get half of his term this time around, it'd be worth it."

The next interviewee was an older woman. "Drugs are evil," she snapped. "Representative Meany is working to keep them off the streets. That's good enough for me. I hope he *does* run for president," she added.

"Of course, there is the usual fringe element," the reporter pointed out, as the screen showed, to Faye's astonishment, Marian Higgins, the woman she had seen diving at the Lakeview pool.

"Meany's platform is based entirely on maintaining the outmoded, unworkable, and incredibly expensive drug-law enforcement programs," Marian said. "They haven't solved the drug problem in thirty years, so why should they suddenly start working now?"

That was followed by a report about drug-runners from Mexico being captured by the DEA near the border, carrying some 200 kilos of cocaine.

"Humph! And Marian thinks drug enforcement isn't working," Faye muttered.

As she settled down for the evening, nursing gin after gin, she began to reflect on the drug problem, and how much this Representative Meany seemed to be doing about it. The thought popped into her head that maybe she could do something about it!

It was so unexpected an idea that Faye almost spilled her drink. She, Faye McRae, *do* something about a social problem? If Edwin were here, it would never have occurred to her. Edwin had always believed, and so had she, that the best way to deal with other people's problems was to avoid them altogether.

But, now…now she was a widow, and Edwin wasn't here. Maybe she should become involved in helping Congressman Meany get re-elected. If she didn't, what else *would* she do? Sit and watch TV all day until her legs atrophied so that she could no longer even get up to get a drink?

"I have to do *something*," she said aloud.

Tuesday, September 23, 1997

So, the very next day, instead of starting the day out with a drink, she got on the phone, found out where Meany's campaign headquarters was located, *then* had a drink, three Tic Tacs, drove there, and offered her help.

The headquarters was in a strip mall not far from her home. (Of course, in Sun City, *nothing* was really far from home!) It was filled, mostly with women, stuffing envelopes with promotional material. The sound of conversation enlivened the scene. The volunteers looked like they were having such fun and yet, wonder of wonders, doing good at the same time!

However, Faye was given a place next to a dour-looking gentleman she guessed was in his nineties. In front of her was a box of envelopes, an empty box, and two stacks of folded papers. She was to place one copy of each paper into an envelope, and fill the empty box with the filled envelopes. Each envelope didn't take much time, and soon the empty box was filled, taken away, and replaced with another empty box by a roving someone whose job it was to do just that.

The task quickly became routine and Faye's thoughts wandered. *A gin and tonic would certainly make this job go easier!* she thought. She considered bringing some, perhaps in one of those sports bottles, the next day.

"Isn't it good to have a purpose?" she blurted to the man next to her.

"My grandson was killed in a drug raid," he said. "He was running heroin. I've *got* a goddamned purpose!"

"I'm—I'm sorry," she said, flushing. "I mean, we are *doing* something about it, right? Trying to keep others from falling into the trap of drugs?"

The man grunted, and continued stuffing his envelopes.

That gin-and-tonic-in-a-sports-bottle was definitely a good idea.

On the Wagon

Wednesday, September 24, 1997

And so, that evening, she bought a sports bottle on her way home and brought it with her the next morning, filled with nice refreshing gin and tonic.

It was shortly before two that afternoon when her supervisor asked her to come to her office, a smoke-filled room whose door was always closed to keep the fumes from escaping. "Rank hath its privileges," as Mrs. Graves, the supervisor, would rasp to anyone who complained that no smoking was allowed anywhere else in the headquarters. She seldom left her office since that would mean putting out her cigarette.

When Faye saw Mrs. Graves' expression, she felt a pang of anxiety.

"I don't know how to say this," the woman began. Faye always hated when conversations began that way. "But it seems you've been drinking on the job, or maybe before you got here." She then inhaled deeply of the cigarette that seemed glued to her lower lip.

Faye reddened. It had never occurred to her that anyone would catch her if she drank from a sports bottle. "I—I haven't," she stammered.

Mrs. Graves wore a grim expression. "Well, let's see. Your work yesterday was perfect, but today five out of twenty envelopes either have just one page, or two copies of the same page. Then there's the fact that you *smell* of gin. Really, Mrs. McRae!"

"I'm sorry," Faye muttered, humiliated beyond belief. "It won't happen again." *Vodka*, she told herself. *I should drink vodka.*

The supervisor coughed, took another drag, and continued. "The thing is," she rasped, "besides the fact that we have to check your work so carefully, and re-do twenty percent of it, every now and then newspaper or TV reporters show up. How would it look if the volunteers for Representative Meany were drunk on the job?"

"I'm *not* drunk!" Faye spluttered.

"That's not the point," Mrs. Graves insisted. "Representative Meany's anti-drug program includes an educational package, with six million dollars earmarked for helping people use alcohol responsibly. If reporters should get wind of this...well, it wouldn't look good."

Faye just stared, not quite comprehending what her supervisor was telling her.

"And, besides, dear," the woman continued, "I think you may have a...well, a *problem.*"

Faye was close to tears. "I'm sorry," she said. "I'll go."

"I'll get one of the workers to *drive* you home. And tomorrow, if we catch you drinking, we'll have to ask you to leave."

Tomorrow? Faye had thought she was fired! Suddenly buoyant and grateful, she held her hand out to the supervisor. "Thank you," she said. "It won't happen again, I promise!"

But, that night, in the safety of her living room, as she nursed her gin, she began to have second thoughts.

She...she couldn't possibly have a *drinking* problem, could she?

She knew she didn't. But how would it look to someone else? She simply shouldn't have taken alcohol to work. After all, she had never *had* a job before, not even a volunteer job like this one. Edwin drank beers at the auto body shop but he owned the business and could do as he goddamned pleased, as he used to say.

Suddenly, another thought popped into her head: She had been drinking when she backed into that car that damaged the Ford

Edwin had so lovingly customized. She knew the gin hadn't caused the accident, but suppose a cop had been on the scene? She would have been arrested, for certain.

A great fear grew in her chest as she thought of cutting down on her friend, Mr. Beefeater.

She was a new widow! How could she ease the pain of bereavement? How could she survive?

Of course, if one had a drinking problem, one wouldn't be able to quit drinking—and she also knew that, if she wanted to, she could stop. And so, she decided that she *would* stop, after emptying the current supply—there was no point in throwing away perfectly good gin! That would give her a chance to slowly wean herself off it.

Thursday, September 25, 1997

The next day, when she went to work, it was without even a sip of the stuff. She kept busy, making sure she got close enough so Mrs. Graves could smell her alcohol-free breath and before long, the day was over. By the time she got home, however, the stress of not drinking was added to the constant ache of loneliness, so she had two doubles before dinner instead of one. She was wobbly by bedtime and fell on the way to bed, bruising her forehead badly enough that, by morning, it looked like she had been in a fight. When people at work commented on it, she just said that she had tripped on the carpet, but inside she was more determined than ever not to drink again.

Supermarket Attack

Sunday, September 28, 1997

Getting on the wagon single-handedly was an uphill battle. Every night came the decision: Drink or no? Gin meant the evening would pass in a melancholy haze; no gin meant the interminable evening would be followed by an interminable, sleepless night. Her first weekend was the worst—Saturday, without work, was so bleak and lonely that when she finally gave in and had a drink or few, the next thing she knew it was Sunday morning and she was out of gin and everything else.

She would have to buy one more bottle…and quit after *that* was gone, she promised herself.

Still shaky from the night before, she drove to Smith's supermarket where she usually shopped. It was early, and she practically had the place to herself. There were a few other things she needed, and her shopping style was to start at aisle one and work her way to the end of the store where the liquor was. She picked up some tuna fish, a large jar of mayonnaise, a couple of bags of potato chips, sale-priced pork chops, milk, frozen orange juice, and a few other things before getting to the liquor department…

…And seeing it chained off, with a sign saying, "No Liquor Sales Before 11 AM Sunday" and, in smaller letters, "Sorry For The Inconvenience."

Faye checked her watch and found that it was 10:21 AM.

Her head pounded and her stomach was queasy. She knew a little "hair of the dog" was the only way to keep from being sick. But she also knew how resistant supermarket clerks were to selling liquor before the legal time.

Could she wander the store for forty minutes, waiting for eleven o'clock?

Her legs trembled and her stomach heaved. No, if she couldn't get that bottle of gin immediately, she would have to sit down or lie down. Pretending to shop for forty minutes was not an option.

Perhaps she should buy what she had selected, take it home, and come back for the gin but she didn't really trust herself to drive, as shaky as she was. And it was too hot outside to leave the groceries in the car, especially the pork chops.

So she returned the items needing refrigeration to the places she had gotten them, took the remaining items through the checkout stand, and sat in her car waiting for eleven o'clock.

The glare of the September sun was brutal and, added to the heat, it made her headache worse and she closed her eyes trying to soothe the pain.

It was 10:42, according to the old-fashioned, analog clock on the Ford's dashboard.

At least she wasn't the only one waiting for eleven, she thought. A few lanes over in the sparsely-populated parking lot, was a beat-up station wagon with three young men, laughing and listening to some of that horrible boom-boom-boom music the kids liked these days. Even at this distance, the booming made her head pound and she wished they would leave. But they stayed and she tried closing her eyes again, then opened them and checked the clock, hoping it was now time to go in.

10:44.

She wouldn't have to wait forever, she realized. She could enter a minute or two early, which would give her time to get the bottle. She just had to be at the *counter* no sooner than eleven.

Of course, she would need to re-collect the pork chops and milk. What if, by some incredible coincidence, Mrs. Graves, or anyone else from Carvel Meany's re-election headquarters should see her? It wouldn't do for anyone to see her buying *just* liquor on Sunday morning; it would make her look like a lush!

10:49.

10:51.

Another car pulled into the parking lot, one that caught her attention: It was a 1970 Ford Gran Torino, in awful condition, yet sounding like its motor had just been tuned. An interest in cars was one of the few things she and Edwin had in common, and Faye thought what a shame it was that someone would own such a classic car and not keep it in prime condition, outside as well as under the hood.

10:52.

Now, she thought. *I can go in, now.*

She took a deep breath, climbed out of the car, locked it, and began her unsteady trek back across the lot. She felt worse than ever. If she couldn't get a little gin into her, she knew this was going to turn into a migraine. She began to panic. *Just hold on another ten minutes*, she thought. She clutched her purse as if it was the only thing holding her up, and went on.

The boom-boom-boom continued.

Suddenly, something slammed into her, knocking her to the ground. It seemed like someone had tried to grab her purse, but she had been clinging to it too tightly and it went to the ground with her.

Two of the boys she had seen in the other car were over her, reaching for her purse. Their faces were masks of evil, expressions that put terror into her soul with their intensity and hatred.

She tried to scream but the breath had been knocked out of her. She curled up, both arms pulling the purse close, protecting her solar plexus.

"Give it up, bitch!" one of the thugs hissed.

"Now, or we'll fucking kill you!" the other growled.

It's just a purse, that voice inside her said, while she resisted losing anything else. First Edwin, then the car accident, now this…it was too much too bear.

The boys hovered over her in slow motion. Her heart pounded and, in spite of her pain, she felt surprise at the way her adrenaline rush seemed to make time stop. She wondered if she could get up and run into the safety of the store.

But before she could make a move, a blur in purple suddenly came into her field of vision. A leg pumped through the air, smashing the side of one boy's knee. He screamed as it shattered, and his leg folded grotesquely beneath him.

The other boy started toward the new threat but, before he could complete the turn, the purple blur spun, a hand flashed, chopping the boy's throat, and a knee jerked into his groin.

Both attackers writhed on the pavement, moaning.

To Faye's astonishment, the purple blur solidified into Marian Higgins, the woman from the pool!

"Are you all right, darling?" she asked, helping Faye to her feet. "Did they hurt you?"

Faye shook her head, but couldn't yet speak. Out of the corner of her eye, she saw one of the boys roll to his feet, struggling desperately to remove something from the front pocket of his ridiculously oversized jeans.

Faye gathered what was left of her strength and threw herself on him, knocking them both to the ground. There was a sudden explosion right under her, and she thought she had been shot! In a panic, she looked downward and saw that the thug's toes had been blown off his right foot.

Suddenly, there were footsteps, and shouting, and store clerk uniforms, and a big, burly man yanking the other boy to his remaining good leg, and a distant voice saying, "Thank you darling, you can let him go, now! Let go, dear. Let go."

Faye released him and allowed herself to be helped to her feet. The boy's foot was a mass of red, reminding her of Edwin's head when he shot himself. Shaking, she suddenly filled her aching chest with air, and gasped, and sobbed. Marian patted her on the back and held her comfortingly.

A few minutes later, a police car arrived, followed by an ambulance. Faye still had trouble speaking and was disturbed by the blood she knew was drying on her stockings and skirt. Fortunately, Marian was still there, and told the police what had happened. It seems Marian had pulled into the parking lot just before Faye got out of her car, and had seen the two young men leap from theirs and attack her. Their accomplice, driving the boom-boom-boom car, had peeled away when Marian caught up to the two attackers and downed them. "However, I did note his license number," she added helpfully, reciting it to the astonished officer who wrote it down.

The other police officer looked at Marian's petite frame and asked, "How in the world did *you* take these punks? You can't weigh more than a hundred ten!"

"Kung fu, darling," she replied. "I learned it in the seventies and I keep in practice. You fellas can't be everywhere!" She pointed to her T-Shirt and the words that were emblazoned across the front: "Take Care of Yourself. No One Else Will!"

Naughty Words

Faye declined suggestions that she go to the emergency room to be examined and when the police and ambulance were gone and the crowd of employees and shoppers dispersed, Marian and Faye were left alone on the wooden bench in the shade near the store's entrance.

"Now, you're sure you're all right, darling?"

Faye nodded. "I don't know how to thank you," she said. "You saved my life."

Marian chuckled. "Darling, you made up for it by jumping that asshole before he put holes in both of us!"

Faye gasped at the obscenity, but said nothing. Marian chuckled again. "What, you think he wasn't an asshole? Darling, what do you think I should call him? A misguided youth? An underprivileged juvenile? Maybe, a disadvantaged child? What word do you know that describes him better than asshole?"

Faye shook her head. "I just didn't expect to hear a lady like yourself swear like that. It just took me by surprise. Please don't mind me."

Marian looked at Faye appraisingly. "Darling, excuse me, I sometimes use coarse language to emphasize a point. If you insist on thinking of that asshole as something other than what he is, you're keeping yourself from getting angry over what he did to you, instead of working through it so you can let it go!"

Faye wasn't sure what Marian meant. She intended to hate the creeps forever. But she nodded, rather than argue with the woman who had saved her life.

"Now, practice with me," Marian insisted. "Say it. 'Asshole.'"

Faye blushed. "Oh, I couldn't…"

"He *kicked* you! I saw it!" Marian said. "He ran right up to you and kicked you, and tried to take your purse. Say it! He's an asshole!"

"He's an asshole," Faye muttered.

"Louder, darling! Say it like you mean it! Asshole!"

"He's an asshole," Faye said, a little louder.

"Are you so stifled you can't even call the low-life who almost killed you a *bad name?* Louder!"

"Asshole!" Faye shouted. "He's an asshole!" She found herself laughing, hysterically, then crying and laughing at the same time. "He hurt me! Asshole!"

After a bit, with Faye out of breath from laughing and sobbing and shouting, Marian patted her on the back. "Now, darling," she asked, "don't you feel better?"

It was true, Faye realized; she *did* feel better. She was a little embarrassed that passing shoppers had heard her swearing, but, by God, she was splattered with blood and she *deserved* to swear! Heaven knew, Edwin hadn't hesitated to swear, but he would never have tolerated *her* doing it. She had been raised to be a proper lady.

But proper ladies don't get attacked in front of the supermarket. The world had changed, somehow, not for the better but it had changed and there was no point in pretending it hadn't. She had been attacked, attacked by assholes, and it did feel good to say it!

In fact, as Marian had suggested, somehow the hatred she had felt for the *assholes* had dissipated somewhat. She was still angry at being attacked, but it no longer felt so *personal*. Assholes are assholes; they do what they do and it wasn't really a personal attack on her. They were just being assholes.

"You're going to be all right," Marian assessed.

"Yes, I am," responded Faye, in some surprise.

"Can you drive?"

"I think so," Faye answered. "Yes, I believe I can. Thanks to you!" Amazingly, her headache and nausea were gone. She was still a little shaky, but a quick drink and that, too would pass.

"Oh!" She gasped, suddenly remembering that she was still out of gin. "Actually, I still have to pick up the groceries I came for."

Marian looked knowingly at her, with eyes that missed nothing. "You were sitting in your car when I pulled up. Then you got out...that would have been shortly before eleven o'clock. You were going to pick up some booze, weren't you? And you got here too soon, and had to wait until they could sell it to you. Isn't that right?"

Faye's jaw dropped. "Good heavens! You're a mind reader!"

"Not at all, my darling, just fully conscious."

Faye hung her head. "Well, yes. I ran out of liquor and thought I'd buy some this morning."

"And you were going to have a drink, probably before you left the parking lot, weren't you?"

Faye looked at her in wonder, unable to speak.

"Your husband died recently, didn't he?"

Faye shook her head. "How can you *know* all this?"

Marian said, "Darling, this is Sun City. Practically *everyone* has a recently deceased spouse, or will soon. And eighty percent of them will mourn with a bottle of something-or-other, while the other twenty will *celebrate* with a bottle. Liquor sales are a major source of income in this town." Then she winked, adding, "Besides, Vera Daye told me."

Faye held out her trembling hand. "Look at this," she said. "I *need* something to calm down. I deserve it!"

Marian took Faye's extended hand tenderly. "Darling, that's exactly *why* you should not be drinking right now. You've been wounded, both by your husband's death and by those thugs today. Those wounds will never heal if you just keep washing them with alcohol. Sometimes, things have to be *felt* and *acknowledged* in order to really heal."

Faye began to cry. "But I can't," she sobbed. "I don't know how. You're so strong...but I'm just...just..."

Marian held her. "You can be strong, too," she said. "And I can help you, if you like. Would you like a mentor? Someone to help you grow into a new life?"

Faye felt as if someone had just thrown her a life preserver. "Would you? Really?"

"I'd love to, darling. I will see you home now, and you and I can have a nice talk. That's a 1940 Ford coupe, isn't it? Beautifully customized! I'll follow you home."

And the woman who had saved Faye's life, in perhaps more ways than one, turned on her heel and sashayed away.

Living
· · · · · · · · ·

A Real Friend

On the drive home, Faye found her hands were still shaking. She had never before been so close to death! But, when she looked in her rear-view mirror, she could see Marian's beat-up Ford and it gave her some comfort.

At home, Faye was careful to pull onto one side of the driveway so Marian could park next to her. There they were, two classic cars: Faye's beautifully restored and customized 1940 coupe, and Marian's rusted Gran Torino. It occurred to Faye that, when she knew Marian better, she could explain to the older woman how easy and inexpensive it would be to turn her vehicle into a showpiece. Faye was aware that most women didn't know much about cars, and by actually helping she could give back to Marian.

But now was too soon to tell her new friend that her car was a junker, so she kept quiet. Marian accepted her invitation to come inside, and they entered the cool dark of the McRae home.

"The living room, of course," said Faye as they entered. "Would you like to see the rest of the house?"

"If you'd like to show me," Marian replied.

So, Faye took her to see each room, commenting as she went. "That's where my uncle had this beautiful mask from Africa.

Edwin didn't like it and threw it away. I wish I still had it. Here's the guest bedroom, except we never have guests. And the guest bathroom...it's never been used, not since we moved in. And the master bedroom. Here's where I found..." Suddenly, Faye's throat closed up and she was unable to speak.

Marian placed a hand on her back. "Is this where you found your husband's body?" she asked, sympathetically.

Faye nodded, fighting back tears.

Marian smiled kindly, her face looking motherly and wise. "And you've never really talked to anyone about it, have you?"

Faye shook her head, agreeing, but still unable to speak.

"I'm in no hurry," the older woman assured her. "Tell me every little detail."

As the morning turned into afternoon and then into early evening, Faye poured her heart out. She described Uncle Fred, and his passing and bequeathing them the house, and Edwin's suicide, and how she wished it were an accident even though she knew it wasn't.

"He knew how to use it," Faye explained. "The coroner said he had placed the muzzle directly into his mouth and fired. It couldn't have been an accident. But he left no note, even had me mixing a drink for him at the time. Why would a person ask for a drink and then kill himself?"

"He just wanted you out of the room," Marian suggested softly.

"I keep wondering, what did I do wrong? What could I have done to stop him? Was he terrified that his liver was beyond repair? Oh, God, it's all so awful!"

Marian straightened in her seat, becoming suddenly stern. "Listen to me, Faye!" she said, firmly. "Edwin's suicide was *not* about *you*. It was about Edwin and *his* issues. Do you understand me? You were *not* responsible!"

Faye stared at her new friend.

Marian tried another angle. "Did Edwin ever make a really good decision?"

Faye thought. "Well, he did invest in some IBM stock in the sixties that did really well for us. When he sold them in the seventies, he had made enough of a profit to buy the auto body shop he worked in. So, yes, I guess that was a good decision."

"Do you take credit for that decision?"

"Oh, no!" Faye laughed nervously. "He never discussed finances with me."

"So that decision, and its results, was his responsibility."

"Well, yes," Faye answered, wondering where this was leading.

"Then why, oh why, would you take responsibility for a *bad* decision, like his suicide?"

"Well," she replied, "I was Edwin's *wife*. It was my *job* to make him happy!"

Marian tensed slightly, but continued. "And was it his job to make *you* happy? Did he?"

"Oh, yes," Faye said, her voice carrying less conviction than she had intended.

"Truly happy?"

Faye's expression betrayed her years of suffocation.

"Did he respect you, darling? Everyone *deserves* to be respected. And, one more thing, Faye, darling. When's the last time he told you he loved you?"

Except for the hum of the air conditioner, there was silence in the room. Faye's shoulders began to shake in silent sobs. Marian put her arm around Faye and held her until the shaking subsided.

"Darling, you were desperately unhappy. You told yourself you weren't, but you were. *He* made you unhappy, but you didn't kill him. So why blame yourself now? People don't kill themselves because of anything anyone else does. They do it from fear: Fear of losing control, fear of losing power, fear of losing love. It may be fear of facing another day of unbearable pain…or even just fear of facing another day.

"Faye," she continued, firmly, "you, and only you, are responsible for your own happiness."

Faye thought about it and, as she did, tears came again to her eyes. But, they didn't feel the same, she realized. They weren't tears of grief. They were tears of joy, because the truth of Marian's words had gotten through to her. Be responsible for her *own* happiness? Such a thought! And yet, it made sense.

After all, she realized, who else would really care?

Of course, Edwin had made a *practice* of being unhappy. She should have seen to her own joyfulness.

It might be too late for Edwin, but it wasn't too late for *her*. Faye vowed to herself, from that point on, to look for happiness.

It was getting late, and Marian had to leave. "How about an eight o'clock breakfast, tomorrow?" she suggested.

"It will have to be a short breakfast," Faye replied. "I'm doing some volunteer work in the morning."

"Volunteer?" Marian exclaimed, with a surprised look. "Ah, yes, 'The City of Volunteers'—Sun City's motto."

"Well, it's good to give back," Faye explained with barely-concealed pride. "It's for a good cause, and I enjoy it."

"Then, let's make it lunch," Marian suggested. "Let's meet at the little restaurant in the bowling alley on Thunderbird at noon. You know where that is?"

Faye nodded.

"And you can tell me all about the work you're doing!" And then she was out the door.

Special Assignment

Monday, September 29, 1997

When her alarm clock went off, Faye was startled to discover that her head was clear. It had been so long since she had awakened without a hangover, she had forgotten what it felt like. Amazingly, she had fallen asleep moments after placing her head on the pillow. Somehow, pouring her heart out to Marian the evening before had unburdened her. Her sleep had been sound and satisfying, and she was now actually eager to face the new day.

At work, she spent two-and-a-half hours stuffing envelopes and dodging the spittle from the old man coughing next to her, before she was again summoned to the supervisor's office. Nervously, she opened the door quickly so that not too much of the gray cigarette smoke would escape.

"I want to congratulate you on your turn-around," Mrs. Graves rasped. "Your work the last few days has been excellent. Have a cigarette."

Having expected another rebuke, Faye was startled and couldn't prevent herself from smiling. "Thank you," she said, pulling one from the pack offered by Mrs. Graves.

"You know, I did think you might have a drinking problem. Obviously, I was wrong, and I apologize for saying it. Anyway, you're doing great."

A warm feeling filled Faye's heart. She was unaccustomed to praise.

"Now, we have a special assignment coming up that I think you might be perfect for," the supervisor continued. "Representative Meany's office has requested two people from our office to assist him at a speech he's giving tomorrow."

"Assist him? How?"

"Oh, simple things. Mostly working with the TV reporters, handing out cups of coffee, that sort of thing."

"Oh. Well, that sounds simple," Faye agreed. "But—why me?"

The supervisor lowered her voice so that it sounded like a heavy chain being dragged across the ground. "Frankly, dear, most of our volunteers are substantially older than you. It is possible that you may actually be interviewed or appear on the video-tape. I want someone who looks mature, not bedridden, if you know what I mean."

Faye thought of the gentleman who stuffed envelopes next to her and agreed. "Why is it so many of the volunteers *are* so old?" she asked.

"Well," Mrs. Graves considered, "this is Sun City. And I think it is mostly widows and widowers who have the time and inclination to volunteer, and of course most people are widowed fairly late in life. Your husband died while you are still—" the supervisor suddenly realized what she was saying and coughed nervously. "That is, it was a tragedy for *you*, of course, but you *are* among our younger volunteers..."

Self-Serving Pigs

When Faye entered the bowling alley, it took a few moments for her eyes to adjust to the darkness and her ears to adjust to the constant rumble of rolling balls. The café was near the entrance, and it was easy to spot Marian, waving, wearing another of her custom T-shirts. This one had a hand-drawn picture of a piggy bank with an evil grin, with coins falling into its open slot. The coins were labeled, "Your Tax Dollars," and the piggy bank was labeled, "Your Self-Serving Politicians." Faye sighed tolerantly, smiled, and sat down.

The waitress appeared quickly, and Marian ordered first. "I'll have a bacon cheeseburger with extra mayo, lettuce, no tomato, and *no* bun. And some bottled water, please."

Faye looked at her friend with astonishment. "I wish *I* could eat like that!" she groaned. "I've been trying to lose weight for years, and I'm always hungry, but the fat just won't come off." To the waitress, she said, "I'd like the turkey, lettuce and tomato sandwich on whole wheat, no mayo, a small salad and a Diet Coke."

"Faye," Marian said softly, "Perhaps you aren't aware that seven separate studies in the last twenty years have shown that low-fat diets cause weight *gain*, not loss. It's because the fat must be replaced by something; and they replace it with sugar and refined flour."

"Oh, no," Faye protested. "My doctor in San Diego told me—"

"I'm sorry to interrupt," Marian said. "But very few doctors actually study nutrition. Almost no medical schools teach it, you know—and *none* did thirty years ago, when your doctor probably got his license."

Faye was confused. "But all the magazines...the commercials on TV...even the food packages, they all say low-fat!"

"Of course they do, darling," Marian agreed. "Magazines and TV are just advertisements for products that make money. And what could make more money than 'diet' food that makes the people who eat it fatter?"

"Then, what should I eat?"

"If you want to lose weight, cut out all sugar, refined flour, pasta, potatoes—anything with a lot of carbohydrates. Read the labels;

restrict yourself to twenty grams of carbs a day and I guarantee you'll trim up faster than you would believe. And you won't be hungry!"

"Oh," said Faye. "Well, all right, let me have a bacon cheeseburger! –Without the bun," she added.

"Better have water instead of soda," Marian advised. "You need lots of water on this diet, and soft drinks and coffee do *not* substitute."

When the waitress had gone, Faye related the incident with her supervisor to Marian. As she did so, she actually found herself chuckling. "It wasn't really funny, I suppose, but when I thought of me as one of the *younger* people, it was all I could do to not burst out laughing."

Marian was not laughing, however. "You *volunteer* for Carvel Meany?"

Faye collected herself. "Well, yes," she answered. "Well, not directly. I work for his re-election campaign."

"For goodness' sakes, *why*, darling?"

"Well, he's doing so much good, getting drugs off the streets..." Faye suddenly remembered seeing Marian on the news, saying something about the war on drugs not working. "You know," she added, "He is succeeding. Why, I saw on the news recently where they had just picked up some smugglers bringing in 200 kilos of some drugs."

"And what about the 200,000 kilos that make it through?"

"Uh...what?"

"That's only an estimate, which is probably low, but the 'war on drugs' prevents only the smallest fraction of controlled substances— another oxymoron—from reaching users here in this country."

"But that's only because we aren't spending enough money on it!" Faye explained. "With enough money devoted to it, we could seal the borders of the United States so tightly a fly couldn't get through! That's from Representative Meany's flyer."

"Darling, have you ever even *seen* the border?"

"You mean, have I been to Mexico or Canada? No..."

"Do you have any idea how much it would cost to fence off 6,000 miles of border? Look, I just paid $6,000 to have a square mile of property I own upstate fenced. It's just a simple fence to keep cows out—would never keep people from climbing over. A similar fence for both the Mexican and Canadian borders, and forget Alaska, would cost—um—$36,000,000. One high enough and strong enough to discourage humans would be, say, three times that. That's over a 100 million dollars, just for the fence."

"But, we already *have* a fence, I thought."

"In some places. But, how do you fence a river? Or the Great Lakes? Or the 4,000 miles of Pacific and Atlantic seacoast? And, we *have* to have *some* holes. To let tourists through, for example. And, some of those tourists come in with illegal drugs among their souvenirs."

The waitress arrived with their lunch, deftly distributing their plates and bottled water.

"The tourists would all have to be checked, of course," Faye explained as she cut through the two slices of bacon atop her bun-less cheeseburger.

"Strip search *every single person* crossing the border? I just read that, every day, 3,000 immigrants are *caught* illegally crossing the Mexican border into the United States. Imagine how many people come through legally. A strip search takes an hour, so we would have to pay additional customs officials to do the searches and still get them done in one day...and we'd have to pay them enough to keep them honest, because one customs official on the take and there's a hole in your 'air-tight' fence around the country.

"And how will you fence the air? Not only do we have to keep every single small airplane monitored, difficult when small planes can fly too low to be detected by radar, but we would have to intercept small rockets and radio-controlled model airplanes from sending drug payloads over the border."

"Radio-controlled airplanes? How could intoxicated smugglers ever operate one?"

"Darling, the people moving drugs across the border *don't use them*. Any drug mule actually *using* hard drugs would make a very unreliable partner-in-crime. The drug lords wouldn't trust such a person to keep their secrets."

"Then why do they do it?"

"For the money, of course! The sums involved are staggering! Do you realize that in today's market, a single gram of heroin or cocaine costs more than a gram of gold? And, for enough money, these people are more than willing to risk their own lives, and some do not hesitate to take the lives of others."

Faye stamped her foot beneath the restaurant table. "That's why we have to stop them!"

Marian smiled. "We could stop them easily," she said, "if we took away the one reason they run the drugs to start with: The money."

"But if, as you said, most don't get caught, how could we get their money?"

"Oh, we don't have to take it from them directly, darling. All we have to do is lower the price of the drugs they sell to practically *nothing*."

Faye shook her head. "Nothing? I don't understand. If drugs are illegal, how can we control the price at which they sell?"

Marian grinned. "Easily! You just said it yourself. Make drugs— legal!"

"What?" Faye gasped.

"Sure. It's a simple equation. Legal drugs would be cheap, like cigarettes. The drug lords go out of business because there's no black market for something that can be purchased at the local Circle K. Addicts stop mugging people for their wallets because they can *beg* for a couple of dollars if they have to."

"But, what about regular folks? I mean, if heroin was cheap and easy to get, *everyone* would use it!"

"Would you?" Marian asked. "Would you give yourself injections just to experience a drugged stupor that would leave you barely able to walk, much less drive or do things?"

"No, I guess not," thought Faye, thinking that, except for the injection part, it didn't really sound that bad.

"Anyway, the taxes on the drugs would go towards treatment programs to get people off them. Plus, think of the money we're now spending on enforcement and prisons that we could free up to spend on social programs so that people never got so desperate that they would *turn* to hard drugs! No more DEA! A fraction of the current money spent on the Border Patrol and Customs." She took a breath. "And, the bottom line is, the 'war' hasn't worked. It hasn't made any significant difference in the amount of drugs available or in the number of addicts. Users spend 40 to 50 billion dollars a year on illegal drugs, which is less money than taxpayers spend to stop them. And who gets all that money? The system maintaining the border patrols, the drug lords, and the prison corporations!"

Faye shook her head. "This doesn't make sense," she said." I mean, you do make sense, or seem to. But there must be a reason why Representative Meany doesn't agree. There must be a reason why we're not doing it that way!"

"Oh, darling, there is, there is! When there's a 60 billion dollar budget at stake. Don't you think the politicians who vote for it get a little?"

Faye's expression clouded. "Dishonest politicians? Marian, I'm sorry, but I can't believe that everyone we've elected to public office is dishonest!"

"It doesn't take everyone, darling," Marian pointed out. "You're honest, as far as I know, yet if you'd been elected to public office yesterday, and they asked you today for more money towards the 'War On Drugs,' you would say 'Yes.' The question is…is *Meany* honest?"

"Well, of course he is!" Faye said loudly, somewhat flustered.

"You're speaking from your emotions," Marian pointed out. "Have you even *met* the man?"

"Well, I…no. No, I haven't. But I'm about to…" Faye then explained how she had been chosen to assist at Representative Meany's speech the next day.

Marian put her wrinkled, graceful, hand on Faye's pudgy one. "Talk to him, then," she said. "Ask him some of the questions that are running through your mind. See how he answers, not just *what* he answers. Make your own judgment." The older woman grinned. "I'll be very interested in hearing your conclusions," she added.

A Little Swim

Outside the restaurant, Faye looked at the gently swaying fronds of the palms surrounding it. "It certainly is more pleasant here in the fall," she said. "This feels like a warm summer day in San Diego. Except for the lack of humidity, of course."

"What are you doing this afternoon?" Marian asked. "Do you go back to work?"

"No, my shift is over at noon. I will probably just go home."

"And sit in the dark all afternoon? No wonder you look like a mushroom! Why not go to the pool with me, and get in a little swim?"

"Swim? My goodness, I haven't been in the water since the seventies. Edwin didn't like to swim." Her voice dropped to a conspiratorial whisper. "I'm not sure he knew how!" And then she laughed, nervously, as if fearing she might be rebuked. But Marian smiled appreciatively.

"Good for you!" Marian said. "Never sanctify the dead. The dead don't appreciate it and it only annoys the living." She paused. "That's good. I should put that on a shirt. Maybe with a photo of Strom Thurmond," she added, wickedly.

Faye looked puzzled. "But he isn't dead?" she asked.

Marian grinned. "The wickedness is what *makes* it funny!" she said.

Faye put on a good-sport-but-I-still-don't-get-it smile, and said, "Shall I meet you at the Recreation Center?"

"Sure, or we can go together. I'm already wearing a swim suit under my outfit," she said, spreading her arms as if modeling.

"Oh—I don't actually have a swimming suit," Faye said, somewhat relieved that she wouldn't actually have to go—and, oddly, somewhat disappointed, too.

"Not a problem," Marian announced. "I have a friend who runs a marvelous little sports store. We'll pick up a suit and then it's off to the pool!"

So, in spite of herself, Faye found herself at home, putting on a brand-new swimsuit, while Marian waited in the living room. As she had done with the suit she bought before Edwin's death, she inspected herself in the mirror and found she still didn't like what she saw. She almost gave up and removed it, but then, what would she tell Marian? Reluctantly, she returned to the living room and smiled shyly at her new friend.

"Nice swim suit," Marian remarked.

"I—I haven't been swimming in years," Faye explained. "I don't even know why I bought this," she added. "I used to love to swim, though. I thought I might like to do it again…"

"And you will!" Marian encouraged. "There's nothing like letting the water carry you away."

"I look like an elephant in this thing," she said. "Everyone at the pool will laugh at me."

"Darling, practically everyone at the pool is *heavier* than you are! And, certainly, *I* won't laugh at you," Marian said. "Besides, if you can get back into the habit of swimming, you'll start shaping up your sexy self."

"Oh, really, Marian! Sexy, at my age!"

"There's nothin' wrong with your age, except that you take it too seriously. And, besides, I have it on good authority that sensuality doesn't vanish until you hit 106."

"Oh, Marian! How you do go on!" Faye giggled.

At the edge of the pool, Faye hesitated just a moment before jumping in. There was a wild sensation of coolness surrounding her, then a sensation of floating and weightlessness.

It was wonderful.

She found that her weight didn't keep her from swimming. In fact, if anything, she was more buoyant than the last time she had been in a pool. The sensation of stretching her muscles to move within the water felt good. She was amazed at how far she actually could spread her legs and stretch her arms.

Of course, racing as she had done in high school was completely out of the question. But just to let the water enfold her was bliss. And she wouldn't even be here, if not for Marian!

Faye floated peacefully for several minutes. Marian, who had swum a quick lap as soon as they entered the pool, rejoined her and said, "We'll need to swim to the other end. The AquaBabes have this area reserved for practice every Monday, Wednesday, and Friday from two to four."

"The who? Oh, yes, the synchronized swimmers. I saw them practicing."

"They're quite a draw around here," Marian remarked. "People love to see their shows. And I happen to know they have an opening—well, they always have openings; this is Sun City. I bet, if you worked at it, you could get into good enough shape to try out for them!"

"Do you think so?" Faye asked in disbelief. "They looked so graceful—like angels, or mermaids. Oh, I couldn't!"

"Why be so negative? Are you so certain?"

"Look at me, Marian! How could I be made to look like an angel or a mermaid? Let me know when they have an opening for a walrus or a manatee."

"Hey, come on! A little optimism, darling!"

Faye sighed.

"Look, if you were in good shape and had a chance of being accepted, wouldn't you really want to try out for the Aqua-Babes?"

"Well…sure, of course! And then, I'd like to bring peace to the Middle East."

"Seriously. You *can* get into shape, and you *can* be accepted…if you're willing to do the work. Are you?"

Faye thought about it. She, in good physical shape, as she was in her youth? "I don't think there's any amount of work that could perform *that* miracle."

"Welcome to Auntie Marian's Miracle Diet and Exercise Program," the older woman chuckled.

"What?"

"How do you think *I* stay in shape?"

"Swimming?"

"Mostly, and light weights, kung fu, and yoga," Marian agreed. "Also, I have always watched what I eat. But, we'll get into that later. If you want to lose weight and get healthy, I mean, *really* lose weight and get healthy, then you can do it…and we can start now."

"Oh!" Faye exclaimed. She wanted to say, "No," but couldn't think of a way to do it that didn't make her sound lazy and ungrateful. "Okay…"

"Follow me!" Marian ordered. "We're going to do laps. We'll take our time. It's the number of laps you do that counts, not the time it takes to do them."

And so they swam, back and forth, back and forth, always moving slowly so that Faye never really got out of breath, and even though she had been reluctant to begin Marian's regimen, Faye had to admit it felt wonderful.

A Doctor Who Makes House Calls

Tuesday, September 30, 1997

The next morning when she woke up, Faye found she couldn't move. Every muscle in her body screamed in agony. She did manage to get out of bed, heart pounding and neck aching. What was wrong with her? How could she get to Representative Meany's speech?

Obviously, she needed a doctor. But the only doctor she knew in Sun City was the one Edwin had seen for his liver, a specialist. As far as she knew, there was nothing wrong with her liver. This was some sort of muscular spasm, brought on by overexertion, no doubt. Was this a heart attack?

On her night stand was Marian's card, the one that said "Say Something T-Shirts" and had her phone number. Every movement painful, she dialed the number, hoping Marian would be there. Ring... ring... "Talk to me, darling!" It was Marian's voice!

"Marian, this is Faye! I need a doctor!"

"What? Faye, what's wrong? What do you need a doctor for?"

Faye could hear voices and laughter in the background. It certainly seemed early for company, but her pain overrode her curiosity. "My muscles! I can hardly move. I don't know whether it's from swimming yesterday or if I'm getting some awful disease, but I need to see a doctor and I was wondering if you could recommend one?"

"Just a moment, darling." Faye heard muffled voices, as if Marian had covered the mouthpiece with her hand and was conferring with someone.

"Darling, I do happen to know a doctor, one of the best. His name is Robert Thompson, and he'll be right over."

Faye couldn't believe it. "A doctor who makes house calls?"

"He's a friend of mine, darling, and a good man. He's leaving now, and should be there within ten minutes."

After she hung up, Faye struggled to dress herself but her arms wouldn't rise above her shoulders and she finally abandoned the attempt, settling instead for her bathrobe, which at least covered her. Besides, she was sick! A doctor wouldn't mind if a sick person was wearing a bathrobe. It was still more modest than those silly paper things they made you wear at the doctor's office for an examination.

Brushing her teeth was too much effort, though she was able to swish some mouthwash around. She tried to remember when she last had a home visit from a doctor. It was when she had the mumps, she recalled. She had been eleven or twelve, and the doctor had come to her bedside.

The doorbell rang, and Faye made her way into the living room and peeked out the narrow, vertical window next to the door. There was a colored—no, black—man standing there. Who could he be? Faye wondered. She almost didn't answer, not wanting to be occupied in conversation with a stranger at the door when the doctor arrived. She opened the inner door, and said, "Yes?"

"Good morning, Mrs. McRae? I'm Dr. Thompson. Marian Higgins sent me."

"Oh! Well!" Faye said, pretending not to be flustered. "Please, do come in." She stood back so that the doctor could enter. When he did, she saw that he was a very distinguished-looking man, sixtyish, with silvering hair and alert, friendly eyes.

"What seems to be the trouble?" he asked.

"I woke this morning, almost unable to move. Every muscle in my body aches. I'm afraid it might be serious."

"Marian told me you went swimming for the first time in a while. Do you think that might have caused it?" His eyes were bloodshot, and Faye realized that Marian and her friends must have gone for an early morning swim—that's why he was at her house, with the other people she heard in the background on the phone. Faye hoped that she might someday be invited to join them—they seemed like such a jolly bunch!

But, now she was in pain. "I don't see how it could," she said. "This is far too painful to be from a little swimming."

So the doctor examined her, holding her arms and prodding at the muscles connecting her shoulder to her chest. Everywhere he poked, she groaned in pain. He couldn't find a place that didn't hurt. To take her mind off it, she asked, "How do you know Marian?"

"Oh, my goodness!" he boomed. "Marian and I go way back. I knew her in New York in the sixties. My goodness," he added, reflectively, "how much has happened since then!" He produced a stethoscope, placed it on her chest, and asked her to breathe.

Finally, he was done. "Mrs. McRae, there's not a thing wrong with you that more swimming won't cure. Well, except for your lungs. When did you have your last chest X-ray?"

"You mean, mammogram? Just last —"

"No, I mean chest X-ray. To check for lung cancer."

"Lung cancer?" Faye gasped.

"Now, now. I don't mean to say you have lung cancer. I'm just saying that you should be checked for it regularly, since you smoke."

"How do you know I smoke?"

"Mrs. McRae, I can smell it on your breath. And I could hear it in your chest. You are this close—" he held his thumb and forefinger about an inch apart, "—from developing emphysema. And if you develop that, you can just *forget* swimming."

Faye shook her head, near panic. "I can't quit," she said. "I couldn't. I couldn't."

"You can," the doctor insisted. "And you will—if not by intention, then by death. Which do you choose?"

"Please don't make me quit!" Faye pleaded. "I once ran out of cigarettes by accident, and nearly went crazy until I could buy more. My God, I just lost my husband! I've quit drinking! I can't *possibly* give up cigarettes, too!"

"Mrs. McRae, I can help you quit if you want me to. If you don't, that's your decision. But I won't be able to see you again, because I only accept patients who *want* to get well. If you want to commit suicide, that's up to you—but you will have to do it without my help."

Suicide? Instantly, that image of Edwin on the floor returned. Surely, smoking wasn't suicide.

And yet, she did know what they were saying on TV about it. The lung cancers, the lawsuits against the tobacco companies...

Mind spinning, she recalled a photo of Edwin from the war. She had seen it recently, when going through the photo albums after his death. He and a Navy buddy were standing somewhere, arms around each other's shoulders, smoking. They were standing in front of a poster that showed Uncle Sam smoking a cigarette. The text read, "At 6¢ a pack, you can't afford not to smoke!"

After her conversation with Marian the day before, Faye found herself beginning to question the government's motivations. She remembered Marian's easy command of numbers and arithmetic, and started to wonder how cigarettes could have been sold for six cents a pack. Even in those days, it seemed like it would have cost more than that just to package them. At the time, it seemed like a patriotic gesture on the part of the tobacco companies. But, when the war ended, everyone she knew in any of the armed forces smoked, and their spouses were quick to follow. As an investment on the part of the tobacco companies, it seemed like they had made back many millions of times what they had lost on those six-cent-a-pack offerings.

"Question Authority," one of Marian's T-shirts had read. She remembered the cigarette ads on TV, delivered by doctors. Doctors were supposed to be authorities on health, and those ads had been one of the reasons that justified her smoking—if it wasn't harmful to do, why not?

"...when I studied hypnosis," Dr. Thompson was saying. "It can only help if you *want* to stop. But, if you do, I can help you heal."

"What about those patches and gum and things I see advertised?"

Thompson grunted. "They can help ease the chemical craving while you lose the habit of holding a cigarette. But they're expensive—far more expensive than cigarettes—and nicotine is one of the most addictive substances known, so it takes a long, long time to shake it entirely. I've known people who found themselves unable to quit the gum! And did you ever wonder why those things weren't made available for free, from the money won from lawsuits against the tobacco companies?"

"Then, what should I do?"

"Think about it. Decide if you truly want to quit. If you do, call me—here's my card—and we'll schedule a series of hypnosis sessions to help you stick to your resolve to quit."

Thompson got up as if to go, and Faye stood also. "What about my stiffness?"

"Take some ibuprofen or aspirin, and keep moving, even though it hurts. The more you move, the less it will hurt. Do stretching exercises before and after swimming—Marian can show you how."

"Well, thank you, Doctor. What do I owe you?"

"Oh, don't worry about it—I came here as a favor to Marian. If you make an appointment for the hypnosis, you can pay the usual office rates—my receptionist will explain them to you when you call."

So Faye took a few Advil and, sure enough, by the time an hour had passed she could move without pain—stiffly, but without pain.

And, not a moment too soon! Faye would have to hurry if she wanted to get to Lakeview Point, the park next to the Recreational Center, where Representative Meany was to give his speech.

The Great Man's Speech

It being September and the temperature more reasonable, the speech was being given outdoors. When she arrived, Faye saw that the news crews were setting up in an open area where Representative Meany could stand in the shade, lit by light from shiny umbrella-like reflectors, and there would be the peaceful background of the lake. The microphone was set up where he would stand, and in front of that were devices Faye didn't recognize and couldn't imagine the purpose of. Each consisted of a clear glass plate, almost like a windshield that Representative Meany might look through. One device was positioned to the speaker's left, one to the right, and one directly in front.

It all seemed very high tech and, in spite of Marian's dire talk the day before, Faye was very much looking forward to hearing the great man speak and, perhaps, even meeting him.

While looking for the other volunteer, she was surprised to discover it was Mrs. Graves. "I had asked Anita Gilchrist," the supervisor explained, "and she agreed to come. But just this morning she called—arthritis attack. Thank God *you* could make it!"

Faye was also glad—especially considering how stiff she had felt that morning. And now, Mrs. Graves would think of her as being reliable! Faye smiled inside.

Standing next to her supervisor, smelling the cigarette smoke on her, and being outside, Faye automatically lit one herself, then found herself looking at it. *I haven't started to quit, yet,* she thought. Yet, there was Mrs. Graves standing next to her, an omen of how she would look in another ten or twenty years if she didn't quit. Voice of a bulldozer, cigarette ash speckling the front of her clothes, fingertips and teeth stained brown. It wasn't a pretty sight.

Marian didn't smoke. Marian swam, exercised, went places, did things. Faye tried to imagine Mrs. Graves diving into a pool and almost laughed out loud. But she, herself, had gone swimming just the day before and, although she had been in pain when she got up, the fact was she felt very good right now—better than she had in years! She wasn't certain whether it was the swimming or just being outside, doing something worthwhile. She put out the cigarette and had automatically flicked the butt into the lake before she could stop herself.

Mrs. Graves had Faye set up a table for the coffee urn she had brought, some non-dairy creamer, sugar and saccharine, and some Styrofoam cups. There were also some cookies. She then assigned Faye to supply the cameramen and reporters with all they wanted of the beverage. "Little things like that help keep them on our side," Mrs. Graves explained.

Faye poured several cups, placed the non-dairy creamer, sugar packets and a few cookies on a tray, and walked it to the first knot of TV people. She recognized Audrey Flowers, a reporter from Channel 2. *She's much shorter than she looks on television,* Faye thought. The woman and her cameraman accepted coffee from her but otherwise ignored her, continuing to test the recording level of the microphone.

A hubbub from near the water's edge caught Faye's attention and she saw that Representative Meany had arrived, with three men in suits and two men with *very* serious expressions, that Faye suspected might be bodyguards.

To her surprise, there was no crowd. Oh, a few passersby had been attracted to the hubbub, but this speech, apparently, was aimed at a television audience, not a live one. Faye wondered why it was being taped outside, instead of in the studio. Wouldn't everything have been more convenient there? It occurred to her that if she had seen this on television without having been here in person, she would have assumed the speech was delivered to a large crowd.

But, perhaps the congressman merely wanted the pretty lake as a backdrop.

After dispensing coffee to the Channel 2 crew, Faye headed toward the crew from another station, but was distracted when a man called in her direction, "Coffee! –*Por favor.*"

She turned as an oddly dressed man reached for her tray. He wore blue jeans with a thick, hand-tooled leather belt and over-sized gold belt buckle, a white starched shirt, and a white, straw, cowboy hat, and shiny, expensive-looking boots. "Certainly, sir," she said, smiling.

Having delivered coffee to the media representatives, Faye made her way back to the coffee table so she could restock to serve the representative's retinue. As she was pouring, Representative Meany took his place in front of the cameras and the reflective umbrellas were positioned.

"My fellow Arizonans," he began. "It has come to my attention that some of you are concerned that, if re-elected, I might suddenly stop serving as your representative and run for president of this great country. I am here to assure you that nothing could be farther from the truth. I have worked for you tirelessly, night and day, throughout both my previous terms, and I assure you I will do the same this next term, should you re-elect me."

Faye was impressed with the frank and forthright manner in which he spoke. He sounded so unrehearsed. His eyes focused on camera after camera, as if they were actual people, as if he were actually speaking to the audience he knew would be home, watching him.

"Why? Simply because I can serve you better as representative, than as president. As your representative, I can stand on the floor of the House and *fight* to keep the drug lords and racketeers that infiltrate our very government from allowing the drug addicts to roam our streets. I can introduce bills to address the imbalance between the money the drug lords spend to get their satanic product into the hands of our young, and the pittance we now spend to prevent it..."

Making her way to the men that arrived with Representative Meany, Faye quietly began to distribute the cups of coffee, allowing them to choose their own sugar and creamer. She stood just a few feet from the great man. Even though she knew she was not on camera, she found the idea of seeing what all those cameras facing her looked like, irresistible. She turned, and was amazed to find that those three devices with the angled panes of glass were *not* clear glass from this side. Instead, each one displayed, in large, clearly legible letters, words...words which were moving as the congressman spoke.

"...our young people deserve our best efforts..." the glass plates read.

"Our young people deserve our best efforts," the congressman said, as if the thought had just come to him. Faye was shocked. The glass plates—the word "teleprompter" suddenly popped into Faye's mind; she had heard of them but had never seen one—allowed the congressman to look straight into the camera's lens and never seem to be reading. Now, Faye didn't even know if he had written these words himself.

If not, whose words were they? Why wasn't *that* person running for office?

In her dismay, she forgot to serve coffee or even to listen to the rest of the speech. Suddenly it was over, the cameras were turned to their reporters, who each quietly offered an analysis of what they'd just heard, and Representative Meany moved away from the microphones and spoke to one of the men who'd come with him.

"How about that, Bill?" he asked.

"It was fantastic, sir!" the man enthused. "Those little pauses you put in made it seem so sincere, I believed it!"

"But will the voters believe it?" the congressman fretted. "And, if they do, how upset will they be when I *do* start campaigning for President next year?"

"Don't worry about it," Bill responded. "I guarantee, they won't even remember it. In fact, we can probably use this *very speech*, tweaked just a little, to *announce* your candidacy! 'Why? Simply because I can do more good as president, than as representative. As your president, I can *fight* to keep the drug lords and racketeers from infiltrating...' and so on."

"Brilliant, son!" the representative grinned. "Good job! You're still on the payroll!"

Faye was aghast, angry. Not only was Meany lying when he said he wasn't going to run for president, he was so matter-of-fact about it that he didn't even care that she was standing close enough to have overheard him talking about it! And, so were the others! It was as if they were—Faye struggled for a comparison—as if they were packaging a new brand of coffee or mouthwash, instead of campaigning to do good.

But, he would not get away with it, Faye pledged. She placed her coffee tray on the table, nearly knocking it over in her haste, and practically ran to the reporter from Channel 2. "Miss Flowers!" she called. "Miss Flowers!"

"That's *Ms*. Flowers," the young woman corrected. "Yes?"

"I have a story for you!" Faye whispered dramatically.

"Oh? What about?"

"Well, I just overheard Representative Meany talking to one of his men—I think the man *wrote* his *speech!*"

The reporter smiled patiently. "That's not a story, ma'am. I doubt if there's a single politician in the country today who claims to write his own speeches."

"Oh. Oh, but there's more! He said he really *does* intend to run for President, next year!"

"I'm afraid that's not a story, either," the woman sighed. "When a politician wants to run for President, one of the first things he or she does is announce that he or she has *no interest* in running for President. That way, people start thinking of that person and the Presidency in a single thought, where previously they never would have."

Faye paused, nonplussed. "But—but he *lied!*"

Ms. Flowers snapped shut her briefcase and said, "Ma'am, when you find me a politician who *doesn't* lie, call me—*that'll* be a story!"

Faye couldn't believe it. The man had lied to the public, and no one thought it was wrong or even strange. He had presented himself as something he wasn't, and no one thought that was odd, either. Was she the only person in America who thought she voted for honest men who had her best interests at heart?

By now, the cleared area by the lake had been deserted. The coffee table was gone, taken by Mrs. Graves who had waved cheerily at her and called, "See you tomorrow," as if nothing had surprised her, either. And she was in charge of his re-election campaign office!

Too upset to return home, Faye decided to walk around the park she had never before visited. She passed in front of a very pretty fountain and waterfall; then the path meandered up a hill to the waterfall's source, which seemed to come out of the path itself.

Below the hill, the bushes grew close in to the path so that one had the feeling of seclusion. It was very pretty, and just what Faye needed to soothe her mood. However, suddenly appearing, through the trees and bushes twenty or so yards in front of her, was the man in the white straw cowboy hat, the man she had given coffee to before the speech. He was holding a manila envelope and, as she watched, he carefully placed it on the edge of one of the ever-present waste bins, bent over and adjusted the cuff of his right jeans leg. Then, straightening, he continued on his way down the path—forgetting his envelope!

She was about to call him, when a man in a suit walked past her, obviously in a hurry. The man in the cowboy hat was out of sight when the man in the suit nonchalantly picked up the envelope as he passed the trash bin and slipped it into his inside jacket pocket. In a moment, he, too, was gone.

And Faye found herself standing on the path, alone, feeling as if she were waking up from a good dream into the harsh world of reality. Because the second man, the one in the suit, the one who had furtively taken the forgotten envelope, that man was none other than Representative Meany.

Mobility
·········

The Man With All The Answers

That evening, Faye called Marian to share her indignation. "He didn't even write the speech himself!" Faye fumed. "And he had to read it from one of the Teleprompter things!"

"So," said Marian, "you have just witnessed a subtle ruse that deceives an ignorant public into thinking that these clowns are much brighter than they actually are."

Faye held the receiver tightly. "I am livid," she stated. "My first attempt to get involved in politics, and it turns out that, not only is the politician I picked dishonest, but the TV reporters think they *all* are."

"And what do *you* think?"

Faye hesitated. "Well...I just can't believe they are *all* crooked. I mean...Kennedy? Reagan? Roosevelt? I just can't believe it. And our mayor back home in San Diego, several years ago...I *know* he was a good man; Edwin worked on his car. Things just can't be as bad as that."

"What do you intend to do about your volunteer work?"

"Well, I'll have to quit, of course. I'm going in tomorrow to give Mrs. Graves a piece of my mind. She *knows!* And it doesn't bother her."

"I have a suggestion," Marian announced. "Don't quit tomorrow. Call in sick, instead. There's someone I want you to meet. When we get together, we may be able to figure out a way you can really make a difference."

Wednesday, October 1, 1997

The next morning, Marian appeared at Faye's door with a mischievous grin on her face, and a T-shirt that read, in bright red letters, "Doubt Is The Hatpin To The Balloon Of Faith."

"What does that mean?" Faye asked, indicating the shirt.

Marian grinned all the more. "You have to ask, after having your faith pricked by Meany's speech, yesterday?"

Faye's expression fell. "Oh," she said.

"Cheer up. We are on our way to meet my friend, Marvin, the infomaniac."

"'Infomaniac'?" Faye repeated, puzzled.

"You'll see," Marian laughed. "Let's take my car."

Faye was less than enthusiastic about getting into the bucket of bolts her friend drove. The only shiny part of the car was the gleaming hood. She could only imagine the decrepit condition of the interior, because the darkly-tinted windows made it nearly impossible to see inside. However, when she got in, she discovered that it was like new! The upholstery was soft, comfortable, leather and smelled showroom fresh. The dashboard was padded with the same leather. The dials and gauges were certainly not the original equipment. There was a built-in, retractable multi-channel radar detector, a CD player, and a police scanner designed to look like a typical FM radio to the casual observer.

"My goodness!" Faye gasped. "This is beautiful! *Why* did you—" She pictured this interior with the rusted and dented exterior. "Why did you make the inside so—so—nice?"

"It's comfortable, don't you think? And it suits me."

"But—" Faye was still flabbergasted. "The outside! It's so—so—!"

Marian laughed as she started the engine. "Well, darling...no one would think to steal this old wreck, would they?"

Faye was silent for a moment, as the car smoothly pulled out of the driveway. "You mean...you let the exterior of the car go to pot just to keep people from *stealing* it?"

"That, and not having to worry about inconsiderate morons flinging their doors open and putting dents in it. And, besides, from my perspective, it looks and sounds like a brand-new car."

"I just don't understand, Marian. How does it make sense, putting all that time and money into an old car?"

"Darling this is an age of *have and have-not*. A low profile is an advantage in the survival game. And, don't underestimate Clyde, darling!"

"'Clyde?'"

"That's what I christened him. If men can name cars after women, why can't I name mine after a man? Anyway, this sleeper has a lot more going for it than you'd think by looking at him. For one thing, there's a 440 horsepower engine under *that* hood, the biggest production engine ever offered to the American public. It is slightly modified and can take us from zero to sixty in a little less than six seconds. If need be, we can cruise comfortably at 140 miles an hour."

Faye blinked. "Why would anyone ever need to go that fast?"

"You never know!" Marian grinned.

Faye shook her head in puzzlement. "But, I still can't figure it out. Why not just buy a new car?"

"Some years ago, after replacing yet another car when it hit 100,000 miles, I suddenly realized, cars are *made* to fall apart about then. Now, what sense does that make, I asked myself? Why should I spend thousands of dollars on something that won't last the rest of my life? And, especially, why should I do it *over and over?*

"Do you realize that most cars you buy today for, say, $30,000, will start breaking down in five years or less? That would cost about $6,000 a year for the car, and another $1,000 for upkeep, and that doesn't include insurance. All things, considered, we're talking about seven or eight thousand clams a year—for basic transportation! What a racket!"

Faye fidgeted. "Edwin always customized an older car for us, but I never thought about it that way," she said. "Neither did Edwin, I suppose..."

"Hey!" said Marian. "I decided that, if I had to spend that kind of money, why not spend less on one car that would last me forever? So I picked out a '70 Gran Torino with a frame that was in good condition—not hard when the car comes from an era when they actually put some iron and steel into the construction, instead of that lightweight stuff they use today—and began to *really* build it. I constructed the dashboard myself. The wiring is extra heavy-duty. The suspension is high-tech and finely-tuned, and spare parts are available in every junkyard in North and South America. I see no reason why this car won't be a 'goer' on the cheap, for another fifty years—certainly longer than *this* goer," she added, pointing to herself.

And with that, they pulled into the driveway of another cookie cutter Sun City home.

Trust Me

Marian led Faye to the door and rang the bell, three short rings and a long one. Almost immediately they heard the clanks of three locks turning, and then the door opened, revealing a short, bald man with a pale complexion and green, bloodshot eyes flecked with gold. An unlit cigarette dangled from his smiling mouth. "Doodlebug!" he cried to Marian, in an accent tinged by Brooklyn. "This must be ya new friend."

"Marvin, I'd like you to meet Faye McRae." Faye shook his hand; his grip was firm and friendly. They were ushered into the living room of the house, which, to her surprise, Faye found was *literally* full of books. The room contained rows of bookshelves, like a section of a public library, every row full. Marvin continued to lead them into the back of the house; on their way, Faye glanced at some of the titles and discovered they were organized by the Dewey Decimal System, just like in a real library.

"Don't mind the dust," Marvin begged. "The guy who cleans won't be here till Monday."

He led them to what would have been a bedroom, but in this house it looked more like a command center at NASA. Flat monitor screens were mounted on two walls, apparently displaying different cable TV channels. Faye could hear, faintly, the soundtrack of one broadcast—which one, she couldn't tell. Where the monitors weren't mounted, were charts and maps and erasable schedules. A desk ran around three sides of the room, containing three personal computers, each complete with monitor, keyboard, and mouse. Filing cabinets and more bookshelves filled the fourth wall, with the shelves holding mostly reams of paper, racks of floppy disks, tape cartridges, and a few books.

Marvin plopped down into a worn but solid-looking executive office chair and indicated two other chairs for his guests. "Don't mind the papers," he told Faye, who eyed the documents piled in the one she'd been about to sit in. She picked them up but could find no place else for them, so sat down and held them in her lap. "So," he said to her, grinning. "You're the babe who has a job wit' the Mean-man."

"I did volunteer to work for Representative Meany," Faye agreed diffidently. "But I saw his true colors, yesterday, and I'm going to quit." She then repeated the story she had told Marian: About the Teleprompters, the jaded reporter, the speechwriter, and Meany's intention to run for president.

When she was done, Marvin rocked silently in his chair for a moment, then said, "And that surprised ya? Fresh off the boat, ain't ya?"

"Now, Marvin," Marian chided. "Be nice. Faye might be willing to help out."

"Help out with what?" Faye asked.

Marvin shrugged. "Depends," he said, noncommittally. "Here, let me bring ya up to speed on a few other things you might not know about ya pal." He hit a few keys on one of the keyboards on his desk, and a large wall-mounted monitor switched to a photo of a man who looked a lot like Carvel Meany, yet wasn't. Marvin nodded in the monitor's direction. "This is a picture of Gavin Meany, Carvel's old man. Born 1901 in Tennessee. By the time he was twenty-five, he had already made a million smackers in tobacco, lettin' poor blacks farm his land for a fraction of what their crops brought in. That's a million dollars," Marvin added, "in 1926 dollars!

"Because he kept outta the stock market, the 1929 crash didn't affect him at all. Quite the opposite—when prices of food took a nosedive, he used the depression as an excuse to pay his share-croppers even less, knowin' they wouldn't starve to death."

Faye shook her head. "I know about sharecropping," she said. "It gave people who had no property a way to make a living."

"A *meager* living, maybe," Marian agreed. "But, if people like Gavin Meany's father hadn't used his political connections to buy huge parcels of the land at protected prices, the poorer people could have purchased their *own* with government subsidies, as was originally planned."

"Fageddaboudit," Marvin dismissed. "That's not all it was used for." He hit a key and the picture changed to an oil painting of yet another, older gentleman, also bearing the family resemblance. "This here is Chase Meany, III. Born in Ohio in 1840, he was one of the original carpetbaggers who descended on the South after the Civil War, ya know what I mean? He bought land for cheap, land that was 'liberated' by the government from Southern landowners who fought in the war. Tobacco was a big deal crop, but he also grew rye, which he distilled and sold as whiskey all over the country.

"Now, scope this." Another key tap, and the screen showed an old piece of paper with barely legible handwriting on it. "This is a receipt for $5,000, made out to the Anti-Saloon League of Oberlin, Ohio. We have proof of a lotta other donations to temperance leagues and the like, made in the years before the Eighteenth Amendment—Prohibition—was finally ratified."

Faye was puzzled. "I don't get it," she said. "If he *made* whiskey, why would he donate money to make it illegal?"

"When something people want is illegal," Marian explained, "The price goes up. Meany's grandfather and father made a fortune selling illegal whiskey in the twenties."

"Thanks to Meany's contributions and encouragement, the Anti-Saloon League announced way back in 1913 its intention to achieve national prohibition through a constitutional amendment. Wit' other temperance forces, especially the Woman's Christian Temperance Union, the League in 1916 got the two-thirds majorities necessary in both houses of Congress—which actually *included* Chase Meany, who ran on a temperance platform! —and *poof!* — the Eighteenth Amendment to the Constitution of the United States was on the books."

Faye was dumbstruck. "How could a man who made and sold whiskey be elected on a temperance platform? How could he not be found out?"

Marvin shrugged. "It was the days before cable. Before investigative reporters and the *National Enquirer*, even. The only people who might of cheated his ass were the ones he paid off."

"But, his distilleries! How could he hide them?"

"He simply moved the actual production of the whiskey to Mexico. And so, when Chase checked out at the ripe old age of ninety-seven, even though Prohibition had ended, he turned over to Gavin, his only kid, nearly $40 million. Gavin also inherited the distilleries. Hey, not as profitable as during Prohibition, but they still made plenty of loot. That's when he looked to instigate another prohibition."

"Another...prohibition? What do you mean? There's no other prohibition."

Marvin grinned. "Gavin found that Tennessee dirt was ideal for growin' marijuana."

"Marijuana!" Faye gasped.

"He copied his pop and campaigned against it. Didya ever hear of the early thirties movie, *Reefer Insanity?*"

Faye shook her head.

"I can loan ya a video. Gavin wrote and financed the film himself. A short scare piece, y'know, to terrify the audience into believin' that marijuana was a killer, that people smokin' it turned into fiends wit' no sense a fear and couldn't feel pain. It showed them killin' people randomly, includin' the main character's parents."

"I thought it was called *Reefer Madness*," Faye said, hesitantly.

"As propaganda films went, *Reefer Madness* got bigger distribution, probably because it had the government backin' it. But there was a lotta publicity in those days, comin' at people, makin' 'em believe things that weren't true, an' *Reefer Insanity* was Gavin's contribution. But, the deal is, Gavin Meany was *growin'* marijuana, even while he was workin' to make it illegal, just like his old man did wit' alcohol. In 1937, the Marijuana Tax law was hustled through, and that's what gave us the prohibition that still exists today."

Marian spoke up. "Just think: Not only a prohibition of behavior, but of a naturally growing plant!"

Faye was dazed. It had never occurred to her that laws could have been enacted for any reason but the public good. Her brain was churning and the obvious conclusion could not be ignored. "Are you telling me that Carvel is continuing the family business—and is working to keep marijuana illegal *so he can make more money from it?*"

Marian rose and put a friendly hand on Faye's shoulder. "Burns you up, doesn't it, darling?"

Faye sat resolutely, Marvin's papers held tight in her lap as if to protect herself from this onslaught of horrible ideas. "What can I do?"

Marvin chuckled. "Does the name, 'Mata Hari' ring a bell?"

"What?"

Marian explained in more detail what Marvin meant. "Nothing dangerous, darling," Faye was assured. "But if you continue to do the volunteer work you are doing, you may overhear or come across something that we could use. A list of campaign contributors, for example, or the date and time of a planned drug raid. Anything that would help us expose Meany as the hypocritical criminal that he is. And, yes, darling," she added as Faye tried to interrupt, "he is engaged in illegal activities."

Faye looked at the two of them, Marian looming above her and Marvin rocking and swiveling in his chair. She looked again at what must be a hundred thousand dollars' worth of computer equipment, all those books, the whole secret laboratory feel of the place, and asked, "Who do you people think you are? Superman? Exposing a crooked politician is a job for the police!"

In answer, Marvin picked up a volume from a small stack of identical books. He opened it, scrawled something on the first page, rolled over to Faye on his wheeled executive chair, and handed it to her. On the cover, she read,

TRUST ME
A Book of National Disgraces
by
Marvin Cohen

and, on the inside title page, she found handwritten in pen, "To Faye—what you don't know can hurt you. May you never be hurt. Marvin."

Faye was amazed. "You *wrote* this?" She had never met anyone who had written a book, before.

"Sure. I maintain the web site, too."

"Web site?"

Marian patted Faye on the shoulder. "The Internet, darling. So people everywhere in the world, at least, anyone with access to a computer, can benefit from Marvin's research and even do a little research on their own."

"But, why? To find out their congressman's a crook?"

Marvin grunted. "There's a few honest ones out there. Very few. But, if ya can find one, vote for him— or her!" he added. "My web site tells ya who's runnin', who's thinkin' of runnin', and how they're related to the scams bein' perpetrated on the citizens of the world."

Snap of Fingers

Thankfully, Marian didn't say much as she drove back to Faye's house. Faye didn't feel like talking. She was a cauldron of hot, mixed, emotions. She wasn't sure how she felt, but she knew it wasn't good.

Alone at home, she found herself automatically lighting a cigarette. She considered putting it out, but decided she already had too much to think about.

The tobacco industry! In her heart of hearts, she had known smoking was unhealthy but when the doctors and the government and the tobacco industry had sworn it was safe, she had believed them.

When she had finished the cigarette, she picked up the phone and made an appointment with Dr. Thompson. To her surprise, the receptionist seemed to know her, and scheduled her for that very afternoon.

She attempted not to smoke until the appointment, and was actually a little proud of herself when she only gave in twice. She arrived at the doctor's office promptly at two. The waiting room was crowded, but the receptionist was not busy and, in point of fact, looked familiar to her.

"Faye," the woman said, smiling. "It's so nice to see you again." She then added, "We met at the Lakeside Recreation Center a few weeks ago. I'm Vera Daye."

"Oh, yes, I remember you," Faye replied. "You bought that very T-shirt from Marian Higgins, in fact." Faye could barely keep her eyes off Vera's chest, which stretched the cotton almost to the breaking point. She had never seen an older woman with such large, firm breasts before.

"Oh, yes," the woman smiled. "I actually bought it for my nephew, but I liked it so much I decided to keep it."

Faye forced herself to look into the woman's eyes. "I thought everyone in Sun City was retired."

"I'm semi-retired. I like to keep busy, and Dr. Thompson is doing such an important job, I wanted to be a part of it. I have office skills so here I am! Make yourself comfortable," Vera added, turning back to the computer screen.

Faye found an available seat among the inexpensive padded chairs, next to one of the end tables separating every four of them. On the tables were the usual stacks of magazines, although, oddly, she didn't recognize many of the titles. Usually doctors had an assortment of old copies of *People*, *National Geographic*, and *Highlights for Children*; but, here, the magazines seemed more medically oriented than in most doctor's offices she had visited. There were titles for people with glaucoma, AIDS, and cancer. The only recreational-looking magazine she found was called *High Times*; but as she was not interested in rock or mountain climbing, Faye didn't bother opening it.

In less than a minute, Vera escorted her to an examination room. Faye was surprised, but none of the other patients waiting seemed to mind, or even to notice that she was going ahead of them.

She sat for a minute or two in the examination room; then, there was a knock on the door and Dr. Thompson entered. A sincere smile broke over his face when he saw that Faye was his next patient. "I'm so glad to see you again so soon!" he said jovially. Then his smile dimmed. "Are you ill? Surely that stiffness has left you by now?"

"I want to quit smoking," Faye stated resolutely. "I tried, but I can't stop on my own."

"I'm not surprised. Tobacco has always been among the most addictive substances, and the tobacco companies' files show they intentionally bred tobaccos to *increase* the nicotine content. The stuff is harder to quit than heroin."

"You said you could hypnotize me. Can you, really?"

"Most people can be hypnotized, and it *can* help you quit...but it can't *make* you quit if you don't want to."

"I *do* want to!"

Dr. Thompson dimmed the room lights and turned on a tape recorder. "This is our chaperone."

Faye blushed. "Oh, doctor!"

Dr. Thompson chuckled, and said, smiling, "Now, please stare at the corner, where the ceiling meets the walls. That's right. As you stare, you're going to get sleepy..."

Faye's eyes closed almost immediately, and then Dr. Thompson snapped his fingers, startling her into alertness. "We're done," he said.

"Done?" Faye asked, puzzled. "Done with what? When are you going to hypnotize me?"

Dr. Thompson laughed. "It's done! You were an excellent subject. From now on, whenever you have a craving for tobacco, snap that rubber band on your wrist and envision the president of Phillip Morris laughing at you as you weaken. Your indignation will give you the strength to resist for the one minute and forty seconds it takes for the craving to pass."

Faye looked at her wrist and was surprised to discover that there was, indeed, a rubber band stretched around it.

"I'll walk you to the waiting area," the doctor offered, and opened the door. She followed. At the receptionist's station, he said, "Vera, please give Mrs. McRae an appointment for next week." To Faye, he said, "I'll want to see how the post-hypnotic suggestion I gave you is working out."

"Certainly, Doctor," Vera responded. "And all the folks have arrived for the Mexico trip."

"Mexico trip?" Faye asked. "Is that what those people were waiting for? I wondered why you saw me ahead of them."

"That's right," the doctor agreed. "Once each month, I sponsor a trip to the border to pick up prescription medicines."

Faye was, again, puzzled...a feeling that had been growing more and more familiar in the past week or so. "That's a long trip," she said. "Why not just get their prescriptions here?"

Dr. Thompson laughed, gently. "The drug companies charge as much as five times more for medicines in this country than they do in other countries where most people don't have any insurance to pay inflated prices."

"And," Vera added, "most of the doctor's patients do not, in fact, have adequate insurance and are on fixed incomes. So he takes them across the border to buy what they need at prices they can afford."

Faye tried to figure out how this worked. "Do you have to go with them to write the prescriptions?"

"Oh, no, my dear—I can write scripts here. But these folks don't really have enough money for these trips, so I charter a bus and then, while we're there, I help interpret for the patients who don't speak Spanish, and make sure the meds they get are high quality."

"Dr. Thompson is a *saint!* He charters the bus himself," Vera said, in a stage whisper. To Faye's amazement, the doctor's ebony color deepened. He was blushing! She had never seen a black man blush before.

It was endearing, somehow.

"Oh, come now, Vera," he said. "It's office money, and you know it. Tax deductible, and all that."

"This is why I work here," Vera explained to Faye. "It's *good* work."

Dr. Thompson laughed good-naturedly and took Faye's hands in his. "Now, you know why I want Vera working for me," he said. "How lucky I am to have found a receptionist who thinks I'm a saint!"

Faye could hardly breathe. She had never had her hands held by a black man before. They felt like anyone else's hands, not as rough as Edwin's had been, but masculine and warm and strong. And, standing there, so close, she could smell his breath, sweet and, and, *comforting*, somehow.

And his eyes...beautiful, black pools in the midst of milky whiteness, with only a trace of redness.

"—I have to go, now," he was saying, trying to extricate his hands from hers. Now it was Faye, blushing, as she hastily released him, saying, "Oh, yes, goodbye doctor, thanks," and turning away from him before he could notice her embarrassingly red cheeks, she looked to Vera to make her appointment.

She heard the door open and close behind her, heard his voice, muffled, greeting the people waiting for his chartered bus and the trip for medicine.

Vera stared at her and then, suddenly, grinned. "He *is* handsome, isn't he?" she said.

"Who?" Faye asked, faintly. "Oh, you mean Dr. Thompson? I suppose he is..."

Vera laughed as she sat at her computer, pressing keys, and finally announcing, "Yes, next Tuesday at 11. Will that be all right for you?"

"Yes, yes, fine..." Faye responded as in a fog. She accepted the little hand-written appointment card from Vera when it was handed to her.

"Now, if there's any problem, you can call or you can just go to our web site and change your appointment right there."

"Change my own appointment? With a computer?"

"Surely," Vera smiled. "All kinds of businesses are run over the Internet, these days, you know. You are on-line, aren't you?"

"Um—I don't even have a computer."

"Oh..." Vera looked at her sadly. "You really must get one. It's hard to be connected to the modern world, without."

A Soft Voice

Friday, October 31, 1997

Marian had set up a workout schedule for Faye and there didn't seem to be any way Faye could get out of it. After all, Faye had told Marian she was serious about getting into good enough shape to be in the AquaBabes, and to back out now would make her seem to be completely without conviction, not to mention ungrateful for the effort Marian had already put forth. And so, Faye was never late for the sessions. Sometimes Marian picked her up, and sometimes she met Marian there, but she was never late.

They did step aerobics three mornings a week, Tuesday, Thursdays, and Saturdays, which dovetailed nicely with her work schedule at the re-election offices of the detestable Representative Meany. The step aerobics only took an hour; the class was held at the Lakeview recreation center, and she and Faye would follow up with an hour's swim. On Monday and Friday afternoons, they met at the center's weight room for light weightlifting.

"Weightlifting? *Me?*" Faye had exclaimed when Marian suggested it. But, after just a couple of weeks, Marian had to admit that she was slimming down nicely, and she felt better than she had in years. In decades, actually! The good feeling from exercising lasted the rest of the day. Much to Faye's surprise, she was actually enjoying the entire process.

Every day Marian wore a different T-shirt, each with a unique, hand-drawn slogan. On Halloween, as she waited for Marian to finish a set of chest exercises, Faye found her attention drawn to the evilly-grinning jack-o-lantern on Marian's T-shirt, around which was written, "Truth Is The Enemy Of The State," and, in smaller letters, the attribution, "Joseph Goebbels."

"What is it with your shirts, Marian?" Faye asked, suddenly. "I know you make them, but how many do you have?"

Drawing her arms together against the resistance of the machine, Marian timed her laugh to match an exhalation. "Darling," she gasped. "I have…no idea!"

Faye suddenly realized that Marian wasn't the only person in the gym wearing one of her shirts. Although the employees were wearing Halloween costumes, the exercisers were dressed normally in their shorts and T-shirts; and some of them were wearing shirts they had clearly gotten from Marian. A woman doing sit-ups on an exercise mat was wearing one that read, "Question Authority" –Faye had seen Marian wearing that one before. Another woman wore one with a picture of a bee and the words, "Don't Step On My Buzz." Faye had no idea what it meant, but by now she could recognize Marian's handiwork. A man on a treadmill wore another one; his said, "Out With Incumbents!" Still angry at Representative Meany, Faye could strongly agree with that sentiment!

Marian finished her set and rose, trading places with Faye. As Faye sat, Marian expertly adjusted the weight for her friend. When she was clear, Faye placed her arms against the pads, gripped the handholds, concentrated, and exhaled slowly as she drew her elbows together. When the pads met in front of her, she inhaled and allowed her elbows to return to the starting position.

"Excellent form, darling!" Marian encouraged her.

The first few "reps," as the people in the gym called repetitions of an exercise, were always pretty easy. They got tougher as they continued.

This time, however, Faye found she could not complete the second set, and had to abandon the third after only five reps, even with Marian's intense encouragement.

"You can do it!" the older woman barked. "One more! Just one…more!"

It had troubled Faye greatly the first time Marian coached her like that. "You're…asking…too…much!" she had gasped. Marian had explained to her that she needn't reply; there was nothing personal in the goading. It was just a way to help the person exercising concentrate on putting her *all* into each individual rep.

Faye was used to the goading now and could even egg Marian on a little, although her mentor was already in excellent shape and worked weights just to maintain condition. Faye, on the other hand, was growing stronger daily and was disappointed that she hadn't been able to complete all three sets.

"Don't you mind a bit, darling," Marian smiled. "I upped the weight."

"You...what?"

"You've been pressing thirty pounds, but I thought you could do forty...so, this morning, I moved the weights to fifty."

"*Fifty?*"

"Thursday, pressing forty pounds will seem like a breeze! Now, let's run over to the bars. I have a new one that your back will thank me for!" Marian led the way to the horizontal bar on which she had been doing chin-ups, though only recently had she been able to get up to her chin. "Hold on tight, darling," the older woman said, after Faye had wrapped her fingers around the bar. "Now that you can actually support your own weight with your hands, I want you to do this: Draw your knees up to your chest, and throw your head back."

"Oh, my goodness!" Faye panted, as Marian helped her get her feet between her arms and then hook her knees over the bar.

"Now, let go with your hands," Marian commanded.

"Are you sure?" Faye asked, still clutching the bar.

"Absolutely."

Holding her breath, Faye relaxed her grip—and Marian was right, of course; she hung like a bat from the bar.

"Now, relax yourself, darling!" Marian urged. "You're all clenched up. You aren't going anywhere, so relax."

"But I can't relax my legs!" Faye protested. "If they straighten, I'll land on my head!"

"They won't straighten unless you want them to," Marian promised. "You are designed to hang this way—a gift from our arboreal ancestors, no doubt. And, in this position, blood rushes to your brain, which makes it a good position for solving problems. Plus, your weight *pulls* on your spine instead of compressing it, which gives your back a much needed rest."

Upside down, Faye's eyes spotted yet another of Marian's T-shirt designs, although she couldn't quite make out what it said. She kept trying to twist her head into an upright position so she could read it. "Marian, really. What is this T-shirt thing you're doing? I see people wearing them, but what's the point? You make them by hand, right? So, there can't be much money in it."

Marian pointed out the row of stair machines, each machine occupied by a person endlessly stepping his or her way to fitness. "What are they looking at?"

Faye followed her gaze, and answered, "The TV, of course." There was a television set mounted from the ceiling, tilted so the exercisers could watch and loud enough to hear over the clanking and clanging of weights and machines.

"And what's on the TV?"

It looked peculiar upside down, but still familiar. "It looks like the early news on Channel 2. I think that's Audrey Flowers."

"Why do they watch, darling? Why, do you suppose?"

Faye recognized one of Marian's lessons, but she had grown to appreciate them, and was happy to play along. "Um, to keep informed?" She could tell by Marian's expression that she hadn't given the right answer, so she tried again. "To stave off boredom? Because it's there?"

Marian grinned. "All three answers are correct," she said, "but the first answer is the one each of those people would give if you asked them."

"I guess it makes sense not to waste the time," Faye remarked. "This way they can exercise their minds as well as their bodies."

"I'm sure that's what they think they're doing, darling. But they're mistaken."

"Oh?"

Marian's lips tightened as she asked, "Do you know where the news they are hearing comes from?"

"The TV," Faye blurted, then realized that wasn't what Marian meant. "Audrey Flowers," she amended.

"The TV newsreaders—and that's what they mostly do, darling, read—they do write *some* local stories," Marian admitted. "But right now, she's talking about the riots in Belfast—you can see the pictures. Do you think she went to Belfast to report on those riots? Or that anyone else at Channel 2 did?"

"Well—no, I suppose not..."

"Do you think anyone at the station has ever been to Belfast? How about Lebanon, Jerusalem, Chechnya, Iran? Afghanistan? Poland, Syria, China?"

Faye held out her hands. "So, they must get the news from their network," she guessed.

"Have you ever heard of the Associated Press? Or United Press International?"

Faye shook her head, which produced an odd feeling in her ears when upside down. "I've heard of them, but I don't really know anything about them."

Marian scooped up the copy of *The Arizona Republic* someone had left on a bench against the wall. "Look at the beginnings of some of the articles. They all have something in common. Can you see what it is?"

She handed the paper to Faye, who had to turn it upside down to match her orientation. It contained five or so news articles, describing crises in various parts of the globe. The crises were all different, but most articles began with the words, "Associated Press." Faye looked at Marian, questioningly.

Marian explained. "The Associated Press is a national, non-profit, organization that supplies news to practically every newspaper, radio, and TV station in the country. The other, similar, organization in the United States is UPI, United Press International. If a newspaper doesn't get their news from AP, they get it from UPI or one of a very few, smaller, wire services. That's how a local newspaper *gets* national and international news."

"Every article?" Faye asked, waving the sheet in the air, "They never research *anything* on their own?"

"Big papers rewrite the articles they receive from the news services," Marian explained. "But they are still working from a single point of view, from a single source. Do you remember in high school, working on term papers, when you were required to use at least three sources? That was to guarantee that you at least put *some* thought into what the material in the sources meant. It's a lot easier to just copy from one source, a lot more brainless, too. But that's why all the newspapers in the United States, and all the radio and TV stations as well, even the networks, seem to have the same news. They don't often disagree on what has happened. No matter what paper you read or TV anchorman you watch, you are hearing the same voice."

"Whose voice?" Faye asked, the obvious question hanging in the air between them.

Marian wore an irritated look. "I don't know," she said, grimly. "But I know that we need to hear more than one voice if the world is ever to become a better place. My T-shirts give me that voice."

From her unaccustomed vantage point, Faye looked around the gym. Out of, perhaps, twenty people, four, including Marian, were wearing one of Marian's T-shirts. But, they were hand-made shirts and this was just Sun City, one city out of a hundred thousand cities in America. "Compared to these news services of yours," Faye remarked, "it isn't a very loud voice."

"A soft voice is better than no voice at all. And it's *my* forum."

Faye nodded in agreement, producing an odd feeling in her throat. "How do I get down?"

"You're going to have to take a leap of faith, darling."

"I don't like the sound of that," Faye said, her eyes on her friend.

"It really works simply; it's a matter of physics and you can't louse it up. But, this first time, you will have to trust me."

Faye sighed. "Okay," she said. "Tell me what to do."

"Starting swinging back and forth. Forward and back—like you were on a swing." Faye did so, wondering how much of this she could keep up before breakfast arose from wherever it had gone—or is that, 'fell'? This was so confusing...

"Now," Marian continued, "when you reach the apex of your swing, just straighten your legs."

"But I'll fall!" Faye protested, still swinging.

"No, you won't!" Marian promised. "That's the beauty of it. When you straighten your legs at the top of your swing, physics keeps you moving and you land lightly on your feet. I promise!"

Faye swung, back and forth, higher and higher. Then, just as she achieved that moment of rest between rising and falling, she shut her eyes and straightened her legs, no longer clutching the bar with her knees. Because her eyes were shut, she wasn't certain how it happened; but, sure enough, suddenly her feet were, indeed, on the floor and she was right-side up. She opened her eyes to be sure.

"Oh, my goodness!" was all she could gasp.

Marian nodded. "Soon, you'll be able to get into that position on your own," she promised. "You may like it so much, you'll want a gymnastics bar in your bedroom!"

Lost Appetite

Tuesday, November 4, 1997

Faye continued to work for Representative Meany's campaign on Monday, Wednesday, and Friday mornings. She pretended her heart was in the monotonous work she was doing, keeping it exciting by trying to find information that might be useful to Marvin Cohen.

Although she never had the craving for a cigarette while working out at the gym, the monotony of stuffing envelopes or copying papers often found her plucking at the rubber band she always wore around her wrist. She had learned that she had specific feelings, "cravings," Dr. Thompson had called them, when her body wanted her to have a nicotine fix.

She now knew that her cravings never lasted longer than a few minutes. When one started, she would close her eyes, and pluck on the rubber band. Instantly, in accordance with the post-hypnotic suggestion Dr. Thompson had given her, she would see in vivid detail the monstrous man who ran the tobacco companies. He sat at his desk, with piles of medical reports proving the deadliness of cigarettes and the addictiveness of nicotine, and wore an evil, yellow-toothed grin as he laughed and stuffed wads of money into his pocket.

She was proud of herself and announced to all who would listen that she had quit smoking, and explained Dr. Thompson's technique, and never tried to snap her rubber band quietly.

Frank Timmons, the dour-faced man who often sat next to her when she stuffed envelopes, also smoked, and his resentment of her quitting seemed to grow with every workday. "Why can't you just chew gum like those other wimps who quit smoking?" he grumbled.

Frank Timmons wasn't well, Faye knew. Some days he looked worse than others, his skin gray and lifeless, his eyes dull, his movements halting. Today was one of those days, and, in a rush of concern that surprised her, Faye asked, "Aren't you feeling well, Frank?"

Like an ember that has been blown upon, Frank found the energy to hiss, "I am *not*, missy! You try feeling well with chemo three times a week."

"Oh. I'm sorry."

"'Sorry' don't make it better, missy. You can sit there and snap rubber bands all you want, and that ain't gonna make me feel any better, either."

They continued to work in silence for a few minutes, but Faye couldn't let it go. For the first time in her life, she had recognized someone more miserable than she—more miserable than she had been, at her worst—and she wanted to help, somehow.

"I don't have any experience with chemotherapy," she said, "but my husband might have needed it, if he hadn't died first. He had some sort of liver problem, we never knew for sure…but we suspected cancer."

"He was lucky," Frank snapped. "Death would be better."

Faye caught her breath. Edwin's death hadn't *seemed* lucky. "What's the chemo like?" she whispered. "How can it be worse than death?"

She immediately regretted her rhetorical question, and expected him to snap back, again; but perhaps he sensed the sincerity in her voice. After a moment, he spoke softly. "The chemo is nothing. Just shots. It's what it does to your insides that makes it bad. I haven't been able to eat for almost a week, now. I'm nauseous, and if I try to force something down, I throw it back up within the hour. Sometimes I throw up for no reason, just foam comes out." He glared at her, his ferocity briefly returning. "I still got it up *here!*" he hissed, pointing at his temple. "I'm as sharp as I ever was! Other guys, they're doddering around at my age, pissing in their pants. They don't know what's going on, but I *do!* I know I ain't getting any better. But I hate this damned weakness. I hate the nausea. And I hate that it's happening to *me*."

Faye felt her eyes stinging with tears. She hadn't asked what caused the cancer, but in her heart she knew it was cigarettes. Every day that she didn't smoke must have been another slap in the face to him. If he had quit when he was her age, he might well be healthy now. No wonder he was so hostile!

She desperately wanted him to feel better. "Surely they have some medicine that would settle your stomach!" she said.

Frank glowered all the more. "They do," he said. "It's called Marinol, and my doctor's been trying to get it for me. But it costs over a thousand dollars for a month's worth, and my insurance won't cover it. And I sure as hell don't have that kind of money."

South of the Border

Wednesday, November 5, 1997

"Have you ever heard of a drug called Marinol?" Faye asked Marian over breakfast the next morning.

Marian looked startled, before she composed herself and replied, "Yes, I have, darling. Why do you ask?"

Faye spoke of Frank at work, about the cancer and the chemo and the nausea, and the prescription he couldn't afford. "I found out from Dr. Thompson," Faye explained, "that people can buy medicine for less in Mexico. I was thinking, if Frank could buy it in Mexico, he might be able to afford it. He looks *terrible*," she added. "He says he hasn't been able to keep anything down for over a week."

"But why doesn't he just—" Marian seemed to catch herself, and change her mind. "I don't know the exact price, but I'm sure it's cheaper in Mexico. People don't have insurance down there, and the pharmaceutical companies set prices in accordance with what the market will bear; and in Mexico, it doesn't bear much."

"The only problem is, Dr. Thompson charters a bus that goes down there once a month, but he won't be going again until the end of the month. And Frank should have the medicine *now*," said Faye. "So, I was thinking of driving down, myself."

"You were?" Marian seemed pleased and amused at the same time. "Well, good for you, darling. But, do you know where to go? Do you speak Spanish? You don't want to get ripped off while you're down there."

"Ripped off? You mean, robbed?"

"Not exactly. There are dozens of drug stores lined up in every little border town, some more reputable than others. You wouldn't want to pay for a watered-down version of some prescription."

"Oh, no, I wouldn't."

"Besides, *las farmacias* along the border do their own price inflation, catering to us *gringos*. You'd be better off going a little further south, if you had time."

"I guess I hadn't thought it through. I just wanted to do something nice for Frank, but this sounds too complicated."

"Nonsense, darling, it's not complicated at all when you know what you're doing. What would you think about my going with you?"

Faye's jaw dropped. "Oh, my. I hadn't thought of that. I only brought it up because I would be missing a few of our workouts. But, yes, I'd *love* you to come with me!"

"If we're going to help your friend, we'll have to make this soon." She took a small electronic unit from her purse and began to tap on it with a pencil-like object.

"What's that?" Faye asked.

"My Palm Pilot," Marian replied, tapping. "They're a brand new kind of hand-held computer. I have all my appointments in here." After a moment, she said, "Yes, there's nothing I can't put off. If we leave now, and don't waste time, you can have your Marinol in time for work tomorrow morning."

It's Not About The Money

Faye had never in her life made a trip on such little notice. She usually spent fifteen minutes just making sure her purse and gym bag contained everything she might need before going to the supermarket yet, here she was, a flushed and breathless passenger in Marian's amazing automobile.

"We could take my car," Faye said, as they backed out of her driveway. "You always seem to be doing the driving."

Marian smiled as she shifted into first gear and pulled into the traffic. "Not a problem, darling," she said. "And your car wouldn't last a minute in Nogales. In fact, I bet your car insurance has a specific clause against driving in Mexico."

"It does?"

"Unless you paid extra, it does. And you would spend more time worrying about someone stealing your car than you would taking care of business."

"Aren't you worried about *this* car?"

"This car only looks new from the inside," Marian said, looking out over the shiny hood. "No one would *bother* to steal this wreck."

"Why are we heading this way?" Faye asked. "Don't we want to head south?"

"First, we have to get a prescription for the Marinol."

"Oh," Faye said. "I didn't think about that. I don't know if I can talk Frank into giving me a copy of his prescription. Besides, he's not at the headquarters now, and I don't know where he—"

"Relax, darling!" Marian chuckled. "Frank's prescription wouldn't do you any good if you *did* have it. The U.S. Customs folks will only let you bring medicine back across the border for your *own* personal use."

Faye wore a sudden look of dismay. "Then...there's no point in our going, is there?"

Marian unexpectedly pulled into a parking lot that Faye found familiar. "Why, this is Dr. Thompson's building!"

Inside, Vera Daye led them to Dr. Thompson's office where, in just moments, he joined them. "What a nice surprise," he smiled, "to see both you lovely ladies today. How may I be of service?"

Faye explained about Frank, and his chemotherapy, and his prescription for Marinol. "I just thought I'd do him a favor by picking some up in Mexico," she said, "but Marian said I'd need a prescription—in *my* name."

Thompson nodded. "She's right. I'm happy to write you one, of course. I hate to, though—that stuff is only half as good as the real thing."

"The real thing? What is that?"

"Well, marijuana, of course."

Faye was stunned. "Marijuana? Frank needs marijuana?"

"Frank needs to *eat*," Dr. Thompson clarified. "THC, the therapeutic ingredient in marijuana, is the most effective and safest appetite inducer known to man. But marijuana is illegal to grow in most countries and Marinol is just artificial THC."

Faye nodded, relieved. Somehow, the idea that a nice, hygienic, chemical compound had replaced the dangerous weed sounded comforting to her. "Well, that must be just as good, then."

"Well, it isn't," Dr. Thompson replied. "It's an artificial chemical based on one that grows naturally. Artificial drugs are never as effective as their natural counterparts, but the pharmaceutical firms can't patent herbs. So they sell the artificial drugs, instead."

"Are you saying the pharmaceutical firms made marijuana illegal just because they couldn't patent it?"

"I don't know what part they played, but they certainly reaped the benefits. Most herbal cures are good for five or ten different ailments; the pharmaceuticals get to synthesize the active ingredients, make them more potent—also more laden with side effects—and convince doctors that they are the *only* reliable treatment. Most doctors are so swamped with work, they can't take the time to actually read the medical journals; all they really see are the advertisements—which are placed there by the drug companies. So, they prescribe them, and never even bother learning about the herbs."

"And now that the pharmaceuticals are advertising directly on TV, to the consumers, it's even worse," Marian chimed in.

"You said it," Dr. Thompson agreed. "Now I've got patients walking into my office, telling *me* what to prescribe!"

In spite of his grumbling, fifteen minutes later, Faye held in her hand a prescription, made out for her for a three-month's supply of Marinol and they were again on their way.

Marian took 99th Avenue south to I-10, and then headed east towards Tucson. "I hope you like music," she remarked. "I always play some tunes when I set out on a long drive."

Faye heard the sweet sounds of Ray Coniff, Percy Faith, and the others swirl about in her mind and agreed, "Oh, yes. I would *love* to listen to music while we drive. Edwin never would, you know."

Marian slipped a shiny disk into a slot on the dashboard. "Who is that?" Faye asked.

"Just some Stones," the older woman replied.

"Stones?" Faye responded, confused.

The harsh chords of "I Can't Get No Satisfaction" rocked through the car, and Faye realized with horror that the "music" Marian intended to play was, actually, rock'n'roll.

All the way to Mexico!

Faye managed to restrain herself for nearly an hour, then could no longer. "Do you really *like* this stuff?" she said, indicating the in-dash CD player.

Marian quickly lowered the volume of the music. "Well, of course!" she exclaimed. "Why, darling, don't *you* like rock'n'roll?"

"Well—" Sometimes, when Marian asked a question, it forced Faye to re-think her position. She had never really *listened* to rock music. Edwin had hated it, but that was no reason why she should automatically dislike it. What did she dislike about it? "I guess I find it disturbing, somehow," she replied, finally. "So much of it is disloyal, unsettled. Like that 'Satisfaction' song. The singer seems hungry for something he hasn't even identified himself. It just made me feel so—so *unsatisfied* myself."

"Good music, like any good art, inspires in its audience the emotions and feelings the artist wishes to convey."

"Well, I like art that conveys *nice* feelings." Faye explained.

"So, you're telling me you would prefer a song entitled, 'I *Can* Get Satisfaction'?"

"I suppose…"

"You said the song made *you* feel the same lack of satisfaction that the singer, Mick Jagger felt. Did you feel satisfied before that song came on? *Really* satisfied?"

Faye shook her head in puzzlement. "I'm—we're on our way to do a good deed. I'm healthier than I've been in decades. I have a good friend," she smiled, "that I didn't have a year ago. Why wouldn't I be satisfied?"

"Examine your feelings," Marian suggested. "Look for a feeling of pure satisfaction—if you have it, you should be able to find it. Were you—are you—*completely* satisfied with your life, with your world, right now?"

"With the world? Well, maybe not the whole world..."

"Songs like that one, a gigantic hit in the sixties, helped the kids recognize and name the feelings they had. They *were* dissatisfied with the world, and with the lives the adults seemed to have pushed upon them. Rock'n'roll helped galvanize a whole generation into insisting on change."

"The hippies?" Faye gasped in disgust. "Were—*you* a hippy?"

"And proud of it," Marian grinned. "Look, the media dubbed those who were bright enough to see through the government bullshit 'hippies.' Those who couldn't see through it, the media rewarded with the name 'patriots.' But, you know what, darling? Just because it's in the papers, doesn't make it so."

"But, those hippies just threw their lives away! They wasted their youth!" Faye lamented.

"They weren't thrown away and the effort wasn't wasted. We worked to change the evils that we saw, the illegal war in Viet Nam, a dishonest President, racism and sexism and any number of other things."

"But...weren't you a little *old* to be a hippy?"

Marian smiled sweetly. "Darling, when you work to make the world a better place, one is *never* too old."

Rest Stop

When they were a little north of Nogales, Arizona, they stopped at a small rest area to use the ladies' room. There was one truck parked there, unoccupied, when Marian pulled into a space near the building.

"It's best one of us stay with the car," Marian said. "Would you like to go first, darling, or shall I?"

"I'll go, if you don't mind," Faye said, quickly. Her bladder had been full for twenty minutes or so, and she wasn't sure how much longer she could wait.

Public rest rooms always made her a little nervous. She hated using them alone, but she knew Marian would hear her scream if there were a problem, and it did make sense not to leave the car alone. She stepped with quiet apprehension into the ladies' room. It was dirtier than she had feared, but desperate as she was, she carefully covered the toilet seat with paper.

As she sat, she could hear men's voices in conversation. She thought it must be men from the empty truck using the adjoining bathroom.

Their voices seemed to be drifting through the ventilation grate in the wall. Probably the men's room had one just like it; and in the stillness of the desert, she could hear them well enough to understand most of what they said. "General," she heard, followed by a name she couldn't make out, and some unintelligible conversation.

Suddenly, one sentence came through with absolute clarity. "He wants *more* money?"

Fascinated, Faye held her breath but couldn't make out the reply. The first person, though, was angry and his voice boomed back, "I don't give a flying fuck about his children! If he doesn't want to grease the wheels, I'll just find someone else who does. Generals are a dime a dozen and he knows it." His voice sounded oddly familiar, but she couldn't quite place it.

She could barely make out the other man's reply, spoken with a Mexican accent. "Generals don't come cheap, you know. And he's good, *muy bueno*." She heard the sounds of flushing, and footsteps, then two truck doors open and close, the motor start, and the truck pull away.

It was amazing how much one could visualize from a sequence of sounds!

Finishing up, she flushed, and went back into the desert brilliance and got in the car. Instantly, Marian started the engine.

"Aren't you going to go?" Faye asked.

"I can go later," her friend said, backing out of the parking spot and peeling off onto the highway. "We have to catch up to that truck."

"Why?" Faye asked.

"I can't tell you now," Marian said. "I don't want to influence your judgment." They rocketed down the road, the Torino speeding swiftly and smoothly to 100 mph, rapidly approaching the truck.

"We're going so fast!" Faye cried.

"Stop looking at the speedometer and pay attention to that truck. In a moment, we're going to pass and I want you to tell me who you think the passenger is."

True to her word, Marian's Ford moved into the left-hand land and sailed past the truck with absolute ease. Faye had just a moment to see the passenger, whose face was turned towards the driver and thus towards Faye, as well. Her jaw dropped in recognition, because she had only seen the man in person once before, yet she was certain it was him—and it was his voice that she had recognized in the rest room.

She turned to Marian and looked at her, amazement in her eyes.

"That," she said, "was Representative Meany!" And then she gasped, as the figure in the driver's seat came clear in her mind. "And the man driving him—I've seen him before, too!" she cried. "He's the one who left the envelope that I told you about, the one that Representative Meany picked up, that day in the park!"

Aspiration
• • • • • • • •

Coincidence

As the two women continued their journey to the border town of Nogales, Faye found herself both amazed and disbelieving. "How could this happen?" she demanded of Marian. "I wouldn't have expected to see Representative Meany at his own re-election head-quarters, much less run into him at an out-of-the-way rest stop on a side road heading for Mexico."

Marian didn't seem at all perplexed. "I don't think the odds against this meeting are as high as you do, darling, because I have some information that you don't. And let me relieve you of the notion that there is *any such thing* as meaningless coincidence."

"What do you mean?" Faye had that feeling that Marian was about to turn her world on its side, again.

"What's the biggest coincidence that ever happened to you? In your entire life?"

"Running into Carvel Meany, just now!"

Marian laughed. "Well, before today, then."

Faye thought. The *biggest* coincidence? "It would have to be the night I first met Edwin," she said. "I was eighteen, going to a swim meet, and my best friend Barbara, was driving. My goodness," Faye added, thoughtfully, "I haven't thought of Barbara in years.

"Anyway, we were going to join our other friend, Emily, at the meet. Emily had been going on and on about this great guy she met and she was going to introduce us to him."

"And did she?" Marian prompted, as Faye took a sip from her bottle of water.

"Well," Faye continued, "we had just started out, with twenty or so miles to go, when one of the tires went flat. We lived on a farm in Ohio, nowhere near an interstate highway so we were on a country road with little traffic. When Barbara and I checked the trunk, we discovered the spare was also flat. We didn't know *what* we were going to do."

"And what *did* you do?"

"The sun was just setting, but fortunately Barbara remembered passing a farmhouse about a quarter mile back. We ran back to the driveway and up to the house and rang the bell, and this cross-looking woman answered. We explained our predicament, and she called her son down to help.

"Well, he was just the cutest boy I had ever seen! And he liked me, too—I could tell by the way he looked at me. He was a little older than us, and about to leave for a date, he said. But he took the time to take us back to our car, inflate the spare, and put it on for us—and he wouldn't take a dime for his trouble!

"Well! Barbara and I talked of nothing else all the way to the meet. But when we got there, and caught up with Emily—I almost screamed. It turned out the boy she had wanted us to meet was the same boy who had changed our tire!"

Marian smiled as if she had guessed the punch line. "And that was your biggest coincidence?"

"Of course!" Faye grinned. "The boy was Edwin. We married a year later."

Marian nodded. "That's the thing about good coincidences. They guide us along life's path. Do you suppose you would have married Edwin, if the *first* time you had met him was at the meet?"

"Maybe not," Faye confessed. "I think I impressed him at the car, when I knew the correct name of the lug nuts—Barbara just referred to them as 'those things.' Edwin said he had never met a pretty girl before who knew about car parts and tools. So, maybe that is why he married me!"

"Of all times to have a flat, just *before* Edwin left for his date. Of all places to have a flat, a quarter mile from Edwin's house. Of all evenings to have a flat, the *very one* on which Emily intended to introduce you to Edwin. And, of all people to be involved in this chain of events...Edwin, the boy you married and spent most of your life with." Marian paused and shook her head. "How can *anyone* think coincidences are meaningless, when they shape our entire lives?"

"I suppose some people would say, our *lives* are meaningless." Faye suggested, pensively. It dawned on her how the quickly the blush had fallen from the rose of her and Edwin's love, how soon it was that their lives had become mechanical and dry.

"Well, they're *not*," Marian said curtly. "People who say they believe their lives are meaningless are just trying to rationalize not making an effort at living them. Lives take *work!* But it's worthwhile work, and following the coincidences the universe brings us helps ensure that we do it right."

"What do you mean?"

"Those messages come from our Higher Selves," Marian explained. "You can call it God, or your Higher Power, or Mumbo Jumbo god of the jungle, for all I care. But those messages come to each of us, and if you're alert to them, darling, they can make it a lot easier to achieve your life's goal."

Faye laughed, bitterly. "I guess I missed out on my life's goal a long time ago."

"Darling!" Marian exclaimed. "Your life is *ahead* of you! Everything you've experienced, up to now, happened to make you the person you are...*now!* Every day, you get to choose the goals for the rest of your life. My goodness, darling, how old are you?"

Faye grimaced. "Sixty."

"These days, sixty is hardly being on the verge of death. You're in good health, and your health is getting better as you exercise and get the toxins of alcohol, tobacco, and crappy food out of your system. You should be planning for decades of exciting futures, not planning your funeral!"

Faye felt a lump forming in her throat. "Marian...the life I've known isn't the one I *want* any more of."

"The life you knew is over," Marian said, tartly. "So let's focus on what lies ahead. You've just experienced a great coincidence. I've told you that coincidences lead us along our life's path. So! In what direction do you think this coincidence is leading you?"

"I have no idea," Faye said, flatly. "I only overheard a few words, but—"

"You *overheard* Meany talking?" Marian cried with excitement. "In the rest room? What did you hear?"

Faye's face scrunched in concentration. "Well...the man with him said something about another man, a general, I think, wanting more money. And Rep—er, Meany said he didn't care about that, that generals were a dime a dozen."

"No shit! More money?" Marian exhaled, hands gripping her steering wheel.

"What does it mean?"

"Carvel Meany owns land in Mexico," Marian explained excitedly. "He grows cannabis there and he sells it in the States, illegally. Obviously, he has to get his crop through a customs station or he has to smuggle it across the border. Sneaking it through customs is the easier way."

"But, how could he do that?" Faye asked.

"Bribing a customs official is usually a breeze. And I think you overhead a conversation indicating that an official on some level wants a bigger piece of the pie." A thoughtful look came across Marian's face. "That must be why he's driving down to the border himself. It seemed odd that we would see him in a truck instead of a limousine."

"What do you mean?"

"Well, darling, the Mexicans are big on protocol. They each want to think they're important enough to talk to the top man. So, Meany has to do the business himself. But he doesn't want people to *know* he's going to Mexico, so he travels incognito, driven by one of his ranch hands."

"Oh." They rode in silence for a few minutes, then Faye asked, "So...what is this canna stuff that Meany grows?"

"Not 'canna,' darling," Marian chuckled. "*Cannabis sativa.* Marijuana! You remember, Meany's father grew it in Tennessee. When the marijuana laws that he backed got stricter, ironically, he had to stop growing it in the United States. So, he bought a few hundred acres just south of Nogales and moved to Arizona—that's why his son, Carvel, lives here, now."

Faye looked at Marian in disbelief.

"It's a matter of public record," Marian assured her. "Marvin found the records through a Mexican title guaranty company. He can show you copies. I know where his land is. Would you like to see for yourself?"

"You mean...actually *look* at a marijuana field?"

"Just twenty miles south of the border. And we can do some good, at the same time."

Family Plot

Nogales was a town divided, with half in the United States and half in Mexico. Faye was surprised that so few cars were lined up to cross the border into Mexico. "It's not surprising, darling," Marian explained. "It can be dangerous to drive near the border. Most tourists to Nogales just walk in." She pointed out the filled parking lots behind them, on U.S. soil. "Or they take the little shuttle bus. After all, there are really only three reasons to go to Nogales: To get cheap medicine, a cheap drunk, or a cheap whore. And you don't need a car for that stuff."

The official in the booth on the Mexican side of the border asked where they were going. "Nogales, and no further," Marian said sweetly. "For prescriptions."

"May I see your identification, ladies?" he asked. Both women presented their drivers' licenses, which the man examined briefly and returned. He then waved them on.

"Why is it so dangerous to drive here?" Faye asked.

"Well, you know how in the United States, the basic notion of jurisprudence is that a person is considered innocent until proven guilty? It's the opposite in Mexico. Once accused of a crime, even a minor one, a person is considered guilty until proven innocent. So, a frequent occurrence over here is that someone will crash into your car, just a minor accident, but when the policeman—who is in cahoots with the other driver—comes, he arrests you and impounds your car. By the time you can prove your innocence, your car has mysteriously disappeared from the impound."

"What—that's awful!" Faye spluttered. "How can they get away with that?"

Marian shrugged. "The Mexican government isn't any more corrupt than ours, darling. The corruption is just easier to spot. But, don't worry. No one is going to lust after this car."

As a town, Nogales was built along the border Mexico shared with the United States. After a few minutes of threading through densely-packed streets filled with slowly moving old and beat-up cars, they suddenly broke through into the countryside and found themselves speeding down a pot-holed two-lane highway.

"We told that guard we weren't going further than Nogales," Faye said nervously.

"Not much farther, darling," Marian soothed her. "It's a bit off the road, but Marvin has shown me satellite photos of the layout. I don't think we'll have any problem finding the Meany family's acreage. Of course, we *will* have to be plenty cautious."

"Cautious? Of what?"

"Well...what they are doing, *is* illegal. There will certainly be guards, that sort of thing. But if we're careful, we'll probably never see one."

They drove just a few more miles down the highway, then Marian turned off onto a dirt road that Faye hadn't even seen coming. It was well-graded, at first, and other than the huge cloud of brown dust raised behind them, not much different than tooling down the highway. Seeing the cloud in her rear-view mirror, Marian slowed down. "No point in telegraphing our arrival," she said.

As they proceeded, the condition of the road deteriorated to the point where they had to avoid large rocks on the road; the Torino was forced to wind carefully around them.

"This is not the road to Meany's property," Marian shouted as they jounced along, "not directly. But it goes *near* it. We should be able to off-road it a bit to get closer."

"Won't this just destroy your suspension?" Faye asked between jolts.

"Tough suspension," Marian assured her. "We'll be fine."

As they continued, the road quickly deteriorated further, until it was barely passable. "How could anyone navigate *this?*" Faye asked.

"They don't," explained Marian. "About thirty years ago, this road was maintained better. It was used by local farmers to drive over a bridge to a nearby village to go to church. But in 1967 a flash flood destroyed the bridge *and* the church. There's little reason to use this road, now—there are easier ways to get to any place near here."

"Then why aren't we taking an easier way?" Faye shouted between jolts.

"We want to use the *back* door," Marian replied. She turned to Faye and grinned. "Time to turn off!"

"Off?" Before Faye could say anything else, Marian turned completely off the road, driving between stands of juniper and pinion trees. Amazingly, it was actually a smoother ride than the road had been.

After a half-mile or so, Marian pulled the car under the branches of one of the bushy juniper trees and turned it off. "Time to take a short walk," she said. "Meany's property is just a few hundred yards from here."

They stepped out and onto the hard, dry ground. "Watch out for rattlesnakes and scorpions."

Faye gasped. She hadn't realized this would be a *dangerous* adventure. "How do you know exactly where Meany's property is? Have you been here before?"

Marian had opened the trunk of the car and was busily removing a video camera and another small, box-like device. "As I said, I studied Marvin's satellite photos. When you told me you wanted to go to Nogales, I hoped we could work in this side trip."

She handed the box to Faye. "You don't mind holding this for me, do you, darling?"

"Of course not, Marian," the younger woman agreed. "What is it?"

"A GPS—a receiver for the Global Positioning System. It receives signals from two or three satellites in orbit, times them electronically, and uses them to calculate our position on the Earth's surface to within a few yards."

Faye held the device gingerly, as if it might explode. "Oh, my," she cried. "Where did you get this? Is it some sort of CIA secret Marvin acquired?"

Marian laughed. "Of course not, darling. I bought it at Radio Shack."

They walked along the open ground between the low trees. Faye was looking so intently for rattlesnakes and scorpions that it startled her when Marian suddenly stopped and said, "Well, here you are—your first marijuana plant."

Faye looked up, and at first, saw nothing different. There were the same clusters of juniper and pinion trees as before, with occasional small cacti and other plants growing on the ground in between.

But then, she realized that there was something growing *beneath* the pinion tree in front of her. It was a patch of tall plants, of a brilliant, beautiful emerald green, almost as tall as the tree's lowest branches.

Marian aimed the video camera at her. "Okay, darling, just hold the GPS out so I can tape our position. That will serve as proof later that we are where we are—Meany's property just south of Nogales, Mexico." She then panned the camera toward the plants. "Stand near the plants, Faye, to give them scale, so people can see how big they are."

Hesitantly, Faye felt one of the plants. It seemed like any other weed one might find in a garden or, more likely, growing in the woods. It wasn't as beautiful as a rose, but it was pretty in its own, simple way. It certainly wasn't vile. "It's hard to believe that this plant has been the cause of so many laws, arrests, convictions, and ruined lives," Faye remarked.

"Darling," Marian said, "this plant is just a plant. It's human *greed* that caused those laws, arrests, convictions, and ruined lives. Marijuana just grows. It's just a plant." She handed Faye the video camera. "Now," she added, "if you'll excuse me...I didn't get a chance at that rest stop..."

And, with that, Marian stepped around the pinion tree, and Faye heard her unfasten her jeans, pull them down, and begin to urinate. Faye began to giggle. "What is it, darling?" Marian called.

"I can't believe you're tinkling on Meany's property!"

"Darling," Marian chuckled, "it's the least I can do!"

Faye inspected the marijuana plant more closely. She remembered that Dr. Thompson had said that Marinol was not as effective as "real" THC, which he said was in marijuana. What if Frank just *ate marijuana*—would that bring his appetite back? How much would he need, she wondered? Faye had no idea, but, on impulse, she picked a couple of clusters of buds and stuffed them in her back pocket, smiling.

It was a pleasant day, and she hadn't been out in the country in a long time. The sky was a beautiful, deep blue, and the air smelled fresh and clear—much cleaner than in the Valley. "It certainly is beautiful!" she called to Marian.

There was no answer, and Faye stopped smiling. She turned around to find her friend—and found herself staring into the barrel of a rifle.

She stifled a scream. The face at the other end of the barrel was Hispanic, wearing a straw hat. The man also wore a bolo tie, white shirt, and pressed blue jeans, just like the man she had seen in the park in Sun City, and who she had seen driving Meany in his truck a few hours before. It was a different man, but, oddly, he was wearing an almost identical outfit.

That all came to her as her knees buckled. She had never looked into the business end of a rifle, before. *So much for living another sixty years,* she thought. *I'm going to die today.* She focused beyond the barrel to the man's face, and then beyond to Marian, quietly sneaking up behind him.

Faye's eyes gave her away, and the man started to turn, his rifle drifting to the right as he turned—but he was too slow. Marian chopped his neck with the side of her hand; his eyes glazed over, and he collapsed to the ground like a sack of potatoes, Marian grinning mischievously, standing behind him.

"We should go, darling," she said, "before another of these roaming guards wanders by. Or, is there more here you'd like to see?"

Faye stammered, "N—no, I've seen enough." Marian took the GPS from her and guided her quickly back to the car. "Shouldn't we hurry?" Faye asked nervously, as they drove away.

"I don't want to stir up a lot of dust," Marian replied. "In this case, slower is safer than faster."

Faye turned and looked out the rear window. "Did you kill him?" she whispered.

"Not at all. But he'll wish I did, when he wakes up with the stiff neck I gave him!"

Shopping Trip

They bounced back to the dirt road, maintaining a slow pace until they reached the paved road, by which time Faye's teeth had been nearly shaken from her mouth. She kept watch in the side mirror and, as far as she could tell, no one had followed them. She breathed a sigh of relief.

Faye shook her head in amazement. "Well," she said, "that was certainly the wildest adventure I ever had!"

"When we get back to Sun City," Marian said thoughtfully, "I think it will be time for you to start studying kung fu. It will give you a great aerobic workout, and enable you to defend yourself."

"*Defend* myself? Marian, I'm sixty years old! I have *no intention* of ever risking my life, again!"

"Were you 'risking your life' in the parking lot of the supermarket, the day those assholes attacked you?" her friend reminded her.

"No..." Faye replied grudgingly.

"This isn't a safe world," Marian pointed out. "Risk finds us. If you can't protect yourself, who will? What if I'm not there, next time?"

"But kung fu..."

"With only rudimentary training in it," Marian assured her, "you could have disarmed that guard in three different ways. Without," she added, "even breaking a sweat."

Faye tried to imagine herself as someone who could take care of herself in any situation...who didn't need to be rescued. Who, indeed, could rescue others! It was a heady thought and it made Faye's heart pound with excitement.

Minutes later they re-entered Nogales' city limits. After their adventure in the marijuana patch the tangle of the tourists and the madness of the traffic seemed tame. Marian had to circle a block three times before a parking space opened up, but when it did, she grabbed it. Soon, with the vehicle locked, Faye and Marian went on their shopping expedition.

It was like a strip mall of drug stores. For a four-block stretch, there was a shop marked farmacia every three or four doors. Marian picked one, seemingly at random, and they went in.

"*Buenos dias, señora,*" Marian said to the woman behind the counter. "Can you recommend a doctor who can write a prescription for us?" The woman mechanically handed them a mimeographed slip of paper, and Faye followed Marian from the store, puzzled.

"We already have the prescription," Faye reminded her friend when they had got outside.

"The prescription you got from Robert is for the customs people at the border. In order to buy prescription meds in Mexico, you must have a script from a *Mexican* doctor."

"Oh, no! He'll examine me, and find out—"

"Not to worry, darling. This is all standard procedure. See, the address she gave us is just next door."

The doctor's office contained many people but no chairs; they weren't needed because the turnover was so swift. When it was their turn, Faye and Marian stepped to a window and Marian handed the prescription for Marinol and a twenty dollar bill to the receptionist. The receptionist went to the back and returned, in a moment, with a second signed prescription from the local doctor.

Back in the *farmacia*, the woman at the cash register looked at the prescription and blanched. "I—I do not believe we have this in stock," she said in accented English. "I will check." She was gone for several minutes, and had bad news when she returned. "We do not carry this," she said.

"Oh," Faye frowned. "Do you know who does?"

97

"This medicine is very highly regulated," the woman replied. "It is very hard to get. I'm not sure *who* might have it." The cashier then gazed past Faye, looking to the growing line of customers behind her. "You can try other *farmacias*," the woman said, "but I do not think you will find any."

Marian dutifully followed Faye from shop to shop, until they had exhausted the last of the farmacias in the four-block strip. "I can't believe it," Faye said. "This whole trip...for nothing!"

"It does seem odd," Marian commented. "I'm sure I've heard of people buying Marinol here before."

Faye narrowed her eyes and grimaced. "We may as well go," she said.

When they returned to Marian's car, Faye saw her expression darken. "What is it?" Faye asked.

"Someone tried to get into the car," the older woman replied.

"How can you tell? Is a window broken?"

"There's a solid coating of dust on the side of the car from our ride in the country. We haven't opened these doors from the outside since we were there, but the dust is smudged off the handle, here. See?"

"What does it mean?"

"I don't know yet. Let's just get in and see what happens."

So the women got in the car. It started without incident, and they drove around the block and to the hoard of cars waiting to cross back into the United States.

"Something else is fishy," Marian said.

"What's the matter?"

"Well, darling, some people's business requires them to make weekly or even daily trips into Mexico. They can apply for a special tag that, essentially, says, 'I have nothing to declare,' and they're allowed to drive right through the checkpoint. But, today, those lanes are closed, meaning that they're checking *everyone*. It's not unheard of, but it's odd."

"Oh. Well, I suppose it doesn't mean anything to us, only that it will take longer to get through the border than otherwise."

"Perhaps not," Marian nodded. "On the other hand, there's the matter of the white truck that pulled in close behind us the moment we got into line, blocking us from leaving even if we wanted to."

Faye turned and peered through the rear window. It was not just any white truck, but the same make and model as the one they had seen at the rest area, the one Meany and his cohort had been in. It was hard to see who was in it, now, but it could have been Meany, himself, with the same driver.

"My God!" Faye breathed. "I think it is Meany! And he must have just seen me looking at him."

"Not with these tinted windows. But, look," Marian continued, "across the border. Isn't that the Channel 2 news truck?"

Faye had to stretch upwards to see above the cars and beyond the booths, but it did look like the news truck to her. "What does it all mean?" she asked.

Marian took a deep breath. "Well, darling, let's use our thinking caps. When we passed Meany's truck on the way here, they had the opportunity to see my car, as well—it *does* stand out. Suppose our friend with the rifle did contact his boss when he came to. Meany may have figured we were the same two old ladies who passed and recognized him on the road, and came up with a plan to keep us from causing him trouble."

"Plan?"

"You must understand, darling, Meany can't let word get out about marijuana being grown on his property, especially so close to re-election. He may have noticed us when we passed him going into Mexico, and recognized the description of our car when he heard about it from his lackey. So he *knows* we were spying on him."

"I didn't see any 'No Trespassing' signs, not even Spanish signs that might have been warnings. We didn't break any laws. Even knocking out that guard was just self-defense."

Marian shook her head, smiling. "Meany wants to keep his place secret, so he *certainly* isn't going to complain about our trespassing. But he has to do *something* to discredit any story we come out with."

"What can he do? We're just a couple of old ladies from Sun City..."

"Didn't the reaction of that woman in the pharmacy seem odd to you, when you asked for the Marinol?"

"Odd? In what way?"

"I don't know, darling. It just seemed to me that her manner had changed between the time we asked for the address of the doctor and when we returned to fill the prescription. She seemed frightened, somehow."

"Maybe," Faye agreed, halfheartedly.

"According to Robert, Marinol is synthetic THC, the therapeutic ingredient in marijuana. I wonder if dogs can smell it?"

"Dogs? There will be dogs?" Faye asked, her heart suddenly pounding.

"They certainly seem to be doing thorough searches of everyone," Marian pointed out. "And the DEA has plenty of dogs trained to sniff out drugs for operations such as this."

Faye grabbed Marian's sleeve. "I picked some of the marijuana and stuffed some of the buds in my back pocket," she said. "Could they smell that?"

Marian began to chortle as a plan came to mind. "Ah, ha!" she laughed in triumph. "I bet they didn't count on this. You're brilliant, Faye!"

"Are you kidding?" Faye protested. "I brought something into this car that could get us arrested! Me, that is," she amended. "I'll tell them, you didn't know anything about it…"

"Come on, darling. Your slacks and those buds are our way out of this predicament." She reached into the back seat and pulled Faye's gym bag into the front. "See why it's best to travel light? Now, all you need to do is wriggle out of those pants and into your spare pair, without someone outside seeing you."

Speechless, Faye hesitated a mere moment before doing as she was told. Only a month earlier, she hadn't been limber enough to have gotten out of her slacks in such tight quarters. Now, it was almost easy. "And why am I doing this?" Faye asked, more baffled than ever.

"Look, I think these men bribed the *farmacias* to withhold the Marinol from us. Or threatened them, maybe. I think they really got some themselves, and planted it somewhere in or on my car."

"Why? I have a prescription—it's all legal!"

"It's legal *if you declare it.* But we couldn't buy any, so we would have told the customs agent we had nothing to declare—and then the customs agents would have found the medicine, I'm sure. They would have gotten us on perjury!"

"But, I don't understand!" Faye cried. "Why would anyone try to set us up like this?"

"Don't you see, darling?" Marian said wryly. "That guard I *didn't* kill *did* call in a description of our car! They may not know *who* we are, but they know the people in this car were investigating Meany's little marijuana patch and must have followed us."

"So, when that woman suddenly 'ran out' of Marinol—"

"—it was because Meany's lackey told her not to sell it to us. They may have even gotten your name from the prescription," Marian completed.

"And now that we're here at the border, if they get us arrested, that will discount any tale we have to tell about Meany's Mexican property. In fact, with the power he wields, we might have been stuck in jail, incommunicado, until after the election! Maybe *much* longer."

"Then, why did they pull right in behind us?"

Marian's jaw set. "Because, darling, if by chance the agents *didn't* find the Marinol, Meany's men would be right behind us and would, I'm quite certain, have tried to do us in as soon as we hit the open road."

Faye caught her breath. "They can still do that!"

Marian grinned. "Maybe not."

The line moved slowly. They crossed the thick white line marking the border, but the delay was in the U.S. Customs booths. Each car seemed to take forever before passing inspection. Finally, it was their turn, and the man in the booth said, in a friendly manner, "Ladies, do you have anything to declare?"

Marian looked chagrinned. "Well, we do," she said, "but we've lost it."

"What do you mean?" the man asked, smiling pleasantly.

"Well, we came to Mexico to fill a Marinol prescription for my friend—she has the prescription—but I went and dropped it on the floor, and it rolled somewhere, and now I can't find it. I think it may have gone under the seat."

"Well, we can find *that* for you," the officer said. "Please just pull into that lane, and we'll have it for you in a jiffy."

"Certainly, officer," Marian said, shifting gears, and hitting the gas. Instantly the car roared *backwards* and crashed into the truck behind them.

Faye, fortunately, had been wearing her seat belt, and she was only slightly shaken. But Marian seemed completely flustered. "Oh, my God!" she howled.

The customs agent ran out of his booth and to her open window. "Are you all right?" he asked, concerned.

"I don't know *why* I keep doing that," Marian complained, looking and acting as if the first stages of Alzheimer's had crept in. "We'd better check for damage," she added to Faye, nodding meaningfully at the marijuana-tainted slacks Faye had been wearing.

Faye never expected to be in this kind of predicament, much less trying to escape from it. But, now, Marian needed her...Marian, who had twice saved her life. Quickly, before she could change her mind, she opened the car door and stepped outside, folded slacks in hand, knowing exactly what to do.

Marian exited, also, and the two strode purposely to the truck as its occupants also got out. The passenger was, indeed, Representative Meany.

His driver, the same man they had seen driving in Arizona, was livid as he inspected his bumper and broken headlight. "You fucking *puta!*" he cried. "Look what you did to my truck! I will have you arrested!"

"Not here," Marian pointed out, sweetly. "We are on the U.S. side of the border. But I will give you my address and insurance information. Then, when we come to court over this matter, you and your passenger will be summoned as witnesses and you can both tell your side of the story."

Meany inhaled sharply, then made a slight gesture—and the driver, seeing it, instantly swallowed his anger. "Never mind," he said, quietly, cursing under his breath. "It is a small thing."

With both men facing Marian, it was easy for Faye to slip behind them and drop her slacks behind the truck's seat. The passenger turned and faced her as she made her way back to Marian.

"Representative Meany! I'm so sorry we bumped into your truck!" She looked him in the eyes with all the faux admiration she could muster.

The Representative stared at Faye for a moment, and reflexively smiled back—Faye knew it was a habitual gesture, born of politics and not of sincerity, but that was okay—it was working in her favor. "Well, now, who are you?" he asked.

"My name is Faye McRae," she replied boldly. She saw his eyes widen slightly with recognition. He had learned her name from the prescription in the *farmacia*. "I work in your re-election campaign headquarters," Faye replied, pretending she hadn't caught the man's expression. "And I just *love* your speeches! Especially the one you did last week—I was at the park in Sun City when you read it, uh, said it for the TV news. It was so inspiring!" She shrugged her shoulders as if seized with happiness at meeting the Great Man in person.

She could see him eat it up. The flattery—so shallow a child would have spotted it, but for Meany it was as honest as anything else he said or did, and he couldn't recognize it as phony. He reached out and took her hand, and she allowed him to and even gave it a little squeeze. "I'm so happy to meet an enthusiastic constituent," he said. "But what are you doing in Mexico?"

"Just filling a prescription," she said. "Or, *trying* to."

Meany bestowed a smile upon her. He took her hand and gave it an extra squeeze and then released it, and she and Marian returned to their car.

The moment the door closed, they both heaved nervous sighs. "Oh, my God!" Faye whispered. "Did we get away with it?"

Marian hesitated. "We aren't through customs yet. And he certainly knows who I am from my license plate."

"And he recognized my name, I'm sure of it," Faye agreed.

"Well," Marian concluded, "there's nothing else we can do 'til we get through this inspection."

Putting the car into first, rather than reverse, Marian pulled into the inspection station where she and Faye were invited to stand aside while an agent inspected their car. A drug-sniffing dog made the first pass, finding nothing. But, then, the agent himself found the vial of Marinol, duct taped to the underside of the front seat. "This is a strange situation," he said. "I was told you had dropped the medicine, but it looks as if you intended to smuggle it in. Yet, you did declare it, and the law doesn't say *how* you have to take it into the country." He scratched his head. "You say you have a prescription for it?"

"Yes, sir!" Faye responded, handing it to him.

The man looked it over and then gave Faye a once over. "This is highly controlled medicine," he said, "usually prescribed for people on chemotherapy, who are too nauseous to eat. Begging your pardon, ma'am, but you don't look underfed to me."

"I have an appetite problem," she snapped, realizing that she *didn't* look as if she were starving to death. "Look!" She displayed her driver's license photo to the agent to prove her point. And the photo took her by surprise, as well; clearly it was a photo of her, but the woman in the picture was fat, pale, and sour looking. She knew the months spent under Marian's tutelage had made a difference, but this was the first time she had realized just *how* big a difference it had made.

Nevertheless, she worked up a display of righteous indignation. "That was issued just six months ago," she said. "I've lost sixty pounds in two months. Why do you think I need the Marinol? Would you like to present me with a dinner, so you can watch me throw up?" It was easy to imagine poor old Frank here, who *really* needed the medicine, getting the same third degree from the insensitive inspector.

"No, no, I believe you," the agent protested.

Just then, a ruckus from an adjacent station caught their attention. The drug-sniffing dog had discovered Faye's slacks in Meany's truck. A cameraman and reporter from the waiting news truck came running, while Meany and his driver started yelling at everyone within earshot, including the dog.

"Uh—you're free to go," their inspector told them. "Have a nice day." And he ran over to join the melee.

Marian and Faye smiled at each other, got in the car, and drove unobtrusively back into the USA.

All The News That Fits

"Did you see that?" Faye laughed with the release of tension and fear. "The reporters in the Channel 2 van just *ran* to Meany's truck. Why do you suppose they were there, anyway?" she added, suddenly puzzled.

"I wonder," Marian said, as she guided her car speedily down the highway. The traffic was thin, thanks to the slow processing of people entering the U.S. from that border station. "The Customs Department might have notified them that a big bust was expected to happen today. There must be *some* reason why the full inspections were given to every single vehicle. When they find what they're looking for, they like to get news coverage."

The sun set in typical, Arizona splendor before they reached I-10; Faye was able to enjoy it more thoroughly than Marian, who had to keep her eyes on the road. It was a blue-and-yellow sunset, with a few puffy, golden clouds suspended against a cerulean blue backdrop, just above the mountains that lay between them and Phoenix.

"Too bad we'll miss the evening news," she said to Marian. "I would love to see how they report Meany's arrest for trying to smuggle marijuana into the country!"

"We won't miss it. Marvin will tape it," Marian pointed out, "and we can see it anytime we want."

"I can't wait!" Faye said, bubbling. "Meany so deserves this! Will it be too late to visit when we get back to Sun City?"

"It's never too late to visit Marvin," Marian said, grinning. "I don't think he ever sleeps."

And so, late that evening, exhausted from the events of the day, Faye and Marian pulled into the *cul de sac* where Marvin's house was located, and parked in front of his house. They got out, and, before they could knock on his door, he opened it and greeted them.

"Ladies!" he called, smiling. "I saw you pull up on my outdoor monitor. Good to see ya! Come on in."

As they made their way past the bookshelves to his command center, Marian handed him the video camera and explained what was on it. "GPS code, marijuana plant, the whole deal."

"That's fuckin' *great!*" Marvin enthused.

"But it may be moot. Meany got busted going through customs, right behind us, and the news van was there!"

"No shit! What time?"

"When we passed through, about five thirty."

"We want to see the Channel 2 News, if you taped it," Faye added.

"Taped it? I *watched* it," Marvin said, his eyebrows knotted. "I didn't see nothin' about Meany."

"Really?" Marian exclaimed.

"Maybe there wasn't time to get the story back to the station? After all, we didn't get here until just now."

"Naw," Marvin disagreed. "They use satellite uplinks. There was plenty of time."

"Maybe it'll be on the late news?"

Marvin glanced at one of the several clocks he had positioned between the computers and other equipment. "We can see," he said. "It'll be on in just a few minutes."

"Had you heard anything about a big border drug bust taking place today?" Marian asked.

"No," he replied. "And I usually do hear about those. I have my spies," he added to Faye. Eyes twinkling, he nodded to Marian, "You're one of the best. So, before the news comes on, tell me what we're gonna see. What happened?"

With Faye occasionally adding details, Marian recounted the story. When she described backing into Meany's truck, Marvin laughed out loud. "Good for you, babe!" he said. At the story's conclusion, Marvin agreed that Meany's "butt was dust," as he put it. "This will be interesting," he said in anticipation.

As Channel 2's late night news started, Marvin turned up the sound and they gathered to watch it on one of the big wall monitors. On the other monitor was the news from a different station, sound muted. "If we see Meany's picture," Marvin explained, "I can switch the sound. And both channels are being recorded," he added.

The first reported story on Channel 2 regarded boxer Mike Tyson, while the other station reported a group protest in front of the White House. Watching both stations at once on different monitors, Faye could tell from the identical video clips that the stations were running the same stories, but in different sequence. "My goodness!"

Faye gasped. "They really *do* get their news from the same place!"

Eventually both stations got to local news. Both reported a Phoenix town hall meeting regarding a proposed light rail transportation system. Then Channel 2 reported on the opening of a new mall, while the other station ran video of a car fire.

"At least, the local stories are different," Faye remarked. But neither station broadcast one word about a Meany marijuana bust. When the news was over, Letterman appeared on one screen and Leno on the other, and Marvin, Marian and Faye sat, staring at each other in disbelief.

Finally, Marian spoke. "Well, they've certainly had enough time to write the story by now."

Marvin nodded grimly. "We knew our pal Meany has friends in high places."

"What do you mean?" Faye asked.

"If the powers-that-be want Meany in Congress, no stories will appear that might jeopardize his re-election."

"How can that be?" Faye asked, angrily.

"Hey, that's the way it is," Marvin said. "We know that TV and radio stations, and newspapers, receive their national and international news from the same wire services. But this was a local story...so I thought there was a chance it might get through. Oh, well." And he smiled apologetically, and shrugged his shoulders and held open his empty palms.

And Faye swallowed her frustration.

To Have A Friend

Thursday, November 6, 1997

The next day, at Meany's re-election headquarters, Faye managed to pull Frank Timmons aside. "Whattya want?" he snarled in his usual dour manner.

"I have something for you," she said, smiling. "Come outside with me." And she headed for the door, sensing him rising a moment later to follow.

"Okay, what?" he asked, after the door closed behind them. His expression combined curiosity with suspicion.

Faye handed him the bottle of Marinol. Faye had transferred the pills to a vial Dr. Thompson had given her, with Frank's name on it. She could see his eyes traverse the words several times, disbelieving. Finally, he spoke. "What, are you a drug store, now? How much do you want for these?"

"It's a gift," Faye explained. "I was in Mexico, yesterday, and I remembered you telling me you needed these, so I picked up a month's supply for you. I hope it helps," she added.

"Mexico?"

"My doctor, Dr. Thompson—his name and phone number are on the label—wrote out a prescription so we could get it legally and inexpensively."

"Can't have been *that* inexpensive," Frank growled. "What do I owe you?"

Faye felt the love of all mankind well up in her heart. "You don't owe me anything," she explained, "because you didn't ask me to do this. If these pills help you, you can get a refill prescription from Dr. Thompson. He has a bus that goes once a month to Mexico, and a lot of his patients take it to get their prescriptions filled at lower prices. You could do that, too."

Frank glared at her. "Why did you do this?"

Faye took a deep breath and decided not to get into a confrontation over this.. "Because I could," she smiled. "I hope they help." And she turned and walked inside, and returned to her station.

Frank entered a few moments later, but headed directly to the men's room. He was gone over five minutes, and when he returned, he wouldn't look at her. But Faye could tell he had been crying.

And, for the rest of their shift, while he didn't speak to her, he didn't growl at her, either—not even when she snapped her rubber band.

Try-Outs

Saturday, November 8, 1997

Faye stood at the edge of the pool. She had been practicing for this moment for weeks. There was a pleasant pounding of anticipation in her heart and a few butterflies in her stomach. She was breathing deeply, and the sensation of the air filling her smoke-free lungs was satisfying and, also, exciting.

Another part of the thrill was knowing that there were more women around her, each one ready to dive into the water on cue.

The cue came. Faye allowed herself to fall forward, gracefully, her arms gently rising so she would meet the water fingertips first. She didn't rush herself; neither did she hesitate. Gravity did all the work; she simply allowed it to. With no resistance, she entered the water cleanly, perfectly, exactly in time with the others.

Surrounded, now, by the cool, blue water, she tucked her head and rolled forward in an underwater somersault. Her fingertips touched those of the women beside her, and they rose in unison.

It was like being weightless. Nothing held her down; she floated like a cloud, or like an angel, the other angels in formation alongside her.

The women proceeded to execute the short set of movements they'd been given; then, Beatrice Smith, the woman in charge of the AquaBabes, gave the signal and the women swam back to the side of the pool.

"Sit on the edge of the pool, ladies," Beatrice commanded.

Placing her hands on the cement, Faye considered that, just a few months earlier, she would have been as likely to raise herself from the dead, as to raise her bulk out of a pool. But that was then, and this was now. She weighed far less, and her arms were far stronger. One gentle heave, and her behind was on the concrete, between her two companions.

"The following swimmers may stay: Number one, three, number five, seven, number nine, number nine, and twelve," Beatrice called from her seat across the pool. "For the rest of you, thank you very much for trying out. We hope you'll try out again, next time. *After* you've gotten in a little more practice," she added.

Faye could scarcely breathe. *She* was number twelve!

Past Beatrice, sitting on the balcony, Faye could see her friends, Marian and Dr. Thompson, watching. Even at that distance, Marian's smile and bright eyes were visible. And Dr. Thompson actually rose to his feet, grinning and clasping his hands over his head in triumph.

For a second, Faye had a flash in which Edwin was there in Dr. Thompson's place. But Edwin would never have given her a victory sign; Edwin never grinned, and he probably wouldn't even have come to the tryouts to give her moral support.

That she had a doctor—a *friend*—who cared enough to take time out of his day to be here for her, filled her with joy.

Beatrice continued speaking to the new AquaBabes; she informed them of the rehearsal schedule, the importance of *never* missing a rehearsal, and her expectations of them in general. She spoke crisply, in a no-nonsense manner, yet there was a kindness that made her seem far less intimidating than she first appeared.

When Beatrice's speech was over, she dismissed them and Faye ran up the ramp to the balcony. Excitedly, she shouted, "I can't believe it!"

"I can," Marian stated. "You've worked hard for this."

Faye grasped the woman's hands, looked into her eyes, and said, "I couldn't have done it without you."

Marian shook her head and gave Faye a hug. "You did this yourself, and you have *yourself* to be proud of."

"Hey," Dr. Thompson boomed, "if we're giving out hugs, where's mine?" He wrapped his powerful arms around Faye and gently squeezed. And although Faye would have said, a moment ago, that she couldn't have been happier—his hug did, indeed, add exquisitely to her pleasure.

Say Something

They ordered lunch from the poolside café and waiting for their food to arrive, Faye took the time to examine Marian's T-shirt. This one said, "Thinking Too Much Causes Most Unhappiness" and, in smaller letters, "Thinking Too Little Causes The Rest" and Faye actually laughed because she got this one.

"Have you sold many of those?" Faye asked, pointing to the shirt.

"Yeah, a couple," Marian responded.

"Only a couple?" Dr. Thompson interjected. "That's a good slogan. I would have thought more."

"Hey, Robert, I have a small clientele," Marian reminded him. "Even if it is a small forum, it's *my* forum."

"Why does it have to be a small forum?" Faye asked. "T-shirts are easy to make; we made some to promote the body shop. There are T-shirt shops in every mall, with designs and slogans on thermal transfers. People come in and pick the transfer they like, then the shopkeeper irons them onto a shirt, whatever color and size the customer wants. Why can't you sell them transfers with your designs?"

"The shops all get their designs from a very small number of national distributors," Marian explained. "*That's* why all the stores seem to have the same messages," she added.

"It's another variation of a central distribution point for media," Dr. Thompson stated. "No matter who owns the actual stores, they wind up selling the same messages."

"Are you saying that the same people own all the media? TV, newspapers, even T-shirts?" Faye asked.

"That's what Marvin says," Marian agreed.

"The Internet, too?"

There was a long pause. Marian and Dr. Thompson exchanged looks. "Well," Marian finally said, "not the Internet. No one 'owns' the Internet."

"Then, why not sell your T-shirt designs on the Internet?"

For the first time since Faye had known her, Marian seemed truly surprised. "I don't know. Maybe I could. Maybe *we* could," she added, nodding at Faye.

"Why me?" Faye asked.

"Well, it *was* your idea—you should share in its success. Besides, who knows how long I'll be around? I'd love to know my forum was going to outlast me."

"You'll be around another forty years," Dr. Thompson grinned. "You'll bury us all."

Marian dismissed his wisecrack and said, "Let's make a date to talk with Marvin about how practical this idea might be."

Faye agreed, wondering if the day could possibly become more perfect than it already was.

"Speaking of dates," Marian continued, "I believe Dr. Thompson wants to ask you something."

Faye turned to the handsome man. "Yes?" she inquired.

Thompson turned that deep shade that Faye now recognized as blushing. "Well," he said shyly. "I was going to wait for a more opportune moment, but...well..."

Faye had no idea what he was trying to say. "Yes?" she said, encouragingly.

"Well...you've obviously managed to quit smoking...you don't need any more hypnosis from me, and you're in good health...so you won't be needing me as your doctor in the immediate future...and, um...um..."

"What Robert is trying to say," Marian interpreted, "is that there is a singles' dance here at the rec center tomorrow night, and he'd like to know if you would consider going with him."

Faye was stunned. Suddenly, those pleasant butterflies in her stomach turned unpleasant. And Marian and Dr. Thompson were both looking at her, expecting her to speak—to say, "Yes!" But she didn't know how to say that she couldn't *possibly* date a colored man.

And yet, people did do that sort of thing these days—and he was very nice, probably the nicest man she had ever met, and he was *very* handsome. One by one, she mentally ticked off every reason she had ever heard for why a white woman shouldn't become romantically involved with a black man; every single one either made no sense, or didn't apply, or had fallen with changing fashion.

Of course, she would never be able to fall in love with him. But what if he fell in love with her? It would be wrong to lead him on. Faye was in agony. What should she say?

Both Marian and Dr. Thompson were still looking at her expectantly. Faye got another glimpse of Marian's T-shirt, and thought, *I'm thinking too much...*

"I'd love to!" she cried, surprising herself.

Good People

Sunday, November 9, 1997

It was with more than a little trepidation that Faye dressed for her date. A date! She hadn't gone on a date in decades, not since before she and Edwin were married, of course. And now she was about to go to a dance with a doctor. She, Faye McRae, was going to go dancing with a doctor.

She didn't have formal clothes. Being married to a glorified mechanic didn't offer opportunities to be formal but she did have a dress she had worn as matron of honor at her best friend Barbara's wedding. That had been years ago, and she had only kept it for sentimental reasons—especially after Barbara's death from breast cancer, over—*my goodness!* thought Faye. *Has it really been more than twenty years?*

Amazingly, Faye's exercise and subsequent weight reduction allowed her to fit into the dress as though it had been purchased the day before. It had been hanging in a yellowing plastic bag, and smelled a touch musty; she hung it in the open so it could air out. It was blue, with blue chiffon sleeves; so out-of-style that it had come back into style and Faye had seen an actress wear something similar on the Emmy's just a few weeks previously.

While the clothes aired, she hopped into her car to get her hair done. *I'm making such a fuss!* she chided herself. But there was no ignoring it; she felt like a schoolgirl. She had more jitters than she had before the AquaBabes tryout.

While dressing, it seemed strange that Marian wasn't there. Marian and she had been together so much these past months, that she had developed a best-friend feeling about her. But Marian hadn't offered, and hadn't called, so Faye was on her own—as, perhaps, she should be.

She sat in her living room, waiting for the appointed time—Dr. Thompson had said six o'clock—but she started sitting at four-thirty, and again found herself agonizing over the implications of going to a dance with a black man. And, again, telling herself that such thoughts were silly and old-fashioned, and irrelevant to the life she now led.

By a quarter to six, she was convincing herself that he wasn't coming at all; that she had made a fool of herself and that the only good thing was that no one would see her all gussied up and alone.

For the first time in months, she regretted not having any liquor in the house.

She was wondering how she could save face with Marian—"Well, I changed my mind and cancelled"—when the doorbell rang. It was exactly six o'clock.

Remembering her mother's advice to never appear too eager when a boy came to call, she yelled, "Just a moment!" then realized he would know her voice came from two feet from the other side of the door. She jumped up, ran to the hall, was about to call again; then realized she was being silly. She took a deep breath, opened the door, and smiled.

Dr. Robert Thompson stood there, smiling sheepishly, holding a bouquet of red roses. "These are for you," he said. "I hope you don't think I'm foolish, but I wanted to get you a little something and these just reminded me of you."

Faye was touched. Edwin had never given her flowers, not even when they were dating. "I'll put them in some water," she said, and took them into the kitchen, where she realized she didn't own a vase. She could buy one tomorrow; but, for now—hastily she poured the milk out of its carton, cut off the top, rinsed and filled it with water, and stuck the beautiful flowers into it, then returned to the living room.

"Do you like steak?" he asked. "I have a favorite restaurant I'd enjoy sharing with you."

"I love steak," she responded. "And with this new diet Marian recommended, I can actually eat all I want!"

"Controlled carbs? Good for you! How do you feel?"

"Better than I have in years," Faye responded truthfully. "I sleep through the night now; I don't get sleepy during the day and I feel so full of energy!"

Then they were in his beautifully kept, white Lincoln Town Car, and then at the restaurant.

Dinner was perfect, and Robert, as he insisted she call him, was a perfect gentleman.

They spoke of their lives. She told of her overbearing father, and how she had thought Edwin would rescue her from that—and how he, in his way, turned out to be just as overbearing. Robert told her about his upbringing in Philadelphia, and how much in love he had been with his wife, Eleanor, until her death from leukemia ten years before. His eyes misted as he shared the agony of knowing, professionally, how slim her chances of recovery were, while trying to be cheerful and encouraging.

"Thank goodness for the grass," he said.

"Marijuana for leukemia, too?" Faye asked, surprised. "I thought it was just for appetite."

Robert shook his head. "When you factor in side effects," he said, "marijuana is a wonderful pain reliever—because it doesn't have any. In fact, it was America's most popular analgesic before 1937. Now it's a crime, but it's easy for *anyone* to get pot—but I got cocky. I have a nice car and nice clothes, and I drove into the seedy side of town once too often. A police officer, just doing his job, wondered what a black man was doing in such a nice car. I foolishly protested; they searched the car, and found half an ounce in the glove compartment." He shrugged. "So I got arrested for possession of a controlled substance. They could have put me in jail for who knows how long, and taken away my license to practice medicine."

"Oh, my!" Faye gasped. "It seems so unfair. You were only trying to help your wife!"

"It *is* unfair. You know, four times as many drug convictions are of blacks than of whites. But I had money. And so my lawyer was able to work out a deal, where I did eighty hours of community service—which I was already doing, anyway—and that was the end of it."

Impulsively, Faye took his hand and squeezed it. "I don't know what to say," she said, eyes watering.

"There's nothing to say. Nothing to do. It's in the past. We honor Eleanor's memory when we take this gift, life, and live it to the fullest. She would have liked you, I'm sure," he added. "She knew good people when she met them."

The Shirt Off Her Back

Monday, November 10, 1997

The next morning, Faye met Marian at Marvin's, to see if Marvin could show them how to set up an Internet site to sell Marian's

T-shirts. They pulled up in front of the house at the same time. "How did it go last night?" Marian asked the moment they were out of their cars.

"It was wonderful!" Faye burst out. Then she laughed. "It's been so long since I went dancing! I felt like I was sixteen again."

Marian smiled with approval, and rang Marvin's doorbell in their code: Three shorts and a long. "How did you and Robert get along?"

Faye blushed. "He's such a gentleman...and what a wonderful dancer! Do you know about his wife dying?"

"Yeah, Robert and I have been close friends since the sixties."

"Oh," Faye said. "Well, I'm not certain he's completely over it, yet. But still he goes on, day after day, doing such good for people! He's such a wonderful man. Thank you so much for introducing us," Faye added.

Marvin opened the door, with an expression of disgust on his face, nodded for them to enter, and closed and locked the door behind them.

"Is there something wrong?" Marian asked him.

"I took that video you made of the GPS reading of Meany's Mexican property," he said. "Sent it to Audrey Flowers, herself. She sounded really interested...and now, *she says they're not.*"

"You kept a copy of the tape, of course," Marian prodded.

"Shit, yeah. Actually, *they* got the copy—I've kept the original, and I made sure they knew that. But it pisses me off that they can suppress a story like this so off-handedly. Shit!"

"There are other TV stations in the area," Faye pointed out.

"Channel 2 was the only one that would even *talk* to me. None of the other stations would even put a news producer on the horn!"

Marian shook her head. "I suppose we shouldn't be surprised."

"I'm not," Marvin growled. "But I'm pissed off, just the same."

There was a pause, and Faye put in, "How about the Internet, for the shirts? If this is a bad time, we could come back..."

"Nah, no time like the present. Hey, at least we can inform the people wit' T-shirts! Have a seat, ladies," Marvin added.

"Okay, here's the deal. You wanna web site to sell your T-shirts, right?" Faye and Marian nodded. "Well, first, you need a web host.

That's a company that owns a computer you can put your web site on, got it? I can recommend a few."

"You have a computer," Faye pointed out. "Why can't we just keep the site on yours?"

"You can. I do keep my server up all day, every day. That'll save ya about $10.95 a month."

"We'll be happy to pay you for it," Faye offered.

"Nah, no problem," the author assured them. "I'm hostin' my own web site, already."

"So, we have a host. What next?"

"You have to have someone design your site. I can do that, or you can do it yourselves, if you wanna take the time to learn the tools. I'd just as soon set up the basic site for ya, but then youse maintain it— add pages when ya want, change the T-shirt designs, and so on."

"Where could we learn how to maintain the site?"

"Well, you can learn from books—it's easy—or you can take classes. The Sun City Computer Club can help you with that, if you're interested."

"Oh."

"Finally, you need to deal wit' the exchange of money."

"I wouldn't want to deal with banks," Marian said. "You know why." She chewed on the corner of her lip. "Well," she said, "what if we tried something new? What if we gave it away?"

Marvin looked at Marian as if she had just grown an extra head. "You ain't gonna stay in business very long that way, Doodlebug," he said.

Marian smiled. "It's just a different business model," she said. "Profit isn't the *only* way to do things, darling. Suppose we make the patterns for my shirts available free of charge. People can print them on those T-shirt transfer sheets they sell for home computer printers—I've seen them for sale at craft stores. People can buy their own shirts, and transfers, and make 'em themselves! I won't need to charge anything."

"But how many people will find us?" Faye asked.

"Depends on if you advertise, and what kind of word-of-mouth you get. Potentially, millions. And, even if you give ya product away, they can make donations."

"Millions? Well!" Marian chuckled and said, "Well, if only one percent of those millions sends me one dollar a month, our breakfasts will be paid for."

Faye wondered why Marian was so reluctant to make use of a bank, which had always seemed like a very sensible institution, and why she was willing to forego a profit but she knew Marian well enough by now to know she didn't do—or avoid—anything without good reason. "What's wrong with banks?" Faye asked.

A wry look crossed Marvin's face, then he laughed and said, "Hey, didn't ya read my book, yet?"

Faye blushed and apologized. "I've been so busy...I did read the first few pages, but..."

Marvin shrugged. "No matter. Here's the deal. In the fourteen hundreds, people didn't have money like we do, right? They mostly bartered, but they did exchange gold or silver for large transactions."

"Okay," Faye agreed.

"Now, gold is *really* heavy. Also, if you're traveling, thieves are likely to try and steal it. Highway robbers, right? So, people used to leave the gold for safekeeping, in the shop of a jeweler or goldsmith. The goldsmith would give them a receipt, and they'd give the receipt to the person they was doin' business wit' and when that person wanted the gold, he could just come by the goldsmith's with the receipt and get it."

"All right, I understand," Faye encouraged, embarrassed that she hadn't read Marvin's book. Somehow, when he'd given it to her, she hadn't realized she would actually be expected to read it.

"But a lotta times, they just used the receipt to pay a bill. Gold is heavy, so the receipts *became* the currency. And that's how paper money was invented."

"But, where do the banks come in?"

"Well, some of the goldsmiths began to realize that they *always* had gold in the safe rooms—and they got this wild idea. Why not *loan* gold, in the form of receipts? They could actually loan somethin' that *didn't exist*, and charge interest for it, too. So a goldsmith who had just a house wit' a safe room could become filthy rich in short order by simply loaning gold that he *didn't have*—in the form of *receipts!*"

"Oh, my!" Faye wondered. "What if everyone brought their receipts in at the same time?"

Marvin shrugged. "Then the goldsmith woulda been fucked. But, apparently it never happened—or happened so seldom as to not make the scam itself unworkable. So, the next thing ya know, goldsmiths become banks and they are *still doing the same exact thing*—loanin' you money they don't have, and charging interest on it. When you repay the principal, it comes out even; but, when you pay the interest, some of your wealth is transferred into their hands. In time, all the wealth of the world *must* flow to the banks. And, since there is no other scam goin' to get it back, it's inevitable that banks will own everything that can be owned—someday, if they don't already."

Faye sat, stunned. The picture Marvin painted was so clear, so simple, except—

"But, Marvin," she pointed out, "how about the Federal Reserve? Isn't it really the *government* that owns everything? Everything in this country, at least," she amended.

"The Federal Reserve is not a branch of the government, darling," Marian explained. "It's a private bank, just like Wells Fargo or Bank One or any of the others."

"What?" asked Faye, surprised. "It can't be; its picture is on the back of the ten dollar bill."

"It is a private bank. It just happens they have an exclusive contract to loan money directly to the government of the United States, so they're the ones that decide what goes on the ten dollar bill."

"That's right," Marvin agreed. "Make no mistake about it. The government does not own a thing—because, thanks to the national debt, *the Federal Reserve Bank owns the government.*"

Awakening

. . . .

Election Day

Tuesday, November 11, 1997

Two weeks passed slowly, with Faye trying to grow eyes in the back of her head. She always felt Meany's shadow behind her. The man knew who she was, and probably where she lived, and she had no idea how far he'd go to silence her. The safest place actually seemed to be the campaign headquarters; he could hardly hold a massacre *there—especially* with so many envelopes yet to be stuffed!

Then it was election day and as strange as it seemed, Faye was invited to Representative Meany's victory party.

"*Victory* party? How can he be so sure he'll win?" Faye asked when her supervisor invited her.

"Oh, honey, everyone who is running calls it a 'victory' party," the gravel-voiced Selma Graves replied. "Half of them will end in drunken victory; the other half will end in drunken misery. Everyone will be hung over the day after, but only half will have jobs." She smiled confidentially. "But he'll win."

"So, what will you be doing, afterwards?" Faye asked.

Selma shrugged. "I'll take a couple of weeks off, then start on the campaign for Carvel's next re-election. I'll give you a call when we start up again, I could use you. It's not easy to find good envelope stuffers, you know!"

Faye smiled sweetly. "Go stuff yourself, dear," she said. "I've stuffed my last envelope. I'm planning to go into a less stressful line of work, maybe counter-espionage." Selma looked startled, then laughed.

The party was to be held at the Phoenician, one of Scottsdale's fanciest resorts, located on one of the buttes that rose out of nothingness in the southeastern Valley. The campaign headquarters had been rather seedy. This was the antithesis. After admiring it, the valet took her car and she walked into the sumptuous lobby of the hotel in which the restaurant was located. There were fountains everywhere, and crystal chandeliers, and sculptures; well-dressed people chatted casually in a way that made her think they wanted to be seen there chatting casually.

A concierge and signs directed her to the ballroom that Selma had booked, and Faye wondered where the money had come from. Then she considered Meany and sighed.

It reminded her of a wedding reception. There was a buffet table with shrimp, cold cuts, fruits and crisp vegetables. There was an open bar, at which Faye looked longingly but avoided. There was a musical combo, a bass player, a man with one of those electronic keyboards and a woman who sang the blues to their accompaniment. There were men in black suits and string ties and women in dressy suits. *At least they aren't wearing gowns,* Faye thought.

Tobacco smoke hung thick in the air. As many reformed smokers do, she found the smell disgusting—especially the stench of cigars, which many of the men present were smoking.

It was all so incredible. Faye felt as if she were in a surreal fantasy. Here she was, a woman who, just weeks before, had been on Representative Meany's marijuana farm in Mexico and now, here she was, at his election victory party.

She could see him working the crowd, passing from group to group, accepting their congratulations, shaking their hands and pounding their backs. She noticed that he spoke only to the men; for the women he had fatherly smiles but no conversation.

"Surprised to see you here," a voice said behind her, and she turned to find Frank Timmons.

"Frank!" she cried, genuinely glad to see him. "How are you?"

"*Much* better," he replied gratefully. "I've been able to keep my food down, and I have a lot more energy. Thanks to you," he added.

Faye smiled. "I was just the middle-man. I'm just so glad you're feeling better," she replied. "Do you think he'll win?"

Frank indicated the large-screen TV at one end of the room, displaying the election returns. "He's held 73 percent of the vote pretty much all day," he said. "At this point, the only way he can lose is if everyone against him waited 'til now to vote."

Faye shook her head. "It's just so hard to believe," she said, forgetting for a moment that Frank thought she was a Meany supporter.

"What is?"

"Oh, well, that it's all almost over," Faye responded quickly. "All those envelopes! All that folding! What a pain in the ass! And now, finally, here we are on election night. To think all that work's come to an end…well, it's just amazing."

"My work is just beginning," Frank muttered. "Those drug pushers are everywhere, seducing innocent children, killing them."

"They're everywhere, all right," Faye agreed, quietly. "Some, where you'd never suspect."

Frank looked sharply at her. "What do *you* know? Where? *Who?*"

Faye hesitated. Could she trust him? "I know someone who is growing marijuana," she said. "Someone who makes fighting it a public issue."

"Marijuana?" Frank barked. "That's no drug. *Heroin* is a drug. Heroin killed my grandson."

Blinking, Faye said, "But, Representative Meany is fighting marijuana. When we first met, you said you were stuffing envelopes to help get him elected to fight drugs."

"I had to say that," the old man whispered. "I didn't know who you were. But I've watched you. I seen the look in your eye when Meany comes in or even when Graves talks about him. You don't like him any more than I do!"

Faye shook her head. "But—then—why were you there? Why are you *here?*"

"I could ask you the same," Frank challenged.

"Selma invited me," Faye replied. "And I wanted to see if a hypocrite could actually win an election."

Frank's eyes narrowed. "Hypocrite?"

"Last week, when my friend and I went to Mexico to get your medicine, we made a side-trip to some property Meany owns. I saw with my own eyes, he *grows* marijuana."

Frank was silent a moment, eyeing one of the other guests, a dark-haired man with a curiously flat face and piggish nose. Frank returned his attention to her. "Hypocrite is the least of it," he continued. "Marijuana is the least of it. He's been running heroin."

"What?" Faye gasped.

"You heard me, lady. 'H.' He's the asshole who sold it to my grandson."

Faye was dumbfounded. "You're kidding! Representative Meany? Sold heroin to a kid? I can't believe it!" she whispered back. "Really, I can't. It would be too stupid. What if he got caught?"

"He didn't sell it directly," Frank explained. "My grandson, Mickey, didn't have a job and couldn't steal enough money from his parents without getting caught. So these bastards hired him to run the shit for 'em. Who'd suspect him? He was just seventeen, ya know what I mean? And before too long, they began to trust him. One day he walked in on a meeting between his connection and some bigwigs. I guess they trusted him, because they didn't kill him on the spot. But he visited me one day while the news was on, and he recognized Meany as the big shot from that meeting and he told me about it. The cops found his body shortly after."

"I thought you said he was killed in a drug raid."

"The newspaper said he actually died of an overdose *before* the SWAT team showed up. They killed *everyone else there* in the shootout—you *must* have seen it on TV."

"That must have been before we moved to the Valley."

"Whatever. Well, I *know* it was Meany who tipped off the cops."

"Really? But you just said he was a part of the gang."

The old man's eyes grew moist. "Mickey found a drug rehab clinic. He wanted to quit. I thought he *had* quit." Frank laughed bitterly. "I figured Meany was maybe gathering evidence on them. But *he never took credit for the drug raid.* He *always* takes credit. That's how I knew. It was a setup! Meany got rid of all the *witnesses.*"

"Oh, my!" Faye moaned. She then shared the details of being followed by Meany in Mexico, and how he had tried to trick her friend, Marian, and her into not declaring the Marinol. "I really think he would have run us off the road, if we hadn't gotten *him* caught, instead. And, now that he knows who we are—who *I* am—well, the main reason I came tonight was to be so much in his face he won't dare have me killed."

"Didn't help Mickey," Frank growled.

"You don't understand. I intend to get photographed with Meany tonight. If there are photos of us together, it will be that much harder for him to pretend he isn't connected to my murder—especially with the videotape we took of his operation. I'm in that, too—and I'm sure he knows that, as well."

Frank gave Faye an appraising once-over. "Looka here," he replied, with a glint in his eye. He held his suit jacket slightly open so that only Faye could see, tucked behind the belt that cinched his too-large pants, the grip of a pistol. "This is that bastard's last election party," Frank snarled. "He killed Mickey, and he's going to die *tonight.*"

Faye felt as if she were going to faint. "But you stuffed envelopes for him!" she said.

Frank's jaw stiffened. "How else could I get invited here?" he asked. "How else could I be sure of getting close enough to him to do…what I have to do?"

Faye thought furiously. "Frank—Frank! This isn't the answer!" she whispered fiercely.

He stood his ground. "This solves your problem, too, girly!"

She grabbed his lapel. "Come with me." She had to get him out of the room, and heedless of any possible danger to herself, practically dragged the older man out into the hall.

"If he's guilty," Faye continued, "then let's get him convicted! If you assassinate him, he'll just become a martyr. Your story will just sound like the ravings of an old man—an old man on Marinol, I might add. They'll find the drug in your bloodstream and don't think *that* information wouldn't be made public. You've seen Meany's TV ads; doesn't he always point out how this crime or that was committed by someone on marijuana? You'd just be proving his point!"

Faye heard her own impassioned plea from afar, as if she were listening to someone else say it. But it seemed to hit home. She saw Frank's shoulders slump. "You're right," he said. "I didn't think of that." The man started to sob, shaking. "I was prepared to go to jail tonight. I wanted the pain to be gone. I thought, finally, I would be...free."

"I want to get him, too," Faye promised. "But it has to be done right. I don't know *why* the news didn't report his being caught at the border with marijuana, but, I promise you, Frank, I'm *going* to find out what's really going on here. Heroin—my God, heroin! And, somewhere, someplace in this country, there's got to be a newspaper that *will* expose him. And then you and the parents of the other kids he's destroyed will have a chance to look him in the eye as *he's* being hauled off to jail with the addicts he helped create. *That* will be justice."

Just then the musicians played a fanfare, and Faye opened the door to the ballroom in time to see a gray-haired man take the podium. "The results are in," he announced over the loudspeaker. "In Maricopa County, district number..." and he read off the election results for each of the three candidates.

Meany had won by a landslide.

In the joyous celebration that followed, Meany allowed his photo to be taken with many of his supporters. Faye worked her way through the throng, managing to get next to him and throwing her arm around his shoulders just as the flash of a dozen cameras temporarily blinded her and Meany too—he probably had no idea she had been there, and wouldn't until he saw their picture in the paper.

Later, Meany gave a victory speech, voice breaking as he spoke of the dedication of the people who had "made victory possible." There was thunderous applause, and many of the guests burst into tears of joy. Faye and Frank held hands and cried along with them...but for quite a different reason.

All We Need Is Love

Thursday, November 20, 1997

Two days later, in her kitchen having her morning glass of orange juice, her eyes fell on the calendar on the refrigerator door and her heart skipped a beat. The AquaBabe's Aquacade was in two days, and she'd been so distracted by the last frantic week at the re-election headquarters, and the election itself—not to mention her concern that some aspect of her Mexican misadventure might show up at any time to bite her—that she'd lost all track of time.

And, on top of that, Thanksgiving was just one week away.

How could that have happened? How had time gone by so quickly? It had been barely five months since she and Edwin had moved to Sun City; because she had been so involved with the election, the swimming, the health regimen, and her relationships with Marian and Robert, she had hardly thought of Edwin at all. Now, one of the two holidays of the year she and Edwin celebrated was coming up, and she hated the idea of facing it alone.

Marian and Faye went, as usual, for breakfast after their early-morning kung fu class. Marian smiled in anticipation. "Thanksgiving is coming up. I am planning to have Robert, and few other folks I'd like you to meet, over for Thanksgiving dinner. Please, won't you join us?"

"I—I—" Faye was speechless. "You must be a mind reader!" And then her eyes were brimming, and she couldn't speak.

"Well, darling," Marian said as she patted Faye's hand, "you're not the only one who ever had to spend a first Thanksgiving without a loved one."

And the weight that had filled Faye's heart burst like a soap bubble. "Please, can I help—do anything?"

Marian smiled again. "You certainly can! Can you cook a turkey?"

"Can I! Turkey is a specialty of mine. I have a wonderful recipe for sage-and-cornbread stuffing. You'll love it!"

"You're on! My cooking *stinks*," Marian added; and they laughed.

"What time are we going to eat?" Faye asked.

"Around four o'clock, is my guess."

"Then we should start around eight in the morning, you know, clean the bird, get the stuffing into it, get it tented and all."

"Tented?"

"You know, the aluminum foil covering."

"No shit, darling!" Marian cried. "Aluminum foil? No wonder my past turkeys have been turkeys!"

Aquacade

Saturday, November 22, 1997

As far from the pool as the locker room was, Faye could still hear the buzz of the audience gathering outside. People in Sun City came in droves whenever free entertainment was available and the AquaBabes were a big draw, or so Bea, their coach, had told them.

Bitsy Cunningham, a big-boned Amazon with the locker next to hers, commented, "It's cool today. I hope the pool is warm. I'd hate to freeze my ass off out there."

Noticing Bitsy's reddened eyes, Faye replied, "Haven't you been in already?"

"Not yet."

Puzzled, Faye continued dressing, slipping on her red bathing cap. "But, your eyes..." she blurted, realizing too late that Bitsy could have a condition that might be embarrassing to talk about.

"My eyes?" Bitsy asked, then seemed to come to some sort of realization. "Oh—my eyes! Well, I was in my hot tub this morning, before coming here. And it is chlorinated."

"A hot tub! That sounds great!" One's own hot tub, to slip into whenever one wished, sounded divine.

"You're welcome to use mine, anytime," Bitsy offered, generously. "Just call first. You can come and go through the side gate, so you won't have to worry about traipsing through the house."

"Why, thank you!" said Faye. It felt so wonderful to have friends! She hadn't realized, all those years with Edwin, how very lonely she had been.

The recorded music of their opening number blared over the loudspeakers, and the AquaBabes quickly took their positions. At their cue, they stepped gracefully out to the edge of the pool—the audience applauded—and continued into a graceful, shallow dive into the water.

Faye did love swimming, loved the water, loved the music. She had to fight to keep her mind on the moves, though; there was the audience! The music! The other swimmers! It was all a little distracting. She found herself missing a cue now and then and rushing to catch up.

No one seemed to notice, though. They did five numbers, each choreographed differently and in between, she managed to recognize a few faces in the crowd. There were the Beehlers and Vera Daye. Robert Thompson was easy to spot in the sea of white faces and Marian with him. But who was that sitting with them? The next time her face was out of the water, Faye took another look. It was— Frank Timmons, whom she had talked out of killing Representative Meany! She hadn't realized he even knew Robert or Marian, and of course she hadn't seen him since election night. It was amazing— poor old Frank actually looked as if he were *really* enjoying the show.

And then it was over, and the swimmers were drying off in the locker room, and their coach was congratulating them. "It was beautiful," she said, "our best show ever!"

"Thanks to you, Bea!" Bitsy yelled and the girls all joined in applause. Faye's heart warmed. It was just like being in high school again!

As the swimmers dressed and left, Bea tapped Faye on the arm. "Let's talk, Faye," she said, leading Faye to a corner of the room where there was some privacy.

"Yes, Bea?" Faye smiled, wondering what this was about.

"You missed three important cues," Bea told her. "I know it was your first performance. But we take this seriously. I don't know what was on your mind, but you *have* to leave it behind you when you swim with us."

Blushing, Faye wasn't sure what to say. "I didn't realize I was so distracted," she said. "I have a lot on my mind," she added. "I'm very, very, sorry."

Bea put her hands on Faye's shoulders. "Our big Christmas show is just a month away. It's our last performance of the year. We'd love to have you back in the spring, but you *can't* miss any more cues, Faye."

"I'll do my best," Faye promised. She managed to hold herself together until she could get into a stall in the bathroom; closing the door behind her, she sobbed silently, humiliated. She had gotten into shape for this! Worked, exercised, sweated, stuck with a strict diet and gave up alcohol! Shit, she even *quit smoking!* And all that hadn't been good enough.

But what would Marian say? *Darling, you did let yourself get distracted,* she heard in her mind. *Just learn from it, and don't do it next time.* Hearing Marian's voice, even in her imagination, calmed her enough to dry her eyes and emerge from the stall. Looking in the mirror, she was aghast at the redness of her eyes and hoped her friends would assume it was from the chlorine in the pool.

When she returned to her locker to retrieve her towel and wet swim suit, she found Bitsy there doing the same. Bitsy took one look at her and noticed her eyes. "You waited until *after?* Oh, well, to each her own! Here, use my eye drops."

Faye had no idea what she was talking about, but smiled in agreement and accepted the drops. Bitsy lowered her voice and whispered conspiratorially, "We really should get together at my hot tub! I have some *wonderful* new herb."

"It's a date!" Faye agreed, wondering why herbs were so important to Bitsy.

Outside, she intended to introduce Bitsy to Marian and Robert, but the tall woman headed in another direction while Faye was making her way through the crowd to their table. Robert gave a her a big bear hug, whispering, "You were wonderful!" and Marian made it a group hug and kissed her cheek.

"You're quite a swimmer," a familiar, raspy voice added, and Faye turned to see Frank Timmons with his hand extended. She took it warmly and smiled.

"How are you? How are you feeling?" she asked. She had never expected to see him after the election night party. "I hoped I would see you again," she added warmly.

"Much better," the elderly man said, "especially after the treatments I've been getting from Dr. Thompson, here. My appetite is back and I feel a lot stronger."

"I'm so glad! The Marinol helped, then?"

"It helped a lot. But Dr. Thompson's prescribed something even better."

"Now, Frank..." Robert interjected.

"Don't worry, Doc," the old man cackled. "I ain't talkin'."

"All right, let's eat! My treat!" Marian announced, and she got the attention of a waiter.

Nancy Drew and the Case of the Missing Scandal

Monday, November 24, 1997

On Monday, with the pressure of the Aquacade behind her, and the pressure of Meany in front, Faye drove to the Peoria Public Library and asked to be directed to the microfilm area. She expected they would have microfilmed copies of *The Arizona Republic,* Phoenix's largest newspaper, and they did. She was aware that she could probably have gotten Marvin Cohen to look up the article she wanted with a few clicks on his keyboard. But because she had promised Frank Timmons that she would look into his grandson's death, she intended to do as much as she could, bringing what she found to Marvin and Marian for guidance later.

Frank had told her his grandson was killed in October, 1995. Faye figured that was just about a month before Meany's *previous* re-election. That gave her, potentially, thirty-one days' worth of obituaries to read. However, the fates were kind; she found the Michael (Mickey) Timmons' obituary in the October 11th, 1995 edition with his death—by "suicide"—listed as having occurred on October 9th.

Faye tried to remember if she had ever read an obituary that said, outright, that a person had committed suicide. Not even Edwin's had said that; it just seemed too unkind a thing to say, and the cause of death in his obituary had been simply omitted. So why was suicide mentioned here?

And would anyone *intentionally* kill themselves with heroin? Unless a note was left, wouldn't the death be called "accidental"?

Scrolling back to the October 10th edition of the paper, Faye found that the drug bust made the front page. According to the article, an anonymous informant had alerted the police to the goings on in a mini-storage facility not far from downtown Phoenix, and the police had in turn alerted the DEA. A SWAT team had descended upon the place; with no exit, there had been a shootout; and when the police were able to enter the place they found no survivors. The article reported that four men had died with semi-automatic guns in their hands; one teenager—unnamed—had been found in the back, already dead. Forensics had discovered a fatal amount of heroin in his bloodstream and because the teen was dead when the police got there, it was assumed he had overdosed.

Faye pressed the "Print" button on the microfilm reader and a sheet emerged, which she folded and placed in her purse.

She then drove into Phoenix, stopping at the Channel 2 TV station, housed in a particularly attractive building. She walked in confidently and said to the receptionist, "I'm here to see Audrey Flowers."

"I'm sorry, ma'am, but she's just left for the day," the receptionist replied.

Faye moaned, "But this is really important!" She lowered her voice. "It's about her aunt in Sun City. She isn't expected to live through the night."

"Oh, no!" cried the receptionist. "Well, normally I wouldn't mention this, but...well, she only just left. You'll probably find her in the employee parking lot with the balloon."

What is she, a part-time clown or something? Faye wondered to herself, as she thanked the receptionist and hurried outside, then to the back of the building. Faye understood what the reception-ist meant when she spotted Flowers by the bed of a shiny red pickup truck, adjusting the tie-downs for what looked like a huge, hot air balloon. It had all been packed neatly—basket, heater, and bag—in the back of her truck. The most surprising thing to Faye, having seen hot-air balloons in the air almost every day since arriving in Sun City, was that this balloon was jet-black, except for bits of the Channel 2 logo that she could see within the folds.

"Ms. Flowers!" Faye called, waving. The anchorwoman quickly put on her professional smile and beamed it back at Faye.

"I'm in a bit of a hurry," said Audrey Flowers. "Quickly, what can I do for you?"

"Do you remember talking to me at Representative Meany's speech last September?" Faye asked.

Ms. Flowers smiled, thought, and shook her head. "Not really, I'm afraid," she replied. "I meet so many people..."

"Well, no matter," Faye said. "Listen, two weeks ago, I happen to know that Representative Meany was caught in a truck at the Nogales border checkpoint with an illegal substance. I also saw the Channel 2 news truck parked there, and I watched the camera-man run over to Meany's truck when the customs agents found the marijuana. Since a major plank in Meany's campaign platform is based on keeping that substance illegal, I want to know *why* that story never aired."

Flowers looked dumbfounded. "I—I thought you worked *for* his campaign," she stammered.

"I did," Faye replied. "So what?"

Flowers pursed her lips. "I remember seeing that tape," she said. "The border patrol notified us that there would be heightened security that day, so we sent the truck out. Even if they don't catch some celebrity smuggling in some dope, we can usually do a piece on the hassles of crossing the border."

"But you *did* catch a celebrity," Faye pointed out.

"Not really. The truck wasn't registered in Meany's name; it was a miniscule amount and there was no real way of linking it to Meany that wouldn't seem circumstantial. Besides, his election was coming up and it wasn't serious enough to risk a libel suit."

"But, if you simply reported the facts—that he was there, in the truck, when they found the stuff—and let people judge for themselves..."

Flowers smiled. "That was my recommendation," she said. "But at our editorial conference, when we decide what will be broadcast, the producer put the kibosh on the story, and that was that."

"Really?" Faye queried in surprise. "Did he give a reason?"

Flowers shook her head and said, "He doesn't need one."

"What if I told you I have *been* to property in Mexico where I've *seen* the marijuana plants Meany grows? Why, you *know* I have! My friend sent you the videotape we made! And I have reason to believe Meany is also involved in selling heroin! Would that be a story you might run?"

Flowers looked at her and laughed. "Who do you think you are, Nancy Drew?" she asked. "Look, I saw that tape, and it proves nothing—any kid could fake a GPS display. And *you* need to understand that there's probably no more important man in the state right now than Carvel Meany. He's just won his third election to the House, and he may well run for President. He's been a bene- factor to many powerful people, and they tend to overlook a few faults."

"You're saying that selling *heroin* is a 'fault'?"

"I'm saying that circumstantial evidence and rumors are not enough to indict someone with the stature of Representative Meany. And when we play with the big boys, we'd better have big guns or *we're* gonna get shot." She looked Faye in the eye. "You'd better be careful, lady. If you run around slandering someone like Representative Meany, you could easily find your- self in jail."

"Or worse?"

Flowers sighed. "He has a lot of friends, ma'am...and most of them have as much to lose as you allege he does. So, yes, jail might be the least of your worries."

A Matter of Record

After leaving the TV station, Faye drove to the Phoenix police station, parked and went inside. It was a very busy place. Faye tried to relax, focus, look professional, and to separate herself from the greasy teenagers and furtive-looking men the police officers were escorting. The desk sergeant directed her to the Public Records department. All reports were computerized and copies could be requested, for a few dollars each, plus fifty cents for photographs—but because of a backlog it would be a couple of weeks before they could produce the report she wanted. On a hunch, she found the slip of paper, placed in her purse months before, with the phone number of Grant Taylor, the nice police detective who had been so kind to her after Edwin's death. She found a payphone in the foyer of the police station and dialed his number.

"Hello, Grant?" she asked when he picked up. "This is..." she recalled that she had known him before her name change. "This is Nancy McRae," she announced.

"Oh, Mrs. McRae, how are you?" he asked. "I was just thinking about you the other day, wondering if I should stop by."

"I'm doing very well, thank you dear," she said. "So much better, and I don't *need* you to visit, though I'd love to see you anytime. However, that's not why I called. I wondered if you might be able to do me a favor."

"If I can," he offered. "What is it?"

"I need to see a certain police report from Phoenix, from October of 1995. The Public Records department here in Phoenix will give me the report, but it will take weeks. I was wondering if maybe you would be able to get a copy more quickly."

"Oh, sure," he replied. "What is it? What's going on?"

"Nothing important, really," she answered. "I just promised a friend I would try to get some information regarding his grandson's supposed suicide. His body was found in a drug raid on October 9th, 1995."

"Oh." Grant was silent a moment. "That's great, you helping support other surviving family members of a suicide. That's a really good service; it will help in your recovery, too." There was another moment of silence, which he interrupted with, "Yeah, here it is."

"You found it already?" she asked.

"Yeah, our computer systems are linked," he explained. "I remember that, it was a big bust. The Phoenix cops were pis— annoyed as hell, er, heck, when the feds moved in on them. I can print a copy for you and drop it by your house this evening."

"Oh, thank you! Does it say anything about who phoned in the tip that triggered the raid?" Faye asked, too impatient to wait. "Where the person lived, what area the call came from, anything?"

"Well," Grant drawled, "uh...yeah, here it is. It gives the name of the person."

"It does?" Faye was surprised, since the newspaper had said the tip was given anonymously.

"Yeah. Someone from Sun City, in fact...a woman named Selma Graves."

I Want To Turn You On

Thursday, November 27, 1997

Faye, a stickler for promptness, arrived at Marian's house on Thanksgiving morning exactly at eight. She had never been in her friend's house, though she had dropped her off there now and again. She was curious and looked forward to seeing the interior.

Unlike most Sun City homes, Marian's was on a main street and had no front yard. Instead, there was a walled-in patio in the front, and a driveway that opened onto the street. It was an odd arrangement in its way, but it was part of a row of similar homes several blocks long.

Faye pulled her shiny coupe into the driveway, got out, opened the trunk, and removed a shopping bag containing the ingredients for her special stuffing recipe. She rang the bell on the post next to the wrought-iron patio gate. She heard the front door open, and footsteps; in a moment, Marian appeared, smiling.

"Good morning, darling! Isn't it an *exquisite* day!"

It was. The sky was clear blue, of course, and in November this early in the day, the temperature was a perfect seventy degrees.

135

Marian hugged Faye and led her across the patio. Bougainvillea grew against the walls, their brilliant purplish-pink glowing against the contrast of the blue sky, creating a rather private, Secret Garden-like sanctuary. In the center was a fountain, complete with the statue of an athletic Greek god pouring water from a vase. A wooden bench was situated so that one could sit and meditate or gaze at the fountain, smelling the flowers and enjoying the day. Faye wondered how Marian ever left the house.

They entered the house, which was cool and tastefully lit. It was neither cluttered nor sparse; it rather looked like a page from *House Beautiful.* "Marian!" Faye exclaimed. "Your home is lovely!"

"Well, thank you, darling!" Marian responded, pleased. "I'll give you the tour later."

"Could I have it now?" Faye asked, ruefully. "I kind of have to go—I was so afraid I would get here late—"

"Of course you can. But, not the hall bathroom. Let me show you the master bathroom, and then we can get started on the bird."

The kitchen was modest in size but well-equipped; the bird in question was in the sink, with cool water pouring over it from the tap. "Good thing this is November," Marian commented. "Summer tap water around here would almost cook the turkey, instead of just defrosting it."

While Marian untied the legs of the bird and removed the package of giblets, Faye lined up the ingredients for her stuffing on the counter. "I wonder if this is all right?" she said. "There's a lot of carbohydrates in stuffing. Although I did get all whole-grains."

"This is Thanksgiving, darling! No diets today."

"I have new information about Meany," Faye announced.

"Oh?" Marian prompted, and Faye told her about Frank Timmons, and the gun he'd taken to the victory dinner, and the story of his grandson's death, as presented by Frank and expanded by her investigation. Faye amazed Marian with her discovery of Selma Graves' involvement. Marian finished preparing the turkey and gave Faye a hug.

"Darling," she said, "I am so impressed, no kidding! I'm so *proud* of you!"

Faye, her hands still in the mixing bowl with the crumbs and sage and parsnips and walnuts, accepted the hug with pleasure. "I'm glad," she said. "I just wanted to help Frank find peace. I'm not sure what to do next, though."

"We'll talk about it," she said. "Marvin's gonna have some ideas, too."

"Will he be here?" Faye asked.

"Oh, no! He *never* leaves his house. But we can check in with him by phone."

"Why doesn't he leave his house?" Faye asked.

Marian shook her head. "A touch of agoraphobia, perhaps," she said. "That's what Robert says. Or maybe a bit of paranoia. But I'll take him a nice, big sample of our dinner so he won't miss out."

"Well, I hope he likes my stuffing," Faye said, wiping her hands on her apron. "It's ready for the bird when you are."

"Um, actually...there is one herb I'd like to add, if you don't mind," Marian said. "Everyone kind of looks forward to it," she added.

"What herb is that?"

"Well, this one, darling," the older woman replied, removing a bottle from the spice rack.

"Oregano?" asked Faye, looking at the bottle. "That's not really in my recipe..."

"Actually, it isn't oregano, though it does look like it, doesn't it? This is...*cannabis sativa*."

"Hmmm...sounds familiar. Have you mentioned it before?"

"Umm, I might have," Marian replied. "Half the bottle oughta do it."

"*Half the bottle?* It must not be very strong."

"Darling," Marian laughed, "it's stronger than you'd guess. It just doesn't have an overwhelming flavor. Besides, nearly a dozen people will be sharing this stuffing, so it's just about perfect."

Faye laughed. "You make it sound like a prescription." She mixed the herb into the stuffing, then sniffed the half-empty jar. "It smells familiar," she said. "I can't quite place where, but I've smelled this before." She suddenly had a flash of a day in Mexico, a field, picking a handful of buds. "Oh, my God—Marian—this is marijuana, isn't it?"

"You were right when you called it a prescription," the older woman commented. "Most of the people coming to dinner tonight need it for medical reasons."

"Like Frank Timmons? For chemotherapy?"

"Some are undergoing chemotherapy. Vera Daye has glaucoma. Chuck Porter, whom you haven't met, has epilepsy but he hasn't had a seizure in seven years thanks to marijuana. Dave Beadle has high blood pressure that marijuana has kept under control, without side effects. Darling, this stuff is the best, most general medicine that Mother Nature ever invented."

"And you, Marian?" Faye asked. "Why do you take it?"

"Darling," her friend replied. "*I* take it because I like the way it makes me feel."

Faye walked to the kitchen table and sat down in one of the chairs. She had heard so much about the good effects of marijuana in the past few months that discovering her best friend actually used it wasn't as startling as it might have been. And that all the guests would be ingesting this...*all* of them—

"Robert? He uses it too?"

Marian nodded.

"And what's wrong with him?"

Marian smiled. "Nothin' I know of," she said. "I think he just likes the way it makes *him* feel."

Faye hesitated. "How...how *does* it make you feel?"

"Wonderful," Marian replied. "Simply wonderful. Focused. Everything I sense, whether it's a sunset or a symphony or sex, is intensified and marvelous and mystical."

"Wow," was Faye's response. "I guess driving wouldn't be a good idea, then."

"Well, I can't *recommend* driving while high, because of the legal ramifications. But, actually, I do it all the time and I find I drive *better*—because it helps me focus. When I'm driving while high, *nothing* distracts me from driving, just like when I'm embroidering or painting, *nothing* distracts me from that."

Faye rose and returned to stuffing the turkey, but said nothing.

"Well?" Marian asked. "Are you horrified? Frightened? Talk to me!"

Faye stopped stuffing for a moment and looked at her friend. "Have you ever been 'high' while I was with you?"

Marian grinned. "Darling, I'm high *most* of the time."

Faye thought about it. "Well, then…I've never noticed, so I guess the effects can't be *that* pronounced." She frowned. "Do you ever smoke it?"

"Yes, I do, darling. Sometimes."

"But you made me *stop* smoking!"

Marian held her hands out as if to say, stop! "Marijuana has never been linked to cancer, like tobacco has. Anyway, as I said, I only smoke sometimes. I get a more lasting effect from eating it, baked into the bran muffin I eat each morning."

"*Every* morning?" Faye repeated. "You're high, *now?*"

"Right," Marian grinned.

Faye giggled nervously. "Marian…" she began.

"Yes, darling?"

Faye rinsed her hands, dried them, walked over to her friend and put her hands on Marian's shoulders. "Could I—could we—*try* a marijuana cigarette, sometime?"

Marian squeezed Faye's forearms affectionately. "*Right now,* if you want, darling. Why don't you pour the glaze on the bird and put the aluminum tent over it while I roll us a doobie."

Faye looked at her friend blankly. "A what?"

"A joint…a spliff…a fatty…a marijuana cigarette, darling," Marian explained. "You'll find there's a lot of fond nicknames when you deal with weed."

The older woman left for a moment, and Faye poured the light honey glaze Marian had prepared over the turkey; then she pulled out a length of foil, folded it, and placed it over the turkey so it wouldn't dry out while baking. Then Marian was back with a small pack marked "e-z wider double wide," and some matches. Faye watched while she opened the pack and removed one of the thin sheets of paper, forming it into a shallow trough that she held between the thumb and index finger of her left hand. She removed some of the remaining marijuana from the oregano jar, and sprinkled it evenly into the furrow, rolled the paper over the marijuana, licked the length of the exposed edge, fashioning it into a perfectly firm, round cigarette. She lit it as one would light any cigarette, and inhaled deeply.

"Oh, my," Faye tittered. "You look like you've been doing that for years."

"Forty-two years, to be exact," Marian said in an odd, squeaky voice, as she tried not to exhale.

"What's wrong with your voice?" Faye asked.

Marian relaxed and released a small amount of blue smoke from between pursed lips. "Nothing, darling. It's just traditional to hold your breath for as long as you can after inhaling, to absorb as much of the THC as possible."

"'THC?'"

"Tetrahydrocannabinol—the *fun* ingredient. Here, you try."

Heart pounding with excitement at this forbidden adventure, Faye gingerly took the doobie, grinned at Marian, emptied her lungs, put the cigarette gently to her lips, and inhaled. The taste was sweet and musky. She drew in as much as her lungs could hold, and handed the joint back to Marian, all the while holding her breath. While Marian took the next toke, Faye squeaked, "How long do I have to hold it in?"

"Long as you want, darling. There are no rules; you'll have to find out what works best for you."

Faye exhaled explosively, the smoke continuing to hang in front of her. She took a moment to catch her breath, and examined herself. "I don't feel any different," she complained.

"Oh, come on! It takes a couple of hits, depending on the quality of the weed," Marian said. "But, however much it takes to get you high, that's all it will ever take—unlike the way addicts of heroin, cocaine, and alcohol have to take more and more. That's why people sometimes die of alcohol poisoning or heroin or cocaine over-doses, while there's never been a report of someone overdosing on pot."

"In that case," Faye giggled, "I'll try another puff—'hit'." She accepted the joint from Marian.

They traded back and forth a few times, when Faye felt an odd sensation—as if something within her that had been wound very tight, were unwinding. It was a warm feeling, and a happy feeling, and she felt as if the next thing she said, whatever it was, would be fraught with meaning. "I think I might have just felt something," she said, and then giggled because it still seemed like a profound statement, even though a part of her knew it wasn't, which just made her giggle more.

"I'm glad," Marian croaked, then exhaled. "Sometimes, people don't feel anything at all their first time, or even the first few times, especially if they're really hung up. Some people just won't allow themselves to relinquish control. They're the ones who get *nothing* from it, or have an uncomfortable experience."

Faye took another hit and thought about it. "I can understand why people wouldn't want to be out of control," she said. "But I don't feel out of control."

"Darling, control is an illusion, anyway. People spend years trying to control their weight, their aging, their spouses, their children. And it never makes them happy—never. Happiness comes when you give up the need to control, and go with the flow, as we used to say."

"Wow," Faye remarked. "That's so true. When Edwin and I had been married for several years, and I began to see what a jer—what an *asshole* he was—I wanted to change him. I explained, I complained, I nagged. Finally I decided there was nothing I could do to change him, and I let it go. I was still depressed, but at least we weren't fighting. Of course," she added, "heavy drinking helped some." That got her giggling again, and Marian joined her. They giggled their way through the rest of the joint, and then Marian rose, put the jar back in the spice rack, and tossed the papers into a drawer.

"Time to put the turkey in the oven," she said. "This will be a test for you: Can you put a turkey in the oven while high?"

Faye pictured herself, unable to do such a simple task, and had another fit of giggling; when she looked at the turkey's aluminum tent, she was filled with wonder. Aluminum foil was such a beautiful thing! How had she never noticed that before? The way it caught the light, reflecting back to her images of the lights, the window, the red power indicators on the stove, even of herself.

She opened the oven door—how beautiful it, too, was; how seamlessly its form followed its function—and, returning to the turkey, lifted it carefully, it's weight seeming an amazing thing— not that it *had* weight, but the sensation *of* that weight. The heat that rose from the oven seemed inviting and wonderful, and she felt joy in knowing that it would envelope the turkey and turn it into a delicious meal for people she loved.

And she loved everyone! As she closed the oven door, she felt suffused with love for Marian, Robert, old Frank Timmons and even the gravel-voiced Selma Graves, who, Faye now suspected, might be more than she seemed.

Faye turned to Marian. "I did it," she said. "That wasn't difficult. In fact, it was practically a *religious experience*. This marijuana is the best stuff!" She paused. "Oh, wait, I know what they call it in the movies...this is some 'good shit', right?"

Marian approached her and gave her a hug. "You betcha! You have no idea how many times I've wanted to turn you on!"

"Well, why didn't you?"

Marian smiled, her eyes bloodshot. "It had to be the right time. You had to be ready. When I first met you, you were a mess— admit it! And I didn't want you to ever think that pot was a crutch to help you become whole."

Faye looked at her friend, wide-eyed. "That's what all the training was about? The gym, the tai chi, the swimming— all just so you could get me *high?*"

"Partly," Marian admitted. "Do you mind?"

"Mind? It was *worth* it!" She stared at Marian's eyes again. "Your eyes are bloodshot. Are mine, too? Is that from smoking this weed?"

Marian nodded. "I'm afraid so. That's one of the very few negative side-effects."

Faye began laughing uncontrollably.

"What is it?" Marian implored. "Tell me!"

It took Faye several moments to regain control of herself. "All those days I saw you with bloodshot eyes, I thought you had been *swimming!*" She gasped. "Oh, my God—Robert! Vera Daye! I thought they'd all been swimming! But they weren't, were they? They were just high!"

Marian joined her in laughing; then, when they had calmed down, said, "Well, darling, we have a few other things to take care of before the guests arrive. I usually set out a few trays of hors d'oeuvres, you know, crackers and cheese, chips and dip, and I do a tray of deviled eggs. Would you like to fix a cheese plate?"

Faye agreed, and again found herself lost in the wonder of the arrangement of crackers encircling the wedge of cheese.

Party Conversation

The effects of the marijuana had passed by the time the guests began to arrive at two o'clock. The first to arrive was Vera Daye. Marian sent Faye to answer the door, and Vera seemed delighted to see her. "Oh, look at you!" she cried. "Here, let's have a hug."

Getting past Vera's breasts close enough to kiss her cheek was a challenge, but Faye managed. "Let me take your jacket," she offered, and Vera peeled hers off and handed it over. Beneath, she was wearing one of Marian's distinctive T-shirts—the one that read, "White House Interns Have All The Fun." Faye grinned, and led Vera to the kitchen, then placed the jacket on Marian's bed, as Marian had requested.

The next guests were two men in their sixties, strangers to Faye. They introduced themselves as Chuck and Dave, and when Faye took their windbreakers, she found they, too, were wearing T-shirts of Marian's design. One read, "I'm Queer, I'm Here, Get Over It"; the other, "The U.S. Government WAS Patient Zero." Faye made a mental note to ask about that one; moreover, she was starting to wonder if there was some sort of unwritten rule to wear one of Marian's T-shirts to one of her gatherings.

Faye expected the men to immediately turn on the TV to watch the game, but they seemed disinterested in the television. Instead, they first offered to help, and then immediately engaged Faye and Marian in conversation.

"So," said Chuck to Faye, "*you* are Marian's work-in-progress?"

Faye was startled; Marian glowered at the man. "Don't be an asshole! This is Faye's trip, and anything she has accomplished, she has accomplished on her own."

"Oh, but that's not true!" Faye protested. "You gave me tremendous encouragement, you coached me all the way here…"

"Coaching is not the same as *doing*," Marian insisted. "You, and nobody else, can take credit for the turnaround your life has taken."

"So, tell me about your T-shirt," Faye asked Dave. "I can tell it's one of Marian's from the airbrushing, but I don't get the reference."

The two men looked at each other, rolling their eyes. "You've *never* heard of Patient Zero?" Chuck finally asked.

"Sorry, no," Faye shook her head, smiling. "Should I?"

Chuck and Dave sighed as if they shared the same lungs. Dave smiled sadly, and said, "It's not your fault, honey. I'm just still amazed at how straight people can not know about HIV."

"HIV?" Faye thought a moment, then made the connection. "Oh—you mean, AIDS!"

"HIV is not AIDS. It *may* be the virus that eventually causes it, although you wouldn't guess there was any doubt if all your information came from the mass media," Chuck corrected.

"Anyway," Dave continued, "Patient Zero is the mythical first victim of AIDS. There were all these articles about him years ago. He was supposedly a French Canadian flight attendant who fucked his way from one port-of-call to another, spreading HIV wherever he went. Most people, even most gay people—even most people who are HIV positive—*still* believe he existed, although the stories were discredited years ago. The mass media, as usual, printed the retractions in the backs of the newspapers and magazines where they would never be seen."

"But, even if he wasn't Patient Zero, *someone* must have been; right?" Faye asked.

"Maybe not," Vera interjected. "HIV first emerged in the United States in New York, Los Angeles, and San Francisco. It just so happens that the government made available an experimental

Hepatitis B vaccine in those three cities, a year or so before the first symptoms starting showing up."

"Made available?" Dave spluttered. "They asked for volunteers among the gay community." He frowned. "Chuck and I have been together since 1969. We have *never* had sex with anyone else—at least, I know I haven't."

"Me, neither!" Chuck insisted, putting his arm around the other man's shoulder.

"But we both answered the call for volunteers," Dave continued. "What did *we* know? It seemed like a good idea at the time."

Faye caught her breath. "You have AIDS?" she whispered. "Both of you?"

"Not AIDS," Chuck corrected. "We are HIV positive, and doing fine without using those awful meds they try and sell us."

Faye shook her head. "But you're saying the government *infected* you with HIV? Oh, Chuck, Dave—I'm sure you're very nice men but I *can't* believe our government would do such a thing."

"Then you never heard of the Tuskegee Project either, have you?" called Marian, re-entering the room with a tray of devilled eggs.

"No..." Faye admitted.

At that moment, the doorbell rang; Faye excused herself to answer it, and found Robert waiting at the door. A smile spread across her face when she saw him.

"Hiya, Faye! Now it is Thanksgiving!"

"Oh, Robert!" she demurred, shyly.

She led him into the living room where the party was centralized.

"Well, there's no controversy over this bullshit," Marian was saying. "The government admitted it did wrong, and made some nickel-and-dime restitution to the victims."

"What are we talking about?" the doctor asked.

"The Tuskegee Project," Vera, Chuck and Dave replied in unison.

"Oh...*man*." Robert groaned.

"What was it?" Faye asked.

"In 1932," Robert explained, "the Center for Disease Control contacted 399 brothers—black men—who came to public clinics for treatment. They had syphilis, but were told they had 'bad blood' and *got no treatment.* The CDC simply monitored their condition for years, to find out how syphilis behaves in its late stages."

"That's evil!" Faye cried in dismay. "How long did the CDC make the men wait for treatment?"

"In 1972, *The New York Times* reported that this was 'the longest non-therapeutic experiment on human beings in medical history.' By that time, 40 years had gone by, and most of the participants were dead," Robert replied. "This past May, President Clinton made a public apology. Too little, too late, of course. But if you ever notice a lack of trust on the part of blacks regarding the medical establishment, that's part of the reason why."

"And considering it was the CDC that set up that Hep B vaccine test in 1979," Dave added, "you can see why we aren't so certain AIDS was spread by accident."

"It's not even likely to be a natural disease," Vera added.

"That's right," said Chuck. "Genetically, there are bits of SIV, or simian immunodeficiency virus, which could have come from Africa, where the CDC now says the disease originated. But there are also gene sequences that are found only in the Icelandic sheep— and that combination could never have happened by accident."

Although much of the information these people possessed was dismaying, it was amazing how interesting all Marian's friends were! For the briefest of moments, Faye felt inadequate—but then realized that she, too, was one of Marian's friends. The notion made her feel very good...very good, indeed.

The next guest to arrive was, of all people, Bitsy Cunningham, Faye's friend from the AquaBabes, wearing Marian's "Question Authority" T-shirt. "Bitsy!" Faye cried when she opened the door. "I had no idea you knew Marian!"

"I thought *you* might, after I realized you were high after our last show," the big woman grinned. She pulled off her sweater and gave it to Faye.

"I only just got high for the first time, today," Faye said, confused.

Bitsy followed her into the back bedroom where Faye was piling the coats and jackets. "But your eyes were bloodshot," Bitsy explained.

"So were yours," Faye pointed out. "I assumed it was from the chlorine in the pool."

Bitsy laughed as they returned to the kitchen. "Faye thought my eyes were bloodshot because of chlorine in the pool!" Bitsy called out. There was a pause, followed by hearty laughter and communal hugging.

"Now, darlings," Marian chided. "Don't give an innocent a hard time."

"Marian," Faye whispered to her friend, "I didn't know everyone would be wearing your T-shirts! I feel out of place."

Marian gave her a pat. "It's kind of a given," she said. "I'm sorry I didn't think to tell you. But not to worry; I have a pile of them, with new stuff on them, in my workroom off the hallway. Take one and put it on, if you want."

Marian's own bedroom, the master bedroom on the floor plan, was being used to store the guests' jackets and sweaters. It had its own bathroom, which the guests were also using. That meant one of the three other doors in the hall must be the workroom she mentioned.

The first door opened to a spare bedroom. The next door was the hall bathroom with the "out of order" sign, and the workroom would be the door past that. As she passed the hall bathroom, she impulsively turned the knob—what could be so wrong with it that Marian hadn't fixed it before the party? The door opened silently, surprising her with bright lights and a jungle of plant life—plants that smelled unmistakably like marijuana.

Feeling guilty, Faye quickly closed the door and tried the next one and found the workroom, with a day sofa piled with T-shirts. She picked through them, looking for a slogan that would express the way she felt.

Problem was, she wasn't certain *how* she felt. Marian was breaking the law. She was growing marijuana, an illegal plant. It was one thing to be *using* it, quite another to be *growing* it.

Or was it? If it was illegal, how else could one get it but by growing it—or by obtaining it from someone else who grew it?

And there were all those patients of Robert's who needed marijuana for medical reasons. Now, Faye understood where they must get it. Marian was performing a needed service, a humanitarian service, and the law be damned! According to what Marvin and Marian had told her, the law had been passed illegally, anyway. If the *legislators* didn't obey their own laws after creating them, how could they expect anyone else to?

And yet, as she had learned, legislators like Meany, who illegally grew pot themselves, were enthusiastically jailing cancer and HIV patients for using a substance just so they could keep their dinners down.

Faye's eyes fell on a shirt that read, "Just Laws Serve The People. Unjust Laws Serve The Government." It perfectly reflected her feeling, and she put it on.

When she returned to the dining area, the shirt she had chosen was noticed immediately by the group. "Oh, I want one of those!" Chuck cried. He immediately pulled out his wallet and handed Marian a $20 bill.

"Of course, darling!" Marian responded, and then took two more twenties before hurrying to the workroom to fulfill the impromptu orders.

"We've really got to get the web site up and running," Faye said when her friend returned. "You are obviously sitting on a gold mine. I wonder how Marvin is coming with the web pages?" She thought a moment. "Say, if he never leaves his house, how does Marvin shop?"

"He has a boy he trusts who does all those errands for him."

Marian and Faye had timed the various dishes so perfectly, that the several timers they had set started buzzing, dinging and beeping within a minute of each other. The dishes were placed on trivets on a side table, with only the turkey on a platter on the main table. The guests loaded up with the side dishes they preferred, choosing from green bean casserole, mashed potatoes and gravy, Faye's stuffing (with Marian's surprise ingredient), corn on the cob, cranberry relish, crescent rolls and butter, and a leafy green salad.

Then, after seating themselves at the table, the guests watched Marian stand and solemnly cut the turkey, the meat moist and steaming, almost falling from the bones. After the meat had been distributed, they all held hands and Marian spoke.

"Universe of which we are a part, we thank you for the wonderful opportunities we've enjoyed, as well as the challenges we've overcome, in living this past year. We thank Mr. Turkey, here, for helping us to celebrate with his life. We thank the spirit of the vegetables, the corn, the potatoes, and especially the healing spirit of the marijuana plant, without which some of our friends would not be here tonight. We ask only for enlightenment of all humankind, and love for all. Amen."

Then they did dig in. It was easily the most delicious Thanksgiving feast Faye had ever attended; every single dish was perfectly prepared, even if she did say so herself. She had always tended to become distracted while cooking; today, that hadn't happened.

Which reminded her to try her stuffing. She could taste the pot, but only subtly—it wasn't as overpowering as she'd expected. And the taste complimented the pistachios and fresh sage she put in, perfectly.

She also hadn't realized how hungry she was. She and Marian had kept their munchies to a minimum, to save room for the actual meal. Now was the payoff. Faye ate the stuffing, the turkey, and the rest with gusto; then revisited the buffet table, returning with a double helping of stuffing and a little cranberry sauce.

The meal was savored for the better part of an hour; everyone complimented them on the meal and Marian made sure the other guests knew the stuffing had been mostly Faye's recipe.

"And now, darlings," she announced, "it's that time. Time to speak of what we're most thankful for this year. You're first, Faye," she added.

"Oh!" Faye gasped. "Well, I didn't realize I'd be making a speech..." Everyone smiled at her encouragingly. "Hmm...well, this was the year my husband killed himself...and it could have been the worst year of my life." She looked at the other guests, and at Marian. "But you know...it wasn't! Meeting you, Marian...and getting into the AquaBabes, Bitsy...and meeting all of you..." Faye found herself blinking back tears. "Oh, my. So many doors have opened for me that I never knew existed. Amazing! This has been the most amazing year of my life! I am thankful for that."

The guests applauded, and Marian added, "Darling, you ain't seen *nothin'* yet! –Chuck, you're next."

"*I* am most thankful that televangelists have vanished."

There was silence, then Robert pointed out, "Chuck—televangelists haven't vanished."

Chuck nodded regretfully. "I know. I'm being thankful in advance."

Everyone laughed, and Vera spoke up. "I'm grateful for so many things!" she said. "I'm grateful for the new singles' nights at the rec center. I'm grateful for my job with Robert. I'm grateful for my new golf cart. I'm even grateful for this new T-Shirt you made me, Marian!" There was applause, and Vera added, "I'll be wearing it at a wet T-shirt contest if I can start one! Then *everyone* will see your message, Marian!"

"A wet T-shirt contest in Sun City?" Robert laughed. "Not very likely."

"How about a wet shawl contest?" Dave quipped, which broke everyone up.

"Well, *I'm* grateful to *be* here," Bitsy boomed. "With both my breasts, which may not be as impressive as yours, ducks," she added, nodding at Vera, "but I *am* attached to them and I would have lost them if not for the Essiac tea Robert recommended. So, thanks, Robert! And thanks, Essiac. And no thanks, " she added, "to the bastard surgeons who wanted to lop 'em both off!"

"I am thankful for my wonderful partner, Chuck," Dave said when the applause for Bitsy's breasts had died down. "And for the marijuana that has made it possible for me to be here and be off expensive meds. And to Marian, because of—for all the—aw, you know!" He began to cry, and reached for Chuck's hand across the table.

"You know who I'm *really* thankful for," Chuck stage-whispered to him, squeezing his hand.

"I'm most thankful for meeting you, Faye," Robert said quietly. "It has been such a joy to watch you grow these past months."

And then it was Marian's turn. "My dear friends...my darlings...I am most grateful for each one of you. You give me purpose...you are my family."

When they were done, Faye began to rise to help Marian get the desert, but Chuck jumped up ahead of her. "You've done plenty," he told her. "Let me help a little!" And so he and Marian left, and returned to the table with the pies and vanilla ice cream, and everyone groaned, and everyone laughed, and everyone ate a little more.

And all the while, Robert, who sat across from Faye, had been looking at her with what seemed like adoration in his eyes. About thirty minutes after they began eating, the pot in the stuffing kicked in and Faye found herself spellbound whenever their eyes met.

Imagine

After the main course, and finally the desserts of pumpkin and blueberry pie with vanilla ice cream were eaten, Marian led them into her living room. "I want all of you to enjoy my new, surround-sound stereo," she said.

"I had surround-sound in the sixties," Chuck announced. "It sounded great; I never understood why it didn't become popular."

"Well, it's back, and now it has...sub-woofers! And, the best part is, no one has to sit in a special location to enjoy it. Let's try it out with one of my favorites..."

"The Beatles!" everyone shouted in unison. Faye, who remembered Marian's music preference from the trip to Mexico, felt a little trepidation. Marian's choice of music on that trip had been interesting, but it had taken a lot of work to actually hear and understand it. Now, after all that food and the pot, she really just wanted to relax.

"Not the Beatles, actually, but a *former* Beatle."

The delicate sounds of a piano enveloped Faye, and she was hooked. John Lennon began to sing, and it seemed to pierce right through to her soul.

"Imagine there's no heaven..."

Time almost seemed to stand still, allowing her to absorb and consider the lyrics, without missing any. At first, she interpreted "Imagine there's no heaven" as a bad thing, because to her mind that would leave only hell, a depressing concept. *Why in the world would they want to remove the one thing that makes this dreary life worthwhile?*

With the second verse, Faye began to realize Lennon was singing about the *downside* of religion and politics: The Crusades, the Inquisition, all the times that religion had been used as an excuse to destroy a people simply because their notion of God or heaven was different than yours. She remembered Edwin's enthusiasm during the Gulf War: "We should nuke those fuckin' towel-heads off the map!" His response, when she tried to explain the practicality of wearing something wrapped around one's head when spending a lot of time outdoors in 120 degrees, was, "If you like them so much, why don't you live there?"

As the song came to a close, Faye found herself caught up in its theme of freedom from structure, especially the structures that may have been intended to uplift mankind, but in fact had only made things worse.

When the chorus came around the second time, she realized that everyone in the room was singing along—and so was she! She was startled. She had never before felt so much a *part* of a group. And now, not only in the words of the song, she felt they were all *one*.

They listened to more music, and it was like the first piece: Faye really *listened* to it, felt it, became it. She was shocked to realize she had *never* done this before. She wondered if it was because the music she had listened to all her life—Lawrence Welk, Andy Williams, Vicki Carr—had been devoid of any deep meaning, or if it was that the pot helped make the meaning clear.

Finally, it was time to leave—guests began rising and giving everyone else hugs goodbye—and Faye regarded the table covered with dirty dishes. "Don't even think about it, darling," Marian whispered. "That's why I have a dishwasher."

A Night Like This

"I think I'm still high," Faye said, as Robert walked her to his car.

"When you eat pot," the doctor pointed out quietly, "it affects you for a longer time. That's why I wanted to drive you home."

Faye giggled. "I think I would be high tonight even if I had never eaten or smoked the stuff."

"Why do you say that?"

She turned to look at him. "Just being with you," she said.

Robert opened the passenger door of his car for her, then proceeded to the driver's side and got in himself. He started the engine and sighed. "I don't know what it is about you," he said. "I just can't take my eyes off you."

She put her small hand on his large one. "I can't complain. I love it when you look at me!" she replied. Blushing, she continued bravely. "You're sensitive, you're caring, you make a difference in the lives of people you barely know. I didn't know there could even *be* a person like you...and here I am, in your car!"

They drove along the silent, safely lit streets, completely free of traffic, as most of the residents of Sun City preferred to get to bed early. Faye didn't mind the quiet. It seemed to make their conversation more intimate.

Arriving at her door, she fished in her purse for her house keys, every item fascinating her with its beauty, shape, or other attribute. She had no idea she kept so many wonderful things in her purse!

"Thank you so much for driving me home," she said, desperately wanting to invite him in but not wanting to seem like "that" kind of girl.

He put his arms around her. "Will you be all right?" he asked, gently.

"Oh, yes!" she replied. "I'm all right now...more than all right."

"Then," he said, hesitating, "may I...may I kiss you good night?"

"Oh, yes, oh, yes...!" and then his lips were on hers, soft, firm, sweet. The kiss made her breathless, and she parted her lips and then found herself kissing him deeply, passionately, her heart pounding with excitement, a warm glow suffusing her groin.

They stood there, kissing as if they had invented the practice. Finally, Robert broke away.

"I'd better leave," he said huskily, "while I still can."

"Oh, don't!" Faye cried. "Don't—I don't want you to."

He looked at her with longing and regret. "This is your first night high," he said softly. "What if, in the morning, you change your mind? What if you decide it was all a big mistake?"

"Robert, I don't want to be with you because I'm high. I've wanted to be with you since the first day we met, when you came here to look at my strained muscles." She laughed. "I didn't realize it then, but I did see how handsome you are, and how gentle. And I knew that I had loved you forever."

Robert kissed her again, gently. "You bring up feelings I thought I would never have again," he said. "I love you, too. I don't know yet how much, or where it will go. I just know this, right now, is a perfect moment and you're the one who's made it so."

"Then, please," she said, gazing into his eyes. "Come in with me. Don't leave. Stay with me, tonight." She opened the door with her right hand, never releasing his from her left.

He followed her into the cool darkness of her home; he closed the door behind him and she led him into her bedroom. She forced herself not to be distracted by the sensual removal of her clothes. Robert wriggled out of his in almost comic eagerness, kissing her all the while. Now that they had agreed to give in to passion, it overwhelmed them, and they fell on the bed, naked, their bodies blended together in warm embrace.

Faye was amazed at the silky smoothness of Robert's skin, at the gentle touch of his caress. She *knew* this moment had been destined since the beginning of time.

Every touch, every stroke, every moment seemed an eternity of bliss. By comparison, sex with Edwin had been like washing dishes. For a moment she wondered, how much of this pleasure was due to the pot and how much due to Robert, but as each extraneous thought began to intrude, it was as quickly swept away by the sensations and the warmth and the love she felt coursing through her like electrical currents. She had never known, never *imagined*, such ecstasy.

Their passion increased, the pressure intensified, and then they both exploded, as a sun would explode, in light and love and laughter. Yes, they laughed—Faye had never, ever, laughed in bed before. But now, it seemed so wonderful, so natural, and it was delightful to lay with her head in the crook of his arm, with his other hand gently resting on her breast and one leg enfolding hers, to fall asleep with this wonderful man at her side.

The Morning After

Friday, November 28, 1997

When her eyes opened in the morning, her first thought was that of Robert's arm still wrapped around her, and she smiled with the memory of their exquisite night together. Her second thought was how *wonderful* she felt—no hangover! She had wondered if she might feel awkward in the morning. What would she say to him? But he was still asleep, and she knew exactly what to do. She slipped out of his embrace, took a quick shower, and, seeing he was still asleep, went into the kitchen and scrambled some eggs.

Edwin had never asked for a breakfast in bed and she had never felt the desire to make him one. Inspired, she slipped out of the room and, silently closing her bedroom door, she went to the kitchen and set a tray up with both their breakfasts, with eggs and toast and freshly-made coffee.

It was the smell of the coffee that awakened the doctor when Faye returned to the bedroom. She handed him the tray, then crawled back into the bed next to him, and began to eat.

Robert first took a sip of his coffee, then started on the eggs. "These are *delicious!*" he said. "My God, you can cook, too!"

"Hey, remember that was *my* stuffing, yesterday," she pointed out.

"Oh, I do," he replied, finishing his toast. "I had a wonderful dream last night," he added. "I dreamed I was in bed with the most beautiful woman in the world, and that we made love, and the earth trembled. And now I find it wasn't a dream at all—it was real."

"I had the same dream," she said. "I hope to have it again."

Robert carefully replaced his plate on the tray, put Faye's plate on it as well, and lowered it to the floor. He then kissed her, and kissed her again, and then they were making love again, almost as wonderfully as the night before.

After awhile, Robert got up regretfully. "I wish I could stay with you all day but I can't. I have patients this afternoon."

"You're welcome to use the shower," Faye offered.

"Thanks, Faye, but my toothbrush and clean underwear are at home."

"Oh, that's no problem!" Faye cried, embarrassed to sound so eager. But she did hate to let the magic come to an end. "I have a brand-new toothbrush in the medicine chest, I always keep a spare. And you're welcome to any of Edwin's underwear, if you don't mind using them. They are clean, and you're taller than Edwin but I think about the same around the waist...but maybe you don't want to wear another man's underwear, especially a dead man..."

"I'll pass on the underwear, but maybe a fresh pair of socks, if that's okay with you," Robert said. He went into the bathroom; Faye cleaned up the breakfast tray and dishes while he showered. Presently, he emerged with a towel discreetly wrapped around him. "And the socks are where?" he asked.

"Oh—!"Should she have put a pair out while Robert had been in the bathroom? "Silly me. Socks are in the top drawer." Not wanting to stare while he dressed, she busied herself with stretching out the sheets to make the bed while he opened the drawer.

"Jesus!" she heard him cry, and turned to look.

He was holding Edwin's gun as if he'd never seen one before.

"Oh, that's just Edwin's gun," she tried to say lightly.

"You *kept* it?" Robert asked.

"Well...yes," Faye replied. "I didn't think not to. Actually, I've been meaning to give all of his things to Goodwill. I just haven't gotten around to his underwear, yet." She pointed at the revolver. "Edwin always kept that behind the argyle socks he never wore."

Robert put it back.

"I suppose I should give it away, or sell it, or something," Faye remarked lamely, as her guest sat and finished dressing.

"When you're ready," he said. "Don't do it until it seems right to you. Otherwise, it'll be an issue that might give you some trouble down the road."

After he was dressed, she walked him to the door. "You have no idea how wonderful last night was, or how much it meant to me," she said.

He kissed her again and left.

Communication

· · · · · · · · ·

Web of Intrigue

Monday, December 1, 1997

The following Monday found Faye and Marian studying a computer monitor screen at Marvin's. "This," he pointed out to them, "is the button customers'll use to buy this particular shirt. And this other button is used to print the artwork on their own printer, so they can print to an iron-on transfer and make the shirt themselves."

"They can make their own copies of my design?" Marian asked.

"Yeah. You did want that feature, right?"

"Yes, I did. I just didn't realize it would be so easy."

Faye smiled. "I'm amazed you could get so many designs in there. And organized by subject!"

"That helps to keep the user—excuse me, the customer—from bein' overwhelmed," Marvin explained.

"When can we get this up and running?" Marian asked.

Marvin laughed. "It's up, now! Ya been lookin' at it."

"You mean, people can come to the site and buy T-shirts or download artwork *right now?*"

"Technically, yeah," Marvin agreed. "However, no one but us *knows* about the site right now. The next step is to advertise it."

"How do we do that?" Faye asked.

"Ya have a variety a ways, from free to very expensive."

Marian grinned. "Tell us about the free ones, first!"

"That's easy," Marvin said, grinning back. "*Tell* people about it. Send e-mails to your friends who have e-mail, and ask them to tell *their* friends."

"Oh." Marian thought a moment. "Very few people have e-mail."

"More than ya think," Marvin disagreed. "And more every day. By the year 2000, probably most people will have e-mail addresses, so you're just gettin' in position for what's gonna turn out to be a *very* long line."

"Okay," Marian nodded. "I like that. How else do we publicize?"

"Search engines. Web sites that do nuttin' but help people find other sites. They can only do that after visitin' our site, and indexin' *every single word* on it. Say you have shirts with President Clinton's name on 'em. So, anyone who does a search on 'Clinton' will pick up our site name, along wit' a dozen or a thousand others."

"How can we make these search engines come to our site to index it?"

"They'll do it eventually on their own; but I've already submitted 'www.saysomethingshirts.com' to them and within a few days, they should start directin' traffic our way."

"And that's free?" Marian asked.

"It is, now," Marvin assured her. "Most analysts predict that, in two or three years, search engines will charge."

"What are the expensive ways?" Faye asked.

"We can buy TV and radio spots, or rent billboards. I don't really recommend that for a site like this one, but it can be done if you don't mind spendin' the money."

"I prefer using word-of-mouth," Marian said. "What do you think, Faye?"

Faye nodded. "The search engine sounds great. It seems to me that's all we need. It's not like we are trying to compete with Sears or the Gap."

"Printed publicity would be good, too," Marvin pointed out. "Ya could always write a press release and give it to *The Arizona Republic*, or even one of the little local weeklies. They're usually hurtin' for content, and will print just about anything."

"I'll try that," Faye promised.

After showing the ladies how to use a password to access a special page for adding additional designs to the web site, Marvin handed Faye a small square of plastic. "This here's a floppy disk," he said.

"It doesn't *feel* very floppy," she remarked.

"The floppy part's inside. Anyway, that's ya *entire web site* as it stands today. If ya ever want to put it up usin' another host, all you'll need is that disk and some publishing software, which you'll find on the computer I sent ya."

"What? You're sending me a computer?"

"Sure. I've got plenty to spare. It's got the same software on it that I used to create your web site. I also threw in a few books on web site design and programming. Ya don't really need to know all that to manage your site, now that I've designed it but knowledge ain't never a bad thing. And you're one smart babe; you can figger it out."

Faye impulsively threw her arms around the man. "A computer! I can't thank you enough."

"You'll put it to good use," Marvin replied, hugging back. He rose to usher them out. "By the way," he said as he unlocked his front door, "I'm still tryin' to get someone interested in doin' somethin' with that video youse made provin' that Meany's property in Mexico is bein' used to grow weed."

"Have you had any luck?" Marian asked.

Marvin crossed his fingers. "CBS, NBC and ABC all have copies, and I've offered to provide additional info. Since I'm the author of a best-sellin' book, they hafta pay *some* attention to me. So, we'll see what happens."

That's Anarchy

Marian had driven Faye to Marvin's. But instead of taking her directly home, Marian steered her rusty supercar to her own home.

"I thought we were going to my house for dinner," Faye said.

"We are, darling but we have an errand first. And this will give me a chance to show you something you haven't really seen yet."

Once inside, Marian carefully locked the front door behind them and took Faye's jacket. The December cold had hit Sun City with a vengeance. It was odd, because it wasn't really that cold but after the extreme heat of the summer, even a temperature in the forties chilled the bones.

The older woman led Faye into the hallway and unlocked the door to the room that normally would have been the hall bathroom. Faye knew, from her visit on Thanksgiving, that this was where Marian grew her marijuana.

Marian opened the door slowly and took Faye's hand. "My grow room, darling," she said, leading Faye into it as a proud parent might lead someone into a nursery to show off a newborn child. The room was bright from a high-powered halide light reflecting off the aluminum-foil-covered walls.

There was a faint, barely audible ticking, and Faye asked about it. "Those are various timing devices," Marian said proudly. The amount of water the plants receive, the amount of CO_2, the timing of the light—all has to be done just so, and I've got it all automated."

There was a whoosh of something being dispensed into the air, which Faye assumed must be the CO_2. "Whoa! Hi-tech!" said Faye. Five beautiful, bright green plants, each about three feet tall, grew out of pots in the bathtub. Seedlings and smaller plants at various stages of growth were in small pots on wall shelves. Every available space was utilized.

"I know plants needs water and light, but what is the CO_2 for?" asked Faye.

"It speeds up growth and keeps my babies healthy and happy," came the reply. "Plants inhale carbon dioxide—that's the full name for CO_2—and exhale oxygen, the opposite of what animals do. That's why the air isn't *filled* with carbon dioxide. If there weren't any plants, we'd all suffocate."

"Is that why the air in your house is always so fresh?"

"That's the other plants. Every home should be filled with plants. I don't want strangers to be smelling these plants, which you've noticed are a bit pungent. So I've taken precautions with extra venting and deodorizers."

Faye considered her own miserable track record. Edwin had always told her she had a "brown thumb." She could see that was *another* weakness she would have to let go.

"Where did you learn to do all of this?" asked Faye.

"Darling, I've been growing my own weed since 1962. Started outdoors, eventually moved indoors. It's a lot more convenient this way. It also gives me a more consistent product."

"How much will this produce?" Faye asked, curiously.

"I harvest every three months, which gives me plenty for my own use and for a few of Robert's patients."

"Robert's patients?" queried Faye.

"Sure, you know most of them. Bitsy, Chuck, Vera and many, many more," answered Marian.

"You mean you can actually supply all those people from this one little room?" asked Faye.

"This is not the only grow room in Sun City, darling." Marian paused for a moment and continued. "Darling, I trust you implicitly, or I wouldn't be showing you any of this."

"I know that," Faye said, humbly. "I feel honored."

"Just understand that a key part of the deal with growing pot is secrecy...complete and utter secrecy. Don't hip the squares!" Faye pretended to understand the phrase and nodded in agreement. "At present," Marian continued, "there are over one hundred and fifty grow rooms in Sun City and Sun City West...*that I know of.* There are, undoubtedly, more."

Faye's jaw dropped in astonishment. "Over *one hundred fifty...*"

Marian nodded.

Faye's face flushed with the enormity of what she had just learned. "Marian, that—that's civil disobedience on a staggering scale!"

"It's better than that, darling," Marian smirked. "It's anarchy."

Free Hearts

At home, Faye cheerily waved goodbye to Marian, then collapsed onto the easy chair by the door. She knew that Marian was doing the right thing, and she knew she'd come around to agree with it...but *one hundred and fifty rooms?* That wasn't a few people growing a little pot for themselves. That was an industry.

It seemed to Faye that pot was harmless—at least, it had been for her. And she knew that it was also being used medicinally. There was nothing morally wrong, that Faye could see. Yet she was disturbed by the idea of so many people breaking the law.

She was so distracted that it took several minutes before she noticed the red message light blinking on the answering machine. Grateful for something else to think about, she pressed the Play button and smiled at hearing Robert's voice.

"I hope I'm not pushing things," he said, "but would you like to have dinner with me tonight? I'll understand if you don't want to...but I hope you do." There was a long pause, as if he had tried to find the words to express another thought; then he added, "I'll talk to you soon."

Faye called him back, accepting his invitation. "I can't wait to see you," she confessed.

The dinner fare was Thai. "You know the best restaurants!" she enthused, as their waitress, an Asian woman in traditional garb, showed them to a table and handed them menus.

"I remember when we blacks couldn't go into nice restaurants," he said, quietly. "So, maybe now I'm overcompensating."

Faye looked at him, somewhat startled. She had forgotten he was black.

He noticed her look. "I'm sorry," he said. "I'm not trying to lay a guilt trip on you!"

"Oh!" Faye exclaimed. "I didn't even think of it that way. I was just thinking how different our lives have been. I mean, we're both Americans, but it's almost as if—as if we are from different countries. Your America doesn't seem like it was the same place as mine."

The waitress came for their orders, and Faye asked Robert to order for her. "We'll each have the *bah me pud,* please. And, please, bring us chop sticks." The waitress glided away, and Robert gazed into her gray eyes with his dark, soulful ones. "It was different in the fifties and sixties, certainly! Did you have the riots where you were?"

Faye shook her head. "I don't think so," she said.

"I traveled with Dr. Martin Luther King, Jr.," Robert said. "It was the proudest time of my life. We were in the South, where it was illegal to drink from the white folks' water fountain...*and we did!* It was illegal to ride in the front seats of a bus...*and we did!* Such simple acts...but they were against the law, and most folks wouldn't question the law. Millions of people, black and white, were affected by these laws telling us what fountains we could and could not drink from, and those damned fountains kept us all in slavery, in fact."

Faye found herself spellbound, caught up in the images Robert wove. Faye remembered the civil unrest of the sixties, but by the middle of the decade she had been nearly thirty and Edwin only saw a bunch of people who "didn't know their place."

"Then, one day, in Montgomery, Alabama, it all changed. One woman, Rosa Parks," and he spoke her name with reverence, "did what no black had dared before. She got on a public bus...and sat *in the front.*

"She was an old woman. Not even the most hardened bigot dared strike her down. And, God bless her, she changed history. She changed everything."

"Civil...disobedience," Faye said, trying the words on her tongue. They had an uncomfortable feeling, an odd shape. Yet, they were beginning to feel less strange.

"Those who run the country, all countries," Robert said, "make laws they, themselves, have no intention of obeying."

Faye nodded in agreement. Robert was echoing the conversation she'd just had with Marvin and Marian.

"I tell you, we can be sheep who do as we are told, or we can be humans who find out for ourselves what is best for us. My path may not be your path. What is best for me may not be best for you. So, who am *I* to tell you how to live *your* life? What arrogance!"

"But still the laws *are* there...and there are police to enforce it."

"So, we break them quietly...privately. Until someone as brave as Rosa Parks comes along," he said, his voice rising passionately, "and defies the law publicly, and shows it up for the mean-spirited soap bubble it is."

"Anarchy?"

Robert smiled. "Private anarchy. It's what kept us blacks going for those centuries. Our bodies were enchained, but in our hearts, we were free." The waitress appeared with their food. Robert continued, "It just took someone like Rosa Parks to help us see that." He sighed, paused, smiled again and said, "Now, do you know how to use chopsticks?"

Faye shook her head.

"I'll show you how." He gently put his hands on hers to show her how to grip the ivory sticks. Her heart fluttered at his touch.

A Sense of Humor

Tuesday, December 2, 1997

Faye awakened suddenly. She had been dreaming, she couldn't quite remember what; all she retained was the image of many men's legs, running. She couldn't see above their waists; just their legs, running every which way.

She couldn't interpret the dream, but found she had an unexpected intuition. If Meany had gotten Frank Timmons' grandson killed to hide Meany's criminal behavior, maybe others had fallen victim as well?

Without even leaving her bed, she pulled her address book out of the nightstand drawer, and dialed Frank's number. He answered after two rings, and Faye shared her theory with him. "You worked in his re-election office longer than I did. Do you remember anyone dying mysteriously while you were there?"

He was silent for a moment, then replied, "I don't remember any mysterious deaths. But I only worked there six or seven months."

"Well, it was just an idea," Faye said, apologetically.

"Wait!" Frank interrupted. "I said there were no mysterious deaths. But there was a death. We all contributed flowers for the funeral."

"Oh? Who was it, do you remember?"

"His name was Kent Worthington. I didn't know him, but I seen him from time to time. He worked in election finance."

"What did he die of?" Faye asked.

"I'm not sure," the old man replied. "But I'm thinkin' it was suicide."

After hanging up, Faye looked in her West Valley residential phone book and found Worthington, Kent and Michelle. The listing was still that way, which didn't surprise her. She had been brought up in a generation that taught women never to list a phone in their own name, because it implied there was no man at home for protection. Her own phone was still listed under Edwin's name.

The phone was listed with a Surprise address. Surprise was the name of the odd little community situated between Sun City and Sun City West. Without the age restrictions on property ownership that kept the Sun Cities gray, Surprise was home to many of the relatively younger people who provided the Sun Cities' services: Its florists, bankers, doctors, and, yes, its funeral directors.

Before she lost her resolve, Faye dialed the number. "Mrs. Worthington?" she asked, and received a response in the affirmative. "I'm Faye McRae. I worked in Representative Carvel Meany's re-election campaign and I—uh..."

"Oh." The voice sounded distant and distracted, as if Faye had just reminded her the water bill was overdue.

Faye hadn't taken time to plan how she would broach the subject; fortunately, the words came to her. "My husband died a little while ago, of the same—the same way as yours, and I wondered if we might talk..."

"Oh, you poor thing!" Mrs. Worthington cried. "It's awful, isn't it? Of course we could get together. Are you free for lunch?"

Faye jotted down the name of the diner Mrs. Worthington suggested and promised to be there on time, as the younger woman said she would have to return to her job afterwards.

After hanging up, she laid back against her pillow with a sense of satisfaction. Not out of bed yet, and she'd already made progress in her murder mystery! Only now did she realize that Robert hadn't been in bed with her when she awoke, though they had slept together the night before. With his typical consideration, he must have let himself out quietly so as not to disturb her sleep with his early waking.

The diner Michelle Worthington had recommended was decorated with nostalgia from the 1950s. The walls were decorated with pictures of Elvis and James Dean and Marilyn Monroe, and a jukebox was playing "Lollipop, Lollipop" when she entered. It seemed like an unlikely place to discuss two suicides. A young woman in a pink, bobbysoxer's outfit seated her in a booth; Faye asked her to be on the lookout for a friend who would be arriving shortly.

Michelle Worthington was a plump, attractive blonde with watery blue eyes who fidgeted. Some part of her body was in motion every second. She spotted Faye immediately and approached her with a smile and a wave. As Faye shook her pudgy hand, Michelle's smile dimmed only slightly. "Oh, you poor dear, I'm so sorry for your loss. How long has it been?"

"It will be five months on the 28th," Faye replied.

"Oh, I'm so sorry. It's eight months for me," she sympathized. "It still hurts when I think about it. Thank God I have a crummy job to keep me occupied. Otherwise, I *know* I would have gone crazy." She giggled. "Of course, a lot of people say I *am* crazy already, so maybe the job doesn't help after all."

The waiter, a tall, handsome man in his early thirties, approached with menus. He flashed Michelle a brilliant smile. "It's so good to see you again!" he said amiably. "Will your husband be coming in, too?"

"No, he can't make it. He's dead," the woman replied matter-of-factly.

The waiter was taken aback. "Oh," he said. "I'm so sorry. I didn't know." He stood there, helplessly fumbling with the menus, until Michelle took one from him and handed it to Faye.

"I don't need one," Michelle told him. "I'll have the turkey club and Diet Coke."

Faye ordered a salad and the waiter left. "You must have come here together often," she suggested.

"Many times," Michelle admitted.

"How did it happen?" Faye asked, hesitantly. "If I may ask," she added.

"It was the craziest thing," Michelle said, adjusting the positions of the tableware. "He went to work after me, so we always kept his car in the garage and mine in the driveway. That way, I could leave ahead of him. Well, when I got home from work that day, I heard the car running in the garage. So, I opened the door to the garage, and all this smoke and fumes poured out. The police figured the car had been running all day in there. He must have decided to kill himself instead of go to work. How did yours—?" Michelle asked.

The waiter arrived with their lunches, as Faye told Michelle about the gun, and how Edwin sent her to fix a drink and shot himself while she was in the kitchen. "The worst part is that he never left a note. I keep thinking that maybe it was an accident, but it wasn't. You can't accidentally shoot yourself in the mouth." There. She'd said it out loud. She'd said it out loud, and she didn't cry and the world didn't end. She breathed a sigh of relief, but Michelle took it for grief and held her hand.

"Kenny didn't leave a note, either," she said, biting into her sandwich with one hand while dumping catsup on her fries with the other.

"Really? Then how do you know it was suicide?"

"Accidentally running the car in a closed garage until you pass out? What kind of an idiot would do that?"

"Oh."

"He passed out hard, too," the woman continued. "He fell out of the car and actually fractured his skull on the garage floor."

"What?"

"Yeah," Michelle asserted. "Isn't that something? Just *crack*, right on the concrete." She giggled nervously. "I always told him he had a thick skull. He sure picked a hell of a way to show me I was wrong, didn't he?"

"Do you know...*why*...he did it?"

Michelle shook her head emphatically. "Nope. Not a clue. The bastard never told me he was unhappy or anything. I know something at work had disturbed him, something he wouldn't tell me about, which was unusual. But, you know, it was only a temp job anyway; so it's not like he was trapped in the job from hell...like I am. Goodness!" she interrupted herself and looked at her watch. "I've just been talking and talking. They're gonna fire my ass if I don't get back *this minute*." She rose, still chewing the remainder of her sandwich and popping in a couple more French fries. "Listen, honey, here's my card," she added, pulling a business card from her purse and handing it to Faye. "You call me *any* time you need to talk. I know how much it hurts."

Faye looked at the card, which held a greasy thumbprint from where Michelle had gripped it.

Michelle suddenly stopped. She stood, balanced, stock still—the first time Faye had seen her not *moving*. "I know you must think I'm really shallow," she said, softly. "I mean, to make jokes about it and all. But, honey, that's how I've handled trouble *all my life*. I don't know any other way. But, you know, just coming here was a kind of triumph for me." She looked around. "This was Kenny's favorite place to eat. Today is the first time I've been able to come back here." She then flashed Faye a dazzling grin, and was gone.

The waiter returned and looked at the chair Michelle had been sitting in, then toward the restroom door. "Will the other lady be coming back?" he asked.

"I don't think so, not today," Faye replied.

His voice dropped to a low tone; she had to strain to hear him over the jukebox. "I truly didn't mean to eavesdrop," he said. "But did I hear you say that her husband killed himself?"

Faye nodded, surprised to be having a conversation with a waiter.

The man shook his head. "Wow," he said. "He was such a good-humored guy. They used to come in together at least twice a week, and they'd get everyone in the place laughing! He came in with his boss a few times, too; they'd work on papers while they ate. When they stopped coming in, I thought I had done something wrong, or the cook had screwed up their order. It didn't make sense, you know? He didn't seem like the kind of person who would hold a grudge like that. So, it didn't make sense."

"Suicide doesn't make sense," Faye offered. "How did you know he was with his boss?"

"Oh, the boss paid. When men eat lunch together, if they're just pals, they take turns paying. If one always pays, then it's a business lunch because the boss always pays."

"Oh. How about women?" Faye asked, curiously.

"Women always split the check," the waiter grinned, "and take at least half an hour making sure everyone has paid *exactly* their share."

Faye laughed. That was *just* what she and Marian did.

The waiter picked up their plates. "The last time he was here, he got into an argument."

"With his wife?"

"No, he was here with his boss. It wasn't a *big* argument," the man hastened to add.

Faye clutched his wrist, causing the plates he had piled to rattle. "Do you remember what the boss looked like? Do you remember what was said?"

The waiter nodded. "They'd been here together a number of times. I'd recognize him. And the argument was short, just a sentence or two. The guy who comes in with his wife jumped up and said something like, 'You can't do this! Campaign money has to stay in the campaign!' which made me think the other guy might be running for office or something. Then he went outside. His boss gathered the papers and paid for lunch."

Faye wished desperately she had a photo of Meany with her to show the waiter, but she didn't. "If I came back with a photograph, do you think you could identify the boss if it was of him?"

"I'm sure of it," the waiter asserted. "What, are you some kind of cop or detective? You don't think it was suicide, do you?"

"I'm just trying to help a friend," Faye said. "And, no, I don't."

Computers For Dummies

When Faye got home she found two large boxes sitting in front of her garage door. Excitedly, she opened the smaller box. It was a monitor for a computer. In the second box was the computer. There was also a keyboard, one of those mouse things, and numerous wires of various colors and thicknesses. The way the parts were packed suggested this was not a new computer; instead of being protected by Styrofoam or bubble wrap, the parts had been spaced by carefully placed books. There were *Windows For Dummies*, *Introduction to Java*, and several others.

She put down the wires and called Marvin. He answered on the first ring.

"Hey, Faye. You musta gotten the computer I sent over," he said.

"How did you know it was me?" she asked, startled.

"I have that new Caller ID feature on my phone. It tells me who's callin'."

"Oh. Well, yes, I did...and thank you again!"

"You'll need it to maintain ya T-shirt web site."

"I have to tell you—I'm pretty nervous. I don't know if I'll be able to put it together."

Marvin chuckled. "I think ya got the knack, kid," he said. "Start wit' *PCs For Dummies*, it'll tell ya how to wire up the components and you'll be off and runnin' in no time."

And then he hung up, leaving her alone with the monitor and the computer case and the keyboard and wires and...

Faye stared. Taped onto one of the books was a carefully wrapped marijuana cigarette.

Faye caught herself. If she had learned *anything* in the past few months, it was not to be overwhelmed. She took a deep breath, lit the joint, and inhaled deeply. She sat back. *I have an illegal substance in my home,* she thought. Then grinned in satisfaction. *Maybe it's not too late for me to be a rebel.*

As Marvin had suggested, she opened the copy of *PCs For Dummies* and started reading from page one. Sure enough, in less than an hour, following the directions, she had the machine perched on her uncle's desk and wired up. She plugged the "power" cord into the wall socket and flipped the big red switch on the side of what she now knew was the CPU. A light came on in front, but nothing happened on the monitor until she remembered to turn it on, too. In a moment, the screen brightened and she saw the words "Microsoft Windows 95®." She couldn't help but grin. She was now computer literate! She continued to play with the machine, exploring the various pieces of software (the correct term, she now knew, for the programs Marvin had installed) until she suddenly realized that it was dark outside.

Oh, my, Faye thought to herself. *This must be what they call an obsession.* Or, maybe, considering the joint she had been toking on for much of the day, it was simply a productive focus.

Hot Springs

Thursday, December 4, 1997

Obsessed with her new hobby, the next two days passed in a blur. Faye missed a rehearsal of the AquaBabes and even forgot to eat. She had never before been exposed to anything that was so purely logical and it was an unexpected joy. In addition to learning how to work with the web site via her phone line and with an editing program Marvin had included, she was thinking of other things the machine could be used for.

She'd been spending a lot of time on-line and she had only the one phone line. She jumped when a loud knocking came from her doorway. She carefully placed the book she was referring to on the desk and hurried to the door to find Marian.

"You're phone is out of order, darling," the older woman stated matter-of-factly. "I've been trying to call for two days, and it's been busy every time."

"Oh!" Faye cried in embarrassment. "I'm sorry—I didn't think. Marvin sent me a computer, and I've been connected to the Internet most of the time. I'll have to get another phone line, I guess," she added to herself.

"Well, grab a towel. It's high time you got out of the house you've been in for two days. We're going for a soak."

"A soak?" Faye asked. "You mean, a swim? What time is it? Isn't the rec center closed?"

"We're not going to the rec center. Hurry up and get a towel. I'll tell you more about it on the way."

"Well, I'll need my swim suit, too," Faye said as she turned towards her hall.

"No you won't, darling!" Marian called. "Just your towel, and maybe sandals."

They rushed into Marian's car, and in less than ten minute they were stirring up dust on the dirt roads south of Sun City. "All this will be paved and populated within five years, mark my words," Marian stated with some chagrin.

"You think so?"

"No doubt. The greater Phoenix area is growing so fast that the infrastructure can't support it. In a few years, we'll have traffic jams, rush hours—all the things people moved here to get away from. And, at the rate the Valley is growing, it won't have enough water to supply its own population within ten years.

"There's not enough water?"

"Phoenix's supply of water comes from an underground aquifer that contains what they call 'fossil water.' That means the water that fills the aquifer got there thousands or even tens of thousands of years ago. It will take thousands more to refill it, and we are draining it now faster than it can be refilled. When it's empty...well, it won't be pretty."

"But can't something be done?" Faye asked in concern.

"Sure. The people of the Valley could vote on a proposition to stop all new building. But they won't; the builders spend a fortune convincing the construction workers that they'll all lose their jobs if there's a moratorium on building. So they vote against it, and because they look like regular Joes who need their jobs, a majority will support them."

"Well, they *would* lose their jobs, wouldn't they?"

"Those who are building new housing, yes. But the existing housing will need maintenance. In the sun and heat out here, each roof has to be replaced every ten years or so. That alone would keep most of the construction people in the Valley working for the rest of their lives!"

They reached I-10 and Marian turned the car to the West. "Where are we going?" Faye asked.

"It's a little town called Tonopah about thirty miles from here. There's a hot spring located there. It isn't commercially developed. There's nothing in the world more relaxing than a hot soak in natural mineral water—unless it's a hot soak while you're stoned!"

"And why don't I need a swim suit?" Faye asked, fearing the answer.

"Because it's traditional at non-commercial hot springs to soak in the nude."

Faye bit her lip. "I don't know..." she hesitated.

"Relax, darling," Marian urged. "Clothes spoil the relaxation.

And, besides, we're going at night on a weekday...I doubt if there will be anyone else there. Well," she added, "maybe one other person."

Tonopah was, indeed, a little place, consisting of a convenience store, a gasoline station, a darkened building with the name "Alice's Restaurant" hand-painted on the side, and, a quarter mile down a dark, back road, the hot springs. Faye knew where she was, because, in a cleared area that seemed to be the parking lot, there was a water tank on stilts that doubled as a sign with more hand-painted letters: "Hot Spring." The tank was dimly lit by a single light bulb; it couldn't be seen from the highway. There were no other cars in the parking area.

They walked to a small travel trailer parked beyond the lot, where a woman in a lawn chair was sitting at a small table beneath another small light. She was working delicately with pliers and strands of silver; and as her eyes adjusted to the dim light, Faye saw that she was making jewelry. "How pretty!" she exclaimed. "What is it?"

"It's an earring," the woman said. "Marian, dear, how nice to see you again!"

"You, too, Camilla!" Marian gave the woman a hug around the shoulders that didn't require the woman to rise. She then bent over the table and wrote something in a book. "Sign in, darling," she told Faye, who did so.

The jewelry woman started to rise, but Marian motioned her to remain. "Don't be silly," Marian told her. "I know the way perfectly well."

"Even in the dark?"

"Even in the dark!" Marian insisted, and took Faye by the arm. "This way, darling!"

The stars were brilliant now that the moon had set, and Faye found she could make her way without stumbling—especially with her hand on Marian's arm. They passed through a gate into a fenced enclosure. Dimly, Faye could make out five or six large metal tubs and a larger, rectangular, concrete tub that was twelve or fifteen feet long and about four feet wide. Marian led the way to a weathered set of wooden shelves. "This is where we disrobe, darling." She immediately began shucking her street clothes: Shoes first, then slacks and blouse. Hesitating only a little, Faye followed suit. When Marian stripped off her bra and panties, Faye took a deep breath and did the same.

She had never been naked, outdoors, in her life. The cool night air moved around her limbs. She could feel the slightest breeze between her legs, touching her pubic hair and stiffening her nipples. She had expected to feel inhibited and instead, felt wonderfully and exuberantly free.

The ground was covered with some kind of indoor/outdoor carpet; still Faye walked carefully as Marian led the way to the concrete tub. She stepped up onto its rim, then down three steps into the water itself. She moved on into the darkness, and Faye followed.

It was like getting into a really big, hot bath. The floor of the pool was rough but flat. Marian seated herself, the water coming to her chin. She sighed with pleasure as the water enveloped her, and Faye did the same. Only when she had ducked her head into the hot water and emerged, did she realize that she and Marian were not alone.

At the far end of the pool, submerged to her neck in the water, was a woman. She seemed to almost glow in the starlight. Faye couldn't tell how old she was, but a sense of peace that radiated from her implied both vibrancy and agelessness.

Marian turned to the woman and allowed herself to drift over to her. "Norma," she said, softly. The woman's eyelids fluttered; her eyes opened, deep and lustrous in the dim light.

"Marian, dear," she whispered.

The meeting between Marian and the old woman did not seem to have the same quality as her reunion with Camilla, the woman who ran the springs, Faye thought. Camilla was just a friend, a pal. This ageless woman was something special to Marian. Even...something sacred.

"I want you to meet someone," she told the woman. "This is my friend, Faye." Faye half-swam, half-glided to the far end of the tub, trying to keep her breasts under water. "Faye," said Marian, "this is Norma Haverhill."

"How do you do," Faye said formally, offering her hand. Cool fingers rose from the water and took it. Faye was astonished at the firm grip.

"I have been looking forward to meeting you," the woman—Norma—said.

"You...know about me?" Faye asked, surprised.

"Oh, yes. More than you can imagine," Norma affirmed, which made Faye feel slightly uncomfortable. "Come close to me, dear," Norma said. "Let me get a look at you." Faye moved near to the woman. The woman gazed into Faye's eyes for what seemed like an eternity. Faye stared back. She felt as if she were falling into the woman's eyes. Norma's irises were deep and dark, and stars reflected in them. Her lashes were long, the eyelashes of a young woman.

"What do you see?" Faye asked.

"Untried resolve," was the prompt answer. "You have great strength, but have yet to have it tested."

"Oh," Faye said, surprised. The observation was probably accurate, but was unlike anything she had expected to hear.

"Marian has been training you," Norma continued.

"Oh, yes," Faye smiled. "She's taught me to work out, and it's been—"

"Not just exercise," the woman interrupted. "She's been preparing you for the greatest task of your life. Did you not know that?"

"What?" Faye tried to say, *no*, that she did *not* know that. And yet, somehow, she did. In some way the statement felt true to her but she did not know why. She left the rhetorical question unanswered.

The woman nodded. "You *do* know," she said. "Good. Do you know who *I* am?"

"I thought it best," Marian interjected quietly, "to let you explain it to her."

The woman laughed musically. "Always the one to leave me the complex tasks!" she said. "Very well. Faye—may I call you Faye?" Faye nodded. "Faye, dear, when I first met Marian, she was fat, lazy, and ignorant."

Faye turned and stared at her friend. "No!" she cried.

Marian nodded with a rueful grin. "It's true. That was a long, long time ago. I was in my twenties when I first met Norma."

"But she had promise," Norma continued. "She was incredibly intelligent. And she was curious. The reasons for her ignorance were her tendency to believe what those in authority told her...and she had never made an effort to expand her consciousness."

Faye tried to imagine a Marian who did not preach anarchy, or one who did not smoke pot, and failed.

"Now, I want you to understand something," Norma said intently. "Many, many years ago—longer ago than you would guess—*I* was a fat, lazy, ignorant young girl. Then, one day, a woman named Abigail took me under her wing. She taught me how the world worked, and how I could be of some use to the Greater Good. One day, when she thought I was ready, she took me to a secluded glen in the woods and introduced me to the woman who had taught *her*."

Faye felt understanding building up in her chest and filling her throat. "You're saying," she said in amazement, "that you are part of some kind of chain or movement...and that I am, too."

Norma smiled broadly. "You were right, Marian," she said. "This is the one. Good for you!"

"But, what is the movement *for?*" Faye asked.

"You will come to understand in due time," Norma assured her. "I promise."

"Why can't you tell me now?" Faye asked.

"Because you wouldn't believe me," Norma said. "Remember, in *The Wizard of Oz* how Glinda tells Dorothy she had the power to go home all along, but had to learn it for herself? It's something like that."

"But...then...what am I supposed to do?"

Norma spoke with a quiet intensity. "Nothing that you are not doing now," she said. "Follow the causes you are moved to follow. Stand up for what you believe. Your heart knows. Follow it."

Faye took a deep breath. "But I was doing all that. So, why am I here? Why did I have to meet you now?"

The mysterious woman again clasped Faye's hand. "You are about to face your first test. It won't be easy, but knowing Marian and I support you might make it easier."

Faye felt a sudden dread. She knew that her experience with Meany was going to come back to haunt her, and wondered how knowing that a beautiful but mysterious woman "supported" her could ever be of any help.

"You're wondering how knowing that a woman like me is supporting you could ever be of assistance."

Faye's blushing went unseen in the starlight. She wondered if Norma was a mind reader.

"Sometimes," the woman said. "So are you." She arose from the water, droplets glistening on her perfect breasts. "Marian, give her the locket."

Marian said, "I will. It's in my purse."

"Faye, the locket Marian is going to pass onto you was given me by *my* mentor, Abigail Bannister," Norma explained, stepping out of the pool and into the night so quickly, it was as if she had vanished. Faye looked around, but could not see her near the shelves on which they had placed their clothes, or anywhere else in the enclosure.

"Where did she go?" Faye asked of Marian.

"People come and go so quickly here!" Marian laughed, playfully. Faye frowned. "Does she live here, at the spring?"

"No," said Marian. "Frankly, I don't know *where* she lives."

"There were no other cars here when we arrived," Faye said firmly.

"No doubt," Marian agreed. She let her head sink beneath the surface, effectively ending the conversation.

After dressing and saying goodbye to Camilla, they got into Marian's car. Marian started the engine, and then opened her purse and took out something shiny.

"This is Abigail's locket, darling," Marian said, admiring it. "Wow. I never thought this day would come so soon." She held it out to Faye, who threw her hands up to refuse it.

"Give it to me some other time," Faye insisted. "I can't take it from you."

"It's not mine, and it's not yours," Marian said. "It's Norma's, and she wants you to guard it now. Take it. It's all right," she added, when Faye continued to hesitate. "Really. It's all right. Take it."

Reluctantly, Faye accepted the locket. It was old-fashioned, heavy, and made of silver. She popped it open. Marian turned on the overhead light so Faye could examine it more closely. There was a painting of a young girl in the right half, and an elaborately engraved inscription on the left: "To Norma With Love, Abigail."

Final Performance

Saturday, December 6, 1997

Faye placed her AquaBabes swim suit into the gym bag on top of her towel, and zipped the bag shut. Now, there was only one more thing to do before walking over to the rec center for the year's final performance. She went to her refrigerator, bent down and picked up the Roach Motel on the floor next to it and looked inside. There were two, hand-rolled marijuana joints, a gift from Marian. She had gone without for two days to make sure she had one for today. The other she intended to save for an emergency, though she didn't have any idea what would comprise a pot emergency. Perhaps "special occasion" would be a better way of putting it.

Since being introduced to the weed, she hated her stash being so low and she also hated receiving joints from Marian as gifts. She knew that a certain amount of effort went into the growing and preparation of the herb, and that its primary intended recipients were cancer and AIDS patients in Sun City. Faye wondered what kind of gift she should offer in return.

A realization flashed. The *only* appropriate gift...was to join in the effort. Faye must begin growing marijuana, herself. Faye, whose brown thumb had doomed many an innocent plant to the careless mercies of garbage collectors, was going to become a horticulturalist. Oddly, Faye had no doubt that she could learn to grow plants. She knew her heart hadn't been in it before; in fact, she had resented Edwin's assumption that any woman must be able to grow geraniums and such and had been perversely satisfied when it turned out that she could not. But she now had great confidence in her ability to learn *anything*. If the information was in books, or on the Internet, in time she could work it out and master it. It was a heady, powerful feeling. It made her feel strong.

She removed one of the joints, returned the roach motel to its hidden-in-plain-view place, and lit up. She took a hit, held her breath as Marian had taught her, and exhaled. Almost immediately she felt the presence of pleasure the herb engendered. Each time, it seemed as if she could smoke less to get the same result. Apparently the weed was training her body, or she was using the weed to train it—in any case, she was becoming more adept at getting high. She realized it wasn't entirely the effect of marijuana's active ingredients. The high required *her cooperation* to manifest itself.

Faye had had plenty of experience with alcohol, and she knew that if enough was ingested, inebriation would inevitably follow. That's why boys tried to get girls to drink. If they drank, their judgment would suffer and the boy might "get lucky," as they put it when she was in high school and probably still did. Faye knew her judgment, under the influence of marijuana, was intact. It wasn't just her feelings while high; it was also her analysis afterwards of the decisions she'd made while high that proved her point. She had put a computer together, for heaven's sakes—something she might well have found overwhelming without the marijuana's ability to help her focus without being overcome by the plethora of details.

She also liked that, under the influence of the pot, she could use words like *plethora* correctly in her thoughts.

She finished the joint and was ready for the walk to the rec center. Confident that marijuana didn't reduce her reaction time, she still resisted driving while under its influence. Not just because it was illegal; everything about marijuana was illegal except its vilification. She just didn't *quite* trust her judgment in this matter enough to risk other lives in its accuracy.

So she walked the four blocks to the recreation center. She walked briskly in the mild December day, using the trek as a warm-up exercise, taking brisk strides and breathing deeply as she went. In about five minutes she walked down the ramp and went to the changing room where she knew the other AquaBabes would be gathering.

She spotted Bitsy the moment she entered; the Amazon towered over the other ladies, making her impossible to miss. She caught

Bitsy's eye at the same time; Bitsy grinned and then pointed at Faye's eyes, as if to say, *I know what you've been doing!*

"Are you ready, girl?" Bitsy asked as Faye began to undress by her locker.

"I think so," Faye replied. "In fact, I *know* so. I know the routines inside and out and I'm confident I won't be distracted by the audience."

"Good for you, girl!" Bitsy said, clapping her on the shoulder with enough force that Faye had to grab the locker door to steady herself.

The music started, and the women marched out onto the pool deck, taking their places at the pool's edge. They had been coached to look out over the crowd with detached pride, a sensation that exactly matched what Faye was feeling. She saw Marian and Robert and also the gay couple she had met at Thanksgiving, Chuck and Dave. The music started, the opening strains of Tchaikovsky's *Waltz of the Flowers* from *The Nutcracker*. She awaited her cue, completely focused on the music, until she realized she had seen a familiar, but unexpected, face in the crowd.

It was Michelle Worthington, whose husband's mysterious death had been called a suicide.

Only a tremendous act of will kept Faye's mind on what she was doing. She was stoned, and the usual effect was to cause her mind to grab on to whatever caught her attention and not let go—until something else caught her attention. But she needed to keep her mind on the performance; that was why she had *gotten* stoned today. Barring something unexpected and totally riveting, she could do it. She *would* do it.

Her cue came, and she allowed herself to fall in a graceful dive, into the water.

She became one, not only with the water, but with the music as well. Swimming was effortless; indeed, it would have taken an effort not to move in perfect time with the music and the other swimmers. When the ladies were supposed to move together, they did so as if linked by the same, invisible wires. When they were supposed to move in a cascade, Faye's turn came so naturally that she didn't even have to look at her neighbors. She sensed when it was time, or rather, her body sensed it. She didn't move so much as she flowed.

The Waltz of the Flowers concluded, and the quick, Cossack strains of the Russian Dance picked up. The audience laughed in delight as the swimmers cavorted in time, alternately throwing their arms and legs into the air. Then the whimsical notes of the *Dance of the Sugar Plum Fairies* led them into a complex geometric pattern that seemed to coalesce into a different shape at the conclusion of each measure. None of the dancers could see any of these patterns from the water, of course; Beatrice, their coach, had designed them from her balcony vantage point. Faye had memorized her place relative to the other AquaBabes, and flowing into each successive position was done joyfully and effortlessly.

It was over too soon. The AquaBabes emerged from the pool just as the last piece ended; they bowed to thunderous applause. Encores were not an AquaBabes custom and the ladies bowed low, twice, and then filed, heads high, back to the dressing room.

The moment the door closed behind them, the ladies burst into excited chatter. As Bitsy removed her swim suit at the locker next to Faye's, she said, "That was our best performance, ever, don't you think?"

"It seemed to go well," Faye smiled. "The audience seemed to like it."

There were a few hand claps from behind her. Beatrice Smith was standing on a bench, and was clapping for attention. "Ladies, ladies!" she said. The women quieted and turned toward their coach. "Ladies," she continued, "I want to thank you all for a terrific finish for this year's AquaBabes programs. This year's effort will be a hard act to follow!"

The women applauded themselves. Senior citizens all, it saddened Faye to think that next year's lineup of swimmers would likely be missing some of these faces due to illness or death, replaced by newcomers to Sun City like herself.

"As you old-timers know," the coach continued, "Each year we hand out a few awards after the last performance. Angie Hooper, will you come up here, please?"

One of her teammates made her way to the coach's perch. Beatrice handed her a small gold dolphin. "Angie, you get the award for Perfect Attendance again. Including this year, you've made every rehearsal for the past three years—quite an accomplishment!"

The ladies applauded, then resumed dressing as Beatrice continued. "Bitsy Cunningham!" she called. Bitsy looked surprised, then walked to the coach, other teammates melting out of her way. Beatrice handed her a gold dolphin. "Bitsy, you get this years' award for Most Helpful Swimmer. As you know, ladies, Bitsy assisted and helped to train our newcomers on her own time. She's also proved to be invaluable, putting her experience as a lawyer to good use by filing the forms that make us, officially, a non-profit corporation! Thank you, Bitsy!"

There was more applause, and Beatrice called another name. "Faye McRae!"

Faye felt all the blood rush to her head. Her first reaction was that the coach was going to criticize her unexpectedly, as she had after the Thanksgiving performance. She felt the breath go out of her as Bitsy, returning to her locker, saw her expression and grabbed her arm just in time to keep her from stumbling. "Steady, girl!" she whispered, giving her a gentle shove that propelled her the rest of the way to the coach. Dangling in the air before her eyes was another of the gold dolphins. Faye's eyes slowly took in the hand holding the dolphin, then the arm attached to the hand, then the shoulder, then Beatrice Smith's face, smiling warmly at her.

"I think we have all watched with great pleasure as Faye, one of our newest members, has grown into her own as a swimmer and performer. I hope she will be performing with us for many years to come. Faye, this award is yours, as our Most Talented Newcomer."

Her pleasure at being recognized almost bested the applause.

Almost, but not quite.

Transformation

. . . .

Good Things Come In Small Packages

After Faye had dressed, she was eager to find Marian, Robert and the others she knew were waiting for her outside; but at the entrance to the dressing room, she found Michelle Worthington instead.

"I'm so glad I caught you!" Michelle exclaimed, hugging Faye.

Faye hugged her back and greeted her. "Hi! I thought I saw you in the audience. I was a little surprised, since you don't live in Sun City. The AquaBabes don't get a lot of outsiders at these shows."

"Your name was listed with the others in the newspaper article," Michelle explained. "And I knew I needed to see you…"

"Really? About what?" Faye asked curiously.

"Well…maybe we should go to my car. I have something I want you to have."

Puzzled, Faye followed the woman. They slid past the crowd near the pool and went to the parking lot. As they walked across the lot, Michelle spoke softly. "I found a box," she said, and hesitated.

Faye prompted her, "What kind of box?"

"Kenny brought it home from work. Less than a week before he killed hims—before he died. It was odd because I looked for it to give back to Representative Meany's office, but I couldn't find it."

They reached Michelle's car, and Michelle took out her keys and opened the trunk.

"So, where did you find it?"

"I wasn't going to decorate at all this Christmas. It's just been too soon, you know? But then I thought, Kenny would want me to do *something* for the holiday. He loved Christmas. It was his favorite holiday. Also, I had to think of Brian, our son. Kenny always went all out, so I thought, maybe just *one* string of lights around the window, maybe a *small* tree, just for Brian. I went into the attic crawlspace where we keep the decorations, and there was the box he had brought home."

"But you decided not to give it to Meany?"

"Well..." Michelle's face held a tense smile. "After your visit, and I was thinking about whether Kenny had been killed or not...and I thought, maybe I wouldn't be safe if Meany's office knew *I* had the box. So, maybe I should just, you know...get rid of it. On the other hand, if it contained some kind of evidence, I shouldn't just throw it away. So I thought I would give it to you, and you can pass it on to whoever you think is appropriate." She lifted a cardboard file box from the trunk and handed it to Faye.

"What's in there?" Faye asked.

"I don't know," Michelle said firmly. "I did not open it. I don't *want* to know. But, you may find it interesting." Michelle hurried into her car and drove away, leaving Faye holding the box in the middle of the parking lot.

She's frightened, Faye thought. *Just like I was after Edwin's suicide.* She thought about how far she had come since those dark days. Marian had literally saved her life, not to mention her sanity. *Too bad there's no one to help Michelle,* she thought. She then decided to keep an eye on the woman, in case there was some way she could be of assistance.

"Who was that?" Marian asked, from so close behind her Faye almost dropped the box.

"Michelle Worthington," Faye replied. "With a gift."

"Let's put it in my car," Marian offered.

"Thanks," Faye accepted. She saw her other friends strolling in her direction. Marian's amazing rust-bucket was parked nearby. Robert ran to her assistance and took the box from her, placing it in Marian's trunk. He put his arms around Faye and gave her a long, deep kiss.

"You were wonderful," he said softly. "The best swimmer in the show."

Faye beamed with pleasure.

"It was fabulous!" Dave said. "Really, as professional as anything you'd see in New York."

"Just fantastic!" his partner, Chuck, echoed.

Marian closed her trunk and turned around. She was wearing a new T-shirt, one that read, "Pot Is Illegal Because It Cuts Into The CIA's Heroin Sales." Weeks ago, Faye would have challenged her but by now she knew that if Marian said it did, she had reams of proof.

"Marian, I want to help the cause. It isn't right that you keep giving me pot to smoke—which, by the way, I am certain helped me in today's performance. But I want to help grow some, for the sick people who need it."

There was a moment of pleased silence. "Are you sure, darling?" she asked. "It's a real commitment—almost like owning a pet, except this is a pet you have to keep secret."

"Although," Dave quipped, "on the other hand, you don't have to walk it."

"It needs a *lot* of grooming," Chuck added.

Faye laughed at the good-hearted banter. "I'm sure," she said. "I've given it a lot of thought, and I want to do this. But I'll need a lot of help," she added.

"If you like," Dave offered, "Chuck and I can design a hidden grow room for you. Before I retired, I was a cabinetmaker, and Chuck owned a home security company. If you'll pay for the materials, we'll do the work for free."

"A *hidden* grow room? Is that necessary?"

"Have no doubt," Marian warned, "you're breaking the law. It's an unjust, unconstitutional, and unethical law, but it's a law nevertheless. Keeping a low profile is a very good policy."

"But *your* grow room is just a locked bathroom," Faye whispered, looking around to make sure no one else was within earshot. "That's not very hidden."

"We've offered," Chuck interjected.

"I put it together before I met Chuck and Dave," Marian explained. "And I just haven't had time to clear the babies out and give the boys a chance to work their magic."

"Well, I accept your offer," Faye said with gratitude. "Would you like to drop by so you can get an idea of the space we have to work with?"

"Absolutely," Chuck nodded. "Will you be around after lunch?"

"Yeah," Faye replied.

"But it will be a *long* lunch," Marian added. "We're taking you, darling, to celebrate your performance, making the AquaBabes, and your participating throughout the whole season! That's quite an accomplishment for someone who was a tubby just a few months ago!"

"Marian!" Robert chided, but Faye didn't mind. She *had* been fat; she was now as sleek as she had been in high school, and felt even better.

"They gave me an award," she confessed shyly, opening her purse and pulling out the gold dolphin, inscribed with *Most Talented Newcomer, 1997*. Marian took it and passed it on, each person cooing over it and giving Faye an admiring glance.

Faye realized that not since she'd married Edwin, had she had a group of friends with whom she could share her achievements. She felt a rush of tears stinging her eyes. She smiled and said, "Let's eat."

Thinking Out Of The Box

After a splendid lunch in the back room at J. B.'s Restaurant, Marian drove Faye home, with Chuck and Dave following. Marian parked over to the side of Faye's driveway to give the men room to pull up alongside. As Faye unlocked her door, Marian opened her trunk and Chuck lifted the box Michelle had given her, and carried it inside.

Chuck set the box on the coffee table, while Dave inspected Faye's uncle's merchant marine memorabilia. "Oh, my!" he breathed. "Just *look* at this!" He turned to look at Faye. "I didn't realize your husband had been a sailor."

"He wasn't," Faye explained. "This was my uncle's house. He was in the Merchant Marines."

Dave frowned. "Have you...thought of decorating so that it would be *your* house?"

Faye smiled self-deprecatingly. "I'm not really much of a decorator," she said.

"Of course not, honey. You're straight. But that doesn't mean you can't have a nicely decorated home that would reflect *your* personality."

Chuck growled, "There's nothing wrong with Faye's home. Jesus, Dave. Let it be. Let's just look at where she wants to put her grow room."

"We'll talk later, honey," Dave whispered, as Faye led the way into the hall.

"I just figured I would use the hall bathroom, like Marian did," she said.

"The idea," Chuck said, "is to make it look like there's no grow room here at all, *and* like nothing is missing. Let's see what's on the other side of the wall."

"That would be the master bathroom," Faye said, leading them through her bedroom.

Chuck glanced into the bathroom. "Do you ever actually take baths?" he asked, noting the bathtub in the room.

"No, I prefer showers. Besides, this bathtub is too short for a real, relaxing soak."

"You need a hot tub, honey, on the patio," Dave remarked. "Trust me."

Chuck nodded as if he'd made a decision. "If we take out the tubs from both bathrooms, and replaced them with showers, that would give us some room that wouldn't be missed. I think we could reclaim about 20 square feet."

Dave nodded. "That's about right."

"How would I get to it?" Faye asked.

"I can put a secret door in the wall of your shower," Dave explained, his blue eyes twinkling. "In fact, it would be one wall of your shower."

"Will it be expensive?"

"Not at all," Chuck assured her. "Especially after we sell the bathtubs."

"We could also raise money by selling some of your uncle's memorabilia," Dave added, and Chuck punched him in the shoulder. "Ow!" Dave protested.

"Just pay no mind to Dave," Chuck instructed Faye. "He's just a hopeless queen. You keep your home exactly as you want it."

Faye took hold of Dave's arm and squeezed. "I think you're a dear," she told him, "and you're right—I was never in the Merchant Marine, and this isn't my house. Yet. But I'll think about it and I'd love your help."

"We'll strip the hall bathroom first, since you aren't using it, and put in the shower. That way, you'll have a place to wash up while we work on this one."

Dave said, "I'll use the tiles from the hall bathroom for this one, so that the tiles in here will all be the same age. The hall bathroom, which will not have the secret door, will get new tiles unless I can locate enough used ones from a flea market."

"Which he might," agreed Chuck. "You wouldn't *believe* some of the crap he's found at those things."

"When can you start?" Faye asked.

Chuck and Dave exchanged glances, apparently working out a schedule by telepathy. "We could actually start this afternoon," Chuck stated. "We can't do anything tomorrow, but we're free the rest of the week."

"And that's all it should take," Dave added.

"Wow!" Faye exclaimed. "Well...all right, then! Let's do it!"

"This will be interesting to see," Marian inserted. "Maybe I *will* have you do some work at my house."

When the men left to change into work clothes, Marian and Faye sat in the living room in front of Michelle Worthington's carton.

"I'm excited about the grow room," Faye confessed, "but I *really* want to know what's in this box." She removed the cardboard lid. Faye looked down at manila folders filled with papers, some to near bursting; a musty smell rose from the box. She handed a folder to Marian and opened one, herself. "Well," she suggested, "let's see what we've got."

The women each opened a folder. Faye's was filled with receipts. She read the top one, for $4,000 to Carvel Meany.

"Who's Ellie Lilly?" Faye asked Marian.

The older woman corrected her pronunciation. "It's one of the biggest pharmaceutical makers in the world."

"Why would they donate money to Meany?" Faye asked.

"Simple," Marian said grimly. "They manufacture the number one antidepressant on the market...one of the biggest competitors, if you want to call it that, to marijuana."

"Competitor?"

"Well, sort of," Marian clarified. "Marijuana is free to anyone who grows it, and anyone can grow it. That antidepressant is expensive, and is manufactured *only* by license from that company, so they get the profits from every single pill."

"Oh," Faye said. "But $4,000 isn't really very much."

"Look at the other receipts," Marian instructed.

The next receipt was from the same company, but the amount was $40,000 and the recipient was Selma Graves! The receipt after that was also for $40,000 but had been given to Ken Worthington.

"I don't understand," Faye said. "Why did they donate money, but give it to Selma Graves? Or Michelle's husband? It doesn't make sense."

"Of course it does, darling," Marian explained. "The $4000 donation in Meany's name would be reported on Meany's disclosure documents. It would look suspicious if the company *didn't* donate money to his campaign; they support *everyone's* campaigns, in both parties. But the money given to Graves and Worthington doesn't get reported as a campaign contribution. Graves and Worthington only pay taxes on it, and Meany gets the remainder, tax free and secret."

"But why go to so much effort to hide a contribution?" Faye asked.

"Some states put a cap on how much money a single contributor can supply. This is a simple way around that. Besides, the story gets more interesting than that."

"Really? How so?" Faye asked.

"One of the biggest stockholders in Ely Lilly is the Pulliam family, who until recently owned *The Arizona Republic*, Phoenix's biggest newspaper. *The Republic* is known as one of the most conservative newspapers around; so, of course, they have been very supportive of Meany from the start."

"Oh."

"You know that former President Bush used to be head of the CIA, right?"

"No, but, okay."

"Well, when he left the CIA, he was appointed to Ely Lilly's board of directors. And later, when he ran for president, guess who he chose as his running mate?"

"Dan Quayle," Faye answered.

"Who just happens to be the Pulliam's grandson."

"No!" The web seemed to grow more and more complex. She glanced at the other receipts in her folder. It was money, and more money, all from the same contributor—and all made out to Selma and Ken.

"What've *you* got?" she asked her friend.

Marian held up a fistful of receipts. "These are from a major whiskey manufacturer," she said. "Of course, they don't want to see marijuana legalized. And the fact that Meany is a majority stockholder in this company, which his family founded, doesn't hurt."

Faye took the next folder from the box. "This looks like a cotton farming company," she said.

"Hemp, the actual marijuana plant, produces a fiber superior to cotton's. The cotton industry would collapse if it were legal to grow hemp."

"But couldn't the cotton farmers just switch?"

"Of course, but the *farmers* don't make much money either way. Hemp can be grown anywhere, which would collapse the value of the cotton farms, which would put the banks that own mortgages on that land out of business. And here," she added, "are receipts showing a major bank's contribution. Wow—another *big* one."

Faye took another folder and glanced at its contents. "How about this? Du Pont!"

"They manufacture pesticides," Marian replied. "Cotton requires more pesticides per acre, than *any other American crop.* Hemp, on the other hand, requires none—it has a natural pesticide built in."

"Which is why it's so easy to grow," Faye completed.

"Du Pont also manufactures many commercial chemicals from petroleum," Marian continued. "in addition to pesticides. But hemp oil is more versatile than petroleum, and is a renewable resource, besides."

"Why can't Du Pont just switch to hemp oil?" Faye asked.

"The major stockholders of Du Pont are oil companies," Marian explained.

"Corporations can own corporations?" Faye asked in surprise.

"Of course they can, darling," Marian replied. "In fact, most do. The image of the common man as stockholder, watering his garden while his dividends arrive in the mail, is a fantasy. Corporations buy other corporations that will support them in whatever they do. Oil companies own chemical companies to provide another market for their product."

Faye put the folders on the coffee table. "Ken Worthington was killed for this material," she said soberly. "How can we make this information public? It's too late for the campaign Meany just won, but maybe for the next..."

"We could turn it over to the authorities," Marian suggested.

Faye sighed. "Why do I think that wouldn't do any good...and might even get us killed?"

"Then let's just put the information on T-shirts and let the corporations *disprove* it—if they can?"

Faye and Marian spent the rest of the afternoon designing a new line of T-shirts, and Faye entered the information into the web site so the shirts would be available to anyone who visited. They were so engrossed, they barely noticed when Chuck and Dave returned, clad in overalls, and began to disassemble her hall bathroom.

"What do we do with the evidence?" Marian pondered at one point. "The beauty of the T-shirts is that the corporations would have to sue for libel, if they dared—and would have to *prove* their innocence, a turnabout from the usual procedure. We might need to have this stuff available, if it did come to court."

"We'll need to make many copies," Faye decided. "We'll hide the originals, but the copies would serve in most cases, I bet. And we'll send them to as many places as we can. Once the information becomes common knowledge, I don't think we'll be in any danger. People don't usually *burn* the barn after the horse has been stolen."

Marian had continued to scan the folders' contents, and suddenly gasped.

"What is it?" Faye asked in concern.

In reply, Marian handed her a receipt.

It had been made out to Frank Timmons.

Isabella

"I understand how Selma and Ken would have served as money-laundering go-betweens for Meany," Faye said to Robert that evening, as they wandered along the walkways of the lake park near 107th and Thunderbird. "But I don't understand why a donation was made out to Frank Timmons. He *hates* Meany, and only started working in his office to get revenge for his grandson's murder. In fact, the date on that receipt was *before* his grandson was killed. So, I don't get it."

Robert took her hand. His face reflected the yellowish glow of the walkway lights, bright enough to discourage muggers but dim enough to be romantic. The air was balmy, with a gentle, flowered breeze just strong enough to make the leaves whisper and her hair dance.

"Frank is a puzzle," Robert agreed. "I can't ethically speak of his case in detail, of course. But I can tell you, his body shows signs of some kind of trauma. He may have been in a car accident of some sort."

"Recently?"

"Within the last few years."

Faye sighed and changed the subject. "It is so *beautiful* here," she said. "So much nicer than San Diego. And so much nicer than Ohio ever was!"

Robert nodded. "It was designed to be," he remarked. "Nothing out of place. Everything perfect."

Faye looked at him. "You sound like you don't approve," she said, surprised.

He looked at her. "There's nothing wrong with designed beauty," he said. "But it can never be more than it was designed to be.

There's no room for happy accidents." He surveyed the lantana bushes blooming around them. "When nature is allowed to run wild..." He tightened his hold on her hand. "Will you go for a ride with me?" he asked.

"Anywhere," she replied, her eyes wide and moist in the soft light.

He took her to his car, which was parked in the lot next to the Lakeview Rec Center. "Where are we going?" she asked.

He smiled mysteriously. "You'll see."

They drove to 99th Avenue and headed north. Robert pushed a cassette into the player and soon the sounds of soft jazz filled the car. Faye rested her head on his powerful shoulder, content just to be with him.

Around them, the night grew darker as they left Sun City far behind. Houses were fewer and farther between. Soon, there were none. The car climbed a hill, and then another. Just as Faye was about to ask, again, where they were going, Robert pulled over to the side of the road. "We're here," he said, simply.

"Where?" Faye could see nothing outside. Instead of answering, Robert got out, walked to her side of the car, opened her door, and helped her out. When he closed the car door behind her, the dome light faded out.

The moon was low in the sky, looking large, casting thick shadows from the Joshua trees that grew near the side of the road. "Where are we going?" she asked.

"There's a long and winding path. I know it by heart; hold my hand."

Calling it a "path" was grandiloquence; if his grip hadn't been so strong and steady she would have fallen several times. They walked up a rise, into a gully, and up another rise. At the top, Faye gasped.

"Oh, my," she said.

Below them was a large lake. The swollen moon balanced on spires on the lake's opposite side and reflected in the dancing waters.

"Lake Pleasant," Robert explained. "Not really natural by itself; it's the result of a dam. But they couldn't tame the land around it."

There were a dozen types of cacti growing around them, and a few scrubby bushes. Faye wasn't a big fan of cactus but she had to admit that, here in the moonlight with Robert, it was lovely.

Robert let go of her hand and crouched. "Hello, Isabella," he said.

"Who are you talking to?" Faye asked.

"Faye," Robert said grandly, looking up at her, "meet Isabella." He seemed to be talking about a plant; Faye was puzzled until she recognized what *kind* of plant it was.

"Oh," she said. "Hello...Isabella."

"Fifteen years ago, I used to kayak on this lake every Wednesday. Most doctors like to play golf; I'd rather paddle. I found Isabella quite by accident. I've taken buds from her but nothing else, left her just as I found her."

"How did she get here?" Faye asked.

Robert shrugged. "I don't know," he replied. "Maybe from some seeds dropped by a couple of stoners. But she could have grown here without human interference. Marijuana grows naturally on all continents except Antarctica, you know. *Earth* wants it here, even if certain politicians wish it would go away."

The breeze stirred her skirt. "This is beautiful," she agreed. "Thank you for bringing me here."

"I've never shown Isabella to another soul," he told her.

"Really," Faye said. "Not even your wife?"

"I could never get Eleanor interested in the outdoors," he said. "How I would have loved to go kayaking with her! But she was frail, even before the leukemia hit."

"When it gets warmer, perhaps you can show *me* how to kayak?" Faye prompted, hesitantly. "I've never done it, but I certainly can swim and I love the water..." She was silenced by his bear hug. As he squeezed her, a warm droplet fell on her neck, cooling quickly. She said nothing, knowing he had just shed a tear.

Then he kissed her, and it was like the first time, thrilling and dazzling and marvelous. And then, amazingly, they made love, standing up, in the open for anyone to see...except, thankfully, there was no one to see.

As always, she was amazed by his size and the fact that he could penetrate so deeply, while they stood, without causing her any discomfort. Eagerly, she assisted, standing on tiptoes and then lowering herself until she had taken all of him. She began to feel the blood rush in her ears; the moonlight and the night and the lake and the plants—even Isabella—contracting into her mind, bunching into a point of consciousness, imploding in a way that left her breathless, speechless, fearless, eternal. Robert's eruption coincided with hers, and they clutched each other with shuddering intensity.

They stood for a long time, prolonging their intimate embrace. Gradually, the night sounds returned as Faye's breathing returned to its normal pace. She realized she was perspiring, and began to shiver from the chill. "I'll get you a blanket," he said, and walked away, leaving her alone in the night. She thought she should be frightened, but she was not. She didn't know much about the outdoors—there were undoubtedly dangers here she knew nothing of, poisonous snakes and scorpions and who knew what. But she trusted him, and, sure enough, he returned shortly with a large sleeping bag. He unzipped it and used it as a blanket, throwing it on the ground and helping her to sit. He then lowered himself next to her, wrapping the blanket around them both.

When she was warmer, which was almost instantly, Robert pulled a joint from his shirt pocket and lit it, allowing her the first hit. She inhaled deeply. In a minute or so, the intensity of the moon doubled, and to her amazement, Faye found that all the plants around them seem to take on a glow.

"You see it?" he asked, seeing her look around.

"That glow?" she answered hesitantly. "Do you see it, too? What is it?"

"It's called an *aura*. All living things have auras. Some people say *everything* has an aura, but I've only seen it around living things."

"Why couldn't I see it before?" Faye demanded.

"You could, if you'd looked. Most people don't train themselves to really see. The pot helps you focus, so you can see. Now that you know the glow is there, you'll be able to find it any time you look."

There were a few moments of silence, then Robert spoke again, his voice pained. "Now...if only I knew I'd be able to find *you* any time I looked."

She knew what he meant, but struggled to keep her tone light. "You have my address, Dr. Thompson."

"That's not what I meant, my dear." Faye knew that. Why, oh why, did women feel they had to play these games with men?

She sighed. It was so difficult to let go, to say what was in her heart. To say it would be a commitment; it would mean it was true and would have to *stay* true. And, who knew how she would feel in the morning? And yet, and yet, she knew she would feel just the same in the harsh light of day as she did right now, in the soft, wavering light of the moon.

"I have fallen in love with you, Robert," she said softly.

Robert fell back from his sitting position; his hold on the blanket brought it with him, and pulled her down, too. "Thank God," he breathed. "The first time I saw you, I knew I had to get you into my life."

"With me just out of bed, and fat, and unable to move?"

"Especially then. See?" he added, laughing at her shocked expression. "You don't have to worry that I'll fall out of love with you when you start to deteriorate!"

"I'm *in* your life, Robert," Faye replied softly. "You just try and get rid of me!"

"I want more than that, Faye," the doctor whispered into her ear, holding her tightly. "I want you to...to be my wife."

The ground beneath her seemed to quake. "*Wife?*"

"You don't have to answer now," Robert said quickly. "Think it over. Talk to Marian; I did." He swallowed. "She thought it was a great idea."

"You asked *Marian* before asking me?" Faye asked, trying to decide if she should be offended. She hit him in mock ferocity, but the blows quickly became caresses and then they were making love again, the sharp-edged Earth cooperating by keeping their area clear of stones, cactus, or other protrusions.

As with Isabella, the Earth wanted them to be there.

A Brand New Me

Monday, December 8, 1997

Sunday flew past; time with Robert always seemed to go so quickly. She got to bed late, so the ringing of the phone Monday morning jolted Faye like an electric shock.

"G'mornin', deares'," she mumbled, still partially asleep, and still dreaming she was with Robert.

"Ms. Faye McRae?" a no-nonsense, woman's voice questioned. Her tone pierced through the veil of sleepiness and Faye came fully alert. She looked at the clock; it was exactly 9 AM.

"Yes," Faye asserted, wondering how she had answered the phone.

"This is Audrey Flowers from Channel 2 News," the voice said.

At last! Faye thought. *She's going to use the evidence on Meany on the news.*

"I was given your name as the owner of the web site that sells the hot new T-shirts I've been seeing throughout the Valley," Flowers continued. "I wondered if you'd consent to be interviewed on that."

"Interviewed? About the web site?" Faye was confused. Did this have nothing to do with Meany, at all?

"Yes," Flowers replied. "The shirts are quite popular, so your web site must be doing well. I think it's exciting that a woman, not only a woman, but a *senior* woman at that, could be making a success out of a male-dominated field like the Internet. I think it's news.

"And," she added, "the exposure won't hurt your sales any. After all, it's basically free advertising."

"Well, yes, I suppose so," Faye agreed. She wondered if she should check with Marian first, but then remembered how emphatic her friend had been about the web site being *Faye's*. And Faye couldn't see any harm. "When would you like to interview me?"

"I think this is hot, and I want to get it on the air as soon as possible. Would you be free to do the interview this afternoon? Say, about one?"

"Oh," Faye said. "I'm not sure I can get into the city today. I have some people coming by to do some construction work…"

"We'll come to you. Is your address—" and she recited Faye's correct address.

"Yes, it is," Faye admitted. "Are you sure you want to come here?"

"Oh yes," the voice on the phone assured her. "We'll want to take video of your computer setup and so on, so people can see you are a professional."

With the arrangements made, Faye hung up the phone and had just started to get out of bed when the doorbell rang. She threw on a robe and found Chuck and Dave at her door, again wearing overalls. Chuck's were well worn; Dave's looked brand-new and included a new-looking western-style handkerchief artfully stuffed into one pocket.

"You're going to start on the front bathroom?" she asked, hopefully.

"Yep," Chuck assured her.

"Okay, then, I'm going to take a shower in mine. Make yourselves at home." She then left them, returned to her bathroom, reached into the tub and turned on the hot water, and pulled the handle that switched on the shower. She slipped out of her nightgown and, gratefully, placed her body under the cascade of water. The warmth flowed down her back and sides, between her thighs and down her legs. It felt wonderful.

She lathered up her hair with shampoo, rinsed and repeated just as it advised on the label. She rubbed her bar of deodorant soap into her washcloth, then lathered her body and scrubbed. A final rinse, and she stepped out of the tub—

Only to scream as she found Dave there, measuring the wall with a measuring tape. Dave yelped in surprise. "I didn't expect you to come out so soon," he explained, turning away quickly. "I just needed this measurement…"

Faye quickly yanked her towel from its rack and pulled it around her. "I, uh…"

"You don't have to be embarrassed," Dave said. "Remember, I'm gay. I have no interest in the female form."

"Uh…"

Dave frowned. "Is *that* what you're using on your hair?" He pointed at the bottle of shampoo resting on the edge of the tub. "No *wonder* it always looks so dry."

Faye found her voice. "My hair looks dry?"

"Well, *yes*." Dave clucked his tongue. "Honey, when you spend as much time in the pool as you do, your hair is *going* to dry up if you don't spend special care on it." He looked at her. "Don't get dressed," he ordered. "I'll be right back, and then we'll get your hair looking its best. Ten minutes!" he added, backing out of the little room.

What an odd little man, Faye thought. She dried herself and put on her white terrycloth robe, a gift to herself four years earlier. She only wore it on special occasions, when she wanted to treat herself luxuriously for some reason. Now, however, she was wearing it for company.

Chuck came to her bedroom doorway and knocked, even though the door was open. "Where's Dave?" he asked.

Faye replied, "He said he'd be right back with something for my hair." She said this with a bemused expression, puzzled over just what had happened.

Chuck punched one fist into the palm of his other hand. "Dammit!" he swore. "That man hasn't stopped talking about your hair since Saturday. There's nothing wrong with your hair, no matter *what* he says!" Chuck assured her.

"That's okay," Faye told him. "As it turns out, I have a television interview today" —spoken in a tone of casualness, as if she had television interviews on a weekly basis— "and it won't hurt to look my best."

Dave returned, laden with a box of plastic bottles of various colors and shapes. "We have to repair the damage already done to your hair," he said, reacting to her look of alarm. "None of it will hurt."

There was a thunderous crash from the hallway.

"My God, what was that?" Faye shouted, running out to investigate, but Dave grabbed her by the hand.

"It's just Chuck smashing through the bathroom wall," he explained. "You shouldn't look. It will just upset you." Another smash came from the master bathroom. "Ah," Dave nodded. "He's broken through."

"But, I thought you were going to do the front bathroom first!" Faye exclaimed.

"Well, we have to remove the wall to take out the tub," Dave explained.

"But, what about *my* bathroom?"

"You'll still be able to use it," Dave assured her, as a cloud of plaster dust billowed through the open bathroom door. "Um, maybe we should work out on your patio. Do you happen to have a large, portable, hairdresser's sink?"

"Are you kidding?" Faye replied, staring at the cloud of dust, thinking about the things in her bathroom she'd have covered up or removed if she'd known the work was to have extended into that bathroom today.

"Okay, then, we'll use the kitchen."

"You have to be careful," Faye cautioned. "I'm going to be on television tonight." And she explained about the interview.

"I promise," Dave said, crossing his fingers. "Scout's honor."

In the kitchen, Dave tried to position a bar stool by the sink in such a way that Faye's head would drop easily into it; but the sizes weren't quite right. He ended up by clearing the counter adjacent to the sink and bidding Faye to lie down on it, with her head under the water tap. She stared upwards into the filter. "You'd better close your eyes," Dave warned, and she did. The water poured onto her face and into her hair. She felt him put his fingertips onto her scalp and massage some sort of lotion into it. She had to admit, it *did* feel wonderful. She tried to relax and go with the experience. She was really sorry, however, that it hadn't occurred to her to smoke a joint first. That would have made it easier, she was sure, to focus on the massage and to ignore the crashing and banging of whatever Chuck was doing in her bathrooms.

She heard the snip of scissors. "I just got my hair cut," she remarked, feeling as if she were losing control.

"I just trimmed a teeny bit," Dave replied. She heard the scissors again. "And a teeny bit more. Don't worry, I've got the strainer in the sink so we won't stop it up."

Dave put stuff in her hair, rinsed, put something else in, rinsed. One of the substances smelled strongly of ammonia. "You aren't coloring my hair?" she demanded.

"No, of course not," he assured her after a pause. "I'm just adding a little *glow.*"

Eventually he was finished and assisted her to a sitting position and then off the counter. He carefully towel-dried her hair, then blow-dried it, working a stylist's brush with one hand and the drier with the other.

"I thought you were a cabinet-maker," Faye remarked.

"I was," Dave admitted. "But, before that, I attended beautician's college."

"You never worked as a hair stylist?"

"No," Dave admitted. "But once it gets into your blood... Anyway, when Chuck and I lived in New York, I used to do the hairstyles for *quite* a few drag queens."

Somehow, Faye did not find this reassuring. But then, Dave produced a large hand-mirror and held it before Faye's face.

A stranger looked back at her. No, not a stranger; it was a long-lost acquaintance, someone she had known years before but hadn't seen in a long time. He hair was no longer streaked with gray; instead, it was vibrant, her own natural brown color but highlighted, as if she'd spent time in the sun.

And the style, itself, was dignified yet youthful—and Dave had accomplished it with a few snips of the scissors and a few bottles of hair stuff.

"Now," Dave said, looking at her appraisingly, "let's see what you intend to wear on this interview."

Faye's heart sank. Most of the clothes in her closet no longer fit her, and she had had neither the time to dispose of the old things nor to buy more than the most rudimentary new wardrobe. She explained this to Dave.

Dave excused himself and trotted into the hallway, stuck his head into the bathroom. "Babe, I'm going to take Faye shopping," he called. "We'll be back in a few."

She heard the blow of a sledgehammer and a curse. "You'd *better* be," Dave's partner growled. "I am *not* carrying this bathtub outta here by myself!"

When they returned, Faye was wearing a powder blue suit, with white blouse, a red-and-navy scarf, and tasteful gold hoop ear-rings. She also wore matching blue pumps, and carried more clothes and shoes in seven shopping bags.

It was quarter to one.

Dave, back in his partner's good graces, was struggling with the unwieldy bathtub as the Channel 2 News van pulled in front of the house. Faye met Audrey Flowers at the door. Flowers looked at her curiously. "We've met before, haven't we?" she asked, unsure.

Faye looked back at the newswoman indignantly. "Yes," she prodded, "I came to you with evidence that Representative Meany owned a marijuana farm in Mexico."

"Really? Well." Flowers smiled. "Well, today is about *your* web site. And, may I say, you *do* look wonderful for TV." Flowers her-self wore a pale yellow suit with pink blouse that Faye thought clashed with her auburn hair. Her assessment was validated by Dave, when he almost dropped his end of the tub at first look at the newswoman. Faye could tell he was not impressed with the woman's outfit, as he mock gagged himself. It was all Faye could do to stifle a giggle.

Faye apologized for the moving of the bathtub as Flowers' cameraman set up his equipment. "We'll come back later to vac-uum up the plaster," Chuck assured Faye. "You won't want the noise while the camera's running." And then they were gone.

The camera was aimed at the office chair Faye used at the computer. Flowers instructed her to sit in it, but facing the sofa alongside rather than the computer itself. "You should have the program you use to create your web site running on the monitor," the woman instructed; and Faye booted up the computer and started *FrontPage*. Then, getting into the spirit of things, she loaded one of the pages for editing, one of the shirts she and Marian had designed a couple of days before.

Faye's Fifteen Minutes

"What does it take to make it big in today's booming 'dot-com' market? Does it take brawn? Money? Major corporate funding? Apparently not, as we discovered when we spoke with Faye

McRae, a resident of Sun City, at her home office and hub of the newest entry into the 'dot-com' world." Flowers turned towards Faye, and the cameraman rotated himself so that the camera could take in Faye at her desk. "Ms. McRae," Flowers continued, "what gave you the idea to create a web site for your T-shirts?"

"Well," said Faye, struggling to maintain a normal tone of voice, "first of all, they're not *my* T-shirts. My friend, Marian Higgins, designs them. And our friend Marvin Cohen actually designed the site. I just maintain it."

"I spoke with Ms. Higgins this morning," Flowers said, in a conversational tone. "She told me that you were in charge of the web site."

"How did you find Marian?" Faye asked curiously.

"I asked people I saw wearing her T-shirt designs. Now," Flowers continued, switching back into broadcast mode, "How much training did it take before you were competent enough to maintain the site?"

"No formal training," Faye replied. "I just read some books Marvin loaned me," she added, pointing to the stack of books on the coffee table.

"You must be aware that most senior citizens shy away from computers," Flowers remarked. "What do you think makes you different?"

Faye considered this. "My friend, Marian, isn't afraid of anything," she said. "I think I learned from her that new things bring more joy than pain. And, besides," she added, "most of the folks *I've* met in Sun City *aren't* afraid of computers. The idea that older people are afraid of computers is probably just stereotyping."

Flowers referred to a three-by-five inch card she held in her hand. "'Don't Step On My Buzz.' What does that mean, exactly?"

Faye smiled a secret smile. "Whatever you want it to, I suppose."

"But it must have some meaning," Flowers insisted.

"A good T-shirt design will have a catch-phrase that means something special to the wearer. It isn't required that everyone who reads the shirt get the same meaning out of it."

"Here's another one," Flowers continued. "'Question Authority.' Isn't that an old sixties' catch phrase?"

"Just because people used it in the sixties doesn't mean it's wrong now," Faye responded. "It's more important today, don't you think?"

"Some people," Flowers suggested carefully, "might interpret such a message as promoting anarchy, rebellion against authority. Some might expect that senior citizens would have outgrown such ideas."

"If by 'anarchy' you mean thinking for oneself, I hope that's *exactly* what it means!" Faye cried. "And if by 'rebelling against authority' you mean refusing to allow our elected officials to forget who it is they're supposed to be working for, I hope we *never* outgrow it!"

"Now, this web site you have," Flowers asked, "what exactly is it for?"

"Well, the URL—that means Universal Resource Locator, but most people just think of it as the web site address—is http://www.saysomethingshirts.com. It contains pictures of the various T-shirt designs we have to offer. People can buy the shirts directly through the web site; they can also print the patterns out for themselves and transfer them onto T-shirts, handbags, raincoats—anything they want."

"I understand you don't charge people for printing the patterns. How can you make a profit?"

Faye smiled. "Anyone can make a profit on the Internet," she said. "We are more interested in getting people to *think*, to become aware of what our government has become and how it is affecting our lives in ways we would never tolerate if we knew it was happening."

Flowers smiled and put down her card. "I think we have all we need, Ms. McRae," she said. "Thank you so much for your cooperation." She rose, and the cameraman lowered the camera and began retrieving wires and cables.

"When will this be on the air?" Faye asked, trying to sound blasé, as if she were interviewed for the television at least once a week and merely wanted to note the broadcast schedule for her records.

"As long as I can complete the editing in time," Flowers said, smiling, "and I expect I *will*—it should be on the news tonight."

Film At Ten

Faye set up the TV and VCR and brought popcorn in to Robert and Marian. "I know it's a little early for a snack, but I thought this would make it more fun." She sat next to Robert on the sofa and held his hand nervously. This was her first public appearance ever, and she was as nervous as a cat in a roomful of rocking chairs.

The local news began with its usual, frantic fanfare and photos of Audrey Flowers and Newt Florsheim, the other anchorperson. The headlines were the usual, tedious politics, local and national. Faye knew she wouldn't have made it up front with the headlines, still the tension built. Commercials came and went. The sports and weather were rehashed. Finally, just before the program was over entirely, Florsheim conversationally said to Flowers, "So, I understand there's a rebellion fomenting in Sun City."

"That's right, Newt," Flowers said, with a patronizing smile. "It seems the sixties aren't over for a group of senior citizens who've brought in modern technology to revive the protests of their youths." Her voice was heard over video shots of several Sun City residents wearing Marian's T-shirts: There was Vera Daye displaying "Question Authority"; a man Faye didn't know wore "What War?" There was another shot of two women wearing T-shirts: "Don't Step On My Buzz" and "Legalize Marijuana NOW." The scene cut to Flowers, standing in front of the rec center, microphone in hand.

"The sixties never ended for some of the residents of Sun City," she intoned. "But now they've been resurrected with a new twist: The Internet." There was another cut to the interior of Faye's living room. "Now, this web site you have," Flowers asked, "what exactly is it for?"

"Well, the web site address is http://www.saysomething-shirts. com," said the televised Faye, sounding tinny and completely unlike herself. "It contains pictures of the various T-shirt designs we have to offer. People can buy the shirts directly through the web site; they can also print the patterns out for themselves and transfer them onto T-shirts, handbags, raincoats—anything they want."

"What gave you the idea to create a web site for your T-shirts?" Flowers asked.

That's odd, Faye thought. She was sure that was not the order in which the questions had been asked.

"Well, first of all, they're not *my* T-shirts."

"But you're selling them on the Internet. If they're not *your* T-shirts, whose are they?"

In the living room, Faye stared slack-jawed at the screen. She didn't remember Flowers having said that, at least, not that way.

"My friend, Marian Higgins, designs them," the televised Faye replied. "And our friend Marvin Cohen, actually designed the site. I just maintain it."

Now the scene cut to Flowers, who was standing outside of Marvin's house. "Marvin Cohen," said the newscaster, "is the reclusive author of the notorious global conspiracy book, *Trust Me.* He lives here in Sun City, but refused to speak with us. Janine Hurley is his neighbor." The camera panned to include a woman in her seventies.

"I haven't seen Mr. Cohen since he moved in six years ago," the woman reported. "As far as I know he never leaves his house. He has groceries delivered to his door," she added with what seemed like envy. The scene cut back to Faye's living room, where Flowers referred to an index card. "'Don't Step On My Buzz.' What does that mean, exactly?"

The camera cut to a close-up of Faye. "Just because people used it in the sixties doesn't mean it's wrong now," Faye responded. "It's more important today, don't you think?"

In the living room, Faye jumped to her feet. "That's not what I said!" she cried. "I mean, I *did*—but not to that question!"

On screen, Flowers said cautiously, "Some people might interpret such a message as promoting anarchy, rebellion against authority. Some might expect that senior citizens would have outgrown such ideas."

Faye's televised face took on an almost maniacal fervor. "If by 'anarchy' you mean thinking for oneself, I hope it does!" she cried.

"And if by 'rebelling against authority' you mean refusing to allow our elected officials to forget who it is they're supposed to be working for, I hope we *never* outgrow it!"

The scene cut again to Flowers standing in front of the rec center. "Is it true, the spirit of the sixties lives on in our senior citizens? Or can it be that the spirit of the self-serving nineties is manifesting itself, instead? We have Faye McRae's final word on the subject:"

Again, the camera cut to a close-up of Faye, smiling sweetly. "Anyone can make a profit on the Internet," she said.

The program returned to the studio, where a grinning Florsheim said to the smug Flowers, "It seems that scam artists never die...they just move to Sun City!"

"So it would seem, Newt. Now, here are some highlights of stories we are investigating *right now* to bring you tomorrow night!" She vanished, as Faye, stunned, clicked the television set off.

The three sat in silence. Finally, Robert said tentatively, "You looked really beautiful on the TV, Faye."

She turned to him. "I didn't say any of that. I didn't say *any* of that! She took my words and put them in a completely different context!"

Marian looked at her thoughtfully. "I don't suppose it occurred to you to tape record the interview yourself? So you could have an accurate record?"

Faye shook her head numbly.

The phone rang, making them all jump. "Oh, God," Faye moaned. "Now the calls start." She picked up the receiver, ready to explain to whoever was calling that it had all been a mistake, when she recognized Marvin's voice.

"Good job, babe!" he chortled in his Brooklyn accent. "The web site is getting almost a hundred hits a minute!"

"What?"

"The server can hardly keep up wit' the demand! I'm gonna hafta move the site to a faster machine!"

Faye still didn't understand. "You mean people are actually visiting the site?"

"By the truckload!" Marvin boomed over the phone. "I saw your interview. Brilliant! You can't buy that kinda publicity!"

"But, it wasn't true!" Faye protested. "The newswoman, she twisted it all around!"

"It doesn't matter *what* people think you said," Marvin assured her. "They got the web site address. And, the page on the monitor behind you! Brilliant, jus' brilliant!"

Marvin hung up. Slowly, Faye hung up the receiver and walked to the TV. She turned it back on and rewound the tape in the VCR until she spotted one of the shots of her sitting at her desk. She hit the "Pause" button.

Marian's eye grew wide.

Robert laughed.

On the screen, behind the image of Faye, was her computer monitor. On it was displayed the page Faye had been working on the day before. The letters were very small, but readable. In fact, she wondered why she hadn't seen them during the original broadcast, and then realized she'd been too upset to pay attention to detail.

The monitor showed a close-up of a T-shirt slogan. The words read,

Carvel Meany: The Best Politician Money Can Buy
Major Chemical Firm: $25,000
Major Pharmaceutical: $8,000
Meany Beverages: $50,000

The remaining list of contributors had scrolled off the monitor screen, but it didn't matter. The point was made: Companies that stood to lose if marijuana were legalized had been major contributors to Meany's campaign.

Marian was shaking her head in pleased wonder. "She didn't read the monitor," she said. "Audrey Flowers didn't know what she'd put on the air. Now, the cat's out of the bag." And she clapped her hands in girlish glee.

Robert smiled at Faye and said, "You really did look beautiful."

View From A Height

Thursday, December 11, 1997

Robert and Faye pulled into the well-kept parking area, still wet from the morning's rain, and parked. "You're sure you don't mind doing this?" the doctor asked.

"No, I don't mind," Faye replied. "I have a question or two to ask him, myself." As she stepped out of the car, she looked into the clear, blue sky and inhaled deeply. "The air smells so *good* today!" she cried.

"Winter rains," Robert remarked. "They clean the air. Thank God for 'em."

Together they walked into the lobby of the seven-story building, the tallest in the Sun City area. The receptionist stood behind a counter, speaking with another visitor. Faye and Robert politely waited their turn, then informed the portly, beehive-haired woman that they were there to see Frank Timmons. She referred to her computer screen, then said, "Of course, dears. He's expecting you. Take the elevator to the top floor," and gave them the apartment number.

The elevator was posh, with highly-polished wood-grain and metallic surfaces. "This seems like a pretty pricey place," Faye marveled. "After the fuss Frank made over not being able to afford the Marinol, I half-expected him to live in a cardboard box."

"Maybe he has no money left after he pays his rent," Robert suggested. "People have different sets of priorities. Maybe a luxury apartment is the one thing he can't bear to part with."

"Or expensive politicians," Faye added grimly.

On the seventh floor, they quickly found the target apartment number and Robert knocked at the door. It was opened almost immediately by Frank Timmons. "Don't stand outside," he said, crossly. "Come in. I need to sit." And he turned without another word, leaving the pair to enter. Faye was taken aback. Seven stories wasn't really that high, and Faye hadn't expected such a dazzling view. The room had an eastern exposure, and Faye could see the purple expanse of the Superstition Mountains, far beyond the rippling buildings of

Phoenix itself. The brown swath of the usually dry Skunk River showed a trickle of sparkling blue as the rainwater drained from the streets of the Valley. Nowhere was there a trace of the yellow-brown smog that usually hung in the air, partly obscuring the mountains that ringed the Valley.

Timmons' lanky frame folded uncomfortably into an over-stuffed chair. Seeing that Faye was entranced by the view, he said, sourly, "Enjoy it while you can. Just ten years ago, when I first moved here, you could see the Superstitions pretty much every day. Now, it's only after a rain that the air is clear enough to see that far."

"I wonder where the pollution came from?" Faye questioned idly, enjoying the sensation of focusing across the expanse.

"No mystery about that," Timmons grumbled. "It's from all the diesel fumes spewed out by the goddamned trucks rolling across the Valley!"

"Diesel?" Faye exclaimed. "I thought that was cleaner than gasoline, once they got the trucks to tune up their engines."

"Not at all," Robert explained. "Sure, a clean engine emits fewer by-products than a dirty one. But diesel is like any other fossil fuel: It spews poisons into the atmosphere and, in a valley like ours, the poisons don't have anywhere to go. So they hang in the air, making that yellow-brown cloud, until a rainstorm washes them into the ground."

"But what about all the farming in the Valley? If the poisons go into the ground…"

"God only knows what they do to the vegetables we grow here. Eventually, they probably make their way into our bodies." Timmons paused, trying and failing to take a deep breath. "The worse part," he coughed, "is that diesel engines were designed to run on hemp oil, not fuel oil. And hemp oil burns into plain old carbon dioxide and water. There'd be no pollution from all those trucks, except from the fat drivers farting."

"Four years ago," Robert remarked, "a man named Louie Wichinsky drove a standard diesel truck from upstate New York to Las Vegas on used Burger King French fry oil instead of diesel fuel.

It worked just fine. But the people who run the government make a fortune on the oil products they control and sell, so trucks still run on diesel instead of plant oils.

But, Frank," the doctor added curiously, "how do *you* know about hemp oil? Most people don't."

"I *grew* hemp for the WWII war effort," Timmons replied with pride. "My old man grew it when I was a kid, but they made it illegal in the thirties. Then, when they needed oils and rope for the war effort, suddenly it became legal again." He pursed his lips as if he were going to spit, but didn't. "The government," he said in disgust. "Legal when they want it, illegal when they don't. Never mind what's good for the people. Or the air," he added.

"You must have made a lot of money growing it," Faye suggested, gesturing around her. "Enough to donate to some of those politicians, perhaps?" Robert looked at her, surprised.

"Me?" Frank laughed. "Naw, I'm poor as a broken-legged church mouse. This condo is owned by my son. He just lets me live here to house sit."

"He must be doing well, then," Faye pressed.

Timmons shrugged, his bony shoulders poking against his pressed plaid cotton shirt. "A fucking lawyer," he said. "Lets me live in his investment condo, but do you think he ever visits? No," he snorted. "The only good he ever did was to father my grandson... and now, *he's* dead."

The old man hobbled to the window, looking out at the view that had captivated Faye. "What's the use?" he said, almost to himself. "A man looks back on a whole life that was spent in service to others. The government, the produce distributors, the children. And now, look at me, without a pot to piss in or a child to care for me in my old age."

In one respect, Faye thought, the man looked preposterous, complaining about his poverty in the midst of such well-appointed surroundings. And yet, she felt a lump in her throat. She knew how he felt. She had spent *her* life in service to her husband, also without reward. The life she was now creating for herself was infinitely more satisfying yet she was a quarter-century younger than Frank and he was dying of cancer. Any chance to improve his life seemed to have passed.

"You said on the phone you wanted to tell us something," Robert prodded gently. The old man turned around.

"I've been having…dreams," he said.

"Dreams," Robert echoed. "What kind of dreams?"

"About Mikey's death," he said. "In them, I watch him killed."

"Oh," Faye cooed in sympathy.

"There's more," he said, his voice trembling. "The dreams are getting clearer. I can almost make out the figure who actually jabbed the needle into his arm."

"But you don't know *who* did it," Faye said. "You weren't there."

Timmons bit his lower lip and cast his eyes toward the floor. "I wonder," he whispered.

Faye was confused. "Are you saying you were there?"

"I don't know," Timmons said. "I mean, of *course* I wasn't. I was at home when it happened. It was a complete shock when my son came to tell me. But the dreams—they're so damned *real!*"

Robert sat down at one end of the sofa that faced the windows. He pressed his fingertips together reflectively. "In the dreams…are you assisting in the murder in any way?"

"No!" Timmons cried in horror. "I'm just watching. I'm tied to a chair, and gagged, and I'm being forced to watch. First, they cut his belly open while he screams in terror. Then, someone jabs the needle into him and he stops screaming, and then he stops breathing. And I have to watch the whole thing."

"Well, you *know* it isn't a real memory," Faye assured him. "The police report said he died of a drug overdose. It didn't say anything about an abdominal wound."

"You may be feeling guilt over his death," Robert suggested. "It's called survivor guilt. If you like, we can try hypnosis to find out what your buried feelings are. I can recommend a psychologist, or I can do it myself, if you prefer. If the issues are too deep-seated, you might need that psychologist, after all."

"Hypnosis, eh?" Frank muttered, shaking his head. He continued to gaze out the window.

"What do you think, Frank?" Faye asked. "Robert hypnotized me to quit smoking, and it worked, as you know. He's really very good."

Timmons muttered something that Faye couldn't make out, and she asked him to repeat. He spoke again, with more volume.

"When I was a young man, we heard about hypnosis. It was supposed to be bad for you, like playing with fire. And vitamin pills weren't supposed to be needed, and cigarettes were good for you, and the government was supposed to be here to *help*." He turned around, his face a mask of confusion and disillusionment.

"You're supposed to get *smarter* when you get old. Everything you've learned is supposed to add up, so you know more and more. But I don't."

He returned to the easy chair and lowered himself heavily into it. "In fact I feel like I know less and less. Don't know why I bothered trying to learn *anything*, when it's all wrong, anyway."

Faye smiled sympathetically at the old man. "Maybe discovering that what you thought was right is wrong, is getting smarter."

Timmons shrugged and nodded at the doctor. "Go ahead," he said. "Do it. Open up my head and see if you find anything there at all. My bet is it'll be empty as a politician's promise."

Frank agreed to come to Robert's office the next morning, and, at Frank's request, Faye promised to be present. A chill walked down her spine. For some reason, she feared what the session would reveal.

Blasts From The Past

As Robert drove her home, he asked, "What was that about donating money to politicians? Frank doesn't have any money."

Faye told Robert about the receipt she had found in the carton Michelle Worthington had given her. "$1,000!" she exclaimed. "Where would he get money like that?"

"But he didn't seem to know what you were talking about," Robert remarked.

"I know," Faye admitted. "Another mystery."

At home, she found there were two messages on her answering machine. She tapped the "Play" button and listened as she booted up her computer.

The first message was from Marvin. "Faye, you won't *believe* the hits you're gettin' on your web site! We're gonna hafta talk about allowin' *some* ads or somethin'. It'd be a fuckin' *shame* not to make somethin' from all this exposure! Anyway, call me. I wanna have youse over for dinner, to celebrate."

The second message caused her to stop what she was doing and press the "Repeat" button so she could hear it again. "Ms. McRae?" a female stranger's voice asked. "This is Donna Monroe from Global Virtual Properties. I'd like to congratulate you on your very successful web site. Please give me a call as soon as it is convenient to discuss the possible sale of your site to my company. I think you'll be very pleased at the amount we are prepared to offer."

Surprised, Faye found herself dialing before she'd had a chance to wonder how the caller had gotten her phone number. The message had included an office extension, which Faye also dialed. Someone with the caller's voice picked up immediately.

"Hello," Faye said. "I'm Faye McRae, and you—"

"Yes, Ms. McRae!" the woman exclaimed, exhaling as if she'd been holding her breath since V-J Day. "Yes, congratulations on your web site!"

"Thank you," Faye responded politely. "How did you find out about it?"

"I understand you managed to get some TV coverage," the woman replied, though her words didn't actually answer the question Faye had asked. "For a web designer, that's a dream come true! You have a future in web site promotion, that's for sure."

"Well, I don't expect to do any other web sites," Faye remarked.

"Nonsense!" the woman exclaimed. "Putting together a site, promoting it, and then selling it for many times your investment is how money is *made* on the Internet."

"Well, I haven't really invested anything," said Faye.

"All the better! All the proceeds from the sale will be profit, then."

"What sale?" Faye asked. She felt as if the woman were one step ahead of her in a game she didn't understand.

"The sale of your site, of course! Of..." there was a pause, as if the mysterious Ms. Monroe were referring to something. "Say-something-shirts-dot-com."

"That site isn't for sale," said Faye bluntly.

"Well, of course it is!" the woman insisted. "That's why people *create* web sites—to sell them."

"That's not why we created this one," said Faye.

Ms. Monroe made noises that sounded like she was trying to strangle a goose. "I don't understand," she said. The woman seemed truly puzzled.

"The purpose of the site is to provide a few of us with a voice," Faye explained. "And it gives people who agree with what we have to say, the opportunity to speak out with us."

"A voice?" Monroe repeated, puzzled. "What is it you *do* at your site?"

"Don't you *know?*" Faye asked.

"I've never actually seen it," the woman on the phone admitted. "The decisions as to which sites to buy are made by my boss...or, rather, *his* boss."

"Well, you should at least visit a site before you call it's owner to make an offer, don't you think?" Faye challenged, amused. "I would think that would comprise minimal good manners, not to mention making good business sense."

"I can't," the woman explained.

"Sure you can," Faye assured her. "You've got a computer at your desk, don't you?"

"Yes, but they don't put the Internet on our desktop computers."

"They *don't?*" Faye was shocked. "How do they expect you to discuss a web site you've never seen?"

"It isn't about the web site, honey," the woman confided in a chummy manner. "It's about the money. It's always about the money. For example, GSI is prepared to offer you—"

"I really don't care," Faye interrupted. "We didn't create this site for money, in spite of what you think. Thanks for your call, but we really aren't interested." And Faye hung up, as she would with any telemarketer.

She sat before her computer, surfing. When she had started investigating Mickey Timmons' death, she had done so at the library, looking up back issues of the newspaper on microfilm. It had occurred to her on the way home from Frank's apartment that she might be able to turn up other information if she plugged his grandson's name into an Internet search engine. She had learned that some newspapers were starting to make back issues available on-line, which was cheaper than microfilm. Perhaps she could find an article that would prove to Frank his dreams were just—what did Robert call it? —survivor guilt.

She could certainly understand survivor guilt. She had had it herself, after Edwin's suicide, even though no one had named her condition. If she could help ease Frank's torment, that would be a good thing.

She brought up her favorite search engine, Alta Vista, typed in "Michael Timmons and clicked on the Search button. She wasn't sure that there would be any hits at all; but there were more than thirty. They showed up as page titles, with the first few lines of text from the page printed beneath.

She was able to eliminate most of them almost immediately, as they were genealogical references to people who'd been born in the 1800s. Two others referred to a doctor of physics at a midwestern university. Another was a home page yet some other Michael Timmons had constructed as a school project. He lived in Denver, and the page showed a picture of him and his dog, family, and girl-friend. Two hits remained.

The first of the remaining hits was from *The Arizona Republic*, and was Mickey's obituary, which she had already read on micro-film. *But, my!* she thought, *this certainly took a lot less time to find!*

The second and last hit surprised her. It was an entry from the Phoenix police blotter. This was not the official report she had obtained; it was actually an entry, presumably made by the police department dispatcher on the department's own computer system, which was somehow and for some reason made available to the Internet.

At the top of the page was that October, 1995 date and a time in late afternoon. "Found," the text began, with the address of the storage facility, "dead, four cauc. males, shot, three hisp. males, one black male, prob. gang or drug related. No identification. One body, minor cauc male, abdominal mutilation, identified as Michael Timmons by drvrs lic." The page continued with Mickey's home address. Apparently, the entire dispatcher's entry was exposed on the Internet, just as he or she had originally typed it. If Faye had known about this weeks ago! —but, apparently, not even Marvin knew the police blotter was on-line, or he'd have said something about it. Faye felt a sense of enormity, sensed that the Internet, something new that was still in its infancy, was already so complex and powerful it might never be controlled.

She fingered her locket, the one given her by Norma Haverhill at the hot springs. She wore it every day, now, and found herself fingering it often. Originally, she did so because it was something new around her neck and she wanted to make sure it was still there and secure. But now, she found that holding it between her thumb and forefinger seemed to help her concentrate when faced with a knotty problem.

Police blotter entries, Faye intuited, must be made by officers calling in from the scene. The reports are made later. Reports might contain conclusions, as did the one she'd read regarding Mickey's death. The blotter entries would just be factual: This was found, this person called, this other body had no identification, and so on.

And reports, Faye realized with a chill, could also *omit* information. Nothing had been said in the police report about Mickey's body having been mutilated. Faye had thought there might be a newspaper story that would have more information, but she'd expected it to basically corroborate the police report, and thus prove that Frank's dreams were just that—dreams.

She had *not* expected to find his dreams had been accurate.

Still holding the locket, Faye had the sudden urge to look up another name: Abigail Bannister, whom Norma Haverhill had said was the original owner of the locket Faye now wore. She did so. There was one entry.

The name was found in a historical article on the burning of witches in Salem in the 1600s. Faye was about to close the page in disappointment when she came upon a painting of that long-ago Abigail, accompanying the article. An odd feeling swept over Faye, as if she were dreaming.

The portrait was identical to the one in her locket.

My Dinner At Andre's

A crash from the back of the house, followed by the unmistakable smell of plaster dust, reminded Faye that Chuck and Dave were still working on her bathrooms. She wondered if she would be able to use either one. The voice calling, "We're all right!" from her bedroom did little to reassure her.

With some trepidation, she wandered to the source of commotion and found Chuck on the floor, the bathroom sink in his lap, made ghostly by the dust from the dry wall that partially obscured Dave. Since they had already said they were all right, Faye said, "I'm going out to dinner. Will you be gone when I get back, or would you like me to bring you something?" *And will I be able to use my bathroom?* She thought, but didn't say aloud.

"We'll probably be a couple more hours," Chuck said, and sneezed.

"Where are you going, honey?" Dave asked. "Is *he* taking you?" Chuck shot him a frigid glance, but Dave ignored it.

"I don't know *where* I'm going," Faye said. "And no one's taking me. I thought I'd call Marian, though."

"Okay, then, you've got to go to Andre's," Dave stated. "French cuisine. Have you *been*, yet?"

"No," Faye replied. "Where is it?"

"Well, it's all the way into town," Dave admitted.

"Why would they want to go *there*?" Chuck demanded of his partner.

"Because the food is to *die* for," Dave replied. "And they won't have to worry about men ogling them while they're there."

"They'll get ogled," Chuck said, wryly.

"I don't care about being ogled," Faye grinned. "But food to die for sounds good. And with two hours to kill, a trip into Phoenix doesn't sound like a bad idea."

So, while he and Chuck swept up chunks of dry wall, Dave recited detailed directions to the restaurant, which Faye wrote down. She then called Marian. "Are you up for a fancy dinner?" she asked, when her friend picked up.

"Mmm. Sounds good!" Marian replied. "I've taken out a chicken, but it's still frozen. When should I pick you up?"

"*I'll* pick *you* up," Faye insisted. "You're always driving me around. How about thirty minutes?"

"I'll be ready, darling," her friend replied, and hung up.

After verifying that the hall bathroom was no more usable than the one off the bedroom, Faye stood in front of her closet, trying to choose an outfit. Dave's voice called from the bathroom, "The powder blue with the pale yellow trim."

How does he do that? Faye wondered. Dave always seemed to know when she was trying to select clothes. It was a little annoying, more than a little disconcerting yet she suspected she would miss him when the work was completed.

The dress he recommended—and how did he know the contents of her closet, anyway? —was in easy reach; Faye took it by the hanger and laid it on her bed. "And the navy pumps," Dave called.

She stopped at the rec center where she showered and changed. In the large mirror, she examined herself. The dress, which she had purchased while shopping with Dave a couple of weeks ago, was flattering and her newly-colored hair set it off perfectly. With a gasp, Faye suddenly realized how much younger she looked. It was hard to say *how* young, exactly; she had, in fact, never looked as she did now. Faye was sixty; when she was fifty, she was already gray and obese, though at the time she had thought of the weight as middle-aged spread. When she was forty, she'd started turning gray. She'd started putting the weight on at thirty, but no one looking at her would think she was *that* young. Still, she thought, if she told someone she was fifty, they certainly wouldn't have argued.

As she pulled into Marian's driveway, the door to Marian's house opened and Marian stepped out, wearing an ankle-length skirt and wrapped in a shawl; Faye couldn't make out more detail in the twilight. Marian strolled to the passenger side of Faye's car, opened the door, and got in. She gave Faye a hug. "Dinner!" she cried. "How fun! Where are we going?"

"A place Dave recommended," Faye replied, "in downtown Phoenix. I know it's a bit of a drive, but I had to get out of there before the plaster dust drove me nuts."

As they drove east on Thunderbird, Faye brought Marian up to date on her various projects: The grow room remodeling, of course; and the odd offer she'd received for the web site. She shared the progress in her investigation into Mickey Timmons' murder.

When they reached I-17, Faye took it southward a few miles, then exited and resumed her eastward drive on Indian School Road. Soon they were in an area made up of bars, clubs and restaurants, and Marian pointed out the sign for Andre's. Faye found a parking space; they left the car and entered the restaurant.

The place was crowded, and there was a stunning hostess, dressed in a floor-length, black gown, who asked Faye if she had a reservation. "I didn't realize I needed one," she replied in dismay.

"Are you Faye and Marian?" the hostess asked, smiling.

"Yes," Faye replied slowly.

"Then, you *do* have a reservation," the hostess grinned. "Please follow me to your table."

"Dave must have made the reservation for us after I left the house," Faye guessed out loud. She looked around the room as she and Marian followed the hostess and saw, to her surprise, that *all* of the diners, and, for that matter, all of the visible staff—were women.

"Where are the men?" she blurted.

The hostess, apparently assuming the question was not rhetorical and had been directed at her, turned to Faye and smiled. "We don't encourage a male clientele here at Andre's," she said. She indicated a vacant table and said, "Will this suit you?"

Faye said that it would, and she and Marian sat. The hostess gave them their menus and left them to make their choices; but Faye couldn't concentrate.

"How can they keep out men?" she asked. "And *why?*"

Marian was trying to keep from laughing out loud. "Darling, can't you guess? Remember who recommended the restaurant to you?"

"Dave," Faye said, in sudden realization. "Are all these women *lesbians?*" she whispered, eyes wide.

"Well, darling, *we're* not, so I won't guarantee the other women here all are...but I wager most of them are here with each other, as dates."

Faye turned beet red. "I hope you don't think that I..."

"Oh, puh-lease!" Marian interrupted, dismissively.

Desperate to find another subject, Faye mentioned finding the reference on the Internet to Abigail Bannister. "The painting on the page matches the one in the locket *perfectly*," Faye said. "But how can it be the same person? Norma said Abigail was *her* mentor. She *can't* be two hundred years old!"

"I don't know how old Norma is," Marian said, thoughtfully. "When she presented me with that locket, so many years ago, I had no way of looking up Abigail's name or finding any other reference to her. Oh, I suppose I might have, if I'd devoted myself to study in the right direction—but I wouldn't have guessed I'd find her in records of the Salem witch trials, either! What did the page say about her?"

"Oh..." Faye's voice trailed off. "I...well, I was so surprised at finding the painting there, I didn't actually *read* the article," she said. "I will, when I get home. But, still—what can it mean?"

Marian's face took on a reflective expression. "How old do you think *I* am?" she asked.

"Well..." Faye hesitated. She hated being asked that. She had developed a technique that usually, but not always, saved her the embarrassment of guessing too high an age. She would do her best, then subtract five. "I'm sixty, and I know you're a little older than I am...I'll guess sixty-five. But honestly, you're still a knockout."

Marian leaned across the table and took Faye's hand. "Darling," she whispered, "I'll be 92 in April."

Faye stared at her friend. She saw the fresh skin, bright eyes, lustrous hair of a woman at the peak of health. In the last few months, Faye had seen her beat up ruffians, lift weights, garden, swim and dive off the high board.

Faye laughed dismissively. "You're pulling my leg!" she cried.

Marian smiled, her eyes twinkling. "Not at all," she said calmly.

Faye stopped laughing. "How is it possible?" She shook her head, as if to cast out these crazy ideas.

"Proper diet and exercise is seventy-five percent of it," Marian declared. "Reducing stress, which pot helps with, is another ten percent. Good genes don't hurt. And, Faye—you know, marijuana isn't the *only* herb I grow in my garden."

"Oh?"

"Our tradition—that is, the tradition we're following that branded Abigail a witch and that she taught to Norma, and Norma taught to me, and I am teaching you—this tradition makes use of *many* herbs and naturally growing substances for health and healing, as well as attitude shifts and spiritual awareness. Marijuana is currently a big issue because the government is trying so hard to eradicate it, but it is just one of many valuable plants in our pharmacopoeia."

Faye stared at Marian. She shook her head, unable to think of a thing to say. "Tradition?" she finally repeated.

Marian smiled. "By now, darling, you know that most of what you—and everyone else—thought was so, is in fact lies. Have you given any thought to where religion might fit into this new reality you're developing?"

Faye buried her head in her hands. "Oh, no," she mock wailed. "Not that, too!"

Marian plunged ahead. "There is evidence that, ten thousand years ago, people worshipped, not God, but a Goddess. An Earth Mother figure. In the tradition, she taught womankind which plants had what properties—how to identify natural antibiotics, stimulants, sedatives, hallucinogens, and so on. She taught when to use which kind of drug, and when not to. Women, you see, were the first doctors. Men, with their hunting, supplemented a diet that was mostly vegetarian."

Faye breathed a sigh of relief. "Okay, I have heard some of that before."

"About five thousand years ago," Marian continued, "something happened—it isn't clear what, but something—and the original Goddess religion was suppressed, and replaced with a male-dominated religion. The credit for creating the earth and the universe was transferred to a male god from the Goddess."

"Jehovah," Faye supplied.

"This was actually before Jehovah, or Yahweh as he is more properly known, showed up in the ancient texts. The first name given to this god was Marduk, but as the centuries passed, the name changed many times. What did not change was the essence of this religion of domination: Men were given 'dominion' over plants, animals, and even females of their own species. That one word has justified all the extinction of species, leveling of forests, and raping of the Earth that our society now prides itself on. And what's more, women bought into this farce for some unknown reason."

"Maybe we were just tired of running things," Faye suggested.

"But we didn't," Marian pointed out. "The evidence is that the original religion was one of cooperation, rather than of domination. No one 'ran' anything; people got together, decided what needed to be done, and then worked together to do it."

Faye chuckled. "Too bad that wouldn't work today," she said.

"But it *does* work today!" Marian exclaimed. "Chuck and Dave working on your grow room is just one example. You, Marvin and me working on the web site is another. The fact is, cooperation accomplishes far more than the hierarchical management style ever has."

"Then why don't corporations make use of it?"

"At the corporate level, and I'm talking about the very highest levels—those people aren't interested in accomplishments or even money. The thrill, for them, is in command and manipulation."

"You can't mean that!" Faye laughed. "Not interested in money?"

"I do mean that," Marian assured her. "For that strata of humanity, money is like air. They never doubt it will always be there for them. They don't question it or even think about it, except as a tool. *Power* is where they're at."

"But they still have projects and schedules. If they use command instead of cooperation—well, the extra effort they expend on each one must be enormous..."

"Which results in their aging prematurely. Which brings us back to why I look as young to you as I do. I don't *really* look young. I've just spent most of my life devoting my energy to the things that matter to *me*, instead of foolishness like working for someone else or worrying about what other people think or do. Faye, darling— this is how a 92-year-old *ought* to look. I may not live to be 200, but there's no reason why I shouldn't continue to be healthy and attractive until I do die, whenever that is."

The hostess interrupted their conversation, bearing a sympathetic expression. "Ms. McRae?" she asked Faye. "You're wanted on the phone. It's an emergency."

Faye was astonished. "Who even knows I'm here?" she blurted out.

"Dave," Marian reminded her.

"Oh my God," Faye gasped. "Something's happened to my house!"

The hostess led Faye to a small room between the dining room and the kitchen, where the waitresses prepared salads and tallied up bills. She handed Faye a telephone receiver. "Hello?" Faye asked. "This is Faye."

"I'm so sorry to bother you at dinner," the voice on the phone replied. Faye was surprised, then relieved, then concerned again when she recognized the voice on the line as Robert's.

"Robert, what is it? Are you all right?"

"I'm fine, dear, but I wonder if you could come to Boswell Hospital right away. Frank Timmons has attempted suicide."

Suicide Run

Dinner was already on the table when Faye returned, pale. "What is it, darling?" Marian asked with concern.

"Frank Timmons. He's shot himself, and Robert wants me to come to the hospital right away."

Marian flagged a waitress and explained the emergency. Within minutes, she and Faye were back in Faye's car, with their dinner in a pair of Styrofoam containers.

Marian had offered to drive, but Faye shook her head. "You're not the only one who knows how to step on it," she said, rolling down her window as the car tore out of the parking lot. Faye wove skillfully in and out of lanes, leaving Marian in breathless admiration.

"And your window is opened because...?" Marian shouted over the road noise.

"I want to be able to really look behind us, if I need to change lanes quickly."

Several minutes passed before Marian spoke. "How badly is he wounded?"

"What?" Faye screamed over the roar of the engine and the squealing of tires.

"Was it an accident?" Marian shouted.

Faye nodded, eyes focused sharply on the road and the other cars on it. "I hope so," she said. "Robert didn't say a lot before we hung up."

"I know he's been depressed. Robert told me about his dreams," Marian yelled.

"Oh, good. I wasn't sure how much I should say."

"What?" Marian bellowed, as the inertia of Faye's rapid passing of a truck threw her against the door.

"I said, I wasn't sure how much to say!" Faye cried. "Doctor patient privilege and all that."

"Don't worry about that, darling! Robert keeps me posted on all our patients."

"Our patients? What do you mean, our patients?" Faye screamed, preparing to brake for an red light.

"Myself or the other members of the club are supplying the marijuana and other herbs Robert prescribes," Marian shouted, into the sudden silence after the car came to a screeching stop.

"Well, babe! Aw-*right!*" came a voice from an adjacent car. Faye turned to see a couple of young men grinning conspiratorially. The passenger reached out to Faye, and in his hand she was astonished to see a lit doobie.

"Uh, no thanks, we're in a hurry!" Faye called just as the light turned green. Then she floored the accelerator, leaving the young men behind them in a cloud of blue smoke. She darted around a

Volkswagen Rabbit. "A club? What club do you mean?"

"Why, the Sun City Cannabis Club! *You* know; you've met many of the other members and you're soon to be a contributing member."

Faye passed a white Dodge pickup on the right—a tricky move since the right hand lane, at that point, was for parking. However, no cars were actually parked in this business district at night. She stuck her head out the window, pulling back into the lane the moment she saw the Ford had cleared the pickup behind her, earning her a loud honk from the annoyed driver.

"I guess I hadn't thought of it in such a formal fashion," Faye replied. "Is it a real club? With a president, and meetings, and minutes, and rules?"

"No *rules*, darling. This is a cooperative anarchy, remember? We each simply observe, see what needs to be done, and assist as we are able."

"But, really," Faye protested. "Is that really so different than a democracy? Democratic process simply formalizes the whole thing, doesn't it?"

"How would *you* know?" Marian challenged in return. "You've never lived in a democracy."

Faye's tires screeched as the car tore up the entrance ramp to I-17 north. "What do you mean? America is a democracy!" she screamed.

Once on the interstate, Faye slowed down to ten miles an hour over the speed limit, keeping an eye out for police.

"Don't be silly, darling!" Marian scoffed, in a quieter voice now that the engine had resumed its normal purr. "The United States doesn't even *claim* to be a democracy. It calls itself a 'representative democracy,' but it isn't even that."

"But we vote for the people who vote on the issues."

"Why not vote on the issues yourself? That would be a *true* democracy."

"Impractical." Faye saw a patrol car and took her foot off the gas. "Too many issues for people to study. Too difficult to go vote on every one."

"That may have been true once," Marian admitted. "Though one could make a good argument that government has no business being involved in so many issues. But with the Internet and telephones, anyone with an interest can inform themselves of the issues. And everyone can vote from home."

"Then why bother changing things?"

"Because the people you vote for are not *bound* to represent you after they're elected. And, in fact, they don't. If you simply examine the voting records of your senators and representatives, you'll find they don't even follow the Democratic or Republican platforms when they vote. Democrat, Republican—these are just labels, brand names. Once the package is opened, they're all the same...sludge."

"Now, you're just being cynical." Faye dodged a minivan that cut in front of her.

"Am I? Then why doesn't this country have decent national health care? Everyone wants it, except some doctors who would face a pay cut if it passed, and the pharmaceutical corporations that would have to reduce their obscenely inflated prices. Even the First Lady seems to be behind it. So why did Congress overwhelmingly vote it down?"

"The Republicans control Congress," Faye reminded her friend.

"That's what the papers say. But what does that *mean?* The Democrats voted the bill down, too."

Faye frowned. "Well, if people would just really *study* the candidates, and vote for one who *would* vote as his or her constituents wished..."

"How would he get elected? Large corporations supply the money for campaigning. TV ads are prohibitively expensive except for those with corporate backing. So are newspaper ads. Besides, it barely matters anymore *who* you vote for."

"How so?"

"There's been something new added," Marian informed her. "There are now two companies selling electronic voting machines. The machines are computer based, darling. The companies that make them are not required to reveal what the software is that runs them, or how they work—trade secrets, you know. And here's the kicker—*they don't leave a paper trail.* That is, there's no paper on which you wrote, or punched holes, or anything. A recount is instantaneous, but it always gives precisely the same counts."

"What's wrong with that?" Faye asked. "It makes sense, actually. And it's not that different from the scenario you just presented, of voting by telephone."

"There is one difference," Marian said. "The two companies are each owned by politicians, both of whom won the first elections in which the machines were used, even though those politicians displaced incumbents, and the polls showed them to be light years behind the competition."

Faye was so overwhelmed by the implications of this news that she almost missed the turnoff onto Thunderbird. The wheels squealed again as she jerked the car to the right. They made it onto the exit ramp, much to the annoyance of the driver of the car they cut in front of. At the end of the ramp, she turned the vehicle towards Sun City.

Finally, she shook her head. "When word of that gets out," she said, "there's no way other districts will vote to bring in those new machines."

"The powers-that-be *want* those machines," Marian insisted, "because they make elections easier to control. It doesn't take a gypsy to see how this will play out. In the next big election—that would be the 2000 Presidential election—I predict that newly-designed paper ballots will be used in one or two states. The ballots will look fancy and modern, but people will find them confusing and will, after the election, claim to have accidentally voted for the wrong candidate. There will be a big fuss made, a lot of recounts. It will probably develop that the man who won the popular vote loses the actual election, thanks to that Electoral College nonsense. The end result will be that people will demand the old, mechanical voting machines be tossed out—and there are the new, paperless, computerized machines just waiting in the wings. By the election of 2004, every major district will have them."

"No way," Faye grinned.

"Watch and see," Marian replied. "Wanna bet?" She held out her hand, which Faye shook quickly, before returning both her hands to the steering wheel.

Once Upon A Dream

Robert met them at the door to Frank's room. He kissed Faye and flashed a relieved smile at Marian.

"What happened?" Marian asked, speaking at the same time as Faye, who inquired, "How is he?"

"He's resting and in stable condition," the doctor reported. "He tried to shoot himself in the head, but just grazed his temple. He called 911 himself, which is a good sign."

"Why did he do it?" Faye asked.

"I'm not sure," Robert admitted, "but I'm glad you're both here. Something odd's happening, Marian, and you may have more of a handle on it than I do."

"What is it?" Marian asked.

The doctor shook his head. "Let's see if Frank is up to talking. If he is, you'll probably spot it, yourself."

The three of them entered Frank's room, which he occupied alone. He was connected to an oxygen cylinder and an IV drip. Faye was horrified. "I thought you said he was doing well," she whispered.

"This is normal stuff," Robert assured her. "The intravenous drip allows the nurses to sedate him, as well as provide other injections without having to re-puncture his skin each time. And oxygen is something Frank needs anyway for his emphysema."

"The damn oxygen tank isn't worth the trouble it takes to carry," the old man grumbled. Faye was startled, not having realized that Frank was awake.

But she recovered quickly, crossed to him and took one of his gnarled old hands in hers. "How are you, Frank?" she asked solicitously.

"Fucking depressed," he grunted. "I fucking shot myself, you know." Faye thought he sounded more like his old self than he had in some time.

"*Why* did you shoot yourself?" Robert asked, as if asking why Frank had chosen blue trousers instead of green.

But Frank's frown deepened, from his customary grimace to an expression of concern. "I'm not sure," he said.

"What were you thinking about?" Marian asked. "Have you been thinking about this for awhile?"

"No!" the old man replied emphatically. "It just popped into my head last night. I got to thinking about Mickey's death, and those weird dreams I've been having, and suddenly it just seemed like the right thing to do."

"But you didn't go through with it," Faye pointed out.

Frank nodded slowly, causing the starched pillowcase to crease. "Just as I pulled the trigger," he said, hesitantly, "I heard a voice. Right in my ear."

"A voice?" Robert echoed. "You didn't say anything about that before."

Frank laughed, a strangled, raspy sound that contained no merriment. "I didn't want you to think I was crazy!" he admitted.

"What did the voice say?" Faye asked.

Frank answered promptly. "It said, 'I will not fucking kill myself!'"

"Whose voice was it?" Marian asked.

An expression of bemused triumph crossed Frank's face. "Mine."

Robert and the women exchanged puzzled glances.

"What's crazy-sounding about that, Frank?" Robert inquired.

Frank grinned. "I didn't *say* it. I wasn't saying anything. In fact, I was calm as could be. Not scared, not sad, not anything. But I heard the voice, my voice, as if it was comin' outta thin air."

Robert turned to Marian, concern on his face. "What do you think?"

Marian looked at her watch. "When did you smoke your last joint, Frank?"

Frank looked troubled. "About an hour before...before the dreams started in again."

Robert was troubled, too. "It may be that Frank is one of the few people who don't tolerate marijuana well. If pot is causing these nightmares and depression, we'll have to find a substitute to treat his nausea and lack of appetite. Not that there's a good one," he added.

"Nonsense," Marian snapped, tartly. "I don't believe marijuana is causing these nightmares. I think it's *releasing* them."

"You mean...?"

"Exactly," Marian agreed with the unspoken premise.

"What?" asked Faye, confused.

"Did you ever read *The Manchurian Candidate?*" Marian asked her. "Or see the movie?"

"No," Faye admitted. "I remember hearing of it, but I don't remember what it was about."

"It was about brainwashing," Marian sighed. "And how a person could be turned into a programmed killer without even being aware of it." She laughed. "Oh, how Marvin's going to enjoy this if it turns out to be true!"

"Why would Marvin enjoy seeing Frank in the hospital?" Faye cried in dismay.

"Not this, darling," Marian assured her. "But he's so convinced that everything can be explained as part of a global conspiracy, and of course brainwashed killers is a staple of those theories."

Faye caught her breath, her eyes wide. "Remember, I told you— Frank, forgive me, but I told Marian about..."

Frank nodded, but Robert looked blank. Faye gave him a wan smile. "Frank brought a gun with him to Carvel Meany's victory party. He was...going to shoot Meany for the death of his grandson."

"Should've done it, too, the sonofabitch," Frank grumbled.

Robert came to a decision. "We're going to have to try hypnosis," he said. "And it won't wait until morning. Nurse!" he called, as a white-garbed woman passed in the hall outside.

"Yes, doctor?" she queried respectfully, stepping into the room.

"We'll need *absolute privacy* in here, do you understand? No interruptions."

"Yes, doctor. I'll put a sign on the door." And she returned to the hall, closing the door softly behind her.

"You ladies had better sit over there, out of earshot, while I put Frank under," Robert recommended. "In the event you *can* hear, maintain the intention of *not* being hypnotized. Things are confusing enough without recreating *On A Clear Day You Can See Forever.*"

Faye and Marian made themselves comfortable in the room's two visitor chairs while Robert sat beside Frank on the bed and spoke softly to him. Marian took Faye's hand and squeezed. Faye was almost surprised to find herself relaxing a little. She hadn't realized how tense she had become.

In a few minutes, Robert waved them over and spoke in a normal tone of voice. "Approach, ladies. He's under."

"So quickly?" Faye asked, softly.

"Well, this isn't the first time," Robert reminded her. "I hypnotized him weeks ago to help him stop smoking. And, like any hypnotist, I gave him a post-hypnotic suggestion that would make it easier to put him under again if I need to."

"And we don't have to whisper?"

"No, he can only hear the sound of my voice, and that only when I prefix it with his name."

"What would happen if you left right now? You know, dropped dead or lost your voice or something?" Faye asked, curiously.

"He would drop into a natural sleep in an hour or two, and awaken in the morning not remembering any of it." He turned towards the entranced man on the bed. "Frank," he said. "Can you hear me?"

"Yes." Frank's voice was calm and neutral, a tone Faye had never heard from him before.

"Your mind is like a video tape recorder," Robert told him. "Tonight, we're going to rewind the tape and play back some scenes from the past. Do you understand?"

"Yes."

"Some of these scenes may have been disturbing to you the first time you experienced them. You do not need to be disturbed by anything now. You will just be watching reruns, on a TV screen. Do you understand?"

"Yes."

"Let's run the tape back to your, your tenth birthday. I will count backwards from ten to zero, including the zero, as you wind the tape back. Do you understand?"

"Yes."

"Ten…nine…eight…" Robert completed the count and asked, "The tape is rewound. You are watching your tenth birthday on the TV screen. What do you see?"

There was a pause.

"Frank?" the doctor said. "Do you see anything?"

The old man's voice changed tone. Although he was supposed to just be watching the scene on a TV, he seemed to become the young boy he once had been. "It's a tree," he said. "Yeah, a tree."

"Why are you looking at a tree?" the doctor asked.

"I have to pick a branch from it."

"Why, Frank? Why do you need a tree branch?"

"My old man's gonna switch me and he sent me out for the branch to do it with."

"Why is he going to switch you, Frank?"

"Because I opened one of my birthday presents before I was s'posed to." He spoke in a higher, younger, tone than Faye was accustomed to, but she noted he spoke without fear or, indeed, any emotion.

"What present was it?" the doctor asked.

"A new slingshot," Frank answered promptly.

"Frank, we're now going to wind the tape forward a few years," Robert announced. As the ladies listened, the doctor guided Frank into recalling three more memories of his past: The day he joined the Army, the day he got married, the day his son was born. The memories were believable to Faye; only in talking to Frank, later, would she be able to verify that they were genuine.

"We visited those scenes from the past, scenes that were not particularly sensitive, to get the patient used to the technique," Robert explained to Faye and Marian. "Now we'll visit the day in question." He turned to Frank. "Frank," Robert said, "we are now going to wind the video tape forward again, to October…"

Robert faltered, and Faye whispered, "October 9, 1995."

Robert repeated the date, and counted forward from zero to ten—"including the zero," as he said every time he was about to count—and asked Frank to report what he saw on the TV.

"It's a room," the old man stated, neutrally.

"Is it a room you recognize?" Robert asked.

"I've never seen it before," was the reply. "It looks like the inside of one of those rental storage units."

"Rewind the tape some," the doctor requested. "Go back to the point in time when you made the decision that resulted in you coming to this room." He counted, backward, and asked, "Where are you now?"

"In my apartment," Frank said. His voice had resumed its gravelly quality.

"What are you doing?"

"Talking to Mickey."

"Is he there?"

"Yes," Frank replied.

"What are you talking about?"

"His drug problem," Frank said. "He says he's been running drugs to support his habit and he can't get out of it."

"What do you tell him in response?"

"I'm going to go with him, tell the bastards that fucked him up that I'll fuck *them* up if they don't leave him alone."

"And do you go?"

"Yes. I take my gun with me, just in case."

Robert cleared his throat. "Frank, move ahead. You follow Mickey?"

"No, *he follows me*. He gave me the address."

"Tell me what happens."

"I bang on the door," Frank said, in that curiously detached tone. "It slides up. A man is there, a tough-looking guy. I tell him I'm Mickey's grandfather and I want to talk to his boss. He lets us in."

Frank went on to describe how he and Mickey found the small storage unit outfitted as an office, with a desk and a few chairs.

There were three other people there, he said, all men. One of them was measuring a white powder and pouring it into Zip-Loc bags.

"The boss ain't here," one of the men growled when Frank made his demand.

"Yes, I am," said a voice behind them. Frank spun around, startled, to find Representative Carvel Meany, who he recognized from the news on TV, and a woman he did not know.

"What's going on here?" The woman yelled. "Who are these people?"

At her orders, the three men quickly subdued Frank. His gun was found almost instantly and taken away, and he and Mickey were tied into two of the chairs.

"It really does look like a TV show!" Frank commented at one point, the only time his natural personality seemed to escape from its trance.

Meany and the woman got into an argument. She accused him of idiocy, incompetence, and other things Frank did not recognize. The crux of the argument, though, was what was to be done with Frank and the kid.

Frank swore, "All we want to do is go home and never think about you people again!" But the woman wouldn't buy it.

Frank quoted her exactly: "'I could use a man like you,'" she had said. "'But you'll need to be programmed, first.'"

"She said, 'Programmed?'" the doctor pressed.

"That's what she said," Frank insisted.

"It takes a great shock to prepare a mind for programming," she had said. "Usually we just kill a baby. But your grandson, here, will do just as well, I think."

Mickey's terror left him speechless. Frank, in completely over his head, had tried to bargain for his grandson's life. Didn't they need him to run their drugs?

"Nonsense," the woman had cackled. "Kids like him are a dime a dozen. Human sacrifices...now, *they're* harder to come by."

Frank was untied, but held tightly by two of the burly men. A long knife, like some kind of surgical tool, was forced into his hand by the third man and held there. Slowly, with Frank struggling uselessly against them, he was forced to stand face-to-face with his beloved grandson, who had been forced into a corner of the room by Meany. And then, staring into Mickey's eyes wet with panicked, betrayed tears, his hand was forced to drive the knife into the boy's abdomen.

He watched as Mickey spit blood, his eyes glazed over, and he sunk to the floor.

And then, nothing. "The TV blew up," Frank-under-hypnosis calmly reported, and fell silent.

The Man of Sun City Candidate

Friday, December 12, 1997

They gathered at Marvin's home: Faye, Marian, and Robert. Frank was still in the hospital, under sedation—a conventional sedative; Robert couldn't prescribe marijuana and expect the hospital to administer it. Marijuana, even for the most humane purposes, and no matter that its unique properties had never been duplicated, was still illegal in Arizona.

Faye, riding with Marian, could see Robert's car parked in Marvin's driveway long before they reached the end of his *cul de sac*. "I just read something about Feng Shui," Faye remarked to her friend. "It's supposed to be bad chi to live in a house positioned at the end of a street like that," she said. "The energy of the road is like an arrow aimed at the house."

"In the old days, that was literally true," Marian responded. "Men on horseback could fire arrows while riding straight at the house." She parked in front of Marvin's home.

It was morning and Faye noted that Marvin was still bleary-eyed. She knew he tended to work late into the wee hours and was not, as they say, a morning person. Not that Faye was feeling all that well, herself. After Marvin closed and locked the door behind them, Faye greeted Robert then said, "I need a cup of coffee!"

"Already cookin'," Marvin rasped.

"How's that agoraphobia going, Marvin?" Robert asked jovially. "You ready to let me help you with that?"

"It ain't paranoia when they're really out to get ya, doc," Marvin responded. "Here, come to the kitchen. It's the only room in the house wit' enough chairs for all a ya."

Once they were seated, Marian started to speak, but Marvin held up his hand for silence. "Wait," he commanded, and stood vigil in front of the coffee maker. When the pot contained enough of the black sludge—*How many spoonsful of coffee did he put in there, anyhow?* Faye wondered—he poured himself a cup of it and downed it. He then poured another cup, set the pot on the table, and took cups from a cabinet for the others, placing them on the table beside the coffee pot. He then took a shoebox from another cabinet, opened it, and in a moment had created a fat joint which he lit, drew from, and passed to Marian. She, in turn, inhaled, passed it to Faye; Faye took a hit and passed it to Robert, who also partook.

Exhaling noisily, Marvin said, "Okay, out wit' it. Must be somethin' big if you're gonna wake me up *this* early."

"We've mentioned Frank Timmons to you," Marian prompted.

"Yeah, the guy whose grandson was killed by Meany and company."

"Well, it now seems as if...Tell me," Marian interrupted herself, "what do you know about brain washing?"

"All there is *to* know," Marvin said, matter-of-factly, "except what it's actually like. I never *done* it, or had it done to me, if that's what ya mean."

"We think Frank Timmons may have been brainwashed by Meany."

"*Meany?!*" Marvin snorted. "You gotta have a *brain* before you can brainwash somebody else!"

"It looks like *someone* must have done it," Robert said. He then proceeded to describe Frank's nightmares and growing depression, and the story he'd told under hypnosis the night before. Faye then added Frank's attempt to shoot Meany at the victory celebration.

Marvin sighed. "Poor bastard," he commented. "Well, here's how you brainwash someone. It isn't hard, if you got no morals. You force the poor bastard to participate in a murder. A loved one, or a baby. Even a pet, if the person you're brainwashin' is a kid.

That causes a split to form in the mind. What they call a split personality. The event is such a painful memory, it gets pushed into this background persona, and the normal personality—what they call the 'front alter' in brainwashin' circles—no longer remembers the event at all."

Faye was aghast—"A *baby?*" she whispered in horror—but Marian retained a business-like composure. "And how does this brainwash a person?"

"Alone, it don't. It just *prepares* the person for brainwashing, like formattin' a computer disk. Then ya use a combination of drugs and hypnosis to fill the new persona wit' the instructions you want carried out. Murder, mayhem, whatever."

"And the front alter, the normal personality—?" Robert began.

"Don't know nothin'," Marvin said flatly.

"And yet," Faye interjected, "Frank *was* starting to remember things. And they depressed him so much, he tried to kill himself."

"No way!" Marvin scoffed. "They always include an instruction for the person to off themselves if for some reason they start to remember. *That's* why Frank tried to do himself in."

"But why did Frank remember anything?" Faye persisted. "Was this just a botched brainwashing job?"

"I can't answer that," Marvin said. "Since he didn't go through wit' shootin' Meany—wish he had! —it does seem like it didn't take. But that's odd. Anyone who knows how to do it, usually knows how to do it, but good. D'ya know who his handler is?"

"Handler?" Robert asked.

"That's what they call the person what knows the trigger code. *That's* the magic words that move the front alter to the back and make the programmed persona available for access."

"Well, it couldn't be Meany," Faye said, considering. "He certainly wouldn't program Frank to kill *him*."

"Unless he wanted to stage an *attempt*," Marian suggested. "For publicity, or something. That might be why you were able to talk Frank out of it so easily."

"No," argued Faye. "He would have had to shoot *and miss* to create a publicity stunt. No," she continued, frowning, "it must be someone who really *does* want Meany dead."

Everyone looked at Marvin.

"Hey, don't look at *me!*" the computer whiz cried. "I never leave the house!" And the others laughed, the tension broken.

Faye shook her head. "I can't believe anyone would sacrifice a *baby*," she said. Having never had one, Faye was particularly sensitive to how precious every infant was. "It can't happen *often.*"

Marvin snorted. "Looked at any milk cartons lately?" he said. "Every year, in America *alone*, over 700,000 children go missing and are never found. Some conspiracy theorists believe that all, or most, of them go to creating a whole fuckin' *army* of brainwashed weapons waitin' to be activated."

The others were stunned into silence. Finally, Faye said, "Is that what *you* believe?"

He shook his head. "I dunno *what* to believe," he said. "But there's a lot of fuckin' babies missing. They must be goin' *somewhere.*"

"So we have two *new* mysteries," Faye said, mulling. "One, who brainwashed Frank, and two, what caused his personalities to spontaneously re-merge?"

"There is a clue to the *who* question," Marian remarked.

"Of course," Faye agreed. "Frank heard a *woman's* voice directing his grandson's murder. So his handler is probably that woman, whoever she is."

"Well, all *I* know," Marvin said, heavily, "is that Meany is involved in this up to his eyebrows. And I *am* gonna put a stop to it."

They all looked at the information specialist. "What do you have in mind?" Robert asked.

"The only thing I got," Marvin said with intensity, "is the proof that he's got that marijuana farm. It's no murder rap, but it's somethin'."

"I thought you had already tried to interest the media in it, and they refused?" Faye pointed out.

"True," Marvin admitted. "But now we got this *other* means of spreadin' info. You don't mind, do you, Doodlebug?" he asked Marian.

"A shirt?" the older woman guessed.

"Yeah. With the latitude and longitude on it. Somethin' like, 'Carvel Meany Grows Marijuana at—' and throw in the coordinates."

"Sounds great!" Marian agreed. "I approve."

"I'll put it on the site today," Faye promised.

Fame

After arranging to meet Robert for dinner that evening, Faye kissed him goodbye and left with Marian for their usual Friday lunch. Along the way, they passed a strip of stores and Faye counted no fewer than five customers wearing Say Something T-Shirts. It was an odd feeling, as if she were suddenly part of something greater than herself. As if the customers, completely unaware of her presence or connection to the shirts they wore, were nevertheless an extension of her.

And the sayings on the shirts, originally written by Marian, were no less an extension of her. Faye stole a glance at her friend, and saw that she, too, had seen the evidence of her "forum" having taken hold. Her face bore an oddly bemused smile, as if she, too, wasn't quite sure how to feel about this peculiar, anonymous fame.

And it didn't stop with the strip mall. "Oh, my!" Faye uttered. "Marian...your shirts are *everywhere!*"

And it was true. Somehow, a fad had been started. Through the years, Faye had always wondered who started the fads and now, it would seem, *she* had started one. With Marian, of course.

"Slow down, please," Faye requested. "I want to see what sayings are the most popular." Marian complied, and the two of them read, "Doubt Is The Hatpin To The Balloon of Faith", a surprising number of "Don't Step On My Buzz" designs, and many of the Meany contributor shirts that had appeared on TV. So many of them, in fact, that Faye was amazed. "They told us in the re-election headquarters the results of polls indicating Meany's popularity," Faye said. "The polls indicated that he was almost universally loved. There's an awful lot of people wearing these shirts for that to be true."

"Oh, my!" Marian laughed. "Darling, you don't believe in *polls*, do you?"

"Oh." Faye thought. "Well, I guess not. I suppose they're manipulated the same way as the newspapers, radio and television."

"And by the same people, naturally."

"Well, still, a lot of people *do* believe them. And all these anti-Meany T-shirts are sure to have an impact on his popularity. He may not win the next election so easily."

"He may be impeached before then, if enough people wear the new design to get the point across."

In the café where they stopped for lunch, their *waitress* was wearing a shirt that featured a winking happy face and the words, "Have A Vice Day." Faye asked, "Pardon me, miss, but can you tell me where you got your T-shirt?"

"Oh, don't you love it? The T-shirt shop in the mall," she said. "They have a whole bunch of designs from some woman who lives right here in Sun City."

"Really?" Marian asked, stiffening. "Are they very expensive?"

"No, in fact they cost less than their other designs. Apparently these designs are free, so they only charge for the shirt and doing the transfer."

"Oh. Well, that's great!" Marian enthused, relaxing. When the waitress had taken their order to the kitchen, Marian said, "I'm glad the T-shirt shop is not charging for designs that cost them nothing. I hope T-shirt shops everywhere are doing the same thing."

At that moment, Faye heard her name from the television set mounted in a corner of the café. It had been running with the volume low when they came in, but of course a person's own name stands out even in a noisy background. Marian had heard it, too, and turned to watch.

The camera panned a group of pedestrians in some city, probably New York. Many of them were wearing...Marian's T-shirts! Faye strained to hear the announcer, the woman who did the humor pieces on CNN. "...by storm," she intoned. The camera switched views, to that of a man walking. "I even saw a businessman wearing one *over* his Arrow shirt and tie." The shirt read, "The War On Poverty Is Over...The Poor Surrendered."

"It's just what *I* want to say," he said. "And when I saw it, I knew I had to make myself one. I printed out the design from the web site, and ironed it onto a blank T-shirt myself."

"Probably the most surprising aspect of all this," the announcer continued, as the camera continued to pan passersby, "is that the originator of the web site, Faye McRae, refuses to charge for the designs and refuses advertising on her site. So, she's literally giving people the shirt off her back. This is Jeannie Most for CNN."

Faye looked at Marian with amazement. "That was *New York!*" she breathed. "Marian...they're wearing your designs *in New York!*"

Marian pondered. "If they're wearing them in New York," she said, "they're probably wearing them in Boston and Miami and L.A. And CNN is watched *everywhere*. If Marvin thought the site was getting a lot of traffic before...!"

Suddenly, Faye's expression darkened. "Marian, they gave *me* credit for the designs," she said. "I don't know why—"

"Darling, don't fret about it!" her friend laughed. "*I* don't mind. What I want to say is important; the fact that I'm the person who said it doesn't mean a thing to me. Besides, my name is on the site, too, and there's a little logo on the shirts. Anyway, I'm the *last* person to expect accuracy in a TV news report!"

Faye laughed in rueful agreement. It wasn't that long ago, she thought, that TV news and the Bible had, to her, been equally sacrosanct.

Not Holding Back

After lunch, Marian dropped Faye at her house. As Faye put her key into the door, she could hear her telephone ring. Of course, that made her fumble as she rushed to get the call. She managed to get the door open without hurting herself, picked up the receiver on what she was sure was the final ring, and heard a slightly familiar woman's voice say, "Ms. McRae?"

"Yes, this is she," Faye replied.

"This is Donna Monroe. We spoke a few days ago. About selling the web site, do you remember?"

"Yes, I remember," Faye said, slightly out of breath, and annoyed that she had hurried to take a call she didn't really want. "What may I do for you?"

"My boss, Malcolm Sketaris, would like to speak to you," the woman's voice stated. "Please hold."

"But I'm—" Faye began, too late. The soft sounds of the seventies had already replaced the woman's voice on the phone. Faye knew she should just hang up, but her curiosity had been piqued. Why in the world would anyone want so badly to purchase her and Marian's web site? Of course, it was a big success, now; but still— it wasn't a money-maker. That was, in fact, part *of* it's success.

After a thirty-second period, which Faye suspected had been carefully timed, the background music was replaced by a deep voice that reeked of authority and good fellowship. "Hi, Faye," the voice intoned. "I'm Malcolm Sketaris, president and CEO of GSI. It's so good to finally speak to you," he added. "I must admit, you've become somewhat of a legend here in our office."

"Really," Faye responded. "And why would that be?"

"Well, my dear, you're the woman who got away. You're the woman who created a web site, and doesn't want to sell it...or is very clever about holding out to boost the price."

"I am not holding out," Faye spoke tartly. "I am not trying to boost the price of something that I don't wish to sell. And I happen to be very busy at this moment, so I do appreciate your call, but as it is wasting your time and mine, I am going to wish you a good afternoon and say goodbye."

"Is your web site safe?" the voice reached her from the receiver she was just about to cradle. She hesitated, then returned it to her ear.

"Safe from what?"

"From hackers," came the prompt reply. "Unscrupulous types who might try to disable or vandalize your site for reasons of their own."

"Hackers?" Faye had heard the term from somewhere. She had a mental picture of pimply geeks sitting in front of computers.

"Yes. They will single out a site for no obvious reason, and find ways to bypass Internet security to flood the site with bogus requests, which overloads it for anyone else. Or they'll actually *change* the pages on your site, usually to something obscene, racist, or violent."

"But I can always change them back," Faye pointed out.

"Sure…when you realize you've been hit. But how many hours or days will go by until then? Here at GSI, our sites are constantly monitored, and we have state-of-the-art firewalls to prevent unauthorized access. What do *you* have?"

"I—I'll have to check with my friend who's hosting the site," Faye admitted. "But I'm sure he's got every kind of protection that's possible to have."

"A personal friend hosts your site? Who is it?"

"Why do you ask?"

"Well, we could supply him with some of our firewall software, if his is inadequate."

"I'm sure it is…"

"But how can you be certain?" the man asked. "I understand you are new to computers. There may be some subtle aspect of web site protection that you wouldn't understand."

Something in the man's tone frightened Faye. "But I'm quite sure *he* does," she said.

"You know, we can *find* who it is," the man continued, in a friendly tone. "When anyone accesses your site, the web address shows up. The company that registers Internet domain names, such as yours, has to post the address of the host."

His tone was friendly, but the message was not. "Fine," Faye said. "Look it up. Enjoy yourself. I am *not* interested in selling, and my friend is certainly not authorized to sell. Good day, Mr. Sketaris."

She hung up and found she was shaking. There had been a horrible threat implied by his friendly-sounding words, somehow she knew it. And the threat was not just of hackers overloading or vandalizing the site.

It was more personal than that.

And Room To Grow In

Saturday, December 13, 1997

Faye awakened to a ringing that took her a moment to recognize. It was her doorbell, but she had been sleeping so soundly that her orientation was stymied. As she rolled to a sitting position, she discovered her arm had been resting on Robert's bare chest and she smiled. They had had a wonderful dinner at a seafood restaurant; she had told him about the peculiar phone offer to buy the web site and he had reassured her that the buyers were simply being overly enthusiastic. Then he had accompanied her home, and they had spent, oh—*hours* in each other's arms.

Whenever Faye considered how much in love she was with the doctor, she was amazed to discover it was even more than it had been the last time she'd considered it. She had never suspected that a person could love so much. Or *be* loved so much; Robert showed it with every word, every touch. It saddened Faye, a bit, to think how many years she'd wasted as the wife of an uncaring, dominating clod but she knew she wouldn't have been ready for Robert if he *had* shown up then. He was married, or grieving; she was married and fat and depressed. It had taken time, and a little help from Marian, to prepare them both for this moment.

But, oh! It was so worth the waiting.

Now, however, her doorbell was ringing and she scurried into a nightgown, quietly, trying not to wake her beloved. She opened the front door to find Chuck and Dave waiting there.

"Did you see it?" Dave bubbled enthusiastically.

"See what?" Faye asked, sleepily.

"She didn't see it, yet," Chuck nudged his partner. "We can show it to her!"

"Show me what?" Faye asked with a trace of impatience. She hadn't yet had her coffee, or even splashed water on her face. She realized too late that her morning visitors could have been bad guys here to shoot her and destroy the web site and she had opened the door without even thinking about it.

"Your new *grow room!*" Dave whispered fiercely. Faye allowed the men to enter, then held up her hand. "Wait a few minutes," she said. "I have…company, and I should wake him."

"Robert spent the night!" Dave giggled to Chuck, who smiled indulgently. "Good for you!"

Faye stepped into the kitchen and primed the coffee maker. Soon the pungent aroma of fresh-brewed java wafted through the air and by the time she was able to pour four cups, Robert had wandered from the bedroom. "Oh!" she heard him yelp in surprise. "Just a moment, guys, let me get my shorts." She returned to the living room with the steaming mugs and found Chuck and Dave both staring in stunned admiration in the direction of the hallway.

"Coffee, gentlemen," she said.

"Oh, my God," Dave breathed. "No wonder you love him!"

The doctor emerged from the hallway, wearing his slacks and undershirt, doing up his belt. Faye handed him his coffee, then, gratefully, took the first sip of her own. "Okay, now. What do you want to show me?"

"Step this way, please," Chuck said, leading the way into the hall bathroom. Dave assumed rear guard, ushering Faye and Robert ahead of him. With the four of them crowded into the little room, Chuck said, "What do you see?"

Faye looked around. "Oh, you've finished the bathroom! Finally, I can shower in my own home."

"No!" protested Dave. "He means, what would you see if you were just visiting the house for the first time?"

Faye glanced around, then took a second, more detailed look. "It's a bathroom," she said, finally.

"It looks like the *old* bathroom," Robert said, "except there's a shower instead of the bathtub. But it looks like it was *built* this way. Those are the original tiles, aren't they?" He leaned into the shower stall and inspected the walls. "That looks like the original grout." He grinned at Chuck. "This bathroom does *not* look like it's been worked on since the house was built."

"Exactly!" Dave crowed in triumph. "No one looking for a grow room, or anything else, would give this room more than a passing glance."

Faye sniffed. "It doesn't even *smell* new," she said. "What happened to the plaster smell?"

"We spent yesterday taking care of that, along with other finishing touches," Chuck explained. "An electronic air ionizer does a great job of removing odors, *any* odors. And, of course, first we vacuumed up the dust with a heavily-filtered machine that did not allow any particles to return to the air."

"And these are the original tiles," Dave pointed out. "They don't look new because they *aren't* new."

"But, where's the grow room?" Robert asked.

"You can't get to it from here," Chuck replied. "Let's all move into the master bath."

With Dave leading the way, the four of them trooped into the hallway, through the master bedroom, and crowded around the tiny master bath. Chuck and Dave stood back to allow Faye and Robert to enter.

This room, too, held no smell of construction. It looked as if it had been built as they saw it: Toilet, small vanity, and a shower that seemed to occupy the same space that her tub had previously held. There was a shower caddy, a rubber-coated wire rack that looked as if she had owned it for years—she hadn't, but its corners were beginning to show a bit of rust; its shelves contained her shampoo, conditioner, and other toiletries she had previously kept on the rim of the bathtub. When she looked, she found subtle deposits of rust on the tiles matching the rust on the corners of the wire rack. It almost convinced *her* that she had been using the rack and the shower since moving in.

But...

"Where's the grow room?" she asked. She inspected the rest of the shower stall. The tiles seemed to be the original ones, looking for all the world as if they had never been touched, even though she knew that more of the wall was tiled now than previously. There was no door that she could see, no knobs, no cracks. Of course, she wasn't certain where to look; she had made a point of leaving the work to the boys and avoiding all the plaster and dust and noise and smell that had been a part of the reconstruction.

Chuck, grinning like a Liberace who'd just been given a piano with 89 keys, squeezed past the lovers and stepped into the shower stall. He grasped the washcloth hanger on the built-in, porcelain soap dish, gave it a slight twist, and gently pulled. Silently and smoothly, a large section of the tiled wall opened like a door, revealing a space in which stood a gleaming aluminum, refrigerator-sized cabinet.

Faye's eyes opened wide and Robert smiled. "What is that?" Faye asked.

"It's my gift to you," Robert replied excitedly. He opened the doors on the device like a game show host displaying the big prize. "It's terrific; it's all self-contained. It'll flower six plants in the upper chamber and start another twelve from seed or cuttings in the lower. That gives you a continuous supply of our favorite herb."

"Wow!" Faye kissed Robert, then looked with concern. "It must have cost a fortune."

"You'll get, maybe, seven harvests a year. That marijuana will help a lot of sick people—and that makes it a good investment."

"I hope I'll be worthy of this," Faye confessed. "I've always had a brown thumb…"

"This amazing appliance has carbon dioxide injection and high spectrum lighting which will guarantee a healthy yield. All the controls are fully automated. All you have to do is occasionally open the doors and check on the babies."

"Tell her about the heat transfer," Dave urged, nudging his partner.

"Well," Chuck began, "you know, what you intend to grow is still illegal. And the government—"

"—purchased by the pharmaceutical giants—" Dave interjected.

"—sometimes goes to ridiculous lengths to enforce the anti-marijuana laws. So, hiding the grow room from prying eyes isn't enough. We need to make sure that the infra-red heat signature is also invisible from outside the house."

"Infra-red heat signature?" Faye thought this was beginning to sound like an episode of *Star Trek*.

"The DEA has specially-equipped airplanes and helicopters," Robert explained. "They have sensors that can examine houses for hot spots, such as a grow room with all the lamps burning might have. If they spot one, they can notify the police to come and investigate more closely. The hot spot may turn out to be from someone growing orchids. But if the police can't find something that explains the hot spot, they'll take the house apart to find out why."

"Oh, my!" Faye breathed in dismay.

"Not to worry, though," Dave assured her. "Tell her, Chuck."

Chuck grinned. "Your house, m'dear, will not have any hot spots."

"The heat from the grow lamps is distributed by baffles so that it heats the roof evenly," Dave said, unable to leave the explanation to his partner.

"The end result," Chuck continued, "is that your house as a whole will appear to be maybe one degree, maybe only half a degree, warmer than it really is—and it will not appear to have any hot spots other than the usual ones over the stove and hot water heaters."

"And this is a very efficient unit. Your electric bill won't be any more than if you started watching TV an extra two hours a day," Dave added.

"Then there's the air," Chuck said. "Marijuana plants *smell*."

"I like the smell!" Faye protested.

"That's not the point," Chuck said easily. "If the smell gets out of the house, or even *in* the house when you have visitors who aren't savvy to what you're up to, it can be a giveaway. So the grow room vent passes through a HEPA filter that captures all particles and cleans most odors and impurities from the air *before* it goes out of the house—"

Dave interrupted excitedly, "And the ventilation creates a negative air pressure in the grow room, so that when the door is open, air travels from the rest of the house into the room, instead of allowing the scent of the plants to travel out of the room into your house."

"So," Dave concluded, "all that's left is for you to get some potting soil and some seeds."

"I suggest, just for paranoia's sake, that you buy a few small bags of potting soil from several different stores—and be sure and pay cash for them, and destroy the receipts."

"Destroy the receipts?"

"Don't throw them out!" Dave warned. "It's not likely that your trash is being searched, but the smart thing is to anticipate every possible security leak and plug it before it happens."

"I feel like a spy," Faye said, smiling wanly.

"You're a revolutionary," Robert pointed out. "That can be even more dangerous. But it doesn't have to be dangerous at all if you keep your wits about you. And you have a lot of people on your side to help and advise."

Faye took the doctor's hand and gave it a squeeze. "Robert, Chuck, Dave," she said, "I don't know how to thank you. But I do say thank you. And you're invited to celebrate when we sample the first harvest!"

No Through Trucks

By noon, Chuck and Dave had gone and Robert, too, had left a bit later. Faye spent a little time on the Internet, and then Marian arrived, as planned, to take her to lunch. Faye showed her the completed grow room and Robert's gift. Marian offered to take Faye on a "Quest for Soil," as she called it. They made stops at the Glendale K-Mart and Target before stopping for lunch, both buying a bag of potting soil at each stop—and paying cash, as Chuck had advised. Then they hit three hardware stores with garden departments.

"Do I really need *this* much soil?" Faye asked as they loaded the last bag into the spacious trunk of Marian's car.

"Shit, no," Marian admitted. "Most of it is for Marvin. He asked me to pick it up for him. You don't mind stopping by Marvin's before I drop you off, do you, darling?"

"Of course not," Faye agreed. "I want to ask him about the odd call I got yesterday."

"Odd call?"

"About the web site. Hold on till we get there, so I only have to explain it once."

They turned right off Bell onto a street marked "No Through Trucks" and then, a quarter mile later, turned again onto the side street that dead-ended at Marvin's hermitage. They each took two bags; Marvin opened the door for them as they approached, his eyes blinking in the unaccustomed sunlight.

"Whoa," he said in lieu of a greeting, "Guess summer's over. It's fuckin' *cool* out here."

"It's December, Marvin," Marian stated flatly. "And it's not *that* cool, just in the high sixties. You've *got* to get out more!"

"Yeah, yeah," Marvin grumbled. "Here, put 'em here," he said, pointing to a cluttered tabletop. "Yeah, just on top o' the papers," he added. "I'll get to 'em later."

As she placed the bags of soil next to the ones Marian had carried, Faye told Marvin about the threatening call she had received from the company that wanted to buy the web site. "Do I have an overactive imagination? Or would someone want this site so much they would harm me to get it? And, if so, *why?*", she asked in conclusion.

"Well, the *why* is obvious," Marvin said. "The main reason to buy a website is to shut it down. Your site is a political one and so someone you've offended wants it stopped. Who did you talk to?"

"The first person who called was a woman, Donna something. But the guy yesterday had an odd name. It was Malcolm...uh, Sketaris, something like that. No," Faye corrected herself, "*exactly* like that. Malcolm Sketaris. Did you ever hear of him?"

"Don't think so," Marvin replied. "Do you remember the company name?"

"I do," Faye said, thankful that her years of working at Edwin's garage had taught her to commit such things to memory. "It was an odd name—Global Virtual Properties."

"Hmm," Marvin grunted. "Not so odd considering they wanna buy a web site. 'Virtual' means real but not physical. A web site is a real place that people can go to, but it doesn't exist in any country or on any map. It's real but it ain't, dig?"

"Virtual," Faye echoed.

"You're catchin' on, kid! Now, let's see what we can find on 'em." He led the way into his computer room, sat, and spent a few moments in the kind of silence that was punctuated by grunts, half-muttered curses, and furious typing. Finally, he said, "Well, damned interesting. They aren't on the web at all."

"Maybe we can find them in the Yellow Pages," Marian suggested helpfully.

"Naw," Marvin scoffed. "You don't get it. They're supposed to be a company that buys web sites. There's no way they wouldn't have a site of their own. If they don't, they ain't real, that's all there is to it."

"How about Sketaris? Can you find anything on him, or is he made up, too?"

Another minute or two of typing and reading, while Faye and Marian looked over his shoulders, and then the information specialist swore. "Fuck! Whaddya know!"

"What?" Faye and Marian asked in unison.

"Sketaris is listed. Or, someone with his name is. He's a major stockholder in a company listed as GVP, the initials of 'Global Virtual Properties'. So the company is real, even though they can't really be in the business they say they are."

"Oh." Faye considered this. "So...are we glad or not?"

Marvin ran his finger down the screen, which was displaying a list of names. "These are the other stockholders. Recognize this one?"

Faye peered more closely at the monitor. "Oh, my!"

Marian leaned closer, saying, "Who? Who is it?"

Faye added her pointed finger to Marvin's, making two darts aimed at the screen. When she spotted the name, she inhaled sharply. "What do you know?" she exhaled.

The name on the screen was that of Selma Graves, Faye's boss at Representative Meany's campaign headquarters.

"I'll see what else I can find," Marvin promised. "With a little stalker hacking, I can get his address, medical prescription list, and high school grade point average. Check with me tomorrow." And he turned to work, effectively ignoring the two women.

Marian smiled at Faye and jerked her head toward the door. Faye followed her out of the room. "He'll be at it for hours, now," she whispered to the younger woman as they traversed the cluttered hallway. "There's no point in staying; he won't even know we're here."

They left quietly, Marian making sure the door locked behind her, and got into the car. Marian started the engine, which quietly propelled them onto the street that aimed itself at Marvin's house. "It'll only take a few minutes to get your garden started. First, we pour some of this soil into your pots."

"What about the seeds?" Faye asked excitedly. "Too bad we can't pick them up at a nursery."

"Not to worry, darling," Marian assured her. "I've got all the seeds you need in that coffee can under your seat. I've been saving them for you since we met."

"Really? How did you know I would need them?" Faye asked, as they reached the end of the street. Marian stopped at the stop sign, and turned on her left blinker as a large gasoline truck turned from the larger thoroughfare onto the street that terminated in Marvin's *cul de sac*.

"That's odd," Marian said in a puzzled tone.

"Well, that's what I think," Faye insisted. "After all, you didn't even get me high until Thanksgiving—"

"That's not what I mean," Marian interrupted. "Trucks are not allowed to drive through this neighborhood. There's a sign saying so out on Bell Road."

"Maybe he missed it," Faye suggested, turning to look at the vehicle as it accelerated past them.

"No, those drivers face a big fine if they drive into a neighborhood. And he can't be making a delivery; there are no gas stations in here. And no room to turn around, either…"

The two women twisted around to watch through the Torino's rear window as the truck receded. It seemed to be accelerating.

"Oh, my God," Marian said, shaking her head helplessly. She made a screeching U-turn.

The truck didn't slow, stop or turn. It kept going straight at Marvin's front door, and crashed right through it, the shiny tank extending beyond the porch, dripping. Marian jammed on the brakes, throwing Faye against her shoulder harness. Then, almost in slow motion, a flare of white and yellow blew from around the truck, followed almost instantly by a deafening roar and a shock wave that shook the car violently enough to slam Faye's head back against the headrest. Before their eyes, Marvin's house was completely engulfed in flame, black smoke erupting from every window like the demons of hell escaping through the mouth of a volcano. As they stared, the house exploded in a shower of sparks and debris that floated, confetti-like, on the cool December air.

The women sat motionless. Faye's hand was on the door handle but seemed unable to move it. "He's gone, darling," Marian said, softly, and began to turn around again.

"But—but—" Faye couldn't believe it. Her mind, her *heart* rejected what her eyes saw plainly not one hundred yards in front of her.

Marian took her right hand from the steering wheel and clutched Faye's left. "It's over, Faye. There's no reason for us to stay here." She guided the vehicle back again onto the road that would take them to Faye's.

As Marian drove, Faye stared at her friend in shock and horror. Marian was driving with emotionless determination. Yet, Faye could see that moisture was gathering in her eyes; and as they turned out onto Bell Road, where they could hear the siren of an approaching fire truck, they both began to cry.

Perception

The Fifth Board

They said nothing during the ride to Faye's home. Marian was grim and Faye felt as if the breath had been permanently knocked out of her. When they arrived, Faye got out and, to her surprise, so did Marian. "I'm coming in," she stated.

"Of course," Faye agreed.

Inside, it was cool, a little too cool to sit quietly. Faye turned on the central heating, something she hadn't done since moving in. But there was a chill now that seemed to seep into her bones. The house seemed dark, after stepping in from the bright day outside; but Faye didn't turn on any lights. Somehow it felt safer to sit in semi-darkness.

Marian sat quietly in the overstuffed chair that was next to the sofa. Faye began to make coffee, but thought better of it and prepared two cups of chamomile tea, knowing that would tend to calm them.

They sat, sipping in silence. *Poor dear,* Faye thought. She didn't know exactly how long Marian and Marvin had been friends, but she knew it was a long time and that they held each other in high regard. *How this must pain her,* Faye thought. Faye didn't want to give in again to the tears she felt pushing out from inside her. As long as Marian needed her support, she was determined to be strong for her.

Minutes passed. Fifteen minutes. Thirty. Faye watched them go by on the big, captain's clock she had inherited from her uncle.

Finally, Marian spoke. "Well, he always said, it isn't paranoia if they're really out to get you."

She placed her teacup on the side table and rose. "Thanks for giving me a chance to calm down," she said, and began to leave.

"Wait a minute!" Faye cried. "You can't leave now! You're— you're—" Faye broke off, unable to complete her thought. "You need to cry! You need to grieve! Your friend is—" And then, Faye broke down into the sobs she'd known were coming.

Marian put her arms around Faye and hugged her. "I'll stay." She quietly guided Faye back to the sofa. She took a joint from her purse, lit it, took a toke, then handed it to Faye, who accepted it automatically and drew in the sweet and pungent smoke.

"I wasn't going to do this," she told Marian. "I've learned not to drown my sorrows. *You* taught me that."

"This isn't alcohol, darling," the older woman said softly. "It will help you focus, and I have to explain something to you." Each woman took another hit, and a third. By then, Faye felt the buzz. The pain of Marvin's death was *not* masked, as it would have been with alcohol. And she did feel focused and would be able to listen to one of Marian's lectures without bursting into tears.

"We've never spoken of your religious beliefs," Marian began. Faye shook her head. "I know you were Catholic," the older woman continued, "and I know you don't go to church on Sundays, but other than that—"

"I left the Church a long time ago," Faye interrupted. "A few years after I was married, I went to our priest to explain how cruel and small-minded Edwin was, and how I wanted out of my marriage. He told me that God had married us, and neither Edwin nor I could ever break that bond. He advised me to go home and be a 'good wife'." Faye laughed, bitterly. "I followed his advice, but I never went back to church."

Marian nodded. "Now, you know from Marvin's book how all the major corporations are interlinked, how there isn't any real competition at the highest levels, and how most of what we've been taught is a lie designed to keep us enriching the military-industrial complex at the expense of our own enrichment or development..."

Faye nodded guiltily. She had not, in fact, ever opened Marvin's book. It was sitting on a shelf in the living room bookcase where she had placed it the day he signed and gave it to her. Perhaps, if she'd read it then, she'd have taken his concerns for his own welfare more seriously. But for now, she simply agreed with Marian, confident that her take on the book's contents was accurate.

But she *would* read the book.

"Well, the organized religions are *part* of that lie," Marian continued. "It's not that there's no God; there *is*. But God is not a *he* or a *she*; and God does *not* have a set of rules you must follow, nor a hell for you to be punished in if you don't follow them. All that is rubbish, designed with no purpose in mind but to keep you attending a church and shelling out money to assuage the guilt that builds up when you break the impossible-to-follow rules the religion tries to foist upon you." Marian's voice had taken on some emotion, at last. It became clear to Faye that her friend had been suppressing her feelings regarding Marvin, and only now, on a different subject, would she allow them to escape.

Faye was puzzled. "But, why would they lie?"

"Because the Establishment *can not tolerate* the thought of people who do not need to go to a priest or minister for religious advice. Religion makes it easy to control people, the way your priest convinced you to stay with a man who was unworthy of you. And what's the biggest fear they use to control us?"

Faye shook her head.

"Fear of death, darling. Take that away, and we become a population that can accept and exercise responsibility for ourselves!"

Faye was amazed. "You don't fear death?" She sighed. "You're a lot braver than I am, Marian."

"Bravery has nothing to do with it," Marian said, dismissively. "Once a person has had a near-death experience, or an out-of-body experience, it's impossible to accept the bullshit presented as 'Truth' by the churches."

Faye took another hit of the joint, and, trying to hold her breath, asked, "*You* had a near-death experience?"

Marian nodded. "A long time ago. It seems like a different life," she added, smiling. "I don't think I ever mentioned my son, Danny, to you."

"I didn't realize you'd ever been married," Faye confessed.

"I wasn't. But I had a son. I was just 18 when he was born. Oh, Faye—he was such a wonderful baby! So quiet, yet alert. So *centered*. And so beautiful! People who saw him were filled with wonder.

"I lived just outside Washington, D.C., and had always been interested in politics. I knew there was something fishy about the wars in Europe. So, when FDR ran on a promise to keep the United States from becoming involved in those wars, I supported him. Just like you supported Meany. I worked for FDR's election, canvassing, raising donations, putting up posters. I was so good they sent me around the country organizing groups. I met him, and I was crazy about Eleanor. And when Franklin was elected, I was so proud and happy! I truly believed he would end the Depression.

"But then, strange things started happening. I had a friend who worked at a printing company in the District. He gave me a call one day, since he knew I had contacts in the White House. He wanted to know why a huge order for military ID tags had come in. If we weren't going to war, why were we going to build up the Army? This was late in 1940 and there was no reason to imagine that we'd be fighting anyone.

"A few months later, more rumors starting flying around the capital. Apparently, several companies had gotten orders for thousands and thousands of leather body bags. Obviously, someone was expecting a war or an attack or something.

"Finally, in November of 1941, a friend in the Red Cross, stationed in Hawaii, wrote me a note saying that they had just received a *huge* shipment of bandages, morphine, and other material that suggested an attack was coming. And, of course, four weeks later, one did."

"You're saying that Pearl Harbor *wasn't* a surprise attack? I never heard of that!" Faye interjected.

"We've already discussed why the newspapers are not good sources of information," Marian reminded her, sharply. "It was as true then as now."

She took a hit of the joint and returned it to its resting place in the ashtray on the coffee table. "Anyway, you're right—the newspapers were filled with the horror of the attack, and how the Japanese had killed innocent people in their crazed desire to conquer the world. People started demanding, or the papers *said* they did, war. And, because the Pearl Harbor attack came shortly after Germany and Japan had signed an agreement that if either were attacked, it was the same as attacking the other, we were now at war with Germany, too."

"You're saying the attack on Pearl Harbor was planned—*allowed*?"

"I'm not the only one. A Joint Session of Congress in 1945 came to the same conclusion. Only by then, FDR was dead. And the newspapers, rather than "weaken the Presidency," never publicized the Joint Session's conclusions." Marian laughed bitterly. "The Presidency *should* be weakened! The framers of the Constitution never intended that the President should be able to lead his people into a war they didn't want, by allowing or even provoking attacks on our home soil. Yet, that's just what FDR did."

"About your near-death experience...?" Faye prompted.

"Oh, yes," Marian smiled. "I do go on, don't I?"

"That's all right."

"Well, Danny, my son, was 18 in 1942 and, of course, he joined the Army. Oh, I tried to talk him out of it. I told him of all the information and rumors I'd heard, and how the war seemed to be a scam. But he was convinced Hitler had to be stopped." Marian shook her head. "I was trying to fight an *entire* culture. The newspapers, the radio, all his friends...even the *songs* told a consistent story."

"Consistent with everything...but the facts?" Faye suggested.

"Exactly," Marian agreed. "So Danny went. And fought. And died in France." Marian's voice didn't break, but she looked like she thought it might.

"I was devastated. All the war widows and mothers were supposed to be well behaved at funerals. It was supposed to be our contribution to the fight for democracy. But I wasn't. I screamed and cried and blamed Danny's death on Roosevelt. I blurted out what I knew. The others there must have thought I was crazy. Certainly, I didn't convince anyone. The military officers took me to an Army hospital and gave me an injection. 'To calm me down,' they said. But it nearly killed me."

Faye listened intently, scarcely breathing.

"I stopped breathing, and they said my heart stopped. Everything went black. And then, I swear, I found myself sitting in something that seemed like a train station. And I was the only one there. Except, then someone came in—and it was Danny!"

Faye blinked. *An hallucination?* she wondered.

"He told me not to cry, not to feel bad, that it was all part of some plan. His life's plan, I mean. And mine. And that his death was intended to motivate me to live the life I was meant to live. And that someone would come to me shortly who would show me the way."

"He said all that?" Faye breathed.

"That was crazy talk for 1943, of course. I had no idea what he was talking about. The New Age spiritual movement was still decades away. But he seemed to be sure of what he was talking about. And he seemed so real, and alive! My grief eased, as he had intended. We spoke a few minutes more, then he told me he had to leave. Suddenly, everything went black again, and I took a huge breath and regained consciousness. Although," she added, "I felt *less* conscious awake, than I had been in that train station. Seeing Danny like that, I realized he wasn't *really* dead, not relative to eternity. And if *he* wasn't, then *no one* is."

Marian shrugged and smiled, her face radiant. "I no longer grieve for anyone who's passed over. I know I'll see them again, eventually."

Faye licked her lips. "How do you know it was really him?" Faye asked. "Perhaps you just wanted to see him so badly that—"

Marian waved her arm to silence her friend and sighed. "They say that the best jailors are the other prisoners. By your own admission, you haven't studied these phenomena before, yet you feel qualified to tell me, who actually *had* the experience, that it was probably my imagination. And where did *you* get that idea? From dozens of talk shows, movies, and TV shows that trivialize these experiences that millions of people have, by either dismissing them as imagination, as you just did, or making them into science fiction."

Faye held her ground. "Still, it's a reasonable question," she insisted.

"Okay, I'll tell you how I know," Marian replied evenly. "In the train station, the last thing Danny told me—very clearly—was, 'Look under the fifth board beneath my bed.' I remembered that and when I got home from the hospital I did that. I moved his bed, and counted the floorboards from the wall. The fifth board was loose; I'd never known that. I removed it, and found Danny's journals, kept since he was twelve years old. *I never knew they were there.* I didn't even know they existed. Danny had never told *anyone* about them! I would never have found them if Danny hadn't told me where they were. So, tell me, Miss Rational: If I made Danny's ghost up, how could it give me information I didn't possess?"

Faye paused, stunned. "I can't answer that."

"Yes, you can," Marian insisted. "You can admit that what *seemed* to happen, is what happened. I spoke with Danny after his death. And, when you do admit it, you'll do what I had to do: Reject *everything* I had learned from the accepted truths, so that I could be open to *real* Truth."

An E-mail From Tonga

Monday, December 15, 1997

Faye didn't do a thing but read the rest of Saturday or Sunday. She concentrated on keeping herself calm. It wasn't easy. The word spread quickly, of course; Robert called and offered to keep her company but she asked him to please understand that she needed to be alone. She was grateful that he seemed to understand. And, perhaps he spread *that* word because there were no other calls.

Faye wasn't overcome with grief, although grief was indeed a part of what she was feeling. But she was also feeling anger, and fear for herself and Marian. It seemed likely that the "accident" they had witnessed, and nearly fallen victim to, themselves—by less than a minute! —was, indeed, the murder of their friend. And why? Because he had a videotape proving that Meany owned a marijuana farm in Mexico? She had far more incriminating evidence in a box in her living room. The difference was that she hadn't called the TV networks to tell them about it.

But Marvin hadn't just called; he'd sent copies of the tape. While copies probably didn't constitute proof as damning as the original, certainly it was good enough for TV news. No, Faye thought, it didn't make sense. There must have been something *else* that Marvin possessed, information, perhaps, that "they" needed destroyed.

And so, she sat curled up with Marvin's book *Trust Me.*

She tried reading both straight and stoned. She could see where being stoned helped her concentrate on the book but here, at home, with no distractions, it didn't seem to make a lot of difference either way. And she became so lost in the book that, when the effects of the joint wore off, she didn't bother to light another one.

Marvin was a good writer. No — *had been* a good writer. No — a *great* writer. He had a way of bringing history alive in a way that no textbook ever had. He described various historical events of the twentieth century, events with which she was vaguely familiar. But he provided the *background* for those events, and brought in names of individuals and corporations that were repeated over and over, and implicated by presence, or financing, or motivation, to be the cause of those events.

The dichotomy between the versions of events as she had been taught in school or that had been reported by the papers, and the underlying story as presented by Marvin, was revealing...and chilling.

She knew, as "everyone" did, that World War I had been sparked by the assassination of Archduke Ferdinand. She remembered, vaguely, that a "lone gunman" had killed the archduke, but because tempers in Europe were ready to flare anyway, the death had triggered the bloody war that followed.

Marvin provided proof that there had been not one, but at least six, gunmen and that the archduke's chauffer was involved. The chauffer left the normal route; five gunmen had been unable to score a direct hit. Finally, at the position of the last gunman, the chauffer backed up and *re-crossed* the position several times, until the Archduke was finally killed!

Of course, Marvin's "proof" was in the form of a lengthy bibliography. He hadn't, personally, been present at the event but others were, and they had published, in the form of memoirs, interviews, and so on, a cohesive description of the event that disproved the "official" version.

And there were dozens of other, damning, revelations: The American corporations and businessmen that had financed Hitler; the suppression of films showing the presence of gunmen on the grassy knoll in Dallas in 1963; the fabrication of the Gulf of Tonkin attack that Lyndon Johnson used to justify an enormous escalation of the conflict in Viet Nam.

Faye booted her computer, intending to look up the bibliographic references. Her "home page," which Internet Explorer opened automatically whenever it was started, failed to load. An error page showed up, instead. That jolted her; it was the home page of *saysomethingshirts.com*, her and Marian's web site. Suddenly, she realized *why*. Marvin had been hosting the web site *on a computer in his house*. His house, which no longer existed. The computer no longer existed, either. Horrified, Faye suddenly knew with certainty why Marvin had been killed.

It had been to silence the web site being hosted in his home.

Faye cradled her head in her hands.

Her chest heaved, her stomach churned and she cried.

Eventually, she calmed down.

And then, biting her lip, she began a search of offshore web site hosting companies.

There were dozens of them, most of them far less expensive than hosts located in the United States. She chose one located in the island republic of Tonga, mostly because it was as remote and untouchable a place as she could imagine. Signing up was all done on line. She gave her credit card number and provided some information, including the domain name *saysomethingshirts.com* and codes with which Marvin had supplied her. She returned to

Marvin's book. Within an hour, she had received an e-mail from TongaHost with instructions for uploading her site. She did so from her backup copy of the site. She received another e-mail thanking her for her patronage and advising that it would be a matter of 48 hours before the domain would be completely transferred and requests for *saysomethingshirts.com* would be directed to the new host.

Faye sat back in her chair. If this was, indeed, the reason for Marvin's murder, the perpetrators were going to be in for a shock.

The Connection

"Please connect me with Detective Grant Taylor," Faye said into the phone. The person who had answered asked her to wait.

"Taylor," came the masculine voice after a few seconds.

"Grant, it's Faye McRae," she identified herself.

"Faye, how are you?" he asked, obviously happy to hear from her.

"I'm all right," she replied, "but I'm shocked at Marvin Cohen's death."

"Oh!" There was a pause. "You knew him?"

"Yes," she admitted. "In fact, I was visiting him seconds before the gasoline truck crashed into his house." Faye had decided to come clean with her policeman friend. She would leave Marian out of the story, if possible. But she needed information and the best way to get it seemed to be cooperation. "Do you think you might have a chance to come by and talk with me about it?" There was no point in having her tale taped by the police department telephone system.

Within the hour Faye's doorbell rang. She peeked out the front window and, seeing Grant, unlocked the deadbolt and opened the door. "Please come in," she smiled. "And sit down. Would you like some herbal tea?"

The detective stared at her. "My God, Mrs. McRae—you look *wonderful!* I can't believe how you've changed since the last time I saw you!"

"I've really turned my life around," she admitted happily. "I've had a lot of help from friends, especially one in particular."

She brought him a cup of steaming Orange Zinger tea and sat across from him. "Marvin was murdered," she stated in a matter-of-fact tone. "I think it was the same people responsible for Mickey Timmons' death."

Grant turned his palms upwards. "It seems to have been an accident," he said, gently. "The kid driving the truck hadn't been doing it long. He got confused about where he was, and accidentally stepped on the accelerator instead of the brake."

"I saw the truck," Faye stated. "I saw the driver's face. He didn't look confused, just...calm. Intent. And the truck began to accelerate from the time it turned the corner until it hit the house—that was no accidental mistaking of pedals."

"Why didn't you report it right away?"

Faye sighed. "I was in shock. I had just been in the house, myself. If it had taken me a minute more to leave, I'd have been killed, too."

Grant nodded understandingly. "What makes you think there's a connection to the Timmons murder?"

"You know I believe Mickey Timmons was murdered by Carvel Meany, or at least by people working for him."

"This is dangerous territory, Mrs. McRae."

"Marvin was in possession of proof that Meany owns a marijuana farm in Mexico. He had let it be known that he had that proof." Faye had decided to withhold mention of the web site. It had already been featured on television; she had a few days before the people who wished to silence the web site would know they had failed.

"I don't see how you can connect the gasoline truck to Meany," Grant pointed out. "He owns distilleries, not refineries."

Faye sighed. She knew it would be difficult. "Who was driving the truck?" she asked. "Do you know, yet?"

"Oh, sure. Brian Worthington, lived in Peoria—"

Faye gasped. "No! Mother Michelle Worthington, father a recent suicide—?"

Grant stared. "Yes! Don't tell me you know *him*, too?"

"No, Faye said, her eyes wild. "I know his mother. And *there's* the connection. Brian's father worked for Meany's campaign, until his death."

Grant, who'd been holding his teacup, set it on the coffee table. "It's a bizarre coincidence," he agreed. "But what motivation could Brian Worthington have for killing Marvin Cohen? Do you think he was so incensed over this evidence you say Cohen had, that he would be willing to kill himself to destroy it?"

"No," Faye said, shaking her head. "I don't think Brian had any motivation at all."

Grant smiled patiently. "A basic premise of criminology is that three factors go into any murder. First, the murderer has to have the means to kill. Brian had the gasoline truck—a little extreme, but certainly an effective weapon. Second, he has to have the *opportunity* to use his weapon. Brian was in the neighborhood. But the third side of the triangle is *motivation*. If Brian didn't have the motivation to kill Cohen, why do it?"

Faye took Grant's left hand in hers. "You don't understand," she said. "Brian wasn't the murderer. He was the *weapon*."

Nonsense

Tuesday, December 16, 1997

There were a surprising number of people at Marvin's funeral, especially considering that the man had spent the last years of his life as a recluse. Of course, he had been a best-selling author; and a few of those present were reporters. Faye even recognized Audrey Flowers. But most of the mourners were typical retirees, obviously citizens of Sun City. The thing that struck Faye oddest about them was that they didn't seem to know each other. They gathered into groups of threes and fours, but there seemed to be no interaction among the groups. Faye mentioned it to Marian.

"Take a good look, darling," her friend advised. "You'll probably never see all the members of the Sun City Cannabis Club in one place again."

Faye inhaled sharply. "*That's* who these people are? Why don't they know each other?"

"For safety's sake," Marian explained. "We're organized along the lines of revolutionaries, as described by Karl Marx's ghostwriter in *The Communist Manifesto*. We form cells. Each member of a cell knows one member of another cell, and that's how we communicate. But it limits liability if a member gets caught. He or she can only reveal the identities of the members of their own cell, and one member of another."

"Then why are they all here?" Faye asked.

Marian sighed. "They all knew Marvin. It's not a perfect system. Most of them know Robert, too, and me, of course. But you'll note they are keeping their distance from me and Robert."

Marian gave the eulogy. It was short, *very* short, and to the point. "Marvin spent his life *doing*," she said. "He spent it investigating, and finding out things the powers-that-be didn't want him to know, and then making sure that forbidden knowledge was made available to the public. We can be true to his memory by encouraging others to read his book, to think, and to question. If we can effect real change in the corrupt way this country, this *world*, is run, his life's work will not have been in vain."

There were a few scattered *amens* as Marian left the podium, very few. The heat of the explosion and subsequent conflagration had been so intense the house and its contents had been reduced to dust. No identifiable remains had been found. Faye, who had been so traumatized at Edwin's funeral, was glad there was nothing to bury. All she had of Marvin were memories, which she would keep with her always.

Faye spotted Audrey Flowers whispering furiously into a handheld cassette recorder. Marian indicated she was ready to go, but Faye held up her hand. "Please, give me a moment," she requested. Determined, Faye walked to the anchorwoman. "I trust you remember me this time?" she interrupted drily.

Flowers did recognize her and blanched. "I got into so much trouble after running the story about your web site—!"

"Too bad," Faye remarked without sympathy. "Marvin got dead."

"You don't really believe he was murdered, do you?" the reporter asked in disbelief. "The police said it was an accident. The boy who was driving died, too, you know. His funeral is tomorrow."

"It was no accident. It's also no accident that you got into trouble for airing the story about my web site. The same people are responsible for both."

Flowers shook her head. "All these conspiracy theories—you're as crazy as Cohen and his friend that gave the eulogy."

"Have you *read* Marvin's book?"

"I don't have to read it to know it's nonsense!"

Faye stamped her foot in frustration. "*Listen* to yourself! How can you know *anything* if you don't look for yourself!"

"By trusting the word of those who know."

"And what if they *don't* know? What if they're lying for their own purposes? For wealth, or power? You're a news reporter. What *won't* people do for wealth or power?"

Flowers snorted. "Not much," she conceded.

"Read Marvin's book," Faye advised. "Just read it. Oh, and tell whoever it is you got into trouble with that killing Marvin did *not* kill the web site. I simply moved it to an offshore host. And there are mirror sites," Faye added, lying but thinking it would be a good idea, "several of them, and other people poised to maintain them if anything happens to me. So, the site is up for keeps! And it will go right on telling the truth about Carvel Meany!" She shouted that last part, knowing that people were watching and listening to her conversation with the newscaster. Some of them were rival reporters, and this might start them investigating whatever they now thought Flowers was on to.

What Kind Of World Would It Be?

A select few gathered at Faye's after the funeral: Faye, Marian, Robert, Dave, Chuck and Vera. Marian's would have been the natural place for them, but Faye specifically asked if she could host, as she wished to speak to them and Marian gave her blessing.

They sat at her kitchen table, drinking Ginko tea with honey and passing spliffs donated by Vera. Faye sat at the head of the table, a table that had probably never before had so many gathered around it. Marian sat to her right, an expression of amused pride on her face. Robert sat to her left, his face shining in adoration, his usual expression when gazing at her. Vera, to Robert's left, looked frightened. Faye knew the funeral had depressed her. People whose jobs expose them to death every day might be more saddened than most when it actually happens, Faye thought. Chuck and Dave sat holding hands, comforting each other.

"I've asked you here," Faye told them soberly, "because I need your help. You have the sharpest minds I know, and I need to work this out because I am probably in danger."

Marian and Robert nodded knowingly. The others displayed expressions of surprise and dismay.

Faye made sure they were all up to date on the Frank Timmons story: How he had tried to kill Meany, how she had talked him out of it. How his grandson was involved with drug runners, and probably Meany, too. How Robert had hypnotized Frank and revealed a hidden memory that suggested that he had been under some kind of mind control that had been enabled by his witnessing, or even being forced to perform, his grandson's murder.

"And now Marvin's been killed," Faye concluded. "Marian and I were there, and I saw the expression on the driver's face as his truck hurtled by us. He was *not* panicky or anything other than calm. I think *he* was under mind control, too."

"Mind control?" Chuck ventured. "Is that really possible? I thought it was just in movies, like *The Naked Gun*."

"That's what I'd like to discuss today. First, is there any evidence at all, real evidence, that mind control exists?"

"Marvin discussed it in his book," Marian remarked. "He believed it existed."

"I realize that. But is there any evidence that *we* actually know of? Robert, you perform hypnosis. What do you think?"

"Wait," Vera interrupted. "No one can be forced to do anything against their will under hypnosis. Everyone knows that!"

"What I'm hoping to do," Faye explained, "is to get past what 'everyone knows.' Marvin believed that most everything you read or see on the TV or hear on the radio is either an out-and-out lie, or a mistruth designed to control people. Okay, if that's so, then we have to start from first principles. What do *we* know? What truths can *we* derive from that?"

Robert spoke. "I know of one way that a person could certainly be goaded to commit, say, murder, using only hypnosis. But it would take time."

"Tell us," Marian prompted.

"Well, suppose I have a patient seeing me to quit smoking; and I put her under, and implant seemingly harmless memories that she won't resist. I tell her that she can remember knowing Bill Clinton as a boy. If I know her real history well enough, I can construct plausible scenarios for her to 'remember.' For example, if I know she used to go to Lake Pleasant as a girl, I could use that to construct a memory of her first meeting with young Bill Clinton."

"But what good would that do?" asked Dave.

"Well, that's just the first step. That, and giving her a post-hypnotic suggestion to return to me for another session in a week. When she comes back, I build on the false memories, adding more. I suggest that these memories have been repressed because of a trauma she endured, being raped by this boy at the lake. I suggest that she will start having nightmares in which these memories are re-lived as dreams."

There was dead silence at the table. Vera frowned, her expression tense. "You mean, she'll dream about being raped by a young Bill Clinton?"

"By the time I'm through with her, I can have her completely convinced that she was raped and tortured by Bill Clinton when she was a teenager. And that he is coming back to do it again."

Chuck scoffed uneasily, "So she'll kill the President? Puh-lease!"

"Not necessarily. I could also convince her that her butcher or TV cable man was Clinton in disguise, there for the sole purpose of killing her. With enough preparation, she'll believe it and might well be goaded into killing anyone."

"Shit." That from Chuck.

"But it would take many visits for that to happen," Vera prompted.

"Yes, it would. Besides, that's not really mind control," Robert assured her. "The subject would have very confused memories, and it wouldn't be hard to track the problem back to me."

Vera seemed relieved. "So, what you just described doesn't really happen."

"Probably not very often," Robert replied. "In my opinion it would be too easy to trace. It might be used for small-time vengeance, for example a therapist trying to do away with an annoying ex-wife. But multiple murders and assassinations are out of the question; FBI psychologists would find the connection between the murderer and the therapist almost immediately."

"But you said that isn't 'real' mind control," Faye prompted. "I take it that, in 'real' mind control, the controller cannot be traced?"

"In true mind control, the only way to the controlled part of the mind is through a keyword or, more frequently, an entire code sequence. The normal persona, the front alter, truly has *no knowledge* of being controlled or even of knowing the controller."

"Front alter?" Faye repeated. "Are you saying *altar*, like in church?"

"No, 'alter' with an 'e', as in 'alter-ego.' The *front* alter is the normal, waking self. The *back* alter may be a trained assassin or worse—and the front alter will know nothing of it."

"How can that be done?" Chuck asked. "Do you know?"

Robert sighed. "Only in a general way. There were articles in the medical journals, back in the fifties. You've heard of split personalities?"

"Like in The *Three Faces Of Eve?*" Dave asked.

"Right," Robert agreed.

"What are the three faces of Eve?" Vera questioned.

"A movie from the fifties," Robert explained.

"Not just *a* movie!" Dave protested. "Joanne Woodward won the 1957 Academy Award for her portrayal of a woman whose childhood abuse triggered multiple personality disorder."

"What a memory you've got!" Marian applauded.

"Oh, puh-*lease!*" Dave scoffed. "The Oscars are the gay man's World Series."

Chuck looked pained. "Talk about being mind controlled," he muttered.

Vera frowned. "But multiple personality disorder isn't for real. It's been proven to be caused by the therapists, themselves!"

The others looked at her, astonished. "Its real name is dissociative disorder. But there were no cases of it prior to 1980. That's when the first books on it were published."

"Vera is right," Robert affirmed. "There is certainly a controversy surrounding the whole thing. But, Vera, there were a *few* cases of it described as far back as the 1800s. There's no doubt that the frequency of DID, or Dissociative Identity Disorder, was exaggerated in the 1980s. Now there is a movement in the medical community that is actively trying to discredit every researcher into the phenomenon. Almost all the organizations dedicated to studying the phenomenon have actually closed and many of the directors and leading researchers have had their malpractice insurance cancelled. Some have even been arrested!"

"So, see! There's no such thing!" Vera shouted triumphantly.

"I'm not so sure," Robert said, shaking his head. "It seems to me very much like the same witch hunt that was mounted against researchers studying the medical benefits of marijuana. It's almost like someone is trying to *suppress* the study of DID."

"Who would do that?" asked Chuck, puzzled.

"I don't know," Robert admitted.

"Marvin believed it was the CIA," Marian pointed out. "Remember, it was supposedly the CIA that did the original experiments with mind control, which *creates* DID and exploits the extra personality, training it to kill on command."

Vera whistled, her little body agitated. "But those experiments were failures!" she insisted. "The CIA gave them up in the fifties."

"Says who?" challenged Dave.

"The CIA," Vera stated, without a trace of irony.

"But if," Marian proposed, carefully, "the experiments *had* succeeded, what would the CIA have said? Would they have announced that they could turn anyone into a killer without that person ever knowing it?"

"Of course not," Vera scoffed. "They would never have said anything at all."

"But the story *was* leaked. So they had to say *something*. Would they announce that the project was still active, or just lie and say the experiments had been discontinued?"

Vera was silent.

Chuck cleared his throat. "So," he said, "that brings us back to *how* it is done...how 'bout it, doc?"

"It's well described in the literature that was published before the suppression began. Basically, a person who is severely traumatized, usually as a child, isolates the memory of that trauma in the mind. The psychic wound seems to split the mind into fragments. Each fragment then develops on its own, without input or awareness of the other fragments."

Chuck shrugged. "So, what's the problem?"

"The problem is, the fragments don't usually develop *fully*. None of the personalities can become fully realized individuals; they have to be re-integrated into a single person." He added, "There have been a *few* cases of people who refused treatment, claiming that they were happy the way they were. That is, each of the personalities claimed it was happy. But that's a small minority of cases, having a condition that is already rare."

"So, where does mind control come in?" Faye asked.

"As I understand it, the trauma is introduced *intentionally*," Robert explained. "The victim is made to watch as an animal, especially a pet, or a baby or beloved family member is killed. Then, while the mind is split open, so to speak, the controllers step in and make suggestions, similar to hypnotic suggestions, that mold the creation of the new personality. The memory of the trauma, itself, is sealed away so that the victim can't remember it at all."

Vera sniffed. "Then why do the survivors of the Holocaust remember it?" she challenged. "Millions of them watched as family members were killed. Why do soldiers remember going to war?"

Robert shrugged. "I don't know. It's possible that the victims of the Holocaust *knew* something horrible was happening. Most of the survivors spent years in the concentration camps and for them to forget the deaths, they would have to suppress the memories of that whole period of their lives, not just a single episode. And soldiers don't go to war overnight, either. They spend weeks, months, training before they ever see battle. And, finally, the bottom line is that I *know some* people repress memories after experiencing a psychic trauma. It may be rare, and I may not know the details of what causes it, but it does happen."

Vera, frowning, shifted in her seat. "I still can't believe it," she said.

"Why not, darling?" Marian asked, gently.

Vera's distress was very near the surface, Faye could tell. Yet it was clear that Vera, herself, wasn't quite certain what the source of her discomfort was. "If it *was* true," she said, "don't you see how it would change the world? How awful it would be? No one would be safe! At any moment, your father or brother or husband could suddenly turn on you, without explanation or remorse. Do *you* want to live in a world like that? I don't!"

Robert cleared his throat, but said nothing. After a few uncomfortable moments, Dave said, "Vera, it seems to me that a weapon like this would only be used rarely for it to be valuable. And it would never be used against *you*. The only people in danger from it would be people who are politically active and inconvenient—"

"—like Marvin," Chuck supplied.

"And John F. Kennedy, apparently shot by some shmuck who had worked a short time for the CIA," Robert added.

"How about the son of Vice-President Bush's friend who tried to assassinate Ronald Reagan a few years ago," Marian added.

"I remember the assassination attempt," Chuck said. "But I didn't know the shooter knew Bush personally."

"When the Secret Service guys apprehended him, he had an invitation in his pocket to a party at the Bush's that same evening," Marian explained. "The Vice President denied knowing him, but it turned out his father was the largest single contributor to Bush's campaign, and the Bushes knew him very well. The kid is still in jail, and has never been able to explain *why* he wanted to kill the President."

"Why doesn't everyone know about this?" Vera wanted to know.

Marian shrugged. "It was reported, at first. Then the media shut up about it, too quickly, I thought."

"What would make them do that?" Vera asked.

Marian grinned. "I guess if you used to be head of the CIA, as Bush was, it isn't hard to convince people that you know too many of their secrets for them to ignore your wishes. Especially if you're a wealthy newspaper publisher or head of network news." She shivered. "I hate to think what would happen if he needed a favor from the Supreme Court!"

"How about Timothy McVeigh, the guy who blew up the Federal Building in Oklahoma?" Robert remarked. "Any chemist knows that the explosive power of the fertilizer in his rented truck wasn't enough to do that much damage, yet he confessed, and went to his trial without ever offering a convincing explanation of why he killed all those people. Now he awaits execution, and *still* has nothing to say?"

"Those were innocent victims!" Vera cried. "That's what I mean!"

"It's very sad," Marian offered, gently. "But the odds of you, personally, being a victim of one is vanishingly small. It's far more likely that you will die from a lightning strike!"

"Or the effects of tobacco," Robert remarked. "If you want to worry about being killed, consider that more than 4,000 people are killed *every month* in the United States alone, from the direct and indirect effects of cigarette smoke. Fewer people than that are killed *yearly* worldwide in terrorist actions. You're in a lot more danger from the tobacco industry than you are from a mind-controlled neighbor."

"Well, if mind control exists, you would never know it by talking to a mind-controlled person," Faye stated. "I did a little research on it on the web. Same as you, Robert, I was surprised how intense the denials I found, were. There are serious organizations in existence studying the medical effects of UFO abductions, telepathy, and the healing effects of crystals. So why would organizations studying the possibility of mind control suddenly be shut down? I can't think of any reason other than suppression.

"Someone—maybe someone with the power to blackmail a lot of people who are powerful in their own right, as you hinted, Marian— someone *really* didn't want word of their secret weapon to leak out."

"Which brings us back to you," Marian said. "Running the web site, you *are* a possible target. Mind control or not—Meany can't like that information being broadcast. It's one thing to have a hundred people revealing the location of his hypocrisy on their T-shirts...it's quite another to have a million reading about it on their computer screens. Darling, I think we'd better let the site stay down," she added regretfully.

"I will *not* shut it down," Faye stated firmly. "If you want to pull out, that's fine. But I will go on using it to announce the truth. Meany *can't* be that significant in the grand scheme of things. He's just a member of the House of Representatives, for heaven's sakes. I will *not* believe he controls an army of mind-controlled assassins."

Robert looked puzzled. "What, then?" he asked. "I thought this was all about Meany possibly killing Marvin because he was hosting the web site. That's what I got from you, when we talked earlier."

Faye shook her head. "That's what I thought, at first," she admitted. "But I remembered that Frank Timmons, who must have been mind-controlled, tried to *kill* Meany. No, I think Meany is in as much danger as I am, probably more."

"From whom, darling?" Marian asked.

Faye shook her head. "I wish I knew," she said. "All I know is that it's a woman."

"My money's on Selma Graves," Marian said.

"No," Faye disagreed. "Frank said he didn't know the voice, remember? He worked for Selma, same as me. So it can't be her. And there's another mystery," she continued.

"What's that?" Chuck asked.

"Why did Frank start to *remember?*"

Last Minute Shopping

Thursday, December 18, 1997

The mall, all two stories of it, was packed with the Christmas shoppers, both the east and west wings. Sun City didn't have a mall of its own but neighboring Glendale did, and today it seemed to be overflowing with the populations of Glendale, Peoria, Sun City, and Surprise. Or, at least, those who weren't working.

Why did I wait so long to shop? Faye wondered hopelessly. But she knew why. She wasn't in the habit of Christmas shopping. In her life with Edwin, there hadn't been many friends, and, for too many years, no other family. Edwin gave pistachios to his employees at the garage each year, a tin of them that came through the mail from some catalog. He sent a tin to Faye's uncle, too, overriding her wish to send her favorite relative something special.

And so, Christmas had slipped her mind until she realized that the big holiday was almost on top of her. She had discovered Christmas was just around the corner when Marian had invited her to attend a Winter solstice party on December 21.

"I don't celebrate Christmas, exactly," her friend had said, "but I do celebrate the season." The solstice party was going to be held, and that was when Faye had blushed furiously and stammered her acceptance. She had been barely aware it was even December.

She would find out from Robert what Marian meant by "celebrating the season." Apparently there would be a tree, and a turkey dinner, and presents—probably everything but a manger or the singing of "Silent Night."

And so, Faye was at the mall, just before the weekend, the last weekend before Christmas. She had at least *some* chance of finding gifts that hadn't been rejected already by a thousand shoppers before her.

The air was filled with the sound of Christmas music blaring from hidden speakers, competing with the din of shoppers. She found herself, at one point, navigating around a long queue of mothers with fidgety children. "What's this line for?" she asked one woman.

The woman stared at her as if she had two heads. "We're getting the kids' pictures. With Santa," she added. Faye looked past her, and saw an open area surrounded by a miniature Santa's Village. There was a sign in quaint script, which read, "Santa's Village." Below that, in more conventional lettering, were prices for having one's photo taken on Santa's lap.

The prices were, to Faye's mind, rather high. She was also somewhat nonplussed to see that the "village" was, in fact, arranged so that one couldn't get to see Santa until *after* one had paid the photographer.

Wistfully, she remembered her childhood, when she had been taken to some department store to see Santa Claus. There was no money involved, she was sure. Looking back, she realized that the store had undoubtedly paid some old man to put on the suit and put up with the children. They had done so, knowing Santa's presence would lure parents into the store who might otherwise have shopped elsewhere. So, it had been a commercial ruse, even then.

But not so blatant! she thought, and continued on her way.

The weather had gotten quite cool, relatively cold, in fact. She got Chuck and Dave matching alpaca sweaters, one in light blue for Chuck, and one in a soft green for Dave. They were on sale, two for $20. She smiled. *Two down, four to go.*

In a gourmet kitchen shop, she found a boxed collection of herbal teas she thought Bitsy might like. "We limit ourselves to $15 a present, no matter what," Robert had advised. But Faye was overcome with the Christmas spirit, and her love for him; she bought him a handsome men's toiletry kit in a leather case that sold for twice the permitted amount. *Three down, three to go.*

She paused at Radio Shack because she spotted one of Marian's T-shirts on a TV tuned to CNN. The commentator was saying, "...groups gathered today to demand an investigation into campaign election reform."

A man appeared on screen, saying, "Representative Meany says he's against marijuana, but he *grows* it! We need a more thorough investigation of people running for office!"

The anchorman reappeared. "When asked for proof of their claim, the group could only offer their T-shirts as evidence."

Faye smiled to herself. The program had intended to belittle the message on her shirts, but it would get at least a *few* people thinking. "There's no such thing as bad publicity," P. T. Barnum had said. Faye continued her shopping.

On her way to a shop where she thought she might find something for Frank, she slowed as she passed a toy store. Oh, how she remembered the dolls she had loved as a girl! But there were no baby dolls on display, at least, not near the door. Instead, there were boxes with clear plastic fronts stacked, each containing some sort of robotic thing. A man was demonstrating the unit for a crowd of onlookers. He took four small dolls wearing what looked like brightly-colored space suits, and put them together. Quickly, he folded arms and legs, and in what looked like a magic trick, the four dolls suddenly became one object—a large robot wielding some sort of ray gun.

"How much is that?" she asked of the man who gave the demonstration.

"Each Power Ranger is $11.95," he replied.

"And what do you call the small dolls?" she asked.

"Those *are* the Power Rangers," the man explained. "They morph into a Megazoid when you put them together."

"You mean you have to buy four Power Rangers in order to make a Megazoid?" Faye asked. "What can you do with the individual dolls?"

"Not much," the man admitted. "In the Power Rangers TV show, the characters always wind up saving the world by combining into the Megazoid. So that's what the kids want to do with them. Quite a racket, isn't it?" he added, confidentially. She left the toy store, bemused. Half the stack of boxes had been sold while she and the man talked.

She found an alligator wallet for Robert and a white tote bag at a leather goods store that would be perfect for Vera. She paid for the items and was just stepping out of the store when she nearly walked into Vera, herself.

Whoops! Thought Faye. There was no reason Vera would assume Faye had just purchased Vera's present, unless Faye gave herself away.

"Vera, dear!" she smiled, and hugged the woman. "What are *you* doing here?" *Well, there's a dumb question!* Faye instantly chided herself. What else would Vera be doing in a mall less than a week before Christmas, but Christmas shopping?

But Vera's expression was not one of Christmas cheer. Her eyes were bloodshot, but Faye could tell it was from crying, not toking;

tear tracks from her mascara wound their way along the wrinkles on her cheeks. She smiled to see Faye, but it was the smile of a woman with friendship on autopilot; there was no real joy in it.

Faye immediately took her arm and steered her towards the food court. "What is it, Vera?" she asked. "What's wrong?" She had to speak loudly to be heard over the noise of the crowd and the canned Christmas music but her words were still as confidential as those spoken in a confessional.

Vera just shook her head. "I need a drink," she said.

"You need a joint." Faye led the way to the exit. Soon, in relative quiet, the two women found themselves sitting on a cement bench that faced a small stage. A band would be playing later but, for now, they had the place to themselves.

So much so that Faye felt confident enough to locate the joint in her purse, take it out, and light it. She took a deep toke, then handed it to Vera. Vera hesitated.

"What's wrong?" Faye asked her.

Vera handed the joint back to Faye without partaking. "I'm so confused," she said. "I don't know what to do."

"Start at the beginning. What are you confused about?" Faye asked.

"Well, I've suffered from depression for a number of years," her friend confessed. "I used to take things like Paxil and Prozac for it, but they left me so fuzzy and listless I could never get anything done. And then my husband died, and I got really depressed."

Faye nodded sympathetically.

"Then I started going to Robert. He took me off everything else, and had me take vitamins and minerals and smoke marijuana. I was pretty nervous," she added, "but I knew that Arizona had voted in favor of medical marijuana, and Robert is a doctor, after all. He introduced me to Marian, she got me the pot, and I used it. I never smoked cigarettes before, so I mostly ate marijuana brownies."

"And you're explaining why you're crying your way through a mall at Christmas time, right?"

"Well, yes. You see, I stopped taking the pot a few days ago. And the depression's come back, as bad as ever. Worse, now that it's Christmas and I can't shop for Harry..." The tears started anew.

Faye put her arms around her friend and hugged. "Why did you stop using the marijuana?" she asked. "I mean, you're the nurse, not me—but aren't you going against your doctor's orders?"

Vera shook her head fearfully. "It was that meeting at your house, the one where you were talking about child abuse and sexual abuse and all that." Faye blinked. It took her a moment to realize that Vera had missed the entire point of the discussion that had occurred around her kitchen table.

"What about it?" Faye prompted.

"I was also starting to get bad dreams," she said. "Like Frank Timmons. Only, I never associated them with the M.J. They didn't start right away. And I didn't have them every night."

"What kind of bad dreams?" Faye asked.

"About...people. People I knew long, long ago. But the dreams weren't real! Those things never happened."

"Then why worry about them?" Faye asked.

Vera shuddered. "My father was a saint," she said, quietly. "He died when I was in my teens. He was the man I judged all other men by. He would never have raised a hand against me, or anyone else! And to dream of him..."

"What?"

Vera's lips made an angry red line across her face. "It doesn't matter," she snapped, "because it never happened. But I don't want dreams like that. So I've stopped using the M.J."

"Well," sighed Faye, "I think it's very important that you tell Robert. He needs to know, so he can try to find you some other medication. I mean, you can't start crying every time you go to the mall!" She stubbed out the joint on the bench and returned the unused portion to her purse.

"I'm okay now," Vera promised. She squeezed Faye's hand. "Thanks for being here."

Faye smiled back. "Now," she said, "I've got one more present to buy. And it's the hardest one."

Vera looked askance.

Faye grinned. "For Marian. It's very hard to guess what item won't trigger some sort of lecture on the injustice of this, that or the other thing!"

Vera laughed, and the sound was good to hear.

"Pardon me, ladies," a voice interrupted from behind them. Faye turned and found herself face-to-face with a police officer.

"Yes?" she asked, surprised at the sudden stab of guilt she felt. Surely he hadn't seen her smoking! Had he?

"Did you happen to notice any teenagers hanging around here?"

"No," replied Faye truthfully. "Why?"

The police officer frowned. "Can't you smell that?" he said. "Someone's been smoking pot out here. And, recently!"

Faye made a show of sniffing. "Oh," she said innocently. "I thought it was just some new perfume."

"Well, that perfume's gonna get some kids' ass in jail! I'll find 'em," he added over his shoulder, as he continued his search.

Faye and Vera stared at each other in disbelief for a moment, then burst into laughter.

Exhuming Buried Memories

That evening, Robert arrived at Faye's for their regular Thursday-night dinner. They had fallen into a comfortable pattern. She made him dinner on Mondays and Thursdays; he cooked for her on Tuesdays and Fridays. Wednesdays and Saturdays they ate out, and Sunday was reserved for each one's private time.

The fact that neither of them had bothered to specify this schedule warmed Faye. It had just happened, so easily and naturally that it seemed to Faye to prove they were meant to be together. Everything with Edwin had been a struggle, a conflict, a wrestling match.

This was just grand.

It was also nice that Robert was never late. At first, this surprised Faye because she knew the reputation doctors have, even in their own offices. She remembered well the hours she had spent waiting in her doctor's office back in San Diego. An appointment at one in the afternoon usually meant being seen sometime after three but woe to the patient who dared to *come in* late!

She had been amazed that, with Robert, she had always been seen promptly on time. From chatting with Vera, Faye knew that all of Robert's patients were treated the same way.

"How do you do it?" she asked him once.

He had explained that, first and foremost, many doctors were in the business for money. "Dr. Casey and Dr. Kildare are not the norm," he said. "That was part of our culture's indoctrination, as Marian would put it. The reality is, doctors double-book just like airlines do. And if no one cancels, which happens frequently these days because it's so hard to get in to see a doctor—because they *do* overbook—then the appointments run later and later. The doctor himself goes home late, because he couldn't bring himself to say no to the fee he'll get from that last patient."

Robert, on the other hand, had intentionally kept his patient list short. "Hell," he said, "I should be retired, anyway. But I never double-book, and if a patient doesn't show, I am grateful for a little unexpected nappy-time!"

Faye couldn't imagine Robert needing, or taking, a nap. He was as healthy and vital, in his way, as Marian was in hers...or, for that matter, Faye now was. Having experienced the improvement herself, in stages that she had worked very hard for, it was impossible for her to think of the process as magic. Yet, she knew the results would seem miraculous to anyone who had known her previously.

They spent minutes kissing at the front door. Another thing about Robert, he never, ever seemed rushed. He moved forward at a steady pace and accomplished a great deal simply by focusing on what he was doing. Faye wondered if he'd always been that way, or if his pot smoking enhanced an ability that would have otherwise been undeveloped.

When they separated, Faye smiled. "Chicken marsala, with string beans and rice pilaf," she said. "How does that sound?"

He smiled brightly. "You already have my heart," he whispered. "You don't have to reach it through my stomach. But—" he added, "keep trying!"

They went to the dining area, where the table was waiting with white brocade tablecloth, the "good" silver, and a single, flickering candle in a silver holder. Robert took his usual seat while Faye went to the kitchen and dished out their dinners. She tried to look as unhurried as Robert. It made her feel sexy and alluring.

When she returned with the meal, she served him first. "I'm worried about Vera," Faye confessed as she handed the man who wanted to marry her his plate.

"You, too?" Robert asked, accepting it. "This looks wonderful," he added. "Smells good, too." He smiled.

Faye smiled back, accepting the compliment. She placed her own plate on the table, and sat.

Robert's face shone in the candlelight. As he cut his chicken, he said, "Yeah, I'm concerned about Vera, too. I let her spend the morning Christmas shopping, and when she got back to the office, she looked as if she'd been crying."

"Did she tell you she's stopped smoking pot?"

Robert frowned, but carefully continued chewing and didn't speak until he'd swallowed. "That isn't good," he said. "She needs —well, that isn't good."

"She told me she has clinical depression, and that she was on antidepressants before you prescribed the marijuana."

The doctor relaxed. "Then you know how important it is for her to be treated. All I need is another suicide attempt among my patients!" As he ate the string beans, his expression became one of bliss. "Oh, my!" he cried. "What did you do to these?"

"I just stir fried them in olive oil with a hint of real butter," she replied, "and added a touch of basil."

"I'll have to remember that."

"Since I'm not Vera's doctor, I'm not bound by any rule of confidentiality," Faye said, "and I want to run something by you. You don't have to say a thing if you don't want to but Vera told me the reason she stopped using pot was that she had begun to have dreams. Disturbing dreams, like Frank did."

"I never heard of marijuana causing bad dreams," Robert interjected.

"Well, I'm starting to think it doesn't cause the dreams—but it may release repressed memories that come up, at first, as dreams."

Robert frowned. "You're thinking that Frank's dreaming about something he did under mind control?"

"And Vera hinted that *her* dreams were of some kind of abuse by her father, which she denied happening so vehemently that I couldn't help but think she was protesting too much."

"So, you think Vera might have been abused or molested as a child?"

"I suspect it. Poor dear. She's so tiny now, I can't even imagine how vulnerable she must have been as a young girl. But she calls her father a saint, and won't even consider the possibility that he might have ever harmed her."

"Hmmm."

Faye loved that their conversation flowed naturally, neither one having to compete to get a word in. Robert tried the rice pilaf, and groaned with satisfaction. Then he looked up from his plate and said, "Did you know Vera has a sister?"

"No," Faye replied. "I don't really know her that well."

"She does," Robert affirmed. "She lives right here in Sun City. And they haven't spoken in six years."

"My goodness!" Faye responded. "Why not?"

Robert lifted his eyebrows in frustration. "Her sister tried to get her to admit she'd been sexually molested by their father when they were children. Her sister remembers it quite clearly, but the shame was so great she never mentioned it until six years ago. Vera was horrified by the stories. She rejects them, and has refused to talk with Ellen ever since."

"So, it *is* true," Faye said, tapping her fingertips on the edge of her now-empty plate. "Smoking pot can bring up buried memories."

Robert nodded, but with reservations. "I would say it probably releases the inhibitions that keep the memories buried in the first place. And, once the memory is revealed, pot's tendency to keep the user focused probably helps the memory come more fully to the foreground, where it can be processed."

"How awful for the person with repressed trauma!" Faye cried.

"Not really," Robert corrected. "After all, repressed trauma can do all kinds of damage, to the mind *and* the body, while it's repressed. Only after it's freed can the sufferer begin to heal. *Any* treatment that releases repressed memories is unpleasant while experiencing it but the results are generally felt to be well worth it."

Faye frowned. "This, of course, brings us to the next logical conclusion."

"Conclusion to what?" Robert asked.

"If Vera suffered childhood trauma that she can't remember, is *she also* mind controlled? Might she suddenly try to murder one of us—namely, *me*?"

Wedding Bell Blues

Saturday, December 20, 1997

Marian and Faye met for breakfast two days later at their usual breakfast restaurant, one of the many places in Sun City offering meals at prices more appropriate for the 1950s than the 1990s. "Sun City residents simply won't pay more," Marian once explained. "And isn't it interesting that the restaurants seem able to turn a profit, anyway."

This morning, Marian was all smiles. "You look happy today," Faye observed. "How are the plans going for your solstice party? Is there anything I can do to help?"

"Nope," the older woman replied, "I'm going to help *you*. Today we are going to start planning your wedding."

"My wedding?" Faye responded, incredulously. "Are you kidding? My wedding won't be complicated enough to need planning. Come on, I'm not eighteen any more! I just figured we'd be off to a justice of the peace, that sort of thing."

"Well, darling, to begin with—no justice of the peace for you. As it happens, *I* am a legally ordained minister, and I'd love to perform the ceremony for you—unless, of course, you really *want* some stranger to do it."

"No, no—of course not! Though I had thought of having you be my matron of honor. Or maid. Or whatever."

"You will need at least two witnesses. Fortunately, you have plenty of friends here who'd be thrilled to stand up for you and Robert."

That was true, Faye thought, in amazement. Marian was her dear friend, her best friend, but certainly not her only friend. She felt close to Vera, and even more to Chuck and Dave, and Bitsy.

And Robert, of course, though he couldn't be a witness at his own wedding. She smiled. She hadn't had so many real friends at one time since high school.

They ordered breakfast—Faye requested a single egg and a fruit medley, with a glass of freshly squeezed orange juice—and Marian took out a stenographer's pad and a pen. "Now," she said, "where would you like the ceremony to be held?"

Faye blinked. She hadn't thought of it, none of it. She loved the *idea* of getting married, but the reality of it was terrifying. "Um..." She paused. "Wait a minute. Let's slow down, okay? I haven't even said yes yet!"

"You can rent space in a church, of course," Marian told her. "Or you can reserve a room at a restaurant. The advantage there is that no one has to leave to go to the reception."

"The reception?" Faye felt overwhelmed.

"Of course, darling. How many people will you invite?"

"I don't know. I only have a few friends..."

"I realize that, darling, but Robert is a professional man. He may want to invite family, or patients, or colleagues. What has he said about this?"

"Nothing," she confessed. "We've hardly talked about this at all."

Marian frowned. "Bad sign. Some guys string their poor ladies along for years."

"Robert wouldn't do that!"

"Of course not, darling. But you'd better think of a space that has plenty of room, just in case. And talk to him about it soon, darling. Most places where weddings are held are reserved months in advance. Though it's not so bad here in Sun City," Marian added thoughtfully. "No one here makes plans very far in advance— they're afraid they won't live long enough to see them through."

Faye laughed uneasily.

"You'll also have to decide how much you want to spend on each plate," the older woman continued.

"Plate?"

"My goodness!" Marian said, catching her breath. "Each meal, per person. The expense of feeding each person." She stared at Faye as if seeing her for the first time. "Didn't you plan your first wedding?"

Faye tried to remember. It seemed so long ago. "I guess not."

Marian's brow furrowed. "Well, who did? These things don't just happen, darling!"

"I—I guess my parents must have done it all. I don't even remember picking out a gown."

"Did you wear one?"

"Yeah, it was beautiful. But I don't remember picking it out. I don't even know how much it cost." She sighed. "I guess I'll have to buy a new gown. I didn't keep my old one."

Marian laughed. "Well, of course you wouldn't want to wear your old one! Obviously, your parents bought into the 'worthless daughter' thing if they spent a lot of money on your wedding."

"What do you mean?"

"Well, darling, you know...weddings aren't all about love; they're also about ownership. In our male-dominated society, young women are assumed to have no intrinsic worth. So the men have to be bribed into the marriage by the offering of many expensive wedding presents, and parents who imply their wealth, and their daughter's eventual inheritance, by throwing a big, expensive party."

Faye wasn't sure what to say. "I'm s-sure Edwin didn't feel he had to be bribed!" she stammered, as their breakfast arrived.

The waitress placed their plates—$4 a plate, Faye found herself estimating, wondering if there were such a thing as a breakfast reception—and, when she left, Marian continued. "Of course he didn't, darling. But these things go far beyond the individuals involved. Remember, if this was just about the two of you, you wouldn't bother at all. You'd just *be* together. A wedding is a public announcement of your commitment to each other. And, as such, it has to conform to the public's expectations of what that announcement should look like." Marian took a bite of her grapefruit. "Afterwards, you're expected to conform to the public's notion of what your commitment should look like, as well."

"I didn't really think about Robert knowing so many people," Faye said, hesitating. "When we're together, I'm always so focused on the moment. I guess I just enjoy being with him. I guess I hadn't thought about the...the whole *package*."

Marian took a sip of her juice. She swallowed. "Well, you know," she said, "you don't just marry a person. You marry their *life.*"

Faye's stomach fluttered.

She would be marrying into Robert's life. The same as she had married into Edwin's life. Robert's life was as different from Edwin's as it was possible to imagine. But Faye wasn't that certain she *wanted* to marry into a new life so quickly. After all, she was only just beginning to discover her *own* new life. She knew, intuitively, that there was a lot more of that to experience and it occurred to her, for the first time, that, maybe...it sounded like blasphemy to her well-trained ears...maybe, she didn't *want* to get married.

Solstice Party

Sunday, December 21, 1997

"What do you think, darlings?" Marian asked, pirouetting prettily to show off the pink, custom-embroidered, hooded sweatshirt Faye had given her. There were murmurs of appreciation, a wolf whistle from Chuck, and a "You go, girl!" from Dave. Marian leaned over Faye, seated in the big easy chair, and gave her a hug. "I love it, darling!" she said, softly, and kissed her friend on the cheek. Faye glowed, gratified that she'd managed to find the right Solstice Day gift.

"I just thought, once in a while, it might be nice for you to have something to wear that wasn't a billboard. I was a little afraid you might think it meant I didn't like your T-shirts, but you know I do; it's just that it's getting a little cool..."

"Oh, you're right, darling, it's much too cool for T-shirts. And I love the embroidery!" On the back of the sweatshirt, and winding around to the front, was an intricate embroidery of a flowering plant. Only on close inspection, would a person realize that it was an exuberant growth of Cannabis sativa. Because it wasn't the typical five-leaved, single plant so often used as a logo by pro-marijuana organizations, only someone truly familiar with the plant would recognize what the shirt represented. "Wherever did you find it?"

Faye grinned. "Not at the mall, that's for sure!" There was general laughter. "No, I found some pictures of marijuana on the Internet, and I took the parts of several that I liked, and put them together. Then I found a shop in Massachusetts that does computerized embroidery."

"Computerized embroidery?" exclaimed Robert, and Frank swore, "I'll be damned!"

"How did you find a company in Massachusetts?" Chuck asked.

"On the Internet," Faye replied, hearing in her voice an "Oh, of course!" tone she realized she would find annoying in someone else. She resolved to not become arrogant over her growing sophistication with the new technology. "I was thinking how clever the printer is that Marvin gave me, and then I wondered if it might be possible to build one that printed with thread, instead of ink. And then I thought, what if there already is one? So I did a search, and sure enough, there is! I called the shop in Massachusetts that makes shirts to order, e-mailed them the picture I made and they sent the sweatshirt via overnight express."

"My!" exclaimed Marian. "I'm very impressed, and very appreciative, Faye."

"So am I!" Robert exclaimed. "I've been using computers in my practice for ten years, and it would never have occurred to me to do what you did." He kissed her with enough intensity to spark applause from Bitsy and a "Get a room!" from Dave.

"I thought it might even be an alternative way to create T-shirts, Marian. And embroidered baseball caps! I'm working on more designs to show you." Faye tried to rein in her enthusiasm, but it was difficult. She enjoyed her discoveries on the computer so much!

Marian stepped to the counter that separated the kitchen area from the dining area, and lifted her flute of champagne. "My darlings, I want to thank you all for being here tonight. You are the best friends and the dearest friends and I love you all more than I could ever say. Cheers to you all!" She held her glass high; the others lifted theirs, and everyone drank.

"Too bad Vera couldn't make it," Faye said softly to Robert, who was sitting next to her on the sofa.

Robert shook his head heavily. "I don't know what's going to become of her," the doctor muttered. "She's slipping away from us, and I don't know how to stop her."

"I knew she was depressed," said Faye, "but I didn't realize it was so serious."

"There's nothing physically wrong with Vera. But emotionally...we really can't talk about this, here, Faye. Later, all right?"

"Of course, darling," Faye agreed, beaming at him. He was such a dear, and so professional, and so correct! Such a pillar, she thought, and then giggled at the *other* meaning in her compliment. The room lights were dim, and she loved the way his face shone in the glow of the multi-colored lights of the Christmas tree. Pardon me, Faye corrected herself, the solstice tree.

Needing a graceful way to change the subject, she spoke up. "Okay, Marian," she demanded lightly. "Why is this a solstice tree instead of a Christmas tree? I mean, I know you want to celebrate the solstice instead of Christmas. But with a tree, and gifts? Why borrow that from Christmas instead of just having Christmas?"

Crucifiction

"That was the very same thing I asked, my first year, honey," Dave admitted.

"We all did," Bitsy added. The tall woman dwarfed the others in the room, except for Robert. But her warm heart and ready humor had endeared her to Faye, even though she hadn't seen much of her since the AquaBabes' last performance.

"Christmas trees pre-date Jesus by thousands of years," Marian explained. "It was the Christians who borrowed the tree, not the other way 'round."

"I know all about that!" Faye interjected. "I went to Catholic school. When St. Boniface was converting the German people to Christianity, he came upon a group of pagans worshipping an oak tree. St. Boniface cut down the oak tree in anger and a young fir tree grew in its place. He took this as a sign of the Christian faith, and used the triangular shape of the fir to represent the Trinity." Faye nodded once, smugly, surprised she could remember so much from so long ago. Of course, she *had* won honors for her high grades in religion class.

"That's the official story," Marian agreed. "But it leaves out the fact that trees have been used in veneration and worship for thousands of years."

"Not always oaks or firs," Chuck remarked. "The Egyptians used palm trees."

"The Romans used fir boughs when celebrating Saturnalia!" Dave added.

"It had to do with celebrating the end of the winter solstice, which we are doing today," said Marian, "even though today is actually the *start* of the solstice."

"The start? I thought today was the whole solstice," Faye maintained. "Isn't it the shortest day of the year?"

"Technically, it's the day when the sun rises at its southernmost point," Marian said. "But it doesn't start moving northward until three days later, December 25 on today's calendar. That's why December 25 is considered the sun's birthday."

"The Son's birthday?" Faye repeated, confused. "What's Jesus got to do with the solstice?"

"Not 'son', darling, 'sun'. The sun in the sky," Marian explained. "December 25, or its equivalent—three days after the solstice—has been celebrated for thousands and thousands of years as the sun's birthday."

"In Sumer, 7,000 years ago," Bitsy interjected, "the god Dumuzi was said to have been born on December 25 to a virgin. Visiting wise men brought gifts, but they inadvertently warned a jealous king of the baby god's birth. He tried to kill the young god by slaughtering babies throughout the land. But Dumuzi's parents were clued in by an angel, and took off."

Faye couldn't quite understand what Bitsy was saying, or why no one else in the room seemed to be shocked. She shook her head. "What?"

"I'm saying, the Jesus story is not an original one. It was told 5,000 years before they say Jesus was born."

Faye was still confused. "It happened twice?" she asked. "Or are you saying that the Sumer people prophesied the real thing 5,000 years in advance?"

"If it's a matter of prophecy, it's happened many times," Bitsy replied. "The god Apollo, the god Tammuz, the god Mithra— thousands of years apart, each of them, but the same story told over and over. Virgin mothers, death on a cross, resurrecting after three days, even Last Suppers—the whole deal." Bitsy sat as if she expected to be challenged.

"Then," Robert interjected, his deep voice gently rumbling, "add to that the fact that there's absolutely no evidence that Jesus ever lived at *all*."

"What?" Faye turned in shock at her lover's blasphemy.

"It's true," Robert said, with a sad smile. "I was astounded when I realized it. But, you know, when I went through medical school, I had to learn to read Latin fluently. We had to read the Roman classics, Caesar, both Plinys, lots of it. There were writers who lived in Galilee between 100 BCE and 100 CE, prolific writers like Philo, who wrote about everything—current events, what people wore, what it was like to live there. And none of them, not one single one, reported the earthquakes and the total eclipse of the sun that supposedly accompanied Jesus' crucifixion, or the raising of the dead that supposedly took place over the whole world at the moment of Jesus' death, let alone his teaching or trial. In fact, no one named Pontius Pilate was ever governor of Judea, according to Roman records. And Jesus was supposed to have been crucified between two thieves, but that wasn't the Roman punishment for theft."

Faye's mouth worked, but she couldn't think of a thing to say.

"I'm sorry to be the one to tell you this, my love." Robert's dark eyes were moist with empathic pain, but it wasn't enough to quell the feeling of panic Faye felt building in her gut.

"How can there be no evidence at all?" she finally whispered. "Jesus' tomb...and birthplace in Bethlehem...pieces of the True Cross discovered in the Holy Land...people go there! They see those things for themselves!"

Frank shrugged. "Tourist traps," he snarled. "Seeing a hole in the ground doesn't prove who might have been born or buried there."

"All set up by Helena," Marian added, "the mother of Constantine, on a visit to the so-called Holy Land in the Fourth Century. And the supposed location of Jesus' birth? Used to be a shrine to Apollo, one of the other sun gods, also born to a virgin on December 25."

"The solstice is on December 21," Dave supplied. "That's when the sun 'dies.' Three days later, when the days lengthen, the sun is 'reborn.' Mankind has worshipped to this story for at least 7,000 years. It just keeps getting re-told for modern audiences, like the 1960s and 1980s rewrites of the 1930s Nancy Drew stories."

"They rewrote the Nancy Drew mysteries?" cried Faye. "No shit! I *loved* those books!"

"And how about the story of the Star of Bethlehem and the Magi and the killing of 14,000 babies?" Frank growled. "*There's* a story that makes no sense!"

"No sense?" Faye moaned weakly.

"Sure," Chuck said, rising to his feet in his earnestness. "The Wise Men—the Magi—these were wealthy men, astrologers, who would not have been traveling alone. They'd have had servants, grooms, flocks, shepherds, and families for all of them, including children—that's how the wealthy traveled in those days."

"But if they did travel alone?" Faye pleaded.

"Then they would never have been able to get in to see Herod," Dave grumbled, "partly because they would have seemed like poor people who were beneath his attention, but mostly because they would have been dead—the reason for those huge caravans was protection against certain attack by highway robbers."

Chuck continued, "So these Magi, astrologers, are following a star they know signifies the birth of a king. And they find that star suddenly vanishes just when they reach Jerusalem, so that they have to drop in on the local king—Herod—to ask directions."

"Men asking directions?" Bitsy snorted. "That *proves* the story is fiction, right there!"

The others laughed, but Chuck ignored her. "They leave and continue on to Bethlehem, where Mary and Joseph are now living in a house. The star reappears like a neon sign, right over the house—and the Magi, with their servants, flocks, herdsmen, grooms, camels, associated families and children—all show up!"

Dave laughed. "You can bet it would be the talk of the town for *years!*"

"Now, after a surprisingly short visit, considering they'd been traveling a year or two just to see this kid, the Magi leave. Herod asked them to come by on their way back to let him know where the baby king was, but an angel appears to them in a dream and they take a different route. So Herod sends soldiers into town to kill every baby under two years old."

Faye nodded in sympathy to those long-ago mothers. The story had always torn at her heart, especially in later years, as she had to accept her childlessness.

"We know a lot about Herod," Robert remarked. "The historian, Flavius Josephus, wrote 40 chapters of his twenty-volume history on the minutiae of Herod's life." The doctor swallowed hard. "There's no way he'd have let that huge caravan go to Bethlehem without sending spies to follow. Those spies would have told him exactly where the baby he wanted was."

"And if not spies, he could have asked anyone in town!" Bitsy exclaimed. "Everyone would have known the house the Magi's caravan went to."

"But, most telling," Robert sighed, "is the fact that Josephus, who detested Herod and wrote entire chapters about his most trivial faults, does *not* record any such killing of the innocents...and neither does anyone else."

He squeezed Faye's chilled hand sympathetically. "I was brought up Baptist," he added. "This wasn't easy for me to face, either."

Faye, feeling weak, found the name of Josephus familiar from her high school religion studies. "But, Josephus—" she protested. "He did mention Jesus in his writings. I'm certain of it!"

"A forgery," Marian stated flatly. "Josephus was, and died, a devout Jew. How in the name of reason could, or would, a devout Jew write these words?" Marian produced a thick, well-thumbed volume from a bookcase, flipped open to a bookmarked page, and dropped the tome in Faye's lap. Through blurring eyes, she followed Marian's finger and read,

> Now there was about this time, Jesus, a wise man, if it
> be lawful to call him a man, for he was a doer of wonderful
> works; a teacher of such men as received the truth with

pleasure. He drew over to him both many of the Jews, and many of the Gentiles. He was Christ; and when Pilate, at the suggestion of the principal men amongst us, had condemned him to the cross, those that loved him at the first did not forsake him; for he appeared to them alive again the third day, as the divine prophets had foretold these and ten thousand other wonderful things concerning him; and the tribe of Christians, so named from him, are not extinct at this day.

Marian gave her time to read the words she'd indicated, and said softly, "Darling, do those words sound like a devout Jew, who doesn't believe the Messiah—the Christ—has yet come, could have written them?"

"I need some air!" Faye leapt to her feet, and ran outside into Marian's walled garden.

She closed the door behind her and leaned against it. The walls were strung with white Christmas lights that twinkled in the cool December air. It all looked so normal, so harmless! Christmas lights, a tree, presents, dinner. But...

Faye, who hadn't attended Mass in decades, still thought of herself as a Catholic. As a girl she'd had a close relationship with Jesus, talking to Him as if He were an invisible friend. She had taken an honor at graduation for having the highest consistent grades in religion for all four years of high school. Often, she had been able to answer questions of theology that had stumped even the nuns.

But that study hadn't been a reaction to love of religion, or even of God. It had been, simply, a search for truth, which Faye had loved more than anything. She smiled, sadly, wondering what had become of that idealistic young lady who had devoured every book she could find on the life of Christ, simply because she wanted to understand every nuance of the greatest encounter humans had ever had with a superior intelligence.

She knew what had become of her. She had evolved into the mature Faye, who was able to appreciate and understand the truths to which Marian had led her. And now she'd been led to an unexpected and disturbing truth, one that shook the bedrock of her very being.

Sure, she had left the church. But, in her mind, there'd always been the knowledge that she could confess her sins and be forgiven. She had known that her friend, Jesus, would understand how that unfeeling priest had driven her away and would forgive her.

But if Jesus didn't exist? What did that leave her with?

It was like finding out her parents hadn't existed. It changed everything, everything she had understood as the basis of the universe and of her life. It was one thing to learn that the president she admired might have run drugs and arms through the Mena Airport in Arkansas, but quite another to learn that God's son might be a myth. It was a shock that left her hollow and shaken.

Of course, Faye could always turn to the sources she knew Marian would have, and study them for herself. But she also knew that, whenever this happened, her studies would only verify the conclusion Marian had already reached. Marian's love of truth, if anything, exceeded Faye's; it was perhaps the thing that drew Faye most to her older friend.

She felt pressure on the door behind her and moved away. She knew from her scent that it was Marian.

"I know it isn't easy," her older friend said, softly. With the door opened a crack, Faye could hear the others still discussing the validity of some of her other beloved Gospel stories—now it sounded like they were on the Crucifixion. "An honest search for truth never is."

"There are almost two billion Christians in the world," Faye breathed. "How can so many people be fooled?"

"Consistency," Marian answered into Faye's ear, putting her arms around her friend's waist from behind. "They tell the story to each other. They believe it and retell it. And, each generation, there are more children who never hear any other story and are encouraged not to question."

Faye patted Marian's hand and slowly pulled away. She knew that being in the cool night air without a sweater wasn't the explanation for the clammy chill that penetrated her.

"Some say there may have been a Jesus," Marian said from the door. "But, in an effort to win converts from Mithra and Sol Invictus, two of the most popular gods of the era, the early Christians borrowed ancient stories wholesale. After all, the details of Jesus' birth aren't *really* important compared to his teachings, are they? And so, a struggling, minor religion grew to fill a third of the world."

"Is that what you think?"

There was a pause. "No. I think that the creators of the original religion of Dumuzi, and their descendents, have re-created the religion in various names and guises for the purpose of enslaving humanity. I can find no evidence for a historical Jesus, or for a historical Mithra, for that matter. But I find evidence of enslavement in every era, on every side."

A Voice Frank Couldn't Recognize

Monday, December 22, 1997

Robert and Faye left the party early. They spent the night together and, as usual, Robert left for work in the morning. Marian, wearing the embroidered sweatshirt Faye had given her, showed up an hour later to take Faye to breakfast.

"Look what you're wearing!" Faye cried, pleased.

"I love it," Marian assured her.

After breakfast, Marian drove Faye back home, where they shared a joint and Faye showed off the latest enhancements to the web site. When she transferred the original site to TongaHost, she had also added some visual tricks she had learned in her continuing study.

"Very impressive," Marian praised, taking a hit and passing the joint to Faye. "You've really made something of this."

Faye accepted the weed and shook her head. "I may be wrong," she said, "but I don't think I could *ever* have gone so far so fast, without being high while I studied."

"Pot can't give you abilities you didn't already possess," Marian pointed out.

"I guess not. But I've always heard that people who smoke a lot of marijuana are listless and unmotivated. That certainly doesn't describe *our* friends!"

Marian hesitated. "It's true," she said, "people who are high are hard to motivate to do *other people's work* for them. That makes marijuana very threatening to the global industrial complex, because its wealth *depends* on leaching the energies of masses of people. But people who toke up are very motivated when it comes to doing something that interests them, and the focusing aspect of weed allows us to accomplish amazing things."

"Then, here's something I want to accomplish," Faye announced. "It seems to me that sitting here, waiting to be attacked, is futile. I know you're not afraid of death, but *I'd* just as soon put it off for awhile!"

"What do you want to do?" Marian inquired quietly.

"I think it's time to find out who's behind the mind control. We know about Frank and Brian. They had one thing in common: Carvel Meany. Or, more specifically, Carvel Meany's reelection campaign. So, the next thing to consider is, was *everyone there* put under mind control?"

"Brian wasn't actually there," Marian reminded her.

"No, but his father was." Faye frowned. "Give me a moment." The computer still running, she referred to the personal address list she had set up in it, then dialed the phone. There was a pause as she waited for an answer, then she said, "Hello, Michelle? It's Faye McRae."

"Hello, Faye." Michelle's voice at the other end of the line sounded far more somber than Faye remembered it. Clearly, the recent death of her son, added to the death of her husband a few months previously, had worn her down to nothing.

"I'm so very sorry for your loss," Faye said. "I lost a friend in the same accident."

There was a pause. "I'm still numb, I guess."

"I understand," Faye assured her. "Please, let me ask you one question."

"All right."

"Did Brian ever visit the Meany re-election campaign headquarters?"

"Not that I know of." There was another pause. "Don't tell me you think *this* is related to Kenny's death, too!"

"I don't know yet," Faye admitted.

"Faye, the world isn't filled with conspiracies!" the voice over the phone shouted. "Everyone isn't out to get you—or me!"

"I suppose not," Faye admitted, though she thought if Michelle had seen her son's blank expression as he sped toward his doom, she might feel differently.

"Besides," Michelle's voice continued, "Brian would have had no reason to go to the campaign headquarters. Representative Meany always came here."

Faye's breath caught. "He did?"

"Yes," Michelle affirmed. "He and that gravel-throated witch who ran the campaign."

"*Selma Graves?*"

"That's the one," Michelle agreed. "I had to clean up a pile of cigarette butts from outside the front door every time she came. And I was always here when they visited. So, you see, there's no way anyone could have gotten to Brian, or I would know."

Faye inhaled sharply, trying not to reveal her new suspicions. "Well, thanks for talking to me," she said. "And, again, please know that I am so very, very sorry about Brian."

"Thank you," Michelle replied, and hung up.

"What is it?" Marian asked, as Faye sat there, pale, clutching the telephone receiver as if it were an anchor.

"I think I found the woman whose voice Frank couldn't recognize."

Emerging From The Shadows

Faye quickly recounted the half of the conversation Marian hadn't heard. "We need to see Selma, I think," she said.

"Selma Graves?" Marian shivered. "I'm not sure I want to meet that woman. From your description, she sounds like she could give lung cancer to a person by merely letting her shadow fall on them."

"It's all about layers," Faye explained, as they climbed into Marian's high-powered rust bucket. She fastened her seat belt as her friend did the same, then peered behind them as Marian backed the vehicle onto the street. "You're doing it, too. Mind control victims or marijuana growers; in each case, if an individual is caught, he or she must not be *able* to reveal the names of any associates."

"That's true," Marian agreed.

"So, why not use mind control on someone, and instruct them to be someone else's handler? That way, even if the handler is caught, he or she won't consciously know who *their* handler is, and the whole investigation would be a bust."

"There is one big difference," Marian pointed out. "The Sun City Cannabis Club is a group of equals. I am not the head of it and neither is anyone else."

"And the difference?"

"Well, the lines of control in an organization of mind-controlled individuals, by necessity, flow just one way, since the individuals don't *know* they are being controlled. So you've described a hierarchy, a pyramid...which implies one, or a very few, individuals at the very top."

Faye exhaled heavily. "You're right," she said. "But I think, given the *possibility* of mind control, that such a hierarchy is inevitable. Once a single, greedy or immoral person became aware of the technique, what would stop him from exercising it?"

"Then, we can only hope that the discovery is recent," Marian said thoughtfully. "And that it hasn't yet infiltrated *every* branch of government, media, and business. So—who do you suspect, darling? Michelle, or Selma? Or Meany himself?"

"I've been thinking about that. Turn left, here, dear. Isn't it obvious? Meany must be the boss."

"Why is that obvious?" Marian stopped for a red light.

"Well, he's the obvious top of the pyramid. He's Selma's boss, and he was Kenny Worthington's boss. It was he who stood to be exposed by the evidence Kenny had compiled. My bet is, he's mind controlled Selma, and Kenny, and then Michelle when he went to the Worthington's house. In a trance, Michelle probably put her own son under control, and maybe even Frank Timmons. Only, *she herself doesn't remember it*."

"But why would Meany want Frank Timmons under mind control? He tried to *kill* Meany, remember?"

"But Frank wasn't operating under mind control when he went to Meany's victory party. He certainly wasn't emotionless, and I was able to talk him out of it pretty easily. My guess is, he developed a hatred of Meany from the evidence he *did* remember, that Meany was involved somehow in the drug ring his grandson had gotten mixed up in."

"It is a puzzle. So, where do I turn?"

Faye nodded toward the corner of a side street. "To the right. We're going to talk with Selma. She's a crusty old broad, but not a bad soul. I'm hoping we may be able to determine whether she is, indeed, mind controlled."

Faye had been to Selma's home just once before, when she had brought a box of stuffed envelopes there before the election but she remembered where it was. Marian continued to follow her directions and soon they found themselves on a street not far from 99th Avenue, in a neighborhood that the locals referred to as Phase One. It looked a lot like Marvin's—and Faye's, and Marian's, and Robert's, for that matter. They pulled up to Selma's house. It was a single-story concrete block affair, one of the first homes built by Del Webb. Marian parked behind a Cadillac in front of Selma's house.

"That's Selma's black Cougar in the driveway," Faye pointed out. "I wonder who's visiting?"

"Someone with a couple of bucks, by the looks of it."

"Maybe it's Selma's secret lover!" Both women laughed.

They walked through the mild December day to the front door and knocked. After a wait of one or two minutes, Marian knocked again loudly. "Maybe she isn't here," Faye said, disappointed.

"Perhaps she and the owner of the Caddy went somewhere."

Suddenly, a cloud of cigarette smoke whirled and danced in the eddies formed by the opening door, making Selma's subsequent manifestation look like a magician's appearing act. Her cheeks were flushed and her eyes dark, and she seemed astounded to recognize her former volunteer standing there.

"Holy shit, what are you doing here?" the wrinkled old woman said in her tearing-of-canvas voice.

"It's nice to see you again, too," Faye responded, smiling. "I'd like you to meet my friend, Marian Higgins. Marian, this is Selma Graves."

"I'm kind of busy," Selma said. "I have company."

"We won't be long," Faye said. "I just needed to ask you a question about Representative Meany's campaign."

"It's over," Selma remarked. "He won. We won't need you again for another year-and-a-half."

"Oh, not that!" Faye laughed. "I just wanted to know if you knew about the illegally high donations his campaign received from a number of multinational corporations."

Selma froze for a moment, then scowled—or so it seemed, as Graves' face wore a permanent scowl. But it seemed to deepen, somehow. "What makes you think that?" Selma asked quietly, her words sounding like a cardboard box being dragged across a concrete floor.

"Well," Faye replied casually, "it's all in the box of evidence Kenny Worthington brought home just before he was killed."

If Faye had any lingering doubt that Selma had conscious knowledge of the mind control plot, it was erased by the look on her face. The leathery skin took on expressions of shock, anger, frustration, and annoyance, all at once. "Perhaps you'd better come in," she said. She opened the door wider. All Faye could see inside was the fog of cigarette smoke. Ironically, a year earlier she wouldn't have hesitated a moment to enter such a den. But now that she had quit smoking, she had to force herself to enter the place. Marian followed.

Inside, the vertical blinds at each window were drawn, allowing just a few bars of daylight to filter through. The furniture was simple and plain, and clean except for the invisible film of nicotine and tar that Faye knew coated everything. It had taken her two weeks to clean it from her own home and she had never smoked as heavily as Selma did.

Reluctantly, Faye and Marian sat on the sofa Selma indicated. "Where is your company?" Marian asked, warily.

Selma lit a fresh cigarette and sat facing them. "Not important," she growled in an even tone. "Now, what is this nonsense about illegal contributions? And about Kenny Worthington being murdered? Everyone knows he committed suicide. It was in the papers."

"Before he died, he brought a box of papers home and gave them to a policeman who's a mutual friend of ours." Faye decided there was no point in telling Selma the exact truth, and she didn't want to endanger Michelle any more than she probably already had. "When the officer found out I was investigating Kenny's death, he gave me the box. It contained the 'other' set of books—the one with the *real* contributions listed, and the money trail that got the amounts laundered and looking like many, many small donations from individuals. It was easy to follow, even for someone like me who doesn't know shit about accounting. So, the question is—did *you* know about this, or are you as shocked as *I* was?"

Selma inhaled, obviously using the pause as a time to formulate a reply. Faye was glad she was still buzzed from the joint she and Marian had shared before coming; she could focus and remain placid for as long as it took.

"I think we should ask the person who knows," she said, finally. "Carvel!" she barked. "Get in here."

And, from the shadows of the smoky hallway, emerged the imposing figure of Carvel Meany.

T'was Brillig, And The Slithy Toves

Marian remained seated, but Faye found herself leaping to her feet without thinking. Faye's impulse came from her deep-rooted respect of authority.

"Representative Meany," she said. She remembered him giving that speech at the Town Hall—how long ago that seemed!—she had only peered at him between bobbing heads. She had gotten a little closer during his speech at the lake, when she heard him admit to his cronies that he had lied on-camera, and she'd been a dozen or so yards from him when she spotted him leaving the envelope for his connection. And then there was the false camaraderie at the victory party, when he'd had his picture taken with her without having any idea who she was. It seemed the closer she got to him, the less she thought of him.

And now, he was less than ten feet away, looking slightly woozy, his tie askew, his jacket open, as if he'd been sleeping.

"I must've taken a nap," he said, obviously confused. "Good afternoon, ladies."

Faye spotted a change in Selma's posture when Meany entered the room. You couldn't deny it, the man was handsome and possessed of regal bearing. Clearly he worked out; the cut of his jacket couldn't hide his firm biceps and the cut of his pants showed off a firm, muscular bottom. Faye stared at him. *I'm acting like a schoolgirl!* she thought, hoping Marian wouldn't notice. She couldn't believe her own reaction. This was an evil man! But what a "hottie."

And it was clear that Selma was attracted to him, as well. Amazing, that Faye had never noticed it before! In the office, Selma's behavior had always been absolutely professional. But now, after the election, in her home...

"Are you ladies friends of Selma's?" the Representative asked, still seemingly confused. *What the hell was Meany doing here?* Faye found herself wondering. Selma and he couldn't be having an affair. He was far younger and better looking than she was. The thought of him in bed with the gravel-throated lizard made Faye's skin crawl.

And yet...Faye recognized the flush on Selma's face when she came to the door, the luster of her eyes. Faye had seen that very same look...on herself, in the mirror, after making love with Robert.

Meany seemed unmoved by the experience, if indeed there'd been one.

"This woman is Faye McRae, one of the workers on your re-election campaign," Selma introduced. Meany automatically extended his hand, then jerked it back. "You!" he cried. "You're the women from the border!" He turned sharply to his host. "Selma, what are *they* doing here?"

Selma glared. "These women have evidence of impropriety in your campaign contributions."

The man's face quickly took on a parental look. "Now, Faye— and Marian—I assure you, any *appearance* of impropriety can be explained. I suppose you're referring to those T-shirts that people have been wearing—"

"*My* shirts?" Marian interjected, suddenly. Everyone looked at her. "The one that gives the location, in latitude and longitude, of your Mexican marijuana farm?"

Meany flushed in anger. "Yes, *that's* the one!" He choked back the last word. "I mean, there *is* no farm!"

"What do you mean, *your* shirts?" Selma demanded.

"I'm the one who designed them!" Marian announced. "And I have the evidence to back them up!"

"And *I* designed the shirt that lists the illegal contributions, and I run the web site that made all these shirts available to people across the country," Faye announced, "so you'd better wake up. These are serious charges and we mean to follow them through."

"*Your* web site?" Selma rasped.

"But that site is down," Meany protested. "An accident destroyed the computer it was running on."

Faye lifted her chin proudly. "Not at all. I simply moved the site to an off-shore host, where you'll *never* be able to destroy it!"

"I bet it'll go down when you stop paying the bill," Selma said, grimly. "Carvel, I have another job for you."

"A job for *me?*" The man sounded truly puzzled. "What do you mean?"

"Beware the jabberwock, my son, the jaws that bite, the claws that catch."

Faye stared at Selma, puzzled. She recognized a poem from *Alice in Wonderland* that she'd been forced to memorize in grade school, but couldn't guess why the woman had uttered a stanza from it.

The words certainly meant something to Meany, though. He straightened, his shoulders thrown back as if he were at attention, and completely lost that expression of confusion, replacing it with one of attentive expectation.

"Beware the jub jub bird," he replied, with all the seriousness reserved for one of his speeches. "and shun the frumious bandersnatch." He looked directly, and *only*, at Selma. "What sword shall I use?"

"Take up your *vorpal* sword!" Selma croaked triumphantly.

It sounded like a command, yet Meany didn't move or take his eyes from Selma's. "Command me," he said in a voice devoid of all emotion.

"Kill these women," Selma demanded, and took two steps back. Faye froze, but Marian assumed a combat position.

"Be ready!" Marian said to Faye, quietly.

"I am," Faye replied steadily.

But Meany, smoothly as a Swiss clock, stepped over to the end table next to the sofa, opened its top drawer, and withdrew a deadly looking pistol. Without blinking or showing any sign he understood what he was doing, he aimed the pistol at Marian, then shifted his aim toward Faye. "Which should I kill first?" he asked, monotoned.

Selma was as excited as Meany was calm. "I don't care!" she screeched, then said, "Faye—kill Faye first, then the other."

The muzzle of the gun was no more than five feet from Faye, aimed straight at her heart. She could see down the barrel almost to the bullet that was waiting for her. Still buzzed, she felt somewhat detached. She wondered if she would actually feel the bullet, or would she just black out?

Meany pulled the hammer back. Faye heard it click into place.

Pygmalion

There was a dark flash from Faye's right, and Marian's sleek body was airborne. Time froze for Faye, and for a moment Marian seemed to hover in the air, twisting slowly. Meany was frozen, too, in the sense that he hadn't yet registered what had happened. Marian's right foot flashed as she spun, connecting with the revolver and smashing it violently from Meany's hand. It spun, crazily, into the vertical blinds covering the door into the patio, bouncing off and onto the carpeted floor where it skipped and slid under the coffee table.

Marian came down, hard, on the table, smashing it. As she began to rise, Faye's training, untested in battle, came to the fore.

She executed a kung fu snap kick, her right leg making a straight line that extended into Meany's belly. He doubled over in obvious pain. By then, Marian had recovered and threw all her weight behind her fists, which she brought down upon the back of Meany's neck. The big man, whom Faye had thought of just moments before as imposing, collapsed like a blown-out tire onto the floor at their feet, his hands stretched toward the wreckage of the coffee table.

Faye and Marian, frozen, still in defensive positions, stared at Selma, who, in turn, stared at Meany's crumpled form.

"You idiot!" she groaned, sadly. "This is the first time you've failed me." She raised her gaze to Faye and Marian. "You have to die," she said. "You know too much."

Faye's breath caught, but Marian seemed unruffled. "What're *you* going to do about it?"

Selma straightened and sneered. "Nothing. Carvel will do that. He's unstoppable. You have no idea."

Faye didn't move. "Tell us," she encouraged.

"I've made him into the ideal man. One who obeys without question. One who defers to my greater wisdom. His strength is mine. My will is his. And no one is going to destroy what I have created!"

Meany stirred. He did not groan or indicate any injury. Slowly, he poked his hand under the splintered coffee table top. "I—I'm *sorry* I failed you," the Congressman whispered. Then, in a single, smooth movement, his hand pulled the still-cocked revolver from beneath the wrecked table, held it to his temple, and pulled the trigger.

The resulting *boom!* was so loud in the enclosed space that Faye was deafened. The recoil threw the pistol under the couch.

The side of Meany's head—the side that faced Selma—exploded, showering her with red and gray and white.

The three women, frozen in horror, stood as corners of an equilateral triangle around the fallen pawn.

Then, with a scream, Selma feinted toward the couch.

Instantly, Faye and Marian both dove at the gun, trying to beat her to it. They collided in mid-air, and landed next to the couch. Faye's fingers found the gun first, but when she realized Marian was clawing for it, too, she relinquished it willingly. The women rolled away and snapped to their feet.

Aside from the dead Congressman, they were alone.

"Where is she?" Marian mouthed. Faye wasn't certain if she were still deaf, or if Marian had merely spoken silently so as not to alert their enemy. In a moment, she heard the roar of a powerful motor and the screech of tires.

"The bitch is trying to escape!" Marian cried, and ran for the door, Faye right behind her. In a sudden panic, she realized that, if Selma escaped them now, she would be able to do them in at her leisure. Worse, their attacker wouldn't have to be Selma. It might be Vera, or Michelle, or any of a dozen or a hundred other people Selma might have at her disposal. They had no way of knowing how broad her reach would be, only that their only chance of defusing it was already speeding away from them.

Outside, all that remained of Selma was the smell of burnt rubber. Marian had turned the key before she'd closed her own door, and, fighting inertia, Faye had to wait until they'd completed a screeching U-turn before she could pull her own door closed.

"Let's hope she's heading for Bell," Marian said through gritted teeth, and turned left at the end of the residential street. Sure enough, the Cougar had turned left onto the major thoroughfare.

"Don't lose her!" Faye cried.

"I don't intend to," Marian said through clenched teeth as the Torino rocketed to the crossroads. The light had just turned red, but Marian ignored that and careened through the intersection, swerving to avoid a car whose driver, a man in his 90s, was creeping at a sedate 15 mph.

There were five or six cars, and a golf cart, positioned between them and their quarry.

"What are you doing?" Faye cried. "Catch her! Catch her!"

"Don't you want to know where she's going?" Marian asked.

Marian never let fewer than four cars get between them and Selma. "Where *is* she going?" Faye asked. At first, Faye thought

Selma might go for the police but when they passed the Surprise Police Department building, she had to reevaluate. They drove past the citrus groves that still grew in Surprise, then some construction in the Sun City West development. Selma never even slowed down.

One of the cars between them turned off onto R. H. Johnson, and now there were just three vehicles between them. Selma turned abruptly onto Grand Avenue, angling northwest towards the expanse of the Arizona wilderness.

"*Where* is she going?" Faye asked, again.

"I don't know," Marian admitted. "A safe place, maybe? To a confederate's lair?" Grand was a two-lane highway at this point, though construction barriers indicated it would soon be enlarged. Faye couldn't imagine why, as there were no buildings out this far. There were also few turn-offs. Each of the remaining cars between them and Selma turned off: One at Jomax, one at Dove Valley, and the last at State Road 74. Then it was just the two vehicles, Selma in her 1996 Mercury Cougar, and, a quarter of a mile behind, Marian and Faye in Marian's 1970 Ford Gran Torino, hurtling up the deserted highway, with only the occasional car passing in the opposite direction.

Selma punched her accelerator the moment no cars remained in front of her, and she was just a speck in the distance on the arrow-straight road. They were easily able to maintain sight of Selma. 100 mph, 110 mph, 120 mph…Faye watched the needle climb in fascination. "Where is she *going?*" Faye asked, for the third time. "And why is she going so *fast?* We aren't catching up to her."

"I don't want to," Marian pointed out. "But why is she going *at all?* might make for a more answerable question."

Faye thought about it. "Yes, why? Why didn't she go for the gun, as she pretended?"

"That's easy. We had just overcome her boyfriend. She knew *she* didn't stand a chance fighting us, so she split."

"Do you really think Meany was her boyfriend?" Faye asked. She was still a little buzzed from the joint she and Marian had shared in her living room. She couldn't imagine going through what she'd been through, drunk, and still be able to handle herself.

"That was obvious, darling, though I'll bet it was a one-sided relationship."

"One-sided?"

"Don't you get it?" Marian laughed uneasily. "He didn't even know where he was. She gave him the mind control trigger over the phone, and told him to come to her. She got laid, and when she heard us knocking on the door, she told him to go to sleep. He took her literally, and awoke as his normal self."

"Do you really think she was forcing him to...have sex with her?"

"Yeah. And if you had a powerful, handsome man at your command...can you honestly say you wouldn't be tempted to do the same?"

"Not me!" Faye retorted. "I think it's disgusting. It's rape."

"Yes, darling, it is rape. But, you see? It's the classic tale *Pygmalion*, the sculptor who creates a statue so beautiful that he falls in love with it. Most people misunderstand the tale. They see it as the story of a twisted, lonely soul who falls in love with a statue. But, really, it's the story of *every* love affair, because we *all* perceive our loved ones as the image of what we want them to be...not what they really are."

"But, I don't understand—why did he kill himself?" Faye wondered. "He wasn't that badly hurt."

Marian shook her head. "Selma said he'd failed her," Faye's friend replied. "I think, when someone is put under mind-control, they're probably given an order to destroy themselves if they fail a mission. Otherwise, they might be captured alive and could, conceivably, give away the identity of their handler."

"But Meany couldn't have given anything away. It would have made more sense to take another shot at us."

"Under mind control, the puppet has no volition, no common sense. He or she simply follows orders."

"Like a computer!" Faye suddenly realized. "He was programmed—and the program with the highest priority was the one to self-destruct in case of failure."

The inhumanity of it sickened her.

Why Don't We Do It In The Road

Selma slowed to a respectable 65 mph, and Marian was forced to slow down as well to remain unnoticed.

"It seems like we'll be driving for awhile," Marian said, in a mystified tone. "Get a joint from my bag, will you, darling? If we've got to run a low-speed chase through the Arizona desert, we might as well enjoy ourselves."

Faye shrugged, and opened Marian's tote. It was a fresh shock to see Selma's gun resting on Marian's flashlight, water bottle, change purse, and the silver cigarette case she knew held the weed. She opened it, found the requested bone, lit it, and placed it between Marian's lips. The older woman inhaled deeply, then nodded. Faye took the joint and took a deep hit from it. "I can't believe we're doing this!"

Marian chuckled in response. "It is pretty funny," she agreed. "Two old ladies chasing another one across the desert."

They never took their attention away from the Mercury Cougar ahead of them; and, in minutes, found themselves at the outskirts of a town.

"Where are we?" Faye asked.

"Coming into Wickenburg," Marian replied. Both cars slowed to 30 mph, Marian well behind Selma.

Selma steered right, and to the right again. They seemed to be in a neighborhood of mobile homes and inexpensive houses. Then, suddenly, they came to the end of the pavement. Selma's car raised an impenetrable cloud of dust above the dirt road. By the time Marian had driven through it, Selma's car was out of sight.

"Damn that bitch!" Marian swore.

"She's still on this road," Faye pointed out. "You can see the dust over the top of the hill. Just follow it!"

Marian did as her friend suggested. They left the flatness of the desert behind and were now in hilly country. They drove up and down but mostly up. They almost lost it on a sudden, sharp curve above a sheer drop of a hundred feet or so, but Marian's skillful driving, the heavy duty shocks and her car's suspension saw them through. At the far end of the curve was a sudden drop into a dry wash, and there, partially hidden by a grove of tamarisk trees, was the black Cougar, surrounded by a dissipating cloud of dust. Marian slowly pulled up right behind it. "This is it, kiddo," she said. "Stay behind me; we'll make a smaller target."

Marian opened her door. There was no sound other than the wind whispering through the brittle leaves. She got out of the car, her large bag slung over her shoulder. Faye slid out after her.

It seemed the draw had once been the site of a small mining community, though there wasn't much left. There was a rusted old windmill whose blades hung crazily from their axle, and a partial brick wall; concrete steps that led nowhere. There was no movement. It was as peaceful as a cemetery.

They both spotted movement at the base of the windmill. "Come on," Marian whispered. They ran silently through the soft sand until they reached a hedge of prickly bushes.

"How do we get past this?" Faye asked.

"Like this," Marian said, grabbing one of the branches. "It's fake. There are no roots, and it wasn't replaced properly." She tossed it aside. They passed through the resulting opening, and reached the windmill just in time to see a large, metal hatch closing over the hole beneath it.

Instinctively, Faye placed a rock to block the hatch from closing completely. As the hatch hit the rock, it automatically opened again.

"That's a considerate mechanism," Marian observed. "Like an elevator door,"

"Do you think that's where Selma went?" Faye asked, in a hushed tone.

"I'd put money on it," Marian replied. "Are you ready, darling? Faye took a deep breath. "Ready as I'll ever be," she promised. "Then, let's do it. Let's go down the rabbit hole."

Enlightenment
· · · · · · · ·

Shafted

The hatch to the shaft had an automated safety mechanism, an anachronism in what seemed to be a 150-year-old ghost town.

The hatch, itself, was an anomaly. The side it normally presented to the outside world seemed ancient and corroded; it seemed as old as the windmill that straddled it. The inner surface was a different story. "What is this?" Faye asked, wonderingly.

"I don't know," Marian replied, examining it. "Some kind of alloy, I suppose. Why, darling?"

"I've never *seen* a material like this."

"We're wasting time," Marian pointed out practically. "We can't let Selma get too far ahead of us. We don't know how deep that shaft is, or how many tunnels extend off it."

Carrying the gun and insisting on entering the shaft first, Marian explained to Faye, "I'll stop every four or five rungs and look below me to see if there's any danger. So, you expect that and don't step down onto me!"

"I won't," Faye promised.

The flashlight came with a belt clip; Marian fastened it to her fanny pack. She was wearing the embroidered, pink hooded sweatshirt that

Faye had given her and Lycra bicycle shorts. Faye was in blue jeans that had been clean but were now splattered with blood, and a pale blue turtleneck sweater. Both wore sneakers, or rather, what the store clerk had referred to as "cross trainers." The difference, apparently, was about $60, but they were very comfortable and had turned out to be a godsend.

Marian timed her entrance into the shaft just as the hatch began its opening oscillation. She quickly lowered herself down the ladder as the hatch started to close. Faye gave her a moment, then began her descent. The hatch made its muffled thud against the rock just as she'd lowered herself far enough into the shaft so the hatch didn't thud into her head.

"Hey," Faye called down, "where are you?"

"Shhh," Marian hushed back. "Let's not make ourselves targets until we *have* to turn on the light."

The ladder was made of metal, with rounded, pipe-like rails and metal rungs. It wasn't new metal, but not so old as to be corroded. Marian's tote bag made more noise rubbing against it than Marian's shoes did. Faye wondered if bringing it had been such a good idea.

One step at a time, they descended. Buzzed, Faye found it easy to focus on the steps rather than the depth or the darkness or the danger of what they were doing. Every now and then, she would hear Marian halt, and she would wait quietly, catching her breath while thinking what a challenge climbing back up was going to be and letting her eyes adjust to the dimness.

Faye had no way of guessing how far they'd descended. The hatch far above them continued to open and close, creating a sort of slow-motion strobe effect to light their way. When the hatch was open, she could barely make out her fingers on the rungs. When it was closed, she couldn't see a thing.

Suddenly, Marian cried, "Oh, shit!"

"What is it?" Faye asked in fright.

"Move up! Move up!" Faye climbed several rungs. She heard her friend grunt behind her, then climb.

"What is it?" Faye asked again.

"No more rungs." Marian's breathing was ragged. "If I didn't do ten pull-ups every day, I'd be at the bottom of the shaft."

"What do we do?"

There was a pause. "I'm going to have to risk the light, darling. Be ready for anything." She heard Marian fumble, then a click as she turned on the flashlight. It threw a bright, yellow circle on the wall of the shaft, which then elongated as Marian aimed it further downward. "Damn," came Marian's voice after a moment.

"What is it?"

"The rungs don't stop, but they're about twenty feet apart. We'll have to climb back up," Marian whispered hoarsely. "Darling, take the light and see if there's anything we missed on the way down."

Faye accepted the flashlight. She pressed the button and aimed it upwards. There was a rectangular shadow on the wall above them, next to the ladder. "I think there is something," Faye whispered. "It might be a tunnel."

"Let's check it out."

Faye began the climb upward and because this was traveled territory, she was more relaxed. Still, it was a forty-foot climb to the tunnel, and climbing up was a lot harder than climbing down.

Finally, they reached the opening. Faye put one foot on the tunnel floor, shifted her weight, and, gratefully, sunk to her knees. Her trembling legs could not have held her upright for another moment.

Even though Marian's passage was made a little more gracefully, she, too, collapsed at the first opportunity.

Finally, her breathing slowing to near normal, Faye found the energy to push the button on the torch. What it revealed was unexpected.

"Shit!" Marian exclaimed, puzzled.

"I thought it was a tunnel," Faye replied, disappointed. "But it's just a goddamned recess in the wall."

"Isn't this odd?" Marian asked, puzzled. "This whole setup. I assumed this was an old mine shaft, but I never imagined one being built like this."

"It's under a windmill," Faye pointed out. "Could it be a dried-up well, rather than a mine?"

"What's that?" Marian queried, pointing to the wall behind Faye. Faye craned her neck to see. It was a box, with a button on it. The box was shiny metal, and the button looked like black plastic. It was foreboding in its commonness.

"What happens if we push it?" Marian proposed.

"What happens if we don't?" challenged Faye.

"Nothing," Marian replied.

Shrugging in agreement, Faye pushed the button.

Nothing happened.

She pushed it again.

Still, nothing happened. Dissatisfied, Faye returned to her former position on the rock floor.

"What should we do?" Faye asked, softly.

"Hush!" Marian commanded.

"What is it?" Faye asked.

"I don't know. Listen." They rose, and Marian took a position in front of Faye, revolver at the ready. The sound, rising from below, a mechanical grinding, grew steadily louder; and a light, though faint, grew gradually brighter. Suddenly, an object appeared before them, and Faye stifled an excited cry.

It was an elevator.

Getting To The Bottom

The track the elevator ran on was the "ladder" the women had been climbing. It looked like a cage. Its walls were an open, iron grillwork; it was illuminated by a single, small-wattage light bulb set in its dome-like roof. The grill covered three walls. The fourth, facing them, was open.

Empty, it hung there, silently inviting them to enter.

Faye and Marian stood, staring.

"What do we do?" Faye finally asked.

"What Selma must have done," Marian replied. "She never climbed down as far as we did. She came down as far as this recess, pressed the button, and was going down on this elevator before you and I got to the hedge."

"The ghost town, outside—it's been deserted for 150 years," said Faye. "I read about it when we first moved here from San

Diego. At one time there was a lot of gold mining in this section of Arizona, but the mines all played out."

"That's right, darling."

"So...why does *this* one have electric elevators and lights?"

Marian shrugged. "I can think of only one way to get an answer." And she led the way into the elevator cage.

There were two buttons inside, arranged one over the other, as in any elevator. Marian pressed the lower one, and the elevator began an uncannily smooth descent.

"Sure beats ladders," Faye muttered. Marian did not respond.

The descent was not speedy. The light from the bulb illuminated the rock wall in front of them. It was smooth and featureless as a piece of paper. "This is nothing like I imagined an old mine would be like," Faye said.

"Me, neither," Marian agreed.

The air began to warm. Faye's ears popped. "How far are we *going?*" she asked.

"To the bottom, I imagine."

And, just then, the elevator stopped at an opening in the rock wall. This *was* a tunnel. It was unlit; the illumination came from the bulb in the elevator cage. Marian aimed her torch into the space. The tunnel was simple, perfectly cut, leading beyond the range of the flashlight.

Somehow, the walls seemed reassuring. The elevator blocked the way behind them; the walls stood guard at their sides. Although they could only move forward, that was also the only direction from which an enemy could attack.

"Should we turn off the flashlight?" Faye asked. "What if Selma is ahead of us, in the dark, just waiting?"

Marian thought, then shook her head. "I don't think Selma is what we have to worry about."

"What do you mean?"

"Well, we have to ask ourselves—why did she come here? There's got to be something here that she believed would protect her from us—and maybe kill us for her."

"*For* her?"

"Sure. She's a mind controller. That means, she's a puppeteer. She gets *others* to do her dirty work for her. She would *hate* to get her own hands dirty. But, maybe she came here because she knew *someone else* was here who would protect her."

Faye felt a sudden chill, in spite of the closeness of the air. "So...someone else is down here? Someone besides Selma?"

Marian shook her head. "I can't see any other conclusion."

"Me, neither," Faye agreed reluctantly. "But what do we do?"

"We remain on guard. There's nothing else we *can* do."

So the two walked forward. Faye held the flashlight, and she held it far from her side so that anyone shooting at it would miss *her*. Marian, at her other side, held the revolver. But there was no movement ahead, and no openings in either side of the tunnel.

The tunnel abruptly widened. The flashlight exposed a circular room, maybe thirty feet wide, into which eleven other tunnels converged. Turning around, Faye realized how easy it would be to get lost; she withdrew her water bottle from Marian's tote, and placed it by the entrance of the tunnel from which they had come.

Suddenly, the room filled with light.

As Faye's irises adjusted, and she could see that the light came from a recess in the wall, and was aimed at the ceiling, illuminating the room with a soft light.

The voice, when it came, was also soft.

The Tool Makers

"So," it said, "you are the ones who have caused so much trouble." The voice was a genderless, rich contralto.

"They don't look like much to me," observed another voice, distinct yet also genderless.

"Who are you?" demanded Marian. "Where are you?"

"Neither of those questions have any importance to us. What is important is that you have obstructed two of our valuable tools. And so you must be neutralized."

"There is another possibility," a third voice interjected. "Perhaps they could be made into tools, to replace the two they destroyed."

Faye could not make out where the voices were coming from, but a speaker sharing the same niche as the light seemed a likelihood. She supposed there must be TV cameras in here, as well—otherwise, why turn on the light at all?

"What destroyed?" Marian demanded. "Meany killed himself, and Selma is still down here, somewhere."

Faye shook her head, grimly. "I don't think we'd make very good tools."

One of the voices actually laughed. "You'd be surprised."

Another added, "The best tools are intelligent, caring, and empathetic—all qualities we find you possess."

"And how would you know a single thing about us?" Marian demanded.

"You would be Marian Higgins," a voice announced. "A native and life-long resident of Arizona. Born in 1935 in Bisbee. Married to Arthur Higgins in 1956..." Faye listened in amazement. The information was authoritative, even believable. But it conflicted with the history Marian had given her.

"And, you, Faye McRae..." the information the voice gave her was completely accurate, but she noticed it consisted entirely of details that were in the public record—nothing that wouldn't have been found on her credit report.

"You took our purses from the car," she guessed. "You want us to think you're all-powerful and mysterious, but you just have our Social Security numbers and a good computer."

"We're far more powerful than you guess, little lady."

"Then why do you have to work through 'tools'?"

"Foolish one," a new voice chuckled. "That's what makes us powerful!"

Faye felt the hair on the back of her neck prickle. "You do *everything* through 'tools'?"

"She's the one," the first voice said. "A quick mind, even if her conclusions are simplistic. How would you like to be the new State Representative from Arizona?"

"What?"

"How do you think we mold the world into the image we desire? Simply by placing tools where they'll do the most good. Selma

Graves was a good tool for years; she recruited Carvel Meany's father before he died, and then him. But her usefulness has ended. *You*, on the other hand, might provide years of entertainment."

With that, two men marched into the room from one of the tunnels. Expressionless, they wore black uniforms with an insignia that Faye didn't recognize. She exchanged glances with Marian, and dropped into a fighting stance.

"Oh, are you going to give us a show?" a voice asked.

One of the men advanced toward Marian, the other toward Faye. The women backed against the wall between two of the tunnel entrances, so that the men could not get behind them. The men never showed any interest at all. And, as soon as they were within two feet of their quarry, Faye and Marian flashed into action. In moments, both men were lying on the floor, unconscious.

"I told you you'd underestimated them," one voice said.

"No matter."

Out of two of the tunnels came four more of the uniformed men, every one staring blankly.

Marian aimed Selma's revolver at the light and put two shots into the recess in the wall. The second shot plunged them into total darkness. Faye felt Marian's hand feeling for her, and held on to it. They began to follow the wall, trying to find the opening marked by Faye's water bottle. Faye moved as quietly as possible, hoping the newly arrived soldiers wouldn't be able to hear them.

"Do you really think we can't see you in the dark?" one of the voices asked, but Faye wasn't fooled. She was sure they could not.

Suddenly, she heard many footsteps and in a moment, she knew the room was filled with men. She could hear them breathing and, soon, they were packed around her. She attempted to lash out at the ones nearest her, and she heard Marian do the same but it was pointless. There were too many of them, and in minutes Faye was packed so tightly into the mob that she couldn't move.

She saw a dim light playing on the ceiling. By its glow she could see that there were dozens and dozens of soldiers packed into the room. Whoever was holding the flashlight, was able to make them part for him; the beam came closer and closer, but it was too far away for Faye to see who held it.

The flashlight wielder got to Marian, first. Faye heard her struggle, and then stop. Her heart pounding with terror, Faye renewed her efforts to break free, but now she felt strong hands gripping her arms and legs, keeping them motionless. And then, a sharp sting! on the side of her neck. Almost immediately, she felt herself relax, her head becoming warm, a pressure building behind her eyes. And she collapsed into a blackness far deeper than that of the underground room with the twelve tunnels.

Detached

"You killed her."

When Faye regained consciousness, her head throbbing, those words ringing in her ears, she was still in blackness. The faint echo of her breathing told her that she was in a smaller space than before, and that she was alone. The words with which she'd awakened had either been spoken over a loudspeaker or had been heard while she was still unconscious. She was on a cot, or something that felt like one and when she tried to arise, the blackness swirled crazily around her and she had to rest for several minutes before she dared another attempt.

While she waited, she tried to imagine how much time had passed since she and Marian had failed to fight off the army of black-uniformed men. She intuitively felt it had been hours, but she wasn't sure how many had actually passed. It couldn't be *too* many, because she was still mellow from the joint she and Marian had shared while chasing Selma. And yet, somehow, that seemed like years ago.

Her head steadier, she swung her legs onto the floor, or, rather, onto a lumpy something that was on the floor next to the cot. Faye felt of it with her hands and realized, to her horror, that it was a body.

As had happened when she and Marian were grieving Marvin's death, Faye felt herself detach. It was as if she was looking over her own shoulder, observing the events from a distance, as though they were happening to someone else, not her. The horror was being experienced by the physical Faye, not the detached Faye just behind her.

Was this body the person Faye was supposed to have killed?

And yet, Faye did not feel as if she'd killed anyone.

She reached for the person's head, so she could tell if it was warm or breathing. But she must have misjudged its location, because there was only space where she'd judged the head to be. She felt in the air, found the shoulders, and reached again for the head—and, again, found nothing. The dread mounting, she brought her hands closer to the shoulders, finding nothing until they sunk into a warm, gooey mass of meat and a thick protrusion of something that could only be bone.

The physical Faye screamed. Her companion had been beheaded. And recently.

The detached Faye forced the physical Faye to calm itself. She felt around the cadaver for anything that might be of use and found, somewhat to her surprise, a flashlight. She turned it on, and the room danced with long shadows and dim recesses. It was a room, cut out of the rock, irregularly. There was a wooden door, closed.

And there was the headless body. Her buzz diminishing, her heart sinking, she knew who it would be even before she shone the flashlight on the clothes it wore, Marian's pink pullover and bicycle shorts.

The bastards. Killed. Marian, she thought. Never mind that stupid voice she'd had in her head when she awoke. She knew perfectly well she hadn't done this. Those voices, those puppeteers, had arranged it. Even if, somehow, she'd been forced to do the deed herself—and she was certain she hadn't—she wasn't any more responsible than Frank Timmons had been for the death of his grandson.

Faye sensed herself becoming ultra-rational. Her emotional self was simply pushed aside. She could hear it screaming, but she soothed it, saying, logically, "I'll grieve with you later. Now, let's get out of here."

The door was not locked, and the hall ended in the large room with the twelve tunnels. Her water bottle still lay before one of them. She ran through it, all the way to the elevator cage at the end. Thinking this was far too easy; she pushed the 'up' button and rode grimly to the top. The climb to the mouth of the shaft was short. The hatch was closed, but the push of a button opened it. She climbed out and stood in the chilly, Arizona night.

Marian was dead. Not just dead, but horribly dead. She had a crazy image of beings, the awful puppet masters, drinking from her skull in glee, that beautiful hair still hanging from it.

She couldn't think about it now. The moon was slightly more than half-full, providing enough light for her to make her way to the dry wash where they'd left the car. She looked for it, but it was gone. So was Selma's. It would be a long, long walk and they'd be after her as soon as they realized she was missing.

Or would they? The voices had said they intended to make her a tool, like Selma and Meany. That meant they intended to put her under mind-control. That was why Marian had been killed; although she didn't remember it, she must have witnessed or even participated in the ritual killing. The horror was supposed to split her mind into fragments, one of which the puppeteers would control. Perhaps they weren't chasing her because they were that certain they had succeeding in enthralling her.

And maybe they had. She had no idea what it would feel like. Perhaps, even now when she thought she was escaping, she was actually on the way to murder someone she'd never met.

And yet...Frank hadn't consciously remembered *any detail* of his participation in his grandson's death, and Faye clearly remembered the horror of finding Marian's decapitated body. Had the ritual to split her mind failed?

If so, sometime soon, someone—her handler—was going to give her the keyword, whatever it was, and she wouldn't respond. More likely, though, she *would*, and would never remember doing it.

Right now, she had to get away from here.

She almost jumped out of her skin when she heard a small crackling in the underbrush. Trying to convince herself if was just an animal, she spun, and had another fright when she saw a human figure in the moonlight. Thankfully, this one was not wearing a uniform. It was a woman, wearing a long dress. Almost glowing, her face seemed familiar. In fact, Faye had seen this woman once before, also in moonlight.

"Norma!" she cried. "Norma Haverhill!"

A Walk In The Moonlight

Tuesday, December 23, 1997

"Follow me, quietly, please," the woman whispered.

They walked quietly along the wash, away from the tamarisks where the cars had been parked. It was dark under the trees, but the moon lit their way as they continued to the base of a hill. Faye followed Norma up a few steps of crumbling cement, through what had once been a house but was now only a floor, and up the hill along a path that Faye could never have traversed if she weren't following someone who knew it well.

The path grew steep and began to switchback its way up the south wall of a little canyon. Then, Norma ducked into an almost hidden glade where the air was cooler and moist—definitely noticeable in the dry Arizona night. Faye followed her and thought she heard the faint trickle of running water. With conviction, the old woman led the way, along a ledge that was blocked by a large boulder.

"This will be hard for you," Faye's mysterious guide sighed softly. "There is a rope you can't see, on the other side of the boulder. To reach it, you will have to step off the ledge. You have to be willing to fall into the canyon and die if it isn't there."

Faye implored her companion. "Why do I have to do this?"

"Because, dearie, the signs tell me your enemies may be looking for you shortly. I can see them searching this entire network of canyons. We're going to the one place they cannot follow."

"What keeps them from following?"

The old woman smiled, a radiant smile. "People who live lives of fear, cannot trust. Have you learned to face your fears? If you have not, you will not be able to follow me. On the trail, or otherwise."

Faye weighed her options. Whoever had murdered Marian so violently wouldn't hesitate to do the same to her. And, frankly, she'd *rather* die from a fall into the canyon than be beheaded by the creatures that lived in the mine.

"I'll follow," she said. "Just tell me what to do."

The boulder loomed in front of them, ominous in the light of the half-moon. "The rope is just out of sight," Norma repeated. "You have to step off the ledge, and grab at it just as you fall. That will get you around to the other side of the boulder, where the path continues." Norma took a deep breath. "Watch me, and follow."

Norma stepped off the ledge as if she were going to fall into the canyon. But she reached around the boulder, and her fall was halted. She dangled, seemingly in mid-air, for a moment, then vanished.

Faye's heart pounded. Somehow she knew this was as much a test as an escape. She thought back on her life, pre-Marian. It *had* been filled with fear, and it hadn't been worth living. She realized that her time with Marian had not produced a finished product; she was still learning, and would gladly spend the rest of her life in that process. Marian was now dead, but Faye had every intention of living on as long as she could continue the lessons and experiences she had begun under Marian's tutelage.

She took a deep breath and gritted her teeth, flexed the fingers in her right hand a time or two and stepped into the air over the canyon.

The instant hollow feeling that exploded in the pit of her stomach was overwhelming, but it didn't keep her from reaching around to the blind side of the boulder. Her fingers touched something coarse and clamped spasmodically around it as Faye prayed it was the rope. It was, and the next moment found her hanging over the black chasm below. Momentum swung her around, then suddenly her feet touched a ledge that was a foot or so lower than the one she'd been on. She wobbled briefly, then found her balance.

Norma was smiling. "Glad you could make it, dearie," she said.

Choosing Your Game

It wasn't exactly a cave, but it was a hollow in the cliff wall that would have protected any occupants from being drenched by a rare Central Arizona rain. It also hid them from view from the canyon rim above them or the valley below.

"Are there any tunnels or holes into this grotto?" Faye asked, shuddering.

"None," Norma assured her. "You're safe here. Would you like some tea?"

"Do you *live* here?" Faye asked.

"Of course not," Norma laughed, softly. "But I do spend a few days every now and then, so I keep a few supplies here." She took two cup-sized cans from behind a rock, and pulled a tab from the bottom of each, then handed one to Faye.

"Be careful, Faye, it'll be hot."

"What is it?"

"Ginseng tea, dearie, in a backpacker's self-heating can. Peel off the lid; it should be ready now. Those chemical heaters work really fast."

Faye opened her can. The contents were steaming, and smelled like fresh soil with an overtone of orange and honey. Norma must have seen her analyze the scent, because she added, "And a little orange leaf for flavor. And a touch of honey."

Faye sipped. It was certainly exotic, and she liked the taste. After a moment, she asked, "How did you know I was here?"

"I didn't," Norma confessed. "Not in the way you think. I watch the winds, and the way the animals move, especially the ones that are special to me. And all the signs said I needed to be here tonight."

"You talk to the *wind?*" Faye blurted.

"No, the wind talks to *me,*" Norma corrected. "Is that so strange? You know that a certain wind means rain is coming, or that a hot day is ahead?"

"Sure, but that's weather," Faye said. "Wind is weather, they're related."

"All things are related, Faye. When you've taken as much time as I have to listen to the wind, and learn what it has to teach, you'll find it has far more to offer than weather reports."

"Did the wind tell you Marian had been killed?" Her voice broke on the last word, and she found herself sobbing.

"Has she, now?" Norma asked softly. She put her arms around the younger woman's shoulders and patted her back. "It's sometimes hard for me to tell. But, dearie, there's no need to grieve."

Faye cried, "What's wrong with you people? Marian didn't grieve over Marvin and now you won't grieve over her!"

The old woman touched Faye's breastbone. "Draw your consciousness here, dear. All the way into your heart. Pretend it's a few weeks after you met Marian. Now, look into your heart and find her there."

For a moment, Faye could only feel the sobs she had smothered. But then, she broke through them, and sure enough! There was a special feeling of Marian, deep in her heart.

"Now," Norma continued, "here in the present...you can still find Marian there, can't you?"

"I can," Faye admitted.

"Now, imagine it is next year or the year after. You've accepted Marian's death. And, yet, look!—she is still there, in your heart, isn't she?"

"She is!" Faye cried joyfully. "She is!" And, suddenly, somehow, she felt a peace descend. Everything seemed amazingly, sublimely, *right*, just as it was. The rock walls, the canned tea, her presence and that of Norma, all seemed as inevitable as day and night.

"You aren't grieving because Marian is dead," Norma whispered. "You grieve because you will miss what you imagine remained for her to give you. Companionship, skills, knowledge, protection, whatever. I tell you, if she *is* dead, then your time with her was done. You may not look forward to the task of finding new companions, skills, and so on. But that task is yours, and would now be yours whether she were alive or not."

Faye shook her head, withdrawing from the older woman's embrace. "She was killed horribly," Faye said. "They beheaded her."

Norma sighed. "Marian has always been a fighter," she said. "She sees life as a conflict to be mastered. Even after years of training, she can never see completely past that illusion."

"Are you saying that life is *not* a conflict?"

"I am saying it is a conflict for those who perceive conflict, and a cooperative effort for those who perceive cooperation."

"How can it be both?" Faye scoffed.

"The same way that the skies can bring joy to a person who perceives beauty, or concern to someone who worries about air pollution."

"But, in truth, isn't it both?" Faye challenged.

"It is," Norma agreed. "Wisdom is in seeing both aspects, all aspects, at the same time."

"So, you're admitting that conflict does exist."

"Of course. But in the same situations that you find conflict, there are many other aspects. I advise that you not dwell on the conflict or you'll miss the other, equally significant aspects."

Faye shook her head. "Norma, I was just in an underground mine or base or something, where I was attacked, drugged, and awoke to find Marian's headless body at my feet. It appears that there is some sort of enormous conspiracy that uses mind control to influence the political system for its own ends, molding public opinion and creating laws that benefit only itself. So, forgive me if I have trouble putting that out of my mind."

Norma smiled. "I advise you to do just that," she said. "It isn't important."

"How can you say such a thing? What if it is a global conspiracy, like our friend Marvin thought—before they killed *him*, too! How could there be any more important information in the world?"

"I can think of something more important."

That caused Faye to pause. "What?" she asked, finally.

"Let me explain it this way," Norma began. "When you were young, did you ever like to play house?"

"Of course," Faye admitted. "When I was six or seven. Or eight."

"Suppose you didn't own any dolls of your own," Norma suggested. "But you had a friend who did. What would you do?"

"Play with her dolls, I suppose," Faye replied.

"Now, suppose your little friend got greedy, and insisted on making all the rules, and deciding which doll wore what dress, and basically hogged the game so that there wasn't any fun in it for you. What would you do then?"

"Stop playing with her, I guess."

"But, in that scenario, you don't own any dolls," Norma reminded her. "What would you play with?"

Faye thought a moment, and shrugged. "I guess I could play with something else. Or make dolls out of sticks."

"Faye, *life* is a game. That conspiracy of yours, they have all the toys—the money—and they make the rules. It's a very attractive game, and a lot of fun for those who benefit—but if it isn't fun for you, stay out of it."

"How can I do that?" Faye protested. "They control *everything!*"

The old woman touched a finger to Faye's forehead. "They don't control that, as long as you don't give it to them," she said.

Faye sighed heavily. "I never even knew it *was* controlled," she said, "until Marian and Marvin helped me see that practically everything I believed was false information. Now that they're both gone, I don't know how I'll be able to keep my mind free."

"It's easy!" Norma cried. "Don't watch TV. Don't watch movies. Don't read newspapers."

"You mean, live in a cave?" Faye blurted, then added, "Sorry. But there has to be another way."

"There is," Norma agreed. "Talk to *people*. Have your *own* experiences. Live your own life, instead of existing vicariously through the fictional lives of others. Find a way to live that doesn't require money, which *they* own. Quietly ignore *their* laws, without drawing attention to yourself."

"Be an anarchist, you mean. Marian used to say that, but I don't see how the world could exist without laws."

"The laws enacted by the global elite are exactly like the rules in dodge ball, or stickball, or playing house—they are arbitrary and part of the game. If you aren't playing the game, the rules don't apply to you."

"I can't break traffic laws, or murder someone!"

"Traffic laws are just a formal description of behaviors that have developed since the invention of the automobile. Tell me, do you stop at red traffic lights because it is the law, or because it is the sensible thing to do?"

"Well, because it's sensible," Faye admitted.

"Now, if the law is the only thing preventing you from murdering me," Norma continued with a smile, "I'm glad that law exists! But if the law prevents murders, why are there so many?"

"I guess the law is more about punishing murderers," Faye observed.

"The vast majority of murders are the result of passions which the media foster and inflame," Norma pointed out. "The very few serial killers who exist, people who kill for fun, would quickly be removed from society by the families of their victims, if the laws didn't prevent that."

"We could go on all night about what life might be like without laws," Faye said. "But the fact is, laws exist."

"The fact is, you can ignore them," Norma insisted. "It all depends on whether you *want* to play their game. But it is a choice. One that may even have unpleasant consequences, as you say Marian experienced. But you have to weigh the choices. Either you play a game whose rules you didn't make, and in which the other players are *so* big and *so* strong that you cannot win—or you play a different game, a game of freedom, with different players and rules *you* make, in which *all* those who choose to play can win."

Faye felt light-headed. "It's going to take me awhile to weigh those choices," she pleaded. "After all, if I'm not going to accept the rules of a global conspiracy without thinking, why should I accept yours?"

The moon had dipped below the canyon rim, leaving the grotto in deep shadow. There was a smile in Norma's voice. "I'm happy to hear you say that. Now, no more on the subject, tonight. Have a marijuana brownie and get some sleep—I have a couple of bed-rolls in the corner."

Norma handed her a piece of heavy cake. She took a bite. "Mmm, good! What's in this besides pot?" she asked.

"Chamomile, and carob rather than chocolate. It will help you sleep."

Just then, Faye spotted a yellow glow sweep the far wall of the narrow canyon. Norma saw it at the same time and put a finger over Faye's lips. She whispered into Faye's ear, "We're safe here, I promise. Take my hand; I'll lead you to your bedroll."

Faye felt several blankets lying on an inflated air mattress. Norma quietly helped her onto them, then laid something that felt like a quilt or a comforter on top of her. Exhausted, she swallowed the last bite of the brownie, then fell into a deep sleep.

Lucid Dreaming

Peace did not come in her dreams. Instead, she found forgotten memories of her time in the mine bubbling from her subconscious. She knew, in the dream, that she was drugged. She was, again, in that room, though in the dream it was dimly lit. She was sitting on the cot, unbound but too drugged to move. Marian's headless body lay on the floor at her feet.

"You killed her," one of those genderless voices spoke, in accusation, it seemed. Faye was too drugged to respond. It was nothing like the buzz she got from smoking marijuana. This was an unpleasant sensation, almost like being caught underwater. Everything moved in slow motion, and her breathing didn't seem to satisfy her need for air.

"You killed her," the voice repeated. The room swam around her. Bile rose in her throat. Beneath it all was the lingering buzz of the joint she and Marian had shared. Marian's last joint, she realized. Last joint. Last joint. Last joint. The thought rolled around and echoed in her mind, her hollow mind. Hollow mind. Hollow mind. What an interesting phrase. Interesting phrase. Phrase. What was the etymology of that word, Faye wondered. Was it related to *phase?* Or *face?*

"You killed her," the voice insisted. Why was someone trying to keep drawing her to that idea? she wondered. It wasn't a pleasant idea. *Idea.* What was the etymology of that? *I* was the first syllable. Obviously, an *idea* was something *I* have in my head, she decided. In fact, she realized with a rush of pleasure, the *dea* part was three of the letters in *head*, jumbled up!

"You killed her," the voice said again. But now she was used to ignoring it. She knew that was how pot worked. It enhanced a selective focus. The thing you wanted to pay attention to, *that* was sharp as a tack. Everything else was there, but unimportant. If one chose to shift focus, one could do so. She could devote complete and total attention to that droning, genderless voice. But why would anyone do that?

"It isn't working," another voice complained. It caught her attention because it was different. Different. *Dif-fer-ent. Fer-rent.* For rent?

"I told you," a third voice supplied. "She took some sort of drug before she ever got here. That's why the sodium pentothal didn't affect her the usual way."

"It's marijuana," the second voice opined. "She must have known, damn her eyes. Now we've wasted a perfectly good rabbit."

A vision of the White Rabbit from *Alice in Wonderland* popped into her head. The White Rabbit jumped down a rabbit hole into a strange and sometimes dangerous place. And now, Faye was in the hole and it was, indeed, strange and dangerous. Faye in Wonderland.

She began to realize that there were four sensations vying for her attention, and she tried to identify them. First, there was the comfortable buzz of the joint she'd shared with Marian. Superimposed on that was the nauseating, heady, stretchy feeling of the sodium pentothal. But there were two more sensations, and it seemed important that she determine what they were. The third sensation was familiar, yet more intense than she was used to. "Oh!" she cried out loud. She knew what it was; it was the fresh high from the marijuana brownie she'd eaten before going to sleep.

But, wait—if she'd gone to sleep, how could she be here, back in her cell in the mine or rabbit hole, whatever—with Marian's body?

It hit her with stunning clarity.

She was asleep. She was dreaming.

She'd heard of this, once, on a TV talk show. It was called "lucid dreaming." She hadn't *really* believed in it and had never had the experience before, but this was definitely it. She was awake and alert yet she knew she was in a dream, *her* dream.

Supposedly, in a lucid dream, the dreamer could make the dream turn out however she wished. Faye took a breath and *intended* to overcome the sodium pentothal. Instantly, the dizziness and nausea were gone. She *intended* the room to be brighter, and suddenly there was a light switch in the wall just beside her. She flipped it up, and the room became comfortably well lit. She *intended* for the body at her feet to be gone, and it vanished.

"That's better," she said, rising to her feet.

"How did she do that?" two of the voices cried in unison.

"I'm in control of this dream now," Faye announced triumphantly. "You will answer my questions."

"You're still dreaming," one of the voices said. "Any answers we give you will come from your own mind, not us. They will mean nothing in the waking world."

"Maybe not," Faye admitted, "but the man on TV who talked about lucid dreaming said you can ask the creatures in your nightmares what they represent. I'm lucid enough to know I can't ask you for information I don't possess. But I may be able to access my *own* subconscious, and give myself information I *do* possess, but am not aware of. Now—first of all—I demand you show yourselves to me in person."

The door to the room opened, and three people shuffled in, looking embarrassed. The first was Wally Cox, the actor who had starred in the old *Mr. Peepers* TV show. Behind him was Don Knotts, "Barney" from the *Andy Griffith Show*. And last was Frank Morgan as the Wizard from *The Wizard of Oz*. The three men stood before her, unwilling to meet her gaze, staring at the toes of their shoes.

"What do you want of me?" Faye demanded.

Mr. Peepers and the Wizard looked at Barney, who shamefacedly looked briefly in her direction. "What we've always wanted," he blustered. "Complete control of this planet."

"We have it pretty good," Mr. Peepers added. "As long as humans stay asleep, we get to have our way."

"What if we don't stay asleep?" Faye challenged.

The little men were silent and she shouted, "Answer me!"

The Wizard looked frightened and said, "You will defeat us."

Barney laughed nervously. "But you can never defeat us! Never!"

"Th-that's right!" Mr. Peepers agreed. "In battle, we are invincible!"

"There's only one way we can be defeated," Barney added, confidently.

"What is that?" Faye demanded. Barney suddenly looked sheepish, like a little boy who'd blurted out a secret.

"This is *my* lucid dream," she stated. "You *will* tell me what I want to know."

The Wizard's shoulders drooped. "The only way to defeat us," he whispered, "is to...ignore us."

Faye laughed. "Be gone. You have no power here!" Faye found herself quoting the Good Witch in the movie. It worked. The three men vanished, leaving Faye in the dream underground cell.

And then she forgot that she knew she was dreaming, and retraced her steps out of the mine, to the point where she saw Norma in the moonlight. Then, suddenly, she was awake for real, back in the grotto, in reflected sunshine, and looking at Norma's face.

Crash Course

The woman smiled. Studying her, Faye realized she had one of those ageless faces. Her skin was youthful but her eyes seemed too wise for the face. In the subdued light of the grotto, Norma seemed to have a glow about her.

In spite of the circumstances and location, Norma was dressed in a unique yet stylish manner, in a Kelly green, ankle-length skirt and daffodil-yellow blouse, with a matching yellow, floppy, broad-brimmed hat and a necklace of fresh flowers, woven together by their stems.

"Good morning, dearie," Norma said. "I hope you slept well, because today we must start a crash course in herbology, among other things. Fortunately, we are in the perfect location for accelerated learning."

"A crash course?" Faye repeated. "Perfect location?"

Norma carried two wet canteens, and handed one to Faye, who opened the cap and drank eagerly. "This canyon is the location of a vortex," Norma continued. "It's very valuable for doing the kind of work I do. Unfortunately, it's also useful to people doing the kind of work *they* do."

"A vortex? What's a vortex?"

"A vortex is an area of increased energy," Norma explained. "You feel it by an increased sense of elation. Sedona is the nearest other place you can find a vortex this strong."

"I don't feel very elated," Faye remarked.

"Of course not," Norma agreed. "It's relative to the way you would be feeling otherwise. And it's very subtle. As you develop your psychic abilities, you'll find that you become sensitive to feelings you never would have noticed before."

"*My* psychic abilities?" Faye exclaimed. "What psychic abilities?"

Norma smiled ruefully. "Faye," she said, "I thought we would have much more time to prepare you. To teach you."

"*Teach* me!" Faye took a moment to digest this. "Look, Norma, my friend is dead. At this point, all I want to do is get back to my old life!"

Norma laughed out loud. "You're *old* life? With an abusive husband, morbid obesity, and a constant alcoholic daze?"

Faye felt her heart sink. No relief ahead, no relief behind...what *did* she want?

There was a lengthy silence. Faye could hear the sound of wind wafting its way through the canyon beyond the grotto, and the faint sound of trickling water, and, occasionally, the echo of the voice of a searcher calling to his mates.

"You caught a glimpse of what the world is really like, behind the façade presented by TV and movies," Norma said softly. "Do you really think you can close your eyes to that now? To discontinue your search for enlightenment?"

"Enlightenment." Faye tasted the word. "After all this, you'd think I'd have the answers by now. But I feel more in the dark than ever."

"That's because you're more aware of the questions," Norma pointed out. "And enlightenment, dearie, is a process—not a destination. It's the questions that lead one along the *path* of enlightenment. Answers are just the tidbits that keep us interested."

"That's all nice theory," Faye pointed out. "But I've got people searching for me *right now* and I've got to *do something about it!*"

"It's just a game, Faye."

"But, we were *forced* to play," Faye protested. "They came after *us.*"

"Not really," Norma corrected. "You've been investigating them for months now. You didn't know it, but this is where your search led you."

"Marian didn't try to stop me!" Faye pointed out.

"Dearie, I am simply pointing out how easy it is to get involved in a game whose game board extends nearly everywhere."

"But—" Faye caught her breath. She felt a burst of commitment. "Now that I've been awakened, how can I ignore what I've learned? Turn a blind eye to what I now see?"

Norma nodded with satisfaction. "Then you take the risk, and follow the path where it leads. Just remember—it's always your choice."

Another Word For Nothing Left To Lose

"I don't see how I can exist in the world without participating in the structure of it," Faye moaned. It was lunchtime, and she was eating a turkey sandwich on multi-grain bread that Norma made. The day outside the grotto was bright and beautiful, and though the night air had been freezing, it was warming quickly in the intense Arizona sunshine.

"The important thing," Norma urged, "is that you never forget you can choose the game you play, and the level at which you play."

"I've read about new games for children in which no one loses. They sound like a waste of time, to me. I can't imagine the kids getting very excited about them."

"Of *course* that's the impression you got!" Norma sighed. "Those articles are, like virtually *anything* you read, designed to mold society into a form the global elite can control. The elite are only safe when we compete with each other, instead of uniting against *them*."

"But, left to themselves—don't kids make up competitive games? Like hide-and-seek, and tag?"

"Do you know for a fact that children invented those games? Don't the younger ones learn them from older ones? How do you know who played the first game of tag?"

Faye nodded reluctantly.

"Faye, indigenous children's games are non-competitive. In the African bush, children play games such as one in which they each link one leg to their neighbor's and hop around in a circle. If one goes down, they *all* go down—and laugh, merrily, as they do so. It's a joy to behold! There's no competition, no jeopardy other than falling—and it's *cooperation* that wins the game for everyone."

"You've been to Africa?" Faye asked.

"Oh, yes. Many times."

"I've always wanted to go to Africa," Faye remarked, wistfully.

"Then go!" invited Norma.

Faye shook her head. "It's too expensive. I'm lucky I've got Uncle Fred's house; I just get by on Edwin's Social Security."

"Do you see how *they* have imprisoned you?" Norma demanded. "They give you a stipend, a small amount of money—too small to really live on; and *you*, or rather Edwin, paid for it originally out of his salary—it's enough to keep you alive, but not enough to allow you to enjoy yourself. What a clever prison! And you paid for the bars."

"I can't exactly go out and get a job," Faye declared, indignantly. "Not at my age!"

"You *can* exactly do that," Norma challenged. "But, if you do, you'll just move into a different cell of the same prison. Working for someone else, again, gives you barely enough to live on, not enough to free yourself."

"There aren't any other options," Faye declared.

"There are three, two obvious ones and one more difficult," Norma replied. "The difficult one is suicide: You can simply declare you're not playing any more and go home. But the other two are more fun. One, you can start your *own* business and be one of the exploiters instead of one of the exploited. Second, you can get out of *their* game entirely. Walk out of your house, hitchhike to the East Coast, board a tramp steamer and offer to cook or do cleaning in exchange for passage to Africa. When you get there, you can live off the land or offer to teach or nurse in exchange for living in a village."

Faye stared at Norma as if she'd grown another head. "Hitchhike?" was all she could say. "Do you know what kind of perverts pick up female hitchhikers?"

"I also know that perfectly fine, generous people offer rides as well," Norma said, "though it's been some time since I took advantage of their services myself. The only reason you think 'perverts' pick up hitchhikers is that *they* don't want us to have that freedom of movement. So, whenever a rare incident occurs in which someone *is* injured or killed hitchhiking—which happens far less than the yearly 50,000 automobile fatalities—the media makes a big thing of it and people will get the impression it happens far more often than it does."

"But why would a global elite, or *any* conspiracy, care?" Faye asked.

"*They* really aren't comfortable with people's mobility," Norma explained. "When people can move freely, they are able to go where wages are higher. The global elite *sets* those wages, intentionally creating areas of poverty and plenty, to increase their own profits. That's why they set up immigration laws and border patrols. And that's why airplane tickets are so expensive. Even so, so many people fly that I expect, any time now, some kind of catastrophe will be arranged in which many people are killed, perhaps in simultaneous air crashes. Or perhaps involving simultaneous hijackings. Hijacking one plane at a time apparently hasn't carried enough of a message; it may take three or four at once to really discourage people from flying." She clucked her tongue against her teeth, as if considering this particular scenario for the first time. "That would affect the price of the stock of the airline or airlines involved," she continued. "So *they* would also have the chance to reap a huge profit by short selling stock in those airlines a day or so in advance."

"Short selling?" Faye asked.

"Yes," Norma clarified, "that's when you buy future stock at a *lower* rate and sell it today at its current high rate, betting that the price will drop by the date you buy it. If it does, you make a fortune."

Faye was confused. "How can you sell stock before it's bought?"

Norma shook her head, amused. "Don't get me started on the stock market. It makes the World Bank seem positively logical and moral by comparison. The point, dearie, is that you *can* live in your home if you like, but you don't *have* to. All the things the media presents as terrifying options—living in a third world country, being homeless, being audited by the IRS—are only terrifying if you choose to be terrified by them. When you're conscious that *they* are sending messages of terror regarding those things, you can investigate the options and make your choices consciously."

"But most of those choices involve living without money or stability."

Norma laughed. "Haven't you realized by now, stability is an illusion? And money is just *their* method of skimming the fruits of your labor, in the form of taxes, interest, service charges, and so on." Norma took Faye's hand. "A few years back, there was a song with the lyric, 'Freedom's just another word for nothing left to lose.'"

"I think I remember that one," Faye remarked.

"I first thought that was negative; it made freedom sound like it wasn't all it was cracked up to be. Well, *their* freedom isn't. Consider this. When you let go of everything, when you have nothing to lose, then you are truly free. Let go of preconceived notions, of media-inspired hates and fears, of any agenda but your own. Experience each day to the fullest, and follow the wind where it may lead. *Then* you are truly free!"

Faye smiled weakly. "It...doesn't sound very practical."

"It *isn't* practical!" Norma cried softly. "It's transcendent—*if* you truly let it *all* go."

Why You Are Here

Wednesday, December 24, 1997

Faye sat on a ledge just outside the grotto, her legs dangling over the 200-foot drop to the dry streambed below. Above her, an overhang hid the sky from her—and the grotto and its environs from the occasional helicopter passing invisibly above.

There was no other sound in the little canyon other than the occasional chirp of a bird or the whisper of the wind through the brittle branches of the tamarisks.

It was almost unbearably peaceful. The villains searching for her seemed quite irrelevant. She had never felt so secure, so safe, so nurtured. It was like being in her mother's womb. Norma would say they were in the womb of Mother Earth.

She had spent the previous day being schooled in the use of medicinal plants by Norma. It had been exhausting, but exciting. Faye found she had a knack for recognizing the properties of a plant by its leaves or roots or berries or blossoms. Having been indoctrinated for weeks in the usefulness of marijuana or, as Norma seemed to prefer to reference it, hemp, learning the miraculous abilities of other plants seemed to be more of the same. Faye felt as if she were awakening to a new world, one in which all humankind's needs were ready to be fulfilled by the planet's wealth of vegetation. The previous world, the one in which she had been sleeping, the world in which the solution to every problem brought new problems, seemed dangerous and dreary by comparison.

She became aware of Norma seated beside her. The woman never seemed to make a sound when she moved. Faye had been alone and, now, she was not. Norma's sudden appearances no longer startled Faye; they were becoming comfortably commonplace, as was this canyon. Familiar. Homey. Home.

"Why are you here, dearie?" Norma asked, softly.

"The day was just so lovely," Faye sighed. "And it's so peaceful here."

Faye's companion smiled. "I mean, why are you here on *Earth?* You must have given it some thought, sometime."

Faye grimaced. "Edwin used to say it was to torment him."

Oddly, at the mention of Edwin, Norma seemed less solid than she had a moment before, almost as if Faye could see through her. "But, I'm not going to think about that now! It's too nice a day." Norma resumed her normal appearance, and Faye dismissed the oddity as a trick of the light.

"You must think about it," Norma urged. "Why are you here? What do you intend to do with your life?"

They were absurd questions. Faye's life was winding down! She had wasted most of it living with Edwin. And yet, the last six months had certainly given her a renewal. Her health was better than it had been in decades; there was no reason to think she wouldn't live for decades more. It might be wise to give Norma's questions serious thought.

"The answer to the first, I suppose, is that I'm just *here*. Why question it?" Faye replied lightly, then added, "The second bears consideration.

"You don't feel there is any purpose to your life? Any reason why the Creator would have bothered to give you life in *this* place and time, rather than any other?"

Faye shook her head. "I haven't yet seen any reason to compel me to believe there even is a Creator. And Marian dashed any reason to believe in Jesus at her solstice party a few nights ago. Religion, apparently, is another tool of this global conspiracy."

Norma laughed. "Don't confuse religion with spirituality!" she cried. "And don't confuse Jesus with the Creator! One may be a myth, but the other is very, very real. Look around you! Isn't this real? Wasn't it created?"

"By the universe, certainly," Faye admitted. "By the natural laws built into it. But by an old man with a beard? I doubt it."

"So do I," Norma agreed. "No *man* made all this, bearded or otherwise. But why can't the universe *be* the Creator? Why would you assume the Creator must be a human?"

"Are you saying God is not a person?"

"We might need to define 'person,' dearie. It seems to me that something as rich and complex as the Universe might well have intention and consciousness, and still not be a person in the sense of having lunch, getting angry, being jealous, or having favorites as the official poppycock insists."

Faye thought about it. "Well, if by Creator you mean the Universe, I guess I can go with that. All the science I've read says the solar system and earth were created from the materials of the universe, floating in space; so I guess there's no argument. But consciousness and intention? How could we know? No one will ever be able to prove that one way or another."

"Maybe not in a court of law," Norma admitted. "But is life *really* about proving things? Wouldn't you agree it's more about *experiencing?*"

Faye nodded in agreement, and Norma continued. "Then, what is your experience? Does it seem to you as if each section of your life's story has flowed into the next? Doesn't each part seem to be the inevitable conclusion of what went before, with the added influence of coincidence and 'chance'? Mightn't a conscious Universe be experienced in that very way?"

Faye considered. In fact, she realized, *every* section of her life was precipitated by a chance encounter or coincidental occurrence. She recalled the chance first meeting of Edwin, and the eerie coincidence of being in the ladies' room at the same time Meany had been in the men's room on the way to Mexico. While the coincidences had not arrived with clockwork precision, they did, indeed, seem to have given shape to her life— and, lately, especially so. There certainly did *seem* to be a pattern to them.

"Many people are here *just* for the experience," Norma continued, as if she knew she had made her point. "But some are here for special reasons. And so, I ask you again: *Why are you here?*"

"Why not ask the universe, if the universe is the one with the plan?" Faye teased.

"*You* may do that," Norma said, tartly. "In fact, I urge you to do so. But I cannot ask for you."

"Why not?"

"Because, dearie, *your* path is *your* path, and mine is mine. We interact with each other, you and I, but each of us *directly* relates to the guiding force of the universe. No one can commune with the Universe for you, but you."

Faye sniffed. "There goes the priesthood," she said.

"Exactly," Norma agreed. "The lie was to tell you that you needed a go-between, when in fact a go-between can only *interfere* with your relationship to the Creator. No one can eat for you, no one can pee for you, and no one can pray for you, dearie. Some things can only be done by oneself."

Faye intended to ask the Universe for her purpose, then stopped short, surprised. "Norma," she said. "I don't know how." She shook her head. "I know how to pray to Jesus; I was brought up Catholic. I can say rosaries until my fingers bleed. But the universe? I suppose I just aim my thoughts to the stars..."

"Ah. Another lie," Norma advised. "The *real* universe, the— what's the word the physicists are using now? —ah, yes, the *multidimensional reality* out of which all things arise can only be reached by focusing *within*."

Faye was puzzled. "Within? Within what?"

Norma touched her breastbone. "Here, dearie. Remember your heart. Close your eyes, and draw your mind as deeply into your heart as you can imagine...and then go deeper still. Keep it up; forty minutes is sufficient. When your thoughts drift, gently nudge them back to your heart. And don't feel bad that other thoughts have intruded— the pushing them aside is the process by which you reach the Creator."

Faye was intrigued. "And then what?"

"And then," Norma assured her, "you will have your answer."

Fulfilling

Thursday, December 25, 1997

That night, after a day full of more intense discussions on the properties and uses of various plants, Faye tried the meditation Norma described but fell asleep. She awoke the next morning to find Norma, sitting cross-legged next to Faye's sleeping bag, contemplating a drinking glass filled with rocks.

"Good morning," Faye yawned, happily, stretching cat-like, fingers and toes pointing in opposite directions. The air was cold, but she was snug and warm. "I haven't slept outside since once or twice as a kid. I feel wonderful!"

"Some of that isn't just sleeping outdoors. Remember, this grotto is the center of an energy vortex and if your personal energy fields are compatible with a vortex, then you can sleep very well here, indeed."

It occurred to Faye that if she got Norma to lecturing, she would be able to stay in the warm sleeping bag a few minutes longer. "Vortex?" She prompted. "We talked about that before, but I still don't really understand it. How about more detail?"

Norma asked a question in return. "What do you know about energy fields?"

"Nothing specific, I guess." Faye stretched again and retreated into the warmth of her bag.

"Heat is a form of energy," Norma remarked. "Where did the warmth of your sleeping bag come from?"

"Me, I guess."

"That's right. Your body produces heat energy, which the fabric and folds of your sleeping bag captured. That's why it seems warmer than the outside air."

"And glad of it!"

Norma smiled in appreciation. "There's also magnetic energy, right? You must have played with magnets at some time."

"Of course," Faye agreed. "Magnets make automotive starters work. Solenoids and alternators, as well. And compasses, of course."

"Some places on the Earth are located where there are anomalies in the Earth's magnetic field. Compasses don't work correctly there, and people report physical sensations—a feeling of elation usually, but sometimes of dread. These are also locations with a disproportionate amount of UFO and ghost sightings."

"Really. How interesting." *Don't stop*, Faye pleaded silently. *I do not want to get up yet!*

"There are also such things as electric fields. You create one when you shuffle across a woolen rug; that's why you get a shock when you touch metal afterwards. Some vortexes are anomalies in the Earth's electrical field."

"How do we find them? With an electric compass?"

Norma smiled. "Something like that. But electrical vortexes are useful in healing. That's the kind that's located here."

"Oh. And that's why I slept so soundly?"

"If you needed healing—and, after your adventure in the mine, I'd guess you did—then, yes, you would sleep soundly here as your body repaired." Norma looked into the glass of rocks she held. "The Indians knew about vortexes, as all indigenous people do. They declared such areas to be sacred ground, which meant anyone from any tribe was free to go there to meditate or pray for healing, without fear of being attacked."

"Why do you have a glass full of rocks?" Faye asked.

Norma held it out for inspection. "Do you really think it is full?"

Faye regarded it. "Yes, of course."

"You're quite certain you could get no more into it?"

"No, it's definitely full."

Norma dipped her hand into a small pile of gravel at her side, and withdrew a handful of the small bits of stone. She held it over the glass of rocks and poured the gravel into the glass. The bits of stone fell between the gaps amid the larger rocks. Norma was able to pour four handfuls of gravel into the glass, before the level of gravel rose to the mouth of the glass.

"Is it full now?" Norma asked.

Faye, realizing this was a trick question, smiled lopsidedly. "I suppose not really, but it does look full to me," she replied.

"Fair enough," Norma said. She dipped her hand into another pile at her side, this one of sand. She had to jiggle the glass before it would accept the sand, but accept it, it did; and this time, she was able to pour three handfuls of sand into the glass before it, once again, seemed full.

"How is it possible," Norma asked, "for me to add something to a glass that is full?"

"You've been adding smaller things," Faye observed. "They fit in the cracks between the larger things that were there before." She grinned. "But it is full, now. I can't imagine even flour working its way between the grains of sand."

Norma smiled, picked up her canteen, opened it, and poured into the glass. Seconds went by, as the crystal-clear liquid dribbled into the glass.

Faye laughed. "Is that it? Or do you have something finer than water?"

"Well, there's gas," Norma pointed out. "If we placed this glass into a chamber filled with pure oxygen, or nitrogen, or carbon dioxide, the water would, given time, be able to absorb a fair amount of it. But I think the point is made."

Faye was puzzled. "And what point is that?"

"That larger things can seem to be important, can even seem able to fill our lives with meaning until we start looking at the finer things. The same is true of everything around us. Buildings, cars, money, clothes, all seem very important. One can try to fill one's life with them, but it's never enough. A life filled with material goods always feels empty, even for the man who has everything."

"Oh, my. That is...profound," Faye marveled.

"Things like art and music are 'finer grained' than material goods, and a clever person will find he can fill even more of his life with art and music, no matter how much he owns. For a while, it will seem satisfying. But even that is not sublime enough, and the hollow feeling will return."

"What is the finest-grained thing, then? What will fulfill our lives?"

"Some would say love, of course. And love does go a long way. Others might say religion, though in the end, religion is no more satisfying than art or music. But, at the end, there is only one, final, ultimately fine substance that can satisfy us forever: God. Or, rather, the permeating awareness of God in all things, including, and especially, ourselves."

Good Vibrations

Norma rose abruptly. "It's time to leave," she said.

"Leave?" Faye asked. "Now?"

"Did you hear that?" the old woman asked.

"What?"

"It was a change in the wind. I've been listening for it. Now, it is time for you to leave."

"And go where?" Faye asked, dismayed. Norma's conviction was such that Faye had already begun to extricate herself from the sleeping bag, even while she had not yet formulated the intention to get up.

"It's time for you to go home," Norma said, insistently.

"Won't they be looking for me there?" Faye returned. "My purse was in Marian's car. They know my address and everything."

"Dearie, I don't know everything. I cannot foretell the future. I only know that Mother Earth says it's now time for you to return to your home. What awaits you there, I cannot say...other than it is your fate, or, rather, the next step on your path."

"That's not very encouraging."

Norma smiled. "You cannot avoid your path, Faye. To try and do so lowers your vibrational frequency. Running joyfully to it, embracing it, works best, especially if you want to keep your frequency up."

"My frequency?"

"All things vibrate. You know that, right?"

"I know sometimes cars vibrate. Edwin used to have to fix them."

"All matter vibrates. In fact, as Einstein discovered—have you ever read Einstein? Fascinating mind! As he showed us, matter, in reality, is just bits of energy that are vibrating very slowly. Rocks and metal have the slowest vibrations, living tissue faster, and spirit has the highest frequency of anything you can find on earth."

"So, I suppose we want to increase the frequency of our vibrations?"

"Any individual can adjust their frequency up or down a notch or two. When you are happy and loving, your frequency rises. When you are frightened, sick or depressed, it drops. In fact, your frequency changes faster than your emotions, so that one could say when your frequency drops enough, you *become* frightened, sick or depressed. We can't be certain which happens first, which causes the other. It's possible that they each cause the other, and wouldn't that be interesting!

"Do you know how radio works?"

"Excuse me?" Faye was thrown by Norma's non-sequitur.

"Radio. You know, those boxes that news, weather, traffic and music come out of?"

"I know the stations use radio waves to send the songs through the air to the radio," Faye told her.

"Do you know how more than one radio station can exist, while you listen to just one station at a time?

"Sure; they're on different channels."

"Different frequencies, you mean, dearie. Frequencies. Yes, there's that word, again! As you adjust the dial up and down, you change the sensitivity of the radio to different frequencies. It's the nature of the device to be able to receive only one station at a time. We humans, on the other hand, can receive a range of frequencies. When our own frequency is high, we can tune in things that naturally exist at those higher frequencies, like angels, UFOs, and so on. At higher frequencies, we can hear the Earth speak to us, and the Universe, too. When we are depressed, we lose contact with all that. The world seems to lose its magic, and we lose ours. But, when we are operating at those higher frequencies...my goodness! All the Universe is at our fingertips. We can manifest whatever we want."

"Except for my purse...because it was in Marian's car...which someone took away."

"And which you don't need. You only have to stroll about five miles into the town of Wickenburg. It will be quite a walk, dearie, but I have no doubt you can make it." She gave Faye detailed directions.

"Won't you be going with me?"

"No, my dear. I have other tasks to attend to. You will have to do this on your own."

"My own?" cried Faye in dismay, and then screamed, as Norma vanished.

Resurrection

Faye had gone back, with some difficulty, around the boulder that guarded the grotto. That placed her in a narrow side canyon; traveling north would have brought her back to the mine entrance so she headed south instead. There was no path, and plenty of rocks and boulders to climb over and around. In spite of the cool air, Faye found herself sweating but there was no real discomfort and in fact, Faye rather enjoyed the exercise.

Before long, she reached the rim of the little canyon and stood surrounded by rolling, sandy hills, cacti and Joshua trees. She could make out a ribbon of dirt road less than a mile away, and headed for it.

Faye found herself thankful for the cool day as she walked the dusty road to Wickenburg. She also thanked Marian, who had talked her into buying the cross trainers. Faye could only imagine the shape her feet would be in if she'd been wearing leather shoes.

Faye found herself enjoying the journey. She had expected to be frightened, jumping at every noise, imagining one of the black-uniformed soldiers behind every cactus. Instead, she felt a change of heart, or, perhaps, of spirit. Some might call it fatalism but she knew through every fiber of her being that she wouldn't die this day. It wasn't her time.

This was such an odd turnabout for her that Faye pondered it for a mile or so. What had changed? What was different? What new information did she possess?

There had been her exposure to Marian these past months. Certainly that woman had never feared death. And now, ironically, she was dead. Faye didn't have any idea how she was going to deal with *that* when she returned to Sun City.

Then there was Norma. It had not been a dream. Norma had vanished, right in front of Faye's eyes, as convincingly as any David Copperfield illusion. One moment she had been there, as real and normal as tea and biscuits, and then she was gone. It hadn't been abrupt, like the special effects on the old *Bewitched* television show; it had been more of a going out of focus. Faye could view the event in her mind and did so, repeatedly, to see if she had missed anything. But no, it seemed as if Norma had really been there one moment and gone the next.

And yet, given Norma's talk a few minutes earlier about how radio stations work, and how finer things can occupy the same time and space as grosser things—Faye couldn't help but wonder if Norma had simply slipped into a higher vibrational frequency— or Faye into a lower one—and that made it impossible for her to continue to perceive Norma, much as turning a radio dial would make a station "vanish."

And the last thing Norma had said? "You will have to do this on your own." That had caused Faye's heart to sink, there was no doubt about that. And Norma had told her that fear and sadness made a person's "vibrations" reduce in frequency.

This implied that Faye and Norma didn't exist at the same frequencies. Or, rather, that Norma existed at some frequency other than that of most people. Could this solve the mysteries that had been accumulating regarding Norma?

Faye had been increasingly uncomfortable with the ages of these people. Marian, who looked 55, claimed to be 92...and had the personal history to back it up. Norma, who looked ageless but not aged, said she'd been mentored by Abigail Bannister, a woman burned as a witch in the 1600s.

But if Norma, and Abigail existed at a different *frequency* than normal people—if they were closer to the *spiritual* frequency than the mortal one—that could explain it. Neither "alive" nor "dead" in the usual sense of the terms, they might well go on forever.

In fact, Faye thought, her pulse quickening—could this be the real message of the resurrection of Christ? That, by releasing himself of the cares of the world, he had not died, but transcended life?

What if Norma lived, not quite in the same universe that Faye occupied but in some parallel one where the vibrations were naturally faster but which otherwise occupied the same space and time as this one? And suppose, due to some peculiarity of the vortex or the marijuana or the life-and-death brush with danger, or all of the above, she had enjoyed a similar high frequency for the past three days?

If Norma lived in a faster-vibration world that co-existed with the "normal" world, she undoubtedly did not do so alone. Could the other denizens of that world, partially and occasionally visible to occupants of this one, be the ghosts and UFOs and fairies and other beings persistently reported, and as vigorously denied?

Might that even really explain why the soldiers had never found them? If Norma, and people in *her* universe could only be seen by people making use of a certain frequency, was it possible that, when Faye was operating at that high frequency, she couldn't be seen by lower-frequency people, either?

Faye was beginning to suspect that the mysteries of what Norma called "metaphysics" were, in fact knowable—and a damn sight more interesting than the politics and murders she had spent the past months investigating.

Imagine—a universe of joy coincident with the universe of fear that most people inhabit. And the way to leave the fearful one for the joyful one is to simply *be* joyful!

There would be many people who would resist such an idea. Indeed, it would seem impossible to those who were living in fear, who were living the kind of life in which Faye herself had been mired just a year before. Not only would they believe they couldn't exist in such a place; they would do whatever they could to prevent others from ascending there. Faye wasn't sure how she knew such a thing, but she did. The phrase, "misery loves company" echoed in her mind. The mass of humanity, frightened, sad, repressed, would be unable to imagine any other condition than their own. "Better the devil we know" was another cliché typical of that mind-set.

As was the cliché of needing to control others. No wonder the "sheeple," as Marian called them, were so anxious to suppress the use of marijuana! The global elite, if there were such a thing, would try to prevent people from using it if it made them impervious to mind control. But, even more, the mass of humanity would be terrified of a substance that might lift them above their accustomed condition of despair. *En masse,* they would lie, they would pressure and, yes, they would kill to avoid facing their own demons, even though doing so meant freedom.

Vera was an example. Poor, dear Vera, who ran from the substance as soon as she realized it might force her to re-examine childhood horrors she had repressed.

Faye, herself, had every reason to be horrified and depressed right now, having days before encountered the headless body of her beloved friend. Yet, she wasn't. She had an understanding, now, that *life* extended far beyond the confines of mortality. Marian still lived in her heart, and her apparent murder had merely been the mechanism of her transcendence.

Having felt as low as is possible, in Faye's estimation, and to now be as free and happy as she was, Faye wanted nothing more than to share her insights and joy with others. But that, she realized, wouldn't be an easy job. She also realized she needed time to formulate an approach, something that wouldn't alienate potential students before she'd had a chance to teach them anything. She could easily imagine someone approaching Edwin with this information. For the first time, she understood how pitiful a creature he'd been. All his apparent arrogance and cruelty and limitations had been the product of his fears, nothing more.

In less than two hours, Faye saw the roofs of houses jutting over the tops of the hills. A few minutes later she was walking along a village street, flanked by dusty pre-fabricated and mobile homes. And then, finally, she was at the main road and a McDonald's. There was no pay phone, but the manager allowed her to place a collect call to Robert.

"Are you all right!" he cried, his voice breaking. "No one knew where you were!"

"I'm fine, but—" Her voice trailed. Robert would be terribly affected by the news of Marian's death; she had to tell him, but not on the phone.

"—but I'm in Wickenburg now, at what is, I guess, the only McDonald's. Would you please come and get me? I don't have my purse or any money," she added. "And I haven't eaten all day."

"Wickenburg?" For a moment, Faye wasn't certain Robert knew where the place was. "I'll be there in one hour," he said. "Don't step outside the restaurant."

Gratefully, Faye handed the manager the telephone receiver.

The Gift of Christmas

And noticed, for the first time, the Christmas decorations.

"Oh, my," she said. "Today...it's Christmas, isn't it?"

"It is," the manager, a kindly man in his forties, said. "And, madam," he said, "I didn't mean to eavesdrop, but I couldn't help but overhear that you haven't eaten today. May I offer you a Combo Meal, your choice?"

Faye was startled. It seemed such a long time since she'd experienced such kindness from a stranger. "Thank you so much!" she said. "And merry, merry Christmas."

There were no customers in the place, and just two employees other than the manager. The employees were gathered around a TV set up in the back. One of them left to fry a burger for Faye.

After a minute or two, the manager brought a wrapped hamburger and some fries and a soda on a tray. Faye regarded the meal hungrily. "I haven't had fries in six months, but I guess they won't kill me...especially after walking five miles."

"What happened, did your car break down?"

"Something like that," Faye replied.

"I can drive you out to it," the manager offered, as Faye hungrily bit off a quarter of her sandwich. "And my son is a pretty fair mechanic. Brad!" he called, and one of the employees looked up.

"No, thanks," Faye said, holding up her palm and shaking her head, trying to swallow before speaking again. "My friend will be here soon, and, um, he can take care of it. He's used to it," she added.

The manager waved off his son's attention.

To change the subject, Faye asked, "What are you doing open on Christmas?"

"It's up to the franchise owners," the man explained. "The corporate headquarters allow us to close on Christmas, but we can open if we want." He sighed. "My wife died last week, and we didn't feel like celebrating. So we decided to come in and feed anyone who showed up." The man smiled tiredly. "We figured, anyone who showed up on Christmas to eat at McDonald's was probably worse off than we were!"

"I'm so sorry to hear about your wife," Faye said, impulsively placing a hand on his, and realizing too late that her fingers were greasy from the French fries. But he didn't seem to notice, and even appeared to take strength from her touch.

"Thanks. She was sick a long time, and it was a blessing. But it's still hard."

Faye remembered something taught to her by Marian and Norma. "I can—that is, if you'd like, I may be able to tell you something that might make it a little easier."

The man stared at her. "Please," he said.

"Close your eyes," Faye instructed, and the man did so. "Remember your wife, years ago, young and healthy and having fun." She could tell by the manager's expression that he could, indeed, remember such a time.

"Now, with your mind, look in your heart. Find the exact spot where that memory, that awareness of your wife, seems to live."

After a moment, the manager smiled and said, "I found it!"

"Now, bring your mind forward, nearer to the present, when your wife was ill. Feel it in your heart in the same area. Is she there?"

"Yes, she is," the man replied, in wonder.

"Now, let your imagination move forward, five or ten years into the future, when your life has moved on. Look in your heart. Is she still there?"

Barely audibly, the man whispered, "She is. She is!"

Faye nodded. "And she always will be. Loving, healthy, vibrant. Death is an illusion. The people we love exist forever, and we reach them through our hearts."

The man reached for her. She still held what was left of her hamburger in one hand, so he grasped her wrists. There were tears in his eyes, and she knew they were tears of joy. "Thank you so much for coming here today," he said. "Now I know why God led us to keep the place open. He was sending His angel."

"I'm no angel!" Faye laughed, feeling her heart warm. She knew, in all certainty, that she had said the right thing, the one thing that would bring peace to this gentle man. And, somehow, she did indeed feel that she had been the servant of a power greater than herself...or, perhaps, one living deep within herself.

The manager stood. "You look like an angel to me."

Government Interference

Faye saw Robert's car pull into the lot, but before she could get outside, he leapt from the car and dashed into the restaurant. "Faye! Faye!" he cried, and scooped her into his powerful embrace, then released her, regarding her with sadness in his eyes.

"Marian's—" he began.

"Dead!" Faye completed. "How did *you* know?"

"The police called me to identify her body," the doctor replied in surprise. "How did *you* know?"

"I was—" Faye cut herself off. "We'd better discuss this in your car."

She thanked the McDonald's manager, who thanked her in return and tried to give Robert a Super-sized Big Mac Combo Meal. "No, thank you," he said, suppressing a shudder. "Our friends have a Christmas dinner waiting for us."

The manager thanked her again, and the couple left and got into Robert's car. Robert started the engine, but instead of driving he put his head on the steering wheel and sobbed. "I thought I'd lost you. No one knew where you went. You've been gone three days, Faye! Three days with no word, no note. And then, when Marian— and Congressman Meany—their bodies were found together in a house in Sun City."

"*Sun City?*" Faye exclaimed. "Robert, she was killed not five miles from here!"

"*What?*" Robert took a deep breath. "This changes everything. Faye, she was found in a house with the body of Congressman Meany."

"Selma Graves' house?"

"Who?" Robert considered. "Yes, I think that *was* the owner. They hadn't located her yet."

"I've had quite an adventure," Faye began, not sure how to condense her adventure in the mine and subsequent transcendence into a believable story.

"Her body was mutilated, Faye," Robert said painfully. "Decapitated. And her hands were removed. The head and hands haven't been found."

"It must have been awful for you," Faye sympathized. "But how did her body get to Selma's house?"

"I don't know," Robert said, backing out of his parking space. "I knew from the lack of blood she'd been killed elsewhere. They didn't give me any chance to examine anything; the police hustled me in and out."

"Then how did you know that was Marian?"

"That beautiful, custom-embroidered sweatshirt you gave her for solstice," the doctor replied. "She was wearing it."

Faye digested this. "How did the police know to ask *you* to identify the body?"

"Marian's purse was found next to her," Robert replied, "with several of my business cards."

"Was *my* purse there?" Faye asked.

"No," Robert replied. "Why would it be?"

Faye's mind was racing. Clearly, the people running the show in the mine had taken Marian's body to Selma's house. Selma was in their bad graces, so they planned to frame her for Marian's, and Meany's, murders, making it look like a lover's triangle turned violent.

"So, the police are now searching for Selma," Faye surmised.

"That's right," Robert affirmed. "An 'all-points bulletin', if they still call it that."

"Robert," Faye said. "Let me tell you what *really* happened." And she did. Robert listened quietly throughout the recitation. When Faye was through, he continued to drive in silence, his brow furrowed in concern.

"Well?" she demanded, finally.

Robert sighed. "Faye...dearest..." He shook his head. "I think we need to work on *that* story a *lot*. *No one* is going to believe it."

"But it's true!"

"Faye! A secret, underground military base? Mind-controlled soldiers? A hidden grotto that can't be detected by helicopters or ground searchers? A mysterious woman who vanishes into thin air?" He shook his head again. "It can't be true! I mean, even if it's what you experienced—" He grabbed at her hand desperately. "I trust you too much to say 'I'm sure *you* believe it.' But, Faye—it's just not possible!"

"Robert—Marvin believed there was a global conspiracy, and secret armies, and hidden bases. You've read his book. You know he was killed. You *know* that conspiracies to create and manipulate laws go back *at least* as far as that 1937 Marijuana Tax Act. So how can you doubt me now? How can you justify the, the *intellectual cowardice* of not following your own beliefs to their logical conclusions?"

Robert seemed to cringe behind the wheel, but he continued to steer. "It's just too big," he whispered, finally. "It's too big to be real."

"What is, is," Faye pointed out, just as they both heard the blast of a siren behind them. She turned to see what the source was. Mere feet from Robert's rear bumper were the flashing red and blue lights of a police car. Through its windshield she could see another...and, through *its* windows, another still.

"Oh, shit," Robert moaned. A fourth car came out of nowhere and slid closely in front of them. Robert instinctively jammed on the brakes, and there was a *crunch!* as the vehicle behind them kissed Robert's bumper.

As Robert and Faye's vehicle came to a stop, men in black suits and others in khaki uniforms spilled out of their vehicles and surrounded them, guns drawn. "FBI!" one of the men shouted. "Come out with your hands up!"

Heart pounding, trembling, Faye carefully opened her door and did as directed. She heard Robert do the same from the drivers' side. Sheriff's deputies spun her around roughly and pushed her up against the side of the automobile. She was frisked. Across the top of the car, she could see Robert's face, his eyes, filled with agony, locked with hers. "You have the right to remain silent," one of the FBI men intoned to Robert. "Anything you say can and will be used against you in a court of law..."

"It's her, all right," one of the deputies, a woman, said. She turned Faye around to face her, and Faye could see she was looking at a photo of her, one that had been taken for publicity with the AquaBabes. She now looked at Faye kindly. "You're safe now, Ms. McRae. We won't let him hurt you again."

"But, he didn't hurt me!" she protested.

"Easy, now," the deputy soothed. "It's a common occurrence, in abductions, for the victim to take sides with her abductor. You'll come to understand that in the days to come."

Behind her was a thud and a grunt, followed by the sound of a falling body. Faye spun. "Robert!" she cried. But she couldn't see him over the top of the car.

"He was trying to resist arrest," the FBI man said, coldly. "He won't resist any more."

The trunk of Robert's car sprung open. "Aha!" someone cried triumphantly. "Look at this!"

Several of the officers shifted position to the back of the car. There were a couple of appreciative whistles.

"What is it?" Faye asked the female deputy. "What have they done to Robert?"

One of the men shouted, "There's enough pot back here to put him away for years!"

Faye felt herself flush beneath the grime that still covered her face. Robert might have been making a Christmas Day visit to some of his housebound patients when she called, Faye thought. This wasn't going to go well.

"Of *course* he's got drugs," the FBI man chortled. "Where else would someone like *him* get enough money for a car like this? Either drugs or pimping, you knew it was going to be one or the other." He looked critically at Faye. "Or both," he added.

The woman deputy ran around the car to the FBI man and whispered something to him. "Oh," he said. "Well, it could still involve white slavery. We *did* find drugs in his car." He nodded in Faye's direction. "Test her for drugs, and we'll know. A woman her age wouldn't have any illegal drugs in her system unless he'd forced them on her."

Faye threw up the hamburger she'd wolfed down. And then everything went black.

Anointing

. . . .

Ride With A Robot

When she came to, the face of the female sheriff's deputy was hovering over her. "Are you all right?" the woman asked with genuine concern.

"I think so," Faye muttered. "Where's Robert?"

The woman shook her head. "We've got him. He won't hurt you any more."

"He's *never* hurt me!" Faye protested, as the deputy helped her to her feet.

"Do you need an ambulance?" the deputy asked.

Faye shook her head. "No," she said, "I don't need a goddamned ambulance. Where are you taking Robert?"

"He's going to FBI headquarters in Phoenix," the deputy explained. "He'll be questioned, and held for arraignment."

"But he didn't *do* anything!" Faye protested.

"Then he'll be released quickly. But I have to tell you, Ms. McRae...we found a lot of marijuana in the trunk of his car. It won't be easy to explain that."

"He's a doctor," Faye shouted. "He prescribes it to his patients."

"That's against federal law," the woman stated.

"It's legal in Arizona!" Faye argued.

"A conflict that will have to be addressed in court. Now, please, get into this car. FBI Agent Barrow has asked to drive you home." She opened a door and, placing her hand on Faye's head so Faye wouldn't hit it on the doorframe, guided her in. Faye was panicky and exhausted. The long walk, indeed, the last several days, were catching up to her. She was furious at what was happening to Robert, but realized there was nothing she could do about it now. The deputy was right; it would be ironed out in court or sooner, but first, Faye had to see to her own freedom and safety or she would be unable to help Robert. Should she try to escape? She was literally surrounded by deputies and agents, in an unfamiliar area, without other transportation. Besides, the woman had told her she was being taken home. Though that might not be a given; she could hear arguing outside the FBI car.

She looked through the glass separating her from the arguers. It was the deputy and two of the FBI men.

"...obviously knows him," the agent who'd knocked Robert out said. "I say, we take her in for questioning."

"She is an innocent victim. The victim of an abduction often comes to identify with their abductor, to believe in the abductors' cause, and even to defend them," said the other agent, the one who'd found the pot in Robert's trunk.

"She's been through a terrible ordeal," said the woman deputy. "Yeah, she needs to be questioned. But would it be so awful to let her get a shower and some sleep, first?"

The first agent was outvoted, and was obviously annoyed by that. Faye suspected he didn't want the deputy, a person who did not work for the FBI, to have a vote at all. But the other agent kept repeating the line that victims identify with their abductors and, even though Faye had certainly not been abducted by anyone—at least, until now—she wouldn't argue if it would get her home. She prayed that *he* would be the agent driving the car. She did not trust the other, the one who had beaten Robert.

Her prayer was answered. When the argument ended and the police and FBI vehicles began to drive away, it was the agent with the abduction fixation who got into the car in which she waited.

"Hi," she greeted, but he kept silent as he turned his key in the ignition. The well-maintained vehicle started smoothly and he pulled around Robert's car, which remained where it had been stopped, in the middle of the southbound lane. One of the deputies was tagging it to be towed. Other deputies were engaged in guiding what little traffic there was, around the congestion.

"I'm Faye McRae," she introduced herself. Still, the agent didn't speak. Once clear of the obstructions, he speeded up, heading swiftly southeast toward the city. But Faye was resolute. This man was *not* going to ignore her.

"Who are you?" she asked.

"I am Agent Desmond Barrow, FBI," he replied. He didn't seem angry or officious, simply focused on driving.

"You're the one who found the pot in Robert's trunk, aren't you?"

"Enough to put him away for years," the agent agreed.

"But he's a *doctor*," Faye informed the agent. "He *prescribes* marijuana to his patients, in accordance with Arizona law."

"Possession of marijuana violates federal law," Barrow replied.

"But it doesn't violate *Arizona* law!" Faye cried. "The voters of this state voted to make medical marijuana legal last year!"

"Possession of marijuana violates federal law," Barrow repeated, in precisely the tone and cadence he'd used the first time.

Faye could recognize thorough indoctrination when she heard it. She decided to broach another subject. "Why did you want me to go home, instead of with Robert to FBI headquarters?"

He was silent for a moment, as if trying to decide which canned speech to recite. Finally, he answered, "You are an innocent victim. The victim of an abduction often comes to identify with their abductor, to believe in the abductors' cause, and even to defend them,"

"Yes, you said that before," Faye agreed. "But I was not abducted. Robert has been my friend for months! And, what you need to know is what *did* happen." She started to describe the underground mine, the black-garbed soldiers, the mysterious voices.

But the agent interrupted. "You are an innocent victim," he said. "The victim of an abduction often comes to identify with their abductor, to believe in the abductors' cause, and even to defend them."

That brought Faye to pause. What the hell was *that?* It didn't really seem to be an appropriate response to what she had said.

His next words, spoken with no emotion whatsoever, floored her.

"No one will ever believe you were in a secret, underground military base. If you insist on telling that story, you will be locked in a sanitarium for patients with Alzheimer's disease. There will be no evidence to support your story. No mine, no soldiers, no tunnels. The smart thing for you to do is to keep your mouth shut, to admit that you were abducted by Dr. Thompson, and that you came to identify with him during your abduction. To do otherwise is a one-way ticket to an insane asylum where no one will ever hear your story. I hope I've made myself clear."

He's one of them, Faye thought, chilled to the bone. On the other hand, as they continued to drive southeast on Highway 60, never deviating from their perfectly legal speed of 55 mph, it seemed that he didn't intend her any actual harm; at least, not now. All she had to do was sit quietly and let him take her home.

He didn't ask her for directions, or even an address. They pulled to a stop in front of Faye's home. Barrow got out, walked around to the passenger side, opened the door and offered his hand to Faye in assistance. She ignored it and got out on her own. She stalked towards her front door, then realized she did not have her purse—it had been in Marian's car and God only knew where *that* was. At the bottom of some dusty draw, she imagined. She turned toward the FBI vehicle, reluctantly ready to request the aid of the advanced lock-picking kit she assumed Agent Barrow would have, only to see it pulling rapidly away from the curb.

"You jerk!" she called, but it wasn't very satisfying. Then, remembering her lessons from Marian, she shouted, *"You fucking asshole!"* That felt a little better, but it still didn't make up for all the pain and frustration of the last three days, which were, even now, not truly over. She spun, ready to use kung fu, if necessary, to break into her own home.

But the door was ajar, revealing only the shadowy abyss of the darkened home.

Home Security

Hesitant, senses on full alert, Faye pushed the door the rest of the way open and stood at the doorway, listening intently. There was no sound from within. She snaked her hand onto the wall switch by the door and switched on the light. Still, there was no sound. She poked her head into the room.

It was in a shambles. Cushions had been torn from the sofa and chairs, ripped to shreds, and scattered here, there, and everywhere. Books had been thrown willy-nilly from the bookcase. Faye's uncle's console TV set had literally been smashed, and her computer was missing.

Numb and trembling, she found her telephone and dialed 911. "My house has been robbed!" she cried. "I just got home, and the door was open and the place is a wreck!"

"I've dispatched a police car to your address," the voice at the other end of the line said, in a professional tone designed to calm anyone. "Is there *any possibility* that the intruder is still in your home?"

"I—well, I don't know," admitted Faye.

"Then, get out—*now!*" The voice commanded. "Wait outside, or better yet, at a neighbor's. The police will be there in minutes."

Faye hung up, and, in her suddenly spooked rush to leave, tripped on one of the ripped-up cushions. If not for her kung fu training, she might well have fallen and broken a hip. However, her reflexes came to her rescue and she instinctively hopped until she regained her balance and ran to the street.

In minutes, a police cruiser pulled up to her curb. "I've been robbed!" she cried, arms waving in the air.

The uniformed policeman got out. "Stay here until I give you the all-clear," he ordered. He ran to her door, then drew his revolver and cautiously entered swinging from one side to the other, looking exactly like any policeman on any TV show.

Ten chilling minutes passed while she waited for him. It suddenly occurred to her that he might find her secret grow room—if the intruder hadn't found it first. And, even if that didn't happen—Faye believed the room was pretty secure—what if she had left a joint in plain sight? She remembered sharing one with Marian the last time she was home, just before they set out to confront Selma. *My—that seems like a month ago! But it was just three days,* Faye thought. In any case, three days or a month, Faye couldn't remember for certain what she had done with the remains of the joint. Worrying about this made the wait doubly stressful.

Finally, the police officer emerged from the house, gun holstered, and waving her in with a relieved grin. She released the pent-up tension with a sigh, but kept her guard up as she returned to her home.

The chaos inside continued to daze her. "Is anything missing?" the officer asked.

She shook her head in despair. "I know my computer was taken," she said. "I haven't checked the rest of the house, yet. The operator on 911 told me to get out of the house immediately."

"That's policy," the officer explained. Through the living room window, Faye saw another police car pull up. "Backup," the officer commented. "I'm afraid the rest of the house is as bad as this; you'd better check to see what else was taken. Jewelry, for example. Or cash."

The officer followed her as she went from room to room. Dishes and drinking glasses had been thrown from the kitchen cabinets and knives, forks and spoons were scattered everywhere. The spice shelf had been thrown into disarray. She knew it would take days to get the kitchen straightened up but nothing seemed to have been stolen.

The dining area was sparsely furnished, with no cabinets or drawers in there to open. Nothing was missing.

The guest bedroom had been trashed. The contents of the dresser drawers, spare linens and towels, had been scattered on the floor. One of the drawers was broken. The mirror over the dresser was smashed and the mattress had been ripped to shreds by a carving knife that lay on the floor.

"Do you recognize that?" the officer asked, indicating the knife.

"Yes, it's mine," Faye admitted. She hadn't realized it was missing from the piles of cutlery in the kitchen. She would need to be more observant.

"Don't touch it," the officer cautioned. "It may be evidence."

"*May* be evidence?" Faye questioned.

"Depending on what crime was committed here," the officer explained. "If it was just vandalism or theft, probably nothing will come of this. Your insurance will pay to replace and repair, and that'll be it. If, on the other hand, some kind of mayhem was involved…"

Faye was still too much in shock to complain that she wanted the perpetrators hung for this, even if it was "just" vandalism. She staggered into the hall bathroom, where the drawers and cabinets were opened—nothing but cleaning supplies, here—and the medicine cabinet had been empty to begin with.

Her master bedroom had been treated with no more respect than the guest bedroom. Her mattress was shredded, her clothes thrown from the closet and the dresser drawers onto the floor. Edwin's argyle socks were lying among his underwear. Seeing them was a sad surprise; she had forgotten about them yet here they were, in plain sight, reminding her of how her life had been turned upside down since the day he shot himself.

Someone entered the room; nerves on edge, Faye jumped a little when the shadow passed by the corner of her eye. She was surprised and pleased to recognize her policeman friend as the newcomer.

"Grant!" she cried. "What are *you* doing here?"

"I left word to be notified if you turned up," the detective explained. "I've been worried about you. And," he added angrily, "no one called me when the FBI picked you up earlier. But the dispatcher contacted me when you reported being robbed."

Faye impulsively hugged him. "But, your Christmas!" she cried in dismay.

Grant smiled indulgently. "Christmas morning was great," he said. "We opened all our presents and had Christmas dinner early this afternoon. I didn't really want to watch *It's A Wonderful Life* for the fourteenth time, so don't worry about it. Now, what happened here?"

The officer heard this as being directed to him. "Seems like a case of vandalism, sir, with petty theft thrown in."

"*Petty?*" Faye fumed. "It was a brand-new computer, with all my files on it!"

"What did it cost?" Grant asked.

"Uh—" Faye hesitated. "It was a gift. I don't know how much it was worth, exactly."

"Well, it was probably more than $500. That makes it grand theft, Officer Rodriguez."

"Yes, sir."

"Anything else missing?" Grant asked, pointedly, of Faye.

"Not that I know of. But it will take me days to get all this cleaned up. And Robert has been arrested!"

"Yeah, I know," Grant replied. "Where were you? You look like you were in a bar fight!"

"It's a long story," she said. "And I'll tell you all about it…but, please, *may* I take a shower? It's been a very long, hard couple of days. And it's clearly not over yet."

"C'mon, Officer, let's leave Ms. McRae so she can clean up. Let's check for evidence in the other rooms."

"There's a knife from the kitchen that was used to shred the mattresses," the officer remarked, as Grant closed the bedroom door behind him.

Faye salvaged a pair of slacks and a blouse from the debris on the floor. She found undies beneath Edwin's socks. She stripped off her soiled clothing, placed them in the hamper and turned the water on in the shower stall.

Amazingly, the shower stall had been untouched, perhaps because its contents could be seen through the glass door, and consisted of naught but shampoo, washcloth, and a bar of soap.

Her real relief came, of course, from seeing that the secret door to her grow room was not open.

But, had it *been* opened? When the shower water ran hot, Faye stepped into the stall and allowed the steamy liquid to flow into her hair and run in rivulets down her aching, dusty body. When she lathered herself up, she saw the white suds run gray down the drain.

She had been filthy.

She explored every crevice with soapy fingers, anxious to remove any trace of her misadventure in the mine. She shampooed her hair not once, not twice, but three times.

She remembered Marian scolding her about the way she shampooed in the rec center showers. "Lather, rinse, repeat!" her friend had scoffed. "Haven't you ever even *tried* to lather and rinse just once, to see if it works better for you?" When Faye admitted she hadn't, Marian ranted on, "Don't you realize, those directions are just a scam to instantly double the sales of shampoo? Unless you have very oily hair—and you don't—you should never have to lather more than once. You'll find it leaves your hair much softer, I'll bet." Faye had taken the hint, and tried it, and omitting the "repeat" did, indeed, leave her hair softer and more manageable.

But not today. Today she wanted no trace of the dust, or mud, or blood to remain on her body.

She would also have to clean her clothes—thoroughly—at the first opportunity. No, *tonight*. There were bloodstains on them. Grant would have seen them, if they hadn't been covered by such a thick layer of dust.

As she rinsed, Faye found herself anxious to check her grow room. She knew there were three joints in a bowl on top of the grow unit. If they were untouched, she would feel confident the secret room had not been compromised. She turned off the water and pulled on the washcloth rack in the special way. The wall slid silently open. The baby marijuana plants were thriving, having grown noticeably since she'd seen them last, three days before. And, she saw with relief, the three joints Marian had given her still waited in the bowl.

She returned the wall to its normal position, a soft *click* indicating it was again locked in place.

She dried herself with the towel that, she was relieved to note, had been left untouched on the rack and slipped into her clean clothes. She looked at herself in the bathroom mirror, and felt like a new woman.

Suddenly, her heart froze. "Grant! Grant!" she shouted, as she dove into the clothes and mattress innards covering the bedroom floor. "Grant!" The bedroom door flung open and Grant stood there, revolver drawn.

"What is it?" the detective cried. "Are you all right?"

"Yes, I'm okay, but I think I know what else was taken," Faye responded, frantically sweeping beneath the clothes with her hand.

"What?"

Faye covered a little more area, then straightened up, sitting on her heels. "Edwin's gun," she said. "He kept it, I kept it, I mean, behind his argyle socks. I'd almost forgotten about it. Edwin's socks are on the floor, but the gun is *gone*."

Fosterized

"You're sure it's missing?" Grant asked quietly.

"Well, no," Faye admitted. "I suppose whoever trashed my home might have moved it, instead of taking it. But the rest of the contents of the drawer are right here, and the gun isn't."

The detective clenched his jaw. "Let me ask you one question," he said. "Did Edwin own any weapons other than the Smith & Wesson .44 magnum?"

"No. He only bought that one because of a robbery attempt at the garage we used to own."

Grant sat on the edge of the ruined mattress and patted his knee two or three times. He was frowning, but not at Faye. Suddenly, he looked her in the eye. "Let me tell you what's gone on since you've been missing," he said.

"Two days ago, we received an anonymous tip that there'd been a murder at the home of a Selma Graves in Sun City. I was assigned to investigate, and I recognized her name—she was the one who called the police to the Timmons murder scene. Remember? I looked it up for you."

"That's right," Faye said, trying to sound surprised.

"In fact, I was first on the scene. When I got there, I found, not one body, but two. One was that of a headless, handless woman. The other was U.S. Representative Carvel Meany—and that made it a federal case, so we had to notify the FBI."

Two days? Faye thought. *That was one day after Meany was actually killed.*

"We found a purse near the woman's body. The license gave her name as Marian Higgins. You, allegedly, were abducted at the time, so you wouldn't know—"

"I was not abducted!" Faye interrupted.

Grant nodded. "We'll get to *your* story in a minute. The point is, you weren't in a position to know that the radio and TV went nuts—a headless woman found in Sun City!—and we found several of Dr. Thompson's business cards in her purse. So we called the doc to identify the body." The detective grimaced. "*We* sure couldn't, since there was no head for dental records and no hands for fingerprints. He *did* identify her, and that should have been the end of his involvement."

"But it wasn't," Faye pointed out. "The FBI arrested him while he was driving me home from Wickenburg!"

"When I got to the Graves home, there was no gun on the scene. I would swear to it. But the FBI report says there *was*—and that it was registered in the name of Edwin McRae—your husband, Faye. The report described it as the same gun that Edwin used to kill himself."

"No!" Faye protested, puzzled. "That isn't possible!"

"It certainly didn't seem likely," Grant admitted. "When I read the report, I wondered if maybe you had just thrown the revolver away after I returned it to you. After all, it *was* the gun that had killed your husband; you might not have wanted to keep it. But then, when Thompson called in a missing persons alert on *you*, it seemed too much for coincidence. If he knew you, the FBI figured, he could have stolen your gun and used it to murder the Representative."

"But you said there was no gun there when you arrived, before the FBI showed up. Doesn't that prove that someone planted Edwin's gun there? Probably the same person who stole it from here?"

Grant sighed. "I'd like to say no federal law enforcement agency would ever falsify evidence," he said. "But the fact is, virtually every government agency's been caught at it at least once. Did you follow the Vince Foster case?"

"The President's friend, right? Committed suicide a few years ago? I remember hearing about it on the news."

"In 1993," the detective agreed. "His body was found in Fort Marcy Park in Virginia, across the Potomac River from Washington, DC. That's a small national park, and park police did the investigation—oddly, the FBI *wasn't* brought in. The photograph the park police took of the crime scene clearly shows a black or dark-barreled pistol next to the body. The government later claimed the gun that shot him was a silver-barreled pistol his wife owned."

"You're kidding! Why would anyone cover up a murder like that?"

"Well, Foster was in charge of an NSA project that electronically monitored bank transactions," the detective pointed out. "I can imagine all sorts of powerful men who wouldn't want *that* done. He was also involved in other things, including the scandal at the First Lady's former real estate business. There's no end of people who might want him dead, but no compelling evidence that he, himself, was one of them."

"He wasn't depressed? I thought he was. I remember something about a 'lost weekend' he spent in bed with the blinds drawn."

Grant shook his head. "That was reported from an anonymous source by *The New York Times*. It was never verified. Neither were any of the other stories about Foster's alleged depression."

Faye shook her head. Grant continued, his frown deepening. "So, why don't you tell me what *did* happen, since you say you weren't abducted?"

Faye explained how she and Marian had gone to Selma's to confront her with evidence that Meany had accepted illegal campaign contributions, and how they had found Meany there. She held nothing back, neither the part where Meany shot at them, nor the part where he killed himself.

"Faye," Grant interrupted, shaking his head. "What you're describing is going to be impossible to testify to in a court of law. I hope to heck you aren't asked to."

"But, why?" Faye asked, sincerely. "It's the truth!"

The detective shook his head again, a wry grin giving him an uncomfortable look. "*I* know you well enough to know you are telling the truth as you saw it," he assured her. "But, Faye—people, a jury, they have an idea how a Congressman behaves. Womanizing they would accept. If you described Meany as shooting you to hide the evidence of illegal contributions, they would believe that; but not that a little old woman, his campaign manager, was giving him orders— or, even less believable, of his being under some kind of spell."

"I'm only telling the truth!"

"So am I, Faye. Now, go on—do you know how your friend, Marian, was killed?"

So Faye continued, describing the chase to the canyons east of Wickenburg, and the climb down the shaft into the underground base, and the attack of the soldiers. As she related her tale, Grant kept shaking his head. Finally, Faye described hiding out in a grotto until this morning. She did not mention Norma.

"Unbelievable!" Grant exclaimed when she was done. "I'm sorry, Ms. McRae. You had me right until the mind-controlled army in the mine."

Faye's shoulder's hunched miserably. "I can't help it, Grant," she wailed. "That's what happened."

"I hope to God no one asks you to tell that story on a witness stand." He sat, uncomfortably, perhaps hoping that Faye would break the silence with a confession that she'd made the whole thing up. When she did not, he remarked, "You hid in a cave for three days? You must have been starving!"

"I *was* hungry; after I got up the nerve to hike into Wickenburg, I had breakfast at a fast food place. I'd lost my purse, but the manager fed me for free."

Grant looked puzzled. "But your purse is in the living room," he said. "I found it in the cushion stuffing while you were taking your shower."

"What?" Faye cried, jumping to her feet. "Let me see it!"

"That's Why I'm A Cop"

Grant led the way to the living room, which now had one big pile of cushion stuffing, instead of the whole floor being covered. There were two uniformed officers pouring through the debris. There was Faye's purse, on the coffee table. "That is yours, isn't it?"

"Yes, it is." *Did I leave a joint in it?* Faye wondered, barely containing her urge to panic.

"You'd better go through it, and make sure nothing is missing."

Faye did just that, at first trying to sort through the contents without removing them from the bag, just in case there *was* a joint in there. But it was too difficult to actually spot what was there and what wasn't and Faye felt as if her attempt at discretion made her behavior look guilty. So she placed each item on the now-cleared coffee table: wallet, change purse, compact, lipstick... It all seemed to be there. And there was nothing illegal.

She opened her wallet. Nothing was missing. But...

"My wallet has been tampered with," she told the detective. "My license isn't in the same pocket I normally keep it in."

"Are you sure?" Grant asked, peering over her shoulder.

"Yes, see? It is supposed to be behind this plastic window, but it's in front of it, as if someone took it out and put it back incorrectly." She described the way the voices seemed to know all about her in the underground Great Room. "And they moved Marian's car, so I figured I would never see that purse again."

Grant sent the uniformed policemen out of the room and sat on the sofa, then winced when he sunk through the ripped cushioning to the springs. He repositioned himself so that he was perched on the edge of the upholstered frame. "Faye," he said. "I know I've warned you several times about getting into the investigation business."

"You have," Faye agreed. "And you're sweet to be concerned, but—"

The detective held up his hand. "Please, Faye. You don't realize what it is you're getting into. As soon as you brought Meany's name into this, I knew you were bound for trouble. Do you realize that if I reported your story, *you* would become the prime suspect for Meany's murder? Good grief, woman! He was killed with a gun from *your* home. He was killed while *you* were there, by your own admission. And you believed him to be guilty of the Michael

Timmons murder, and are a friend of the victim's grandfather. That's your motive!"

Faye flushed. "But I didn't do it! Surely, Grant, you know me well enough to know I wouldn't murder anyone, much less decapitate Marian!"

"Your doctor boyfriend could have done that part," Grant said grimly, but without conviction. "Listen, Faye, *I* know you didn't do it. But it's not up to me!"

"Are you going to turn me in?" Faye asked uncertainly.

Grant looked uncomfortable. "Except for your story, there's no evidence that you were ever in the Graves house. And you told it to me before I read you your Miranda rights, so, it isn't admissible in court, anyway. But, Faye, I have to urge you—in the strongest possible way—to *not* tell anyone else about this underground base, or even of your visit to the Graves house. When we find Graves, you may *have* to tell your story if she implicates you. Otherwise, just keep your mouth shut."

Faye glared at her friend. "Grant, you can't be telling me to withhold evidence! There's an underground military base less than fifty miles from here, and it does *not* belong to the United States government. Someone from there almost certainly killed Marian and brought the body to Selma's house. How can I not report this? How can *you* not report it?"

Grant relaxed like a slowly released spring. "The papers said nothing about her being murdered somewhere else. Hmm." He frowned. "You're right. There wasn't nearly enough blood to account for decapitation in that house. Moreover, the head and hands weren't found. The papers assumed the killer took them as souvenirs. And, with Meany's having shot himself there—the bone and blood in the room definitely came from him, and there *were* powder burns on his right hand—we didn't have a scenario that fit all the facts. You're story actually does fit them." The detective sighed. "Unfortunately, I can't use it."

"Why not?" Faye asked in exasperation.

"Faye...Faye." Grant smiled tiredly. "Everyone watches TV, and everyone gets an idea of what police officers can do. We are portrayed as going off on our own, solving horrendous crimes no matter who perpetrated them, and ending up the hero. Reality is nothing like that."

"Oh?"

"In reality, I have a boss. He tells me what paths I can follow. Oh, he never says 'Don't investigate that.' But he might well tell me that I shouldn't follow a certain lead because someone else is following it for another case, or because we don't want to tip him off because we are after a bigger fish. I can be placed on another case at any time and made to abandon one I was working on. With time, every cop gets a feel for what we'll be allowed to do and what we can't. It's all subtle, unspoken. But it's as real as a glass wall. And I knew, when you first started following leads that led to Meany, that you were running where *I* would fear to tread."

"Why didn't you tell me that?"

Grant grimaced. "Force of habit, I guess. The public doesn't *want* to know that certain people can get away with murder if they're powerful enough. Forget O.J. Simpson. Has anyone been executed for selling tobacco, a product known to kill its customers? Has anyone received a prison sentence for selling aspartame, a product that the FDA refused to approve until President Reagan appointed a new head of the FDA, who immediately approved aspartame, then quit to head the company that makes the stuff? Was anyone even *arrested* for murdering Vince Foster?" Grant's eyes flashed angrily. "No, no, and no."

"Then, Grant—if you're so hamstrung—why do you continue to do it? Why even *be* a policeman?"

The man smiled. "Part of my job is capturing criminals. But mostly, I see it as one of helping the victims. Sun City doesn't see that many murders. But you have lots of suicides, which is what brought you and me together originally. I hope I was able to help you when you needed it."

"Oh, you did!" Faye cried, and impulsively kissed the officer on the cheek. "I don't know what I would have done without you. Those were such dark days," she added.

"Well, helping victims get through those days, that's what I'm about. This job gives me an opportunity to do that. *That's* why I'm a cop."

Friends Indeed

Friday, December 26, 1997

Faye awoke the morning after Christmas in the guest room at Chuck and Dave's.

She had never been to their home before. It was beautiful, with everything in the perfect place. There had been so many pillows on the bed in the guest room that it looked like a display at a mattress outlet. She didn't know what to do with them, so she placed all but one of them neatly in a stack in a corner of the room.

The sheets bore a pattern of light grays, tans and browns. The blankets and pillowcases picked up the colors perfectly, but each in a different pattern. Faye couldn't imagine how long it must have taken the boys to shop for all those different matching patterns.

The room even *smelled* beautiful, fresh with a hint of flowers and grass (the lawn kind) and sunshine. It was like being outside in the hills of California. There was, in fact, no hint of the pungent scent of marijuana, even though Faye knew her friends smoked.

She was there because Grant wouldn't let Faye spend the night at her home. He consented to her staying with friends, as long as she didn't call them from her own phone. He had driven her to Chuck and Dave's home, and wouldn't leave until Chuck had answered the door and let her in.

By then, it was late and Faye couldn't keep her eyes open. Dave earned her eternal gratitude by not pressing her to tell her story before getting a good night's rest.

She had only worn the clothes she had put on at home for a few hours, so she was willing to wear them again. However, there was a full-length terrycloth robe draped over the chair—a robe Faye was reasonably certain hadn't been there the night before. She put it on, stepped into the hallway, found the hall bathroom and stepped inside, where she found a toothbrush on the counter still in the wrapper, and a new tube of toothpaste, in addition to a fresh towel laid on the counter.

After brushing her teeth, she stepped into the tub and closed the glass doors. The showerhead was removable and pulsated, giving her the best shower of her life. She'd had no idea there was such a thing as a "shower massage" and wondered what else she'd missed out on. She found out when she dried herself. The towel was luxury itself, big and plush and thirsty. Faye thought it was like drying oneself with an Angora cat.

When she came out, she was assailed by the smells of a big, country breakfast. She followed her nose to the kitchen, where she found Chuck cooking.

"Good morning, Sunshine!" he called out.

"Sleeping Beauty has arisen!" Dave announced, looking up from the copy of *People* he'd been reading.

"I suppose I overslept a little," Faye confessed. "What time is it? Nine? Ten?"

"Try two-thirty," Dave laughed.

"Two-thirty?" Faye gasped. "In the *afternoon?*"

"You betcha," Chuck assured her. "You want your eggs scrambled? Sausage or bacon? I made both," he added, "just to be sure. So you can *have* both, if you like."

"Why are you making breakfast at two-thirty?" Faye asked. "Not just for *me?*"

"Yes, just for you!" Dave said, rising and giving her a hug. "We're so glad you're all right! You're my *favorite* person," he added in a whisper, directly into her ear.

That was a surprise, and Faye hugged him back. She had grown fond of him, too.

"We eat any old time," Chuck remarked, as he placed a plate loaded with eggs smothered in cheese, sautéed onions, and mushrooms, accompanied by bacon and sausage and a thick slice of melon. It was four times more than she could eat.

Dave brought plates for himself and his partner, and then there was "not-from-concentrate" orange juice, with "all the pulp."

"That's a hint of whole cream and savory in the eggs," Dave bragged.

A half dozen humorous ripostes paraded across her mind, but she realized she was hungry—the only thing she had eaten yesterday had been that burger in Wickenburg. And, although she could *never* have eaten all that food, she did.

Her hosts cleaned their own plates and sat quietly and expectantly until she finally sighed in satisfaction.

"All right, now," Dave said. "What happened? And what happened to Marian?"

Faye's expression fell. "Marian is gone," she said through misting eyes. She hated Marian for deserting her like this.

"We know that," Chuck admitted. "From the Channel 2 News. What happened?"

Faye hesitated. She'd been told twice, now, once by an FBI agent and once by a police detective, that her story was too crazy to be believed. She began to think that maybe she *should* tone it down a little. She also realized that she'd better make it consistent—when Robert's case came to trial, if it did, she didn't want any witnesses who could say that she'd changed her story. If she had to, she could always claim that she had been distraught when talking to Barrow and Grant—besides, *they* were the ones who'd advised her to change her story.

At this point, nothing mattered but freeing Robert. If a more believable testimony would help accomplish that, so be it.

So Faye told an edited version. She didn't explain why she and Marian had gone to Wickenburg, how they had become separated, or that she had found Marian's body. Instead, she emphasized her walk into town so that their impression was that she'd spent days making it. However, she held nothing back when it came to describing Robert's sudden and unexpected arrest.

"So, what are you going to do now?" Dave asked quietly. She loved them for not challenging her on any part of the story, for just accepting it as she told it.

"I have to get to Robert," Faye replied. "I understand he's at the FBI headquarters in Phoenix. I don't know where that is, exactly, but I suppose it's in the phone book."

"We'll go with you if you need us," Chuck offered. "But if you don't...well, we *are* in the middle of a grow room job for another member of the club."

"I won't have a problem," she insisted. "If you could just take me home to get my car, I'd be so grateful. Oh—and if I could use your phone. I'll need to get the insurance adjuster out to check the damage to my home." She set her jaw. "But I've got to see Robert. That's my first priority."

Faye Gets A Lawyer

The insurance adjuster was pulling up to Faye's house as Chuck and Dave arrived with her. Her car was still in the driveway; she had not been in any condition to drive the night before. Now she felt quite able: Still furious, but in control.

The boys insisted on accompanying her into the ruins of her home. *Faye* might have been in control, but Dave was not; he ran from room to room, shrieking. When he finally returned to her in the living room, he was livid. "Don't you worry, baby. We'll make this all right! Better than ever, *you'll* see!"

The chaos in her house was not the adjuster's fault, and Faye did not take it out on him. In fact, she was fiercely calm. She walked him through the damage as he took notes. When he was done, he wrote a check on the spot and offered it to her.

"Don't take it, honey," Chuck warned, whispering in her ear. "You can get more by refusing that first offer." Faye had calculated what it would cost to replace her uncle's Spartan furniture and the clothes—most of which no longer fit her, anyway—and the adjuster's offer was, in fact, much more than she had expected.

When she showed it to the boys, Chuck whistled and Dave quipped, "It's your legs, girlfriend!" So she accepted it, desiring to put an end to this aspect of her misadventure as quickly as possible.

"Don't even think about staying here until you've gotten the place cleaned up," the adjuster advised. "I've included enough to provide you with a couple of weeks at a reasonably-priced hotel."

The moment the adjuster had gone, Dave said, "You are *not* staying at some stuck-up motel when we have a perfectly lovely guest room."

"You've already slept in the sheets," Chuck pointed out, gallantly. "We'll have to wash them, anyway."

"But I thought you had another grow room to do!" Faye exclaimed. "I can't expect you to spend time selecting furniture—"

"Shush!" Dave interrupted. "The next two days are mostly Chuck-type work, anyway. And I won't need any longer than that to decorate *this* place!"

Her purse mysteriously returned, Faye was grateful that she would not have to get a duplicate driver's license or car keys. She supposed she should cancel all her credit cards, but she knew somehow her purse had not been taken by people who needed the physical cards to run charges up on them. So she hopped in her Ford and headed to downtown Phoenix.

The Phoenix FBI headquarters was housed in its own building, on the corner of Indianola and North 2nd Street. It being the day after Christmas, and a Friday, there was very little traffic. Most downtown-type businesses had allowed their employees to have the day off, too, so they could return their Christmas gifts to the out-lying stores whose employees were required to work. Faye found on-street parking just across from the FBI building. As she got out of her car, she was startled to see Bitsy Cunningham, her friend from AquaBabes, about to enter the building. She barely recognized her, since the woman was wearing a severe business suit instead of the swim suit in which Faye was more accustomed to seeing her.

"Bitsy!" Faye called. Her friend turned around and waved excitedly when she caught sight of Faye, running across the street to meet her.

"Faye, darling!" Bitsy cried as she nearly crushed Faye in her beefy arms. "I'm so glad I caught you before you got inside!"

"Why, what's wrong with my being inside?"

"Nothing, except it's best that we agree on a story that can be backed up."

"We?" Faye asked, anxiously. "Why do *we* need a story?"

Bitsy looked blank for a moment, then grinned. "I *am* Robert's lawyer. You did know that, right?"

"Oh." Dimly, Faye recalled someone having once mentioned Bitsy's being a retired lawyer.

"And, of course, you're going to be questioned as soon as you go inside, certainly before they let you see Robert. Now, can you tell me everything here, or do we need to sit down? And I do mean, *everything*. Let me decide what to leave out."

"Bitsy," Faye said, "I've already been told by an FBI agent and a cop that what *really* happened is too unbelievable to be true. Are you sure you don't want the simpler, more believable version?"

Bitsy blinked. "Let's sit in my car," she said. "You tell me what *really* happened."

So Faye followed her into Bitsy's car, and did just that. After a moment, Bitsy got out a notepad and began jotting down notes.

"Well?" Faye prompted, when she was done.

Bitsy sighed. "Your FBI and policeman friend were right," she said. "If you tell that story, *you'll* wind up arrested for Marian's murder, if not Meany's."

Faye sighed. "What if we just leave the part out about the mine? I *did* see Meany shoot himself, and Marian and I *did* follow Selma to Wickenburg. Marian and I *were* separated there, and I truly don't know *how* she was killed or by whom."

Bitsy nodded. "That is much better," she said. "It doesn't implicate you *or* Robert, and it should get Robert off the hook."

"So that's what I'll tell them," Faye said decisively, nodding toward the FBI building.

"I advise against it," Bitsy cautioned. "I do suggest you let *me* do the talking. Give me a dollar."

"What?"

"Give me a dollar," Bitsy repeated, holding out her hand. Faye pulled one out of her purse, noting that whoever had taken her purse to her house hadn't even stolen the money from it. She handed the bill to Bitsy.

"All righty, then," Bitsy said. "I agree to be your representative in this matter for the retainer of one dollar." She slipped the money into her jacket coat pocket. "Now, when we get inside, keep your mouth shut. I'll answer questions for you."

The Lions' Den

Bitsy led the way into the building. Faye was nervous, almost shaking, as Bitsy explained to the receptionist that they were there to see Robert Thompson. "We're his representation," Bitsy explained.

The receptionist, a kindly-looking, gray-haired lady, smiled and asked them to be seated.

Shortly, a man in a dark suit emerged from the inner offices, spotted the women in their seats, and nodded affably. "Good afternoon, Ms. Cunningham. I understand you're Robert Thompson's lawyer. And you are Ms. McRae," he added, directly to Faye. "It was nice of you to come on your own."

"She is here to see her fiancé, Dr. Thompson," Bitsy answered before Faye could open her mouth. "I am her lawyer, also, and we will be willing to answer some questions if you have any."

"That's right," Faye said, rising, unwilling to be a marionette.

"I'm Agent Berkeley Keck. We've been expecting you. Follow me, please."

Inside, the agent led them into a room that looked like any number of conference rooms she'd seen on TV. "Now, Ms. McRae," Keck began. "Please tell us everything you did between December 22 and December 25. I am, of course, particularly interested in how you came to be in Dr. Thompson's car Christmas Day."

Bitsy began to recite for Faye, but to Faye it seemed to make her seem terribly guilty. "Really, Bitsy, I can do this," she said, and repeated the simplified version she and Bitsy had agreed on before coming in.

Keck took notes, questioning once or twice, trying to get time estimates, and asking things like, "How far did you drive on the dirt road?" and "How much water did you have with you?"

Finally, he must have judged her done, because he thanked her and excused himself and left the room, closing the door behind him. "Good job, Faye," Bitsy congratulated her, warning Faye with her eyes not to speak while they seemed to be alone. Faye saw the large mirror built into one wall of the room, knowing it was almost certainly composed of one-way glass.

Then, the door opened, and Robert stepped in. He was handcuffed, and followed closely by a Marine.

Faye wasn't sure what she had expected, but it broke her heart to see Robert handcuffed, and wearing an orange, paper jumpsuit.

"Robert!" The cry escaped from her without intention, in spite of Bitsy's warning to keep her mouth shut. Faye leaped to her feet, sending the chair in which she'd been sitting to the floor. Robert reached out for Faye's outstretched hand.

Faye ran around the table to her lover and wrapped her arms around him.

"Really, Agent Keck, are those handcuffs necessary?" Bitsy asked. The Marine looked to the FBI man.

"You may remove them, Corporal," the agent said to the Marine in response. "But keep alert. The suspect has been charged with *two* murders, plus possession of a large amount of a controlled substance. There's no telling what he might do."

Robert, glared at the FBI man, kissed the top of Faye's head and sat down. Even here, in such degrading circumstances, his natural dignity and strength were untouched. This was not a circumstance to be pitied, simply a problem to be solved. Faye understood and smiled inwardly. She knew Robert better than she'd expected.

"Robert," Bitsy announced, "the abduction charge against you has been dropped."

"Oh, thank God!" Faye exclaimed.

Bitsy shot her a warning look before continuing, "Your supposed victim has made it clear she would have followed you anywhere."

"Then I can go home?" Robert asked, hesitatingly.

"I'm afraid not, Robert. They still believe you mutilated Marian, and killed Meany."

"That's preposterous!" Faye burst out, then hesitated under Bitsy's glower. "I told you what happened!" she cried, before sinking sullenly into a seat, like a schoolgirl caught using a bad word.

The FBI agent replied, not unkindly, "I understand the depth of feeling you may have for this man, Ms. McRae—but the evidence shows he used *your* late husband's gun to kill Meany. His fingerprints are on it, on top of yours and over your late husband's. He also had the surgical skill, and equipment, to decapitate your friend."

"But he's not that kind of person!" Faye cried, as Bitsy looked to heaven and threw up her hands in futility.

"Think so?" the agent challenged. "Don't forget that little matter of the bricks of marijuana we found in the trunk of his car. Pot can make a sane man capable of anything—even murder."

Faye reddened. Her first impulse was to cry, "But marijuana isn't like that at all!" But to do so would merely incriminate her as well.

It was one thing to know, with certainty, that one's position was morally clear; it was quite another to find oneself in the den of a lion who saw you only as a piece of fresh meat. Faye knew instinctively that the FBI wouldn't be the least bit interested in her moral or ethical position regarding marijuana, nor of her personal experience which, even at this date, probably greatly exceeded their own. Their only concern was the letter of the law.

"That wasn't mine," Robert said, obviously tired of repeating himself. "I do prescribe marijuana to some of my patients, but not by the brick!"

"Gentlemen! Gentlemen!" Bitsy interrupted, in her most intimidating voice. "We'll be working that out in court, won't we? How long before you ask for indictment, Agent Keck?"

"We did that this morning," the agent replied. "It wasn't as hard to get a grand jury together the day after Christmas as you might think."

Faye was furious. "Without his lawyer? How dare you—!"

"Faye, Faye!" Bitsy cried, patting Faye on the arm. "That's normal, dear. Upon being arrested, a defendant must be indicted by a grand jury before he or she can be brought to trial. During this grand jury hearing, the defendant is not present. Instead, the prosecutor just lays out his *prima facie*, or initial case. If the grand jury concludes that this evidence is sufficient to indicate that the defendant *probably* committed the crime, then they return an indictment. They do not have to be certain beyond a reasonable doubt, just pretty sure."

"An indictment is not an indication of guilt, Ms. McRae," the agent added. "And if the grand jury had not returned an indictment, Dr. Thompson would have been released. But they did, which means our prosecutor, who, I might add, flew out here from Washington the day before Christmas, was able to convince them that we had a case."

"The day *before* Christmas?" Faye repeated. "You were that sure of yourselves before you even had Robert arrested?"

Keck nodded gently. "We at the FBI, Ms. McRae, don't do shoddy work."

"The next step is arraignment," Bitsy continued. "Robert and I will be present at that, and you may be as well, if you wish. That's when the judge asks for Robert's plea. If he pleads guilty, the next step would be sentencing."

"Why would he do that?" Faye asked.

"It's sometimes done in plea bargaining."

"We'll not be doing that, Ms. Cunningham," the FBI agent assured her seriously. "We have too tight a case, and intend to go the distance."

Bitsy ignored him. "But I'll advise Robert to plead 'not guilty', and then there will be a bail hearing, and, finally, his trial."

"The arraignment will be held Monday," the agent informed Bitsy, as matter-of-factly as if telling her when she could get her teeth cleaned. "I will now leave the three of you, as you requested, Ms. Cunningham. Corporal Tucker will be just outside the door if you need him."

When the echo of the slamming door had subsided, Bitsy remarked, "They are not permitted to have microphones or cameras operating while suspects confer with their lawyers. But…only an idiot would assume they always follow their own rules."

Faye's eyes wandered to the embedded mirror. She understood the message. She was to exercise discretion here, even with the agent gone.

"Robert," she said, "I would have brought you fresh clothes, but my house was ransacked and my furniture and everything in the closet destroyed, including the clothes you had there."

"What?" Robert gasped. "Are you all right?"

"Yes," Faye said, squeezing his hand. "And Dave is going to help me buy new furniture with the insurance check. But, right now, I'm concerned about you. Can I get you anything from your house?"

"They won't let you give him anything, Faye," Bitsy interjected. "Not even clothes. Not till after his arraignment, anyway."

"I don't have my keys with me, anyway" Robert complained. "They took my wallet and personal effects when I was arrested. But Vera has the keys to my office, and there's a spare house key in my desk." He sighed. "Why didn't I ever give you a key?"

"I've never even been in your house," Faye pointed out.

"You haven't?" Robert asked in disbelief. "You're kidding."

"No," Faye said. "Somehow, something always came up..."

He looked at her. "I'm worried about my patients," he said, with a meaningful look.

"I understand," Faye smiled. "I'll look in on them, if you like."

"Thank you!" Robert breathed, gratefully. He shook his head. "This is so insane. It's as if someone wanted an excuse to arrest me!"

Bitsy nodded thoughtfully. "They had the excuse, or made one up, with Meany's being murdered with Faye's husband's gun."

"I only touched that gun once, the morning after that first night I spent at your house," Robert pointed out. "That might have been the excuse to *stop* me, but it was the planted marijuana that allows them to *keep* me."

"And, think about it," Faye offered, her mind racing. "When this goes to trial, it won't be the kindly doctor at trial—it will be a man who was arrested for killing and mutilating his close friend, and murdering a member of Congress."

"And not just any member," Bitsy reflected, "but the one who was most vocal about keeping marijuana illegal. That can't help but influence the outcome."

Faye nodded grimly. "Someone's been stacking the deck."

Fallen Saints

Vera lived in one of the smaller condos in a row of one-floor units. In defiance of local custom, the time of year and the laws of nature, a bright green lawn presented itself defiantly to all who drove by.

Faye did not drive by. She stopped at Vera's unit. The condo association was responsible for the lawn, but each occupant did what they could to make the front porch unique and Vera had approached her decorating with the exuberance she devoted to any project she took on. There were Mexican pots filled with out-of-season plants, statues of saints intermixed with Aztec and Mayan gods, a profuse explosion of Christmas lights, and a prominently displayed U.S. flag whose pole jutted out of the exterior wall.

Faye rang the bell and waited. After a few minutes, she rang again. When Vera opened the door, she was wearing a bathrobe, in spite of the time—it was now late afternoon—and the interior of the house was dark. Vera regarded her in silence; Faye could see she had been crying.

"I'm kind of busy right now," she said.

"I'll just be a moment," Faye promised tactfully. "Robert asked me to pick up the keys to his office."

Vera refused to meet her eyes. "Come in," she said, and led the way.

There was a feeling in the house of not having been cleaned, of not having been aired, of sadness and regret. Faye waited near the door while Vera retreated into the depths of the dwelling for the keys. When she returned, and handed them to Faye, Faye asked, "Vera, dear—are you all right?" Impulsively, she added, "Honey, you don't *look* well."

"I'm the one who told them," she said.

"Told who what?" Faye asked.

"I told the police that Robert knew Marian."

"I don't understand," Faye said, confused. "Why would you be talking to the police?"

"When Marian's body was found, Robert's business card was in her purse. I was in the office, packing my personal things, and I thought, whatever, and took the call. I told them Marian wasn't just a client, but was Robert's personal friend." Vera sighed. "Then, when they asked if I worked there, I told them I had quit and was just getting my things. Of course, they wanted to know *why* I had quit, and I told them about the marijuana Robert prescribed for my depression, and how I'd been having terrible dreams about my father. Oh, Faye, I didn't *mean* to say anything. You know how my mouth just runs on its own!"

"I see." Faye didn't know what else to say.

"Oh, Faye, don't you understand? I thought Robert was a saint, and then I thought he was the devil. If I could have been wrong about him, could I have been wrong about my father?" She sobbed heavily. "My sister seemed so *sure*, and she's been in my dreams, too. Is it possible that...that..." She began sobbing again, and Faye reached around her as best she could, hugging the round little woman.

"You stopped smoking," Faye pointed out. "Have the dreams continued?"

Vera nodded vigorously, her forehead prodding Faye's breast.

"Then it wasn't a product of the marijuana, don't you see?" Faye patted her on the back. "The pot just relaxed the, the barriers your mind had put up, and once the dam was broken, it could only collapse completely."

"What can I do?" Vera said at last, her voice muffled by Faye's blouse. "Do you know how many years it's been since I spoke to my sister? I don't even know what we have in common any more."

"You have the memories of your being abused in common," Faye pointed out. "It seems to me that the one thing a victim of childhood abuse needs most is just to be listened to and believed. Don't you think?"

Faye felt the little woman shake her head. "I don't know," she said.

"Wounds usually heal faster when they're in the open, don't they? Call her, honey. You'll feel better, I promise."

House Call

Vera gave Faye the keys to the office, which got her to the office drawer, in which Robert kept both a spare house key and a scrap of paper with the password to his computer's files.

Faye put her new knowledge to use and soon had a printout of the addresses of the patients she had promised Robert she would help. First, however, she was intent on getting Robert some clothes for his upcoming court appearance so she took the key, drove to his house and let herself in.

It wasn't quite true that she'd never been to Robert's house. She'd been *to* it...just not *in* it. They'd driven up to it on two occasions on their way elsewhere. Robert had invited her in the first time, but they were in a hurry to catch a movie before it started, so she declined. The second time there'd been something caught in her shoe, so she spent the minutes while he ran inside to change a stained tie, adjusting her shoe.

Now, *she* was here but he was not. It was a big house in a neighborhood of big houses. They were still unnaturally close together, but less close together than the less expensive houses that filled most of the town.

When she stepped inside, her eyes were immediately drawn to the wall-wide windows and sliding glass doors that lined the side of the house opposite the entryway. Rather than a small back yard, they provided an unbroken vista past a tidy patio, over a low stone wall, and across a beautiful golf course.

Robert had never spoken much of golf, though now that she thought of it, being a doctor he *must* play. And buying a home on a course suggested that he must like to play.

Or, maybe he just liked the view. In the Valley, living on a golf course was the only way to guarantee being able to see *anything* green out one's window.

The master bedroom, bath and walk-in closet took up a full wing of the house. Though most of the floors were of stone, the entire wing was covered with a maroon, deep-pile, wall-to-wall carpet that Faye would have loved to walk on barefoot. Heavy olive drapes, opened, hung at the sides of the wall-wide window overlooking the golf course. Gauzy white curtains hung the entire width.

The bed was made, covered with a traditional, heavy bedspread, not a comforter. It was dark blue, which went with the maroon and the olive in a well-ordered, masculine way.

Why had Robert never brought Faye here? She looked enviously at the king-sized bed, then turned to the walk-in closet. It, alone, was nearly the size of Faye's bedroom; and was filled with more clothes than she'd seen this side of Wal-Mart. They were fine, too; thick, even fabrics, deep, subtle colors. She chose a suit, a crisp, white shirt, selected a tie from a tasteful assortment. There was a dresser *inside the closet,* and from it she gathered several pairs of under shorts, several undershirts, and a few pairs of socks. She had never tried to outfit anyone for jail before. Of course, this wasn't exactly *jail*; but he was imprisoned. A scan of the closet revealed that Robert didn't own any blue jeans. *Edwin couldn't have lived without blue jeans*, Faye thought. She loved that Robert was so different in every way than Edwin. And yet, she had to admit, there was something appealing about a trim man wearing a snug pair of blue jeans.

She rounded it off with a pair of shoes appropriate for the suit. *This should do the trick*, she thought, determined that Robert look as professional as possible at his hearing.

She carried the clothing through the house to the kitchen at the other end of the house. It was equally large, with an island in the middle, enough counter space to prepare food for an army, a huge, double-door refrigerator, and a casual dinette set at which Queen Elizabeth herself might be comfortable.

She found a lovely Kenneth Cole suitcase in a hall closet and brought it to the table. As she filled it with Robert's clothing, the thought struck her that, perhaps, Robert was *embarrassed* to bring her here—embarrassed at his wealth, embarrassed that *she* might be embarrassed at the contrast between his opulent lifestyle and her modest one.

She stood and looked around the room, trying to imagine herself living here. *Funny*, she thought. *She had imagined Robert moving in with* her. Now, the thought was ludicrous. Robert would never be able to tolerate downgrading to *her* level of living. And he shouldn't have to.

But could Faye tolerate upgrading to his? She looked around again. She had never been materialistic but now, she began to feel that she might have been cheating herself. Certainly, she could never have afforded such a huge house. But, she knew the luxurious towel she'd used at Chuck and Dave's was only a few dollars more expensive than the tissue-thin ones she had always purchased for herself and Edwin. She could easily have lived well, and still stayed within her means.

She picked up the nearest phone—the house had more of them than an AT&T showroom—and called Dave's house. There was no answer, but she left a message. "Dave," she said. "This is Faye. Please, don't shop for things without me. I want to be a part of choosing some…some *nice* things myself."

Then, locking the door behind her, she took the suitcase to her car and headed back for FBI headquarters, where Agent Keck had promised to accept and deliver it to Robert.

Tomorrow, her job as prescription deliverer would begin.

Deliveries

Saturday, December 27, 1997

Faye was awakened by her doorbell earlier than she had planned to arise. Half asleep, she pulled on her robe and stumbled to the door. When she opened it, she was surprised to see a stranger there.

"Yes?" she asked the visitor.

"You're Faye McRae?" the man asked.

"Yes," Faye replied before she could catch herself. What if this were a process server? But instead of a warrant, the visitor handed her a small brown paper bag.

"What's this?" Faye asked, puzzled. "And who are you?"

"I'm one of your fellow club members," the gray-haired man replied, softly. "I understand you're making Doctor Robert's deliveries today. This is my contribution."

"Oh?" Faye inquired politely, still not quite understanding. The man nodded pleasantly, walked quickly to his car, and was gone.

Faye closed her door and looked in the bag. It contained, within a Zip-Loc bag, a smallish amount of loose marijuana buds. "Of course!" Faye exclaimed. When Robert had asked her to see to his patients, *this* was what he meant!

Before she could decide between returning to bed or making coffee, the doorbell rang again. This time she peeked through the side window before opening the door, and was relieved to see a familiar face.

"Dave!" she smiled as she opened the door. "What's up? Come in."

"This," Dave grinning as he entered, "Is Chuck's and my contribution."

"How many more people are going to drop by? Will this be going on all morning?" Faye grimaced. "I haven't even had my *coffee* yet!"

"I don't know, toots," Dave replied. "But you should have all you need for your rounds before ten o'clock."

Faye looked at the bag curiously. "Who arranged all this?" she asked. "Robert couldn't have; he's still in custody."

"This is what we *do*, Faye," Dave explained. "This is what the club is *for*. Every other Saturday, Dr. Robert makes his rounds to his patients that need weed. We drop by with our contributions early in the morning and he delivers it. But Bitsy told us that you would be playing Florence Nightingale today, so here we are."

A tap on the frame of the still-open door revealed another stranger, a woman this time, with a broad smile and a small paper bag. "Here you go, dear, and I'll be sayin' a prayer for every poor soul. Bless you and your mission." And she was gone.

"Wouldn't it make more sense to deliver this stuff all at once?" Faye asked Dave. "Robert could keep it in his safe."

"Well, Robert's never explained it to me," Dave replied. "But it seems to me the less you have around, the safer you're going to be. Remember, this stuff is illegal—except for medical purposes—and the Feds are still arguing about *that*. So we have to be careful. None of us delivers more than an ounce at a time, so if we're busted it's just a misdemeanor. Robert is the only one who really takes a chance...and, today, you."

"Shit," Faye said. She hadn't really considered the risk she'd be taking. But, even as the thought came to mind, she knew it didn't matter—she would certainly risk anything to help Robert keep his promise to his patients.

Mission of Mercy

Feeling like some kind of super-hero, Faye threaded through the quiet, post-Christmas streets of Sun City in search of sick people needing help. Her special power: A few healing bags of marijuana delivered by members of the Sun City Cannabis Club.

She arrived at the first address, a condo not unlike Vera's except this one featured a cactus-and-gravel garden in the front yard rather than a lawn. With one of the little bags in her left hand, Faye knocked with her right, and then knocked again. The door opened immediately on the second knock. A woman stood there, forty-something, lines of concern worn prematurely into her forehead.

"Yes?" she asked.

"I'm here for the benefit of Mr. Kite," Faye replied. "On behalf of his doctor, Robert Thompson. May I come in?"

"Of course," the woman said. "I'm Rita, his daughter. I saw on the news that Dr. Thompson had been arrested. I haven't told father yet." A small sob escaped the woman's lips. "If he can't get his—his medicine, I don't know what he's going to do."

Faye shook the little bag. "I have it here," she said, smiling.

"Oh, thank God!" Rita cried, impulsively throwing her arms around Faye. Embarrassed, the younger woman stepped back. "Forgive me. It's just that father's little smoke every day is the only thing that keeps him going."

"Is he in much pain?" Faye asked, sympathetically.

"Oh, pain isn't the problem," Rita explained. "Here, would you like to see him?"

Rita led Faye to a smallish bedroom. A withered man lay on the bed, asleep. Faye only knew he wasn't dead because she could hear the rasp of his breathing. A wheelchair, next to the bed, acted as a second nightstand, with books and magazines piled on its seat.

"He has advanced MS," Rita explained. "Multiple sclerosis, you know. He's only 66, but his muscles have deteriorated to the point that he can barely move or even breathe. Here, Papa," she said. The old man roused. "I have your medicine." Rita removed a rolling paper from a packet on the nightstand, opened the bag of medicine and deftly rolled a thin joint.

"You do that very well." Faye said.

"I've been doing this daily for two years," Rita replied dryly. "I've gotten good at it."

Faye doubted the wisdom of smoking *anything* when one clearly had trouble breathing but the gentleman smoked as she introduced herself and, in moments, the raspiness eased, and his breathing became stronger, deeper.

"Papa would sleep for most of the day, if it weren't for the marijuana," Rita remarked. "There are no drugs to treat MS, you know, except this one...which the NMSS—the National Multiple Sclerosis

Society—denies works." The woman sighed. "I cut down his dosage of it when I heard the news about Dr. Thompson. I mean, I can't very well fill his prescription at the pharmacy! And he only uses three grams of it a day, but without it he wouldn't even have the strength to eat."

"What news?" Mr. Kite asked, alertly. There was something oddly familiar about him, but Faye couldn't place it.

"Some difficulty getting the marijuana delivered to you," Faye explained vaguely. "But this bag will last you a month," she added, "and by then, I'll be able to bring some more." She bid the old man a good afternoon, then followed his daughter into the living room.

The younger woman's eyes were moist with tears. "You're an angel from heaven," she whispered. "He doesn't deserve this, you know. He spent his life bringing joy to children everywhere, not just me. Even after he was diagnosed with the MS, he just kept at it."

"What was he, a clown?" Faye guessed.

"Oh, no, dear. Don't you know? He was one of the stars of a very famous kid's TV show in the sixties." Rita told her which one, and Faye's eyebrows rose in surprise.

"That's still in reruns," Faye said, awed. "I *thought* I recognized... well, something about him."

Rita nodded. "After his show was cancelled, he still did tours. He was especially moved by children with cancer. He visited children in hospitals, sometimes even took them to Disneyland if their condition permitted it. It just crushed him to find himself with less and less energy every day. Not for himself—for the children he wouldn't be able to see, to bring a little brightness into their world of pain and sickness."

"I'm so sorry," Faye said, squeezing the woman's hand. "This must be so hard for you."

"Oh, no," Rita assured her, smiling through her tears and squeezing Faye's hand back. "Really, it's a privilege. You know what is hard on me, though?"

"What's that?"

"Knowing that the NMSS—the very people who are supposed to be helping people like my father—have denied the experience of thousands of MS sufferers, and announced that in clinical trials they found 'no proof' that marijuana helps them! I ask you, how much proof do they *need*?"

Faye's next stop was another condo, this one on the fourth story of a complex near Grand Avenue. As the owner opened the door, Faye could hear the not-so-distant whistle blast from a locomotive pulling umpteen cars of whatever along the tracks that paralleled the avenue.

The owner, a plump, short woman with gray hair and grayer eyes, gave Faye a bright smile. "May I help you?" she asked.

"I'm here for Dr. Thompson," Faye told her. "Are you Mrs. Henderson?"

"I am," the woman replied. "Wait, let me get my purse." She disappeared briefly, then reappeared with a checkbook. "I'm afraid I can only donate $100," she apologized.

"Wait," Faye said, "a hundred dollars for what?"

"Aren't you collecting for Dr. Thompson's defense fund?"

"Oh, no, Mrs. Henderson. It's too soon for anything like that. I'm just here with your prescription." Faye held out a bag, and Mrs. Henderson laughed, looked around furtively, took Faye's hand and yanked her into the apartment.

"Call me Connie," the woman said, "and please excuse the paranoia."

Faye found an immaculate apartment whose most visible feature was a wall of glass cabinets, every shelf displaying dozens and dozens of little glass figurines.

"How beautiful!" Faye exclaimed.

"My pride and joy," the woman said. "I've collected those from every continent but Antarctica. The oldest one is seventy years old, a gift from my aunt who gave it to me for my third birthday. It's that ballerina, on the center shelf."

Faye looked for and found the piece, a glistening miniature of a small girl in leotard and tutu, balancing on her tiptoes and reaching for the sky. In spite of the small size of the piece, Faye could make out the girl's expression of amazed joy that she *could* stand on toe, and the sudden resulting expansion of her world. Faye could easily imagine the Connie of seventy years ago, receiving the gift, equally dazzled by the discovery that so much story could be crammed into a few ounces of glass. And now, Faye realized, the statuette wasn't *just* of the ballerina; the three-year-old Connie was in there, too.

"I'd love to come back some time and look at all of these," Faye said after a moment. "You have an exquisite collection."

"Now that I have my medicine, I can make some tea and see it."

Faye was puzzled. "What do you mean? You aren't blind, are you?"

"Not exactly," Connie explained. "I have glaucoma, which is a stiffening of the eyeball under internal pressure. On the long term, it leads to blindness but on a day-to-day basis it makes it impossible to focus on close things. I can't look at my collection or even read. I can watch TV, I suppose, but I hate wasting time on that drivel. And my embroidery, well, that's just out of the question."

"You embroider, too?"

"Oh, yes. That's my work, hanging on the wall over the sofa. It won first prize at the Minnesota State Fair in 1967. I was once offered $5,000 for it," she added.

"That's *embroidery*?" Faye exclaimed. She had thought it was a painting, one of those huge landscapes where the closer you look the more you see. But, on close examination, Faye saw the entire piece had, indeed, been embroidered. "Such tiny stitches!" Faye marveled. "What incredible patience you have!"

"Not so much any more," the woman sighed, "though the marijuana helps with that, too. I hate having to be a criminal just in order to see!"

"But marijuana for medical use is legal in Arizona," Faye pointed out.

"Barely. And the feds are trying to block that law. They're actively arresting doctors in California who prescribe marijuana and now they've gotten to Dr. Thompson. Even if he's released, what other doctor will risk being arrested like him? That's why they've made such a media blitz over his arrest!"

"I thought you didn't like to watch TV," Faye kidded.

"I don't *like* to, but I do." Connie grimaced. "I got in the habit of watching the news in the evening, just to keep informed. Funny thing, though...after I got glaucoma, it's as if my eyes were opened. I began to see *through* the lies they tell as if they were facts."

"After you got glaucoma?" Faye repeated.

"Well, it's just a figure of speech, dear. You know, losing my sight gained me my sight, that sort of thing. In literary terms, irony."

"But that means you began to 'see through the lies' *after* you began smoking marijuana, doesn't it?"

"No, it was...it was..." Connie frowned. "You know, maybe it was. I remember the first thing that flew out at me was the suppression of the news reports of CIA drug running out of Mena, Arkansas. It caught my attention, because I was using the marijuana by then for my eyes. So, yes, it was after I started using the stuff."

Faye's mind was racing. "Tell me," she asked her new friend, "is there some sort of national organization for people with glaucoma?"

"Oh, several," Connie replied. "After all, they say there's over two million Americans with it."

"What do they say about using marijuana to ease the symptoms?"

"Strange you should ask," Connie remarked. "For the most part, they are silent on the issue." She pointed to a shelf of books. "Even before I was diagnosed with the disease, I had heard somewhere that marijuana was useful in treating glaucoma. But there isn't a single word on the subject in all those books."

"Really!" Faye exclaimed. "How odd!"

"I did find several studies mentioned in periodicals, however. Every single one of them features a huge headline on the order of 'Marijuana No Cure For Glaucoma'! Well, glory be, no one claimed it was! The articles went on and on about how marijuana couldn't stop the progress of the disease. Well, I *know* that. But nothing else can, either. And, until a cure *does* come along, what can I do about improving my vision *each day?*" She held up the little marijuana bag. "This is it, honey. This is it."

Faye had continued to examine the titles in Connie's bookcase. "*Twenty Cases Suggestive of Reincarnation,*" she read. "Are you interested in reincarnation?"

"Oh, yes," the woman replied. "Funny, I never used to be. I had some odd memories as a child, and we once drove through a town I'd never been in, but I somehow knew where all the streets were.

It wasn't until after I got the glaucoma, though, that I became motivated enough to start looking seriously into the idea of having many different lives."

"After the glaucoma?" Faye repeated. "After the marijuana, too?"

Connie didn't answer, but her expression of sudden understanding spoke volumes.

Faye's second-to-the-last stop of the day was a retired construction worker named Mike Parry. He was 65, ruggedly handsome, with biceps thicker than Faye's thigh. She told him who she was and why she was there, and he invited her inside. Faye had not yet decided whether marijuana users were just friendlier than other people, or didn't want to risk being seen in a public hand-off of the weed.

Once inside he insisted that she accept a glass of water—beer had been his first offering—and led her to his little kitchen. There, she perched on a stool while he—hurriedly, it seemed—opened a box of brownie mix, poured it into a waiting glass bowl, and began to make brownies, adding water and the bag of pot to the recipe.

"Sorry," he said, "but I run out two days ago, and I'm in a world of hurt."

"Why don't you just smoke it?" Faye asked.

"Uh-uh," Mike said, stirring the mixture with a wooden spoon. "Back about ten years ago, when my buddies started droppin' from lung cancer, I decided I better quit smokin'. *Anything*. So I did. But I still needed the pot for pain control, so I just started eatin' it. Turns out, it works better that way—takes twenty minutes to kick in, but when it does, it's got a helluva lot more whack, not to mention stayin' power, than when you smoke it."

"You're in pain?" Faye asked sympathetically. "I'm so sorry. What disease do you have, may I ask? You look so healthy!" she blurted.

Mike laughed, but it was a strained sound. "I don't have no disease," he replied. "I injured myself on the job twenty-five years ago. Fell off a ladder, but that wasn't the bad part. It was the acetylene tank that fell on top of me that done the damage.

"Broke my spine and four ribs," he continued. "I also got a little concussion, but it was the spine what almost killed me. I was on my back in the hospital for six months, and in bed for another eighteen months before they could even start rehab."

"But you got better," Faye pointed out. "I mean, you can walk to the door; you don't even limp."

"I'm okay physically," the man admitted. "But I have been in fucking pain—pardon my French—ever since. I couldn't sleep, and without sleep I couldn't think. Hey, it was my own business, and it collapsed without me there. I tried to start it back up, but I *couldn't think!* I wished to hell I had died in that fall."

Faye, spellbound, leaned forward in her chair. "There were no drugs at all that could stop the pain?"

"Oh, sure there were! There was Demerol, Percocet, even morphine when nothing else did the trick. But all those things, they fucked with my head. The pain might be gone, almost, but I still couldn't think. Look, lady—I ain't the most educated sonov-abitch in the world. But I always prided myself on being a fast thinker. That's how I brought my business up to a twenty-man operation in less than five years. But those drugs, man, I couldn't *think* with 'em!"

"So, what did you do?"

"I stopped takin' 'em. Instead, I smoked one joint each night. That eased the pain enough so's I could sleep. In the morning, yeah, I was in pain but it's amazing how much pain a man can bear if he's gotten a good eight hours—and I could *think* again!"

"And now you eat brownies," Faye concluded. "Just out of curiosity," she asked, "tell me—have you developed an interest in politics or spirituality since you started using pot?"

The man's eyebrows furrowed. "Naw, not really," he said. "'Course, I been usin' it for a long time. Why do you ask?"

"Oh, just a theory I've been playing with. Nothing important."

Faye rose to leave, and Mike, a gentleman in spite of his rough ways, rose to show her out.

"Thanks for this," he said, holding up the empty bag.

"I'll be back with more next month," she promised. "Will that last long enough?" she asked, looking at the brownie pan.

"Oh, yeah," he said. "After it's baked, I cut it into one-inch squares and freeze 'em. I get thirty squares out of a pan, and on months with 31 days I do without one day—just to remind myself how bad off I'd be if I had to live like that all the time."

He opened the door. She stepped through it. She turned to say goodbye, and sensed he wanted to say something. "Yes?" she prompted.

He looked up and down the street. No one was in sight.

"I seen angels," he whispered.

"What?"

"I seen angels," he repeated. "Three times."

"*Angels?*" Faye wasn't sure she'd heard him correctly.

"Yeah," he nodded. "Three times. Once, I was backing my car out of the garage in the rain, and I saw this man in a white robe behind me, waving at me to stop. I jammed on my brakes, and got out to give him hell. He was nowhere in sight, but my five-year-old kid was there—got out of the house, somehow, and wanted to keep me from going to work. But I couldn't see him below the rim of the rear window. If it wasn't for the man in the robe, I woulda run over my own kid. I figger, it had to be an angel."

Faye couldn't disagree.

"The second time was when I fell off the ladder. I was on the cement floor, stunned, and I saw that acetylene tank topple over and get bigger and bigger, fallin' right at me. It was aiming at my head, valve-first, and I couldn't move, 'cause my back was broken, but I didn't know that yet. But I knew I was gonna die. And then this man in a robe, the same man, I think, just was there and reached out and knocked the tank. It still hit me, but blunt side and on my chest. It broke my ribs, but not my skull." He shrugged. "Hadda be an angel, right?"

Faye could barely breathe. After her harrowing experiences over the last few days, it was a relief to talk to someone else who had been through similar ordeals and lived to tell about it. "What about the third time?"

Shyly, he took her hand in both his, and shook it. "Today," he replied. "You. You're my angel today."

Of One Mind

Except for a two-hour break in which Faye and Dave went furniture shopping, and twenty minutes in Bed, Bath And Beyond, Faye spent the day visiting Robert's patients. By the time Faye was able to drop in on Frank Timmons at the hospital, it was already dark, and nearing the end of visiting hours. She had saved him for last, hoping to spend time talking with him—but since she spent so much time with Robert's other patients, there would only be a few minutes.

But now she was there and easily found a parking space, since most other visitors had left for the day. She checked at the front desk, to make sure his room number hadn't changed in the past five days.

It hadn't, and Faye arrived at his door, mildly surprised to find it closed. She thought they only close the doors to patient rooms if a doctor or nurse is actually in with him, perhaps giving a shot or performing an examination. Through the door's glass window she could see the curtains around Frank's bed had been pulled closed.

That seemed odd to her, since Frank's regular doctor was Robert and, as he was being held prisoner by the FBI, he couldn't very well be visiting Frank. She strolled to the nearest nurse's station and asked the woman how long the doctor would be with Frank. The nurse examined a computer screen, and replied that there *was* no doctor seeing him just now.

"Then why is his door closed?" Faye asked.

"He probably just wanted to sleep," the woman suggested. "It can get a bit noisy out here."

"That man is here for acute depression," Faye responded tartly. "He's already tried to kill himself once, and is supposed to be under constant observation. With his curtains drawn, you can't even see him from here!"

The nurse looked up, annoyed, and rose. "We can check on him if you like," she said. Faye followed and waited as the nurse pushed open the door. There was a sudden puff of air from a difference in air pressure between the room and the corridor. The curtains billowed, and Faye saw why instantly: The window at the far end of the room was open.

And Frank was sitting on the windowsill, his back to her.

He turned at the sound of their entry, his face chillingly devoid of expression. It didn't change even as Faye charged him, covering the fifteen feet between the door and the window in a fraction of a second. Frank was wearing a bathrobe, and Faye gripped its collar, pulling it sharply. He fell backward on top of her, where the two of them lay for a moment, stunned.

"I'll get a doctor!" the nurse cried, and bolted into the corridor.

"Are you all right, Frank?" Faye asked, but the man rose silently and began to remount the windowsill.

Faye was desperate. It was clear someone had given Frank another suicide command. She remembered how Meany had been impossible to subdue. There was just one chance; it popped into her head and shocked her with its daring, but she could think of nothing else.

"Beware the jabberwock, my son, the jaws that bite, the claws that catch!" she cried.

Immediately, Frank froze and responded, "Beware the jub jub bird, and shun the frumious bandersnatch." His voice echoed oddly in the room, almost seeming to come from behind her as well as directly from Frank's mouth.

"What sword should I use?" Frank's expression, neutral, as he spoke, was creepy.

"Your vorpal sword!"

"Command me," Frank said.

Faye shivered. It was so obvious he would do *anything* she asked. "Go back to bed," she instructed. Like a device designed for no other task, he obeyed.

He had no sooner pulled the sheets over his chest when the nurse returned with a doctor in tow. "Which of you is hurt?" the doctor asked.

"Neither of us, exactly," Faye replied, thinking fast. "I thought Frank was trying to jump out of the window but he wasn't—*were you Frank?*"

There was a terrifying moment of silence. Then Frank's scratchy voice said, "I wasn't."

"What are you saying?" the nurse cried. "Look, the protective grill from the window has been removed." She leaned outward. "This couldn't have been done without tools."

"Who cares?" Faye said, dismissively. She wanted the nurse and the doctor out of the way as quickly as possible. "I'm not hurt and Frank didn't get hurt, either. Frank, tell us, did you get hurt?"

"I didn't get hurt."

"I'd better check you out, anyway," the doctor insisted, and Faye held her breath. Frank lay still, neither cooperating nor fighting the doctor's examination, ignoring the doctor's requests until Faye repeated them. Finally, the doctor was satisfied that Frank had only suffered a small bruise on his right forearm.

"Nurse, I want that window repaired *stat*," the doctor ordered. She scurried out. The doctor gazed at Frank for a moment, jaw clenched, then turned and left.

Now Faye was left alone with Frank who, clearly, was under the thrall of mind control. For the time being, and as amazing as it seemed, Faye was his 'handler.'

If only Robert were here! If only Marian were here! Even Marvin, or Norma; even *Dave* would have been a comfort. But, no. Here was Faye, responsible for another human being in the most bizarre possible way. Obviously, Frank would calmly kill himself if she asked; certainly he would kill someone else.

Faye recalled the Lord High Executioner in a high school production of Gilbert and Sullivan's *The Mikado*. He sang, "I have a little list." *Who doesn't have a little list?* Faye wondered. Who hasn't been annoyed by a supermarket clerk, cheated by an auto mechanic, driven to distraction by an officious clerk? That she could, conceivably, have anyone executed with no risk whatsoever to herself, was a terrifying proposition. It was easy to say *now* that she would never use such a weapon, but she wasn't certain she would always be able to trust herself not to.

If she'd had this power in those dark days after Edwin's death, she might well have been tempted to order Frank to kill *her*.

Which brought up the obvious question. "Frank, who *told* you to kill yourself?"

Frank didn't hesitate to answer. "No one."

That was a surprise. "Then why were you sitting on the windowsill?" she asked.

"A man told me to jump out the window."

"Oh." The command hadn't specifically, been to *kill* himself; it was to *jump out the window*. In this state, Frank could only answer exactly what was asked.

She would have to be more specific. "Do you know who the man was? Or is?" she amended.

"No."

"Have you ever seen him before?"

"No."

"Have you ever heard his voice before?"

"No."

They were interrupted by a man in a maintenance uniform. "Hi, folks!" he called cheerily. "Understand the window's broke?" He breezed past them, looked out the window, and leaned out as the nurse had done. "Jesus!" he cried. "The whole grill is gone! How'd that happen?" Oblivious to the room's occupants, he strode out the room and was gone.

Faye was anxious to get Frank out of the hospital. Whoever had tried to kill him before would surely be back to finish the job—and, whoever it was, had the ability to come into a hospital room and remove a protective grill from the window without being observed...or, without being *reported*, which was even scarier.

But this was rather like querying the computer. Faye found the experience frustrating and yet exhilarating at the same time. Still, Frank's answers so far hadn't been enlightening. And, in any case, this whole mind control thing left a bad taste in Faye's mouth.

"Frank, is it possible for me to command your mind to heal? To glue together however many alternate personalities you may have?"

Frank hesitated, the first time he had done so while in this state. But Faye realized she had asked a question that might not have a simple, factual, answer. "Yes," he replied after a moment. "I will do whatever you ask."

"What I ask," Faye stated as clearly as she could, "is for you to do *what's best for Frank*. And I need to know what that is. If you tell me, I can help you do it."

Frank said nothing, and Faye realized that she hadn't actually asked a question or issued a command. "Frank," she said, finally, "tell me what will happen to your mind if I order you to, uh, stitch together your various personalities so you can become a whole, conscious person again?"

Again there was a pause, but not an indefinite one and Faye could see Frank was considering. Finally, he replied, "I would not be controllable. No one would be able to command me."

"But, what would happen to *you*?" Faye was nearly out of patience.

"I would remember everything," Frank responded simply, unemotionally.

"Does that include the death of your grandson?"

"Yes."

Faye hesitated. That was what she was afraid of. She knew that Frank had to integrate those memories eventually but was he ready for it to happen all at once? What if the shock caused his mind to shatter again, this time into pieces that no one could control?

"Frank, didn't you say you were starting to remember his death? How much of it had you recalled?"

"The front alter now remembers almost everything. The barriers between the alters grow weaker every day."

"Do you know why?"

Frank answered immediately. "It seems to be a side effect of the marijuana the front alter was taking. It caused the front alter to focus so intently on the missing parts of its memory, that it broke through the walls separating the alters."

"Are you saying that your personalities would have reintegrated in time, anyway?"

"If the doses of marijuana had continued to be administered, yes."

No wonder the conspiracy was so intent on keeping marijuana illegal! Faye decided to bite the bullet. "All right, then," she announced.

"Do it. Become a whole person. Meld all these alters together, remember everything. Make it so the only person you obey is yourself. Hide nothing from yourself. Do it now."

Faye hesitated. Should she say anything else? Would she have to rouse him, as Robert roused him from an hypnotic state? But Frank saved her from further questions by stretching and opening his eyes just as if he were awakening from a nap. He blinked as he looked at her, an expression on his face that she had never before seen: One of calm wonder.

"Hello, Faye," he said, quietly.

"How are you?" she asked in a worried tone.

"I'm fine." He smiled. "I'm *really* fine. Thank you so much!"

"How much do you remember?"

"Everything."

"Everything?"

"Everything. I remember you pulling me out of the window, the bastard ordering me to step out of it. I remember Mickey's murder. And I remember you giving me my mind back."

Faye made a decision. "Do you think you're well enough to go home?" she asked.

Frank nodded affably. "I'm here because I tried to kill myself. But that wasn't really me. And now that I'm *me*, it won't happen again."

"Then I've got to get you home. You're still in danger if you stay here. Whoever got to you before, can get to you again. And if they find they can't control you, they might decide you're too dangerous to keep alive." She looked around. "Where are your things?"

"I don't have much here," the old man admitted, sitting up. "The clothes I came in, they're in that closet. And my toothbrush is in the bathroom."

With growing panic, Faye ran to the bathroom and threw open the door—and squealed. The room wasn't empty. A man stood there, calm, immobile.

"Good God!" she cried, in fear. "Desmond Barrow, what are *you* doing in Frank's bathroom?"

"I await your command," he replied.

And Faye gave him one.

No Distractions

That night, Faye checked in to see how her house was coming along. The damaged furniture, bric-a-brac, and destroyed items of clothing were gone. Faye had assigned Dave the job of ensuring that nothing salvageable of her personal or sentimental items be thrown away. Items he thought she'd want to keep were in relatively neat piles in the otherwise bare kitchen. In short, it looked like the previous tenant had simply moved out.

Tonight would be her second night as their guest. "But not until very late," she warned. "I need to spend a little time alone. I hope you understand."

They said they did, and so, after making sure that Dave hadn't been too enthusiastic in throwing things away, she got into her car and headed west.

She had toyed with the idea of returning to the Wickenburg site but she wasn't ready for that. Instead, she turned north at 99th Avenue and headed for Lake Pleasant.

On this night between Christmas and New Year's, there was no traffic on the two-lane highway. The further away she drove from the valley, the brighter the stars became. When she got to the spot Robert had shown her, she parked at the side of the road and stepped onto the path that led to the lake. The night was cool, and she was glad she'd worn the parka she'd bought that evening. After her three days in the canyon, she'd become adept at navigating in the dark. And, though the moon was just a sliver, the stars themselves were easily bright enough to show the way.

She sat where she and Robert had made love. She found herself smiling as she remembered that sacred night. She lit a doobie Chuck had given her, and inhaled deeply. By the time she'd had two more hits, she was nicely stoned. The reflection of the stars danced on the water and the stars themselves seemed to dance in the sky. The air took on a life of its own, shimmering in the darkness. Nowhere could she see an unnatural light or hear a human-made sound.

"Another beautiful night in Paradise," said Norma, sitting down next to her.

Faye did not jump. She had almost expected the intrusion.

"You have questions," Norma observed.

Faye took another hit and passed the joint to Norma. "I talked to people yesterday," Faye said. "Some of Robert's patients who've been using marijuana for months. I found that they *all* had a sense of increased integrity and heightened spiritual awareness since they started using it, though most of them wouldn't use those words. And I found that the social institutions that were formed to support these sick people had gone to preposterous lengths to keep them from using marijuana in treatment, in spite of enormous anecdotal evidence of its effectiveness." She took a breath and continued.

"My gut tells me that those two facts are connected, and that the connection is important. But I can't quite figure out *how*."

"Yes, you can," Normal told her. "In fact, you *have*."

"Well, it's become obvious that marijuana makes mind control impossible."

"There are many types of mind control, Faye. What you experienced in the mine, and since, is a very minor part of the bigger game. Oh, it makes great theatre and would make a thrilling book or movie, but it's nothing!"—she snapped her fingers—"compared to the more subtle levels of mind control exercised on far greater numbers of people everywhere."

"You mean, TV and movies and newspapers..."

"Exactly. And manipulation of the culture through other, even more subtle, means. People who are smoking hemp focus more on their *own* thoughts than they do on those of others. That makes them less susceptible to *any* kind of control."

"Marian told me how people who are stoned like to make their own decisions, and I got from our dear friend, Marvin, how the global elite enrich themselves through the financing of wars and everything else. But, Norma, something is missing. I love pot, it's great, and I've seen how much it can help people. But marijuana can't be the fulcrum of all this! The point of the 'game,' as you put it, *can't* just be a battle of Big Business vs. Marijuana. I refuse to believe the universe could, at its core, be that banal."

"Of course it isn't," Norma agreed. "In fact, this battle, as you call it, isn't about hemp at all. It's about control of the human soul."

"The soul? You mean that thing we don't want to lose, and go to church to have saved?"

Norma laughed merrily. "That misconception is, of course, part of the deception. Your soul is not a wart. You can't sell it; you can't lose it. It isn't a *part* of you— it is you. It is the deeper being from which the earthly you, sitting here, arises. It is also the well to which you will eventually return. And, when you do, you will no longer be a plaything for the game masters to manipulate."

"You mean, when I die. Well, that will happen to everyone sooner or later! I guess it's a pretty short game."

"I *don't* mean when you die. You see, the universe isn't so shallow as to only include the living world, and the game isn't so simple as, when you die, you're out. Your soul, your *self*, continues in a cycle of rebirth, and as long as it does, you remain a pawn in the game."

"If the goal is to stop being reborn, why don't we? Just stop, I mean?"

"Because, when we die, we bring our most-cherished beliefs with us. If we've been trained to look outside ourselves for God, we'll do that *after* death as well. If we've been trained to believe we must achieve some kind of perfection, we'll look for ways to do *that*. And if we've come to see ourselves as fundamentally powerless in the face of karma, or government, or family, we'll create that kind of experience."

"Create it?"

"Be born into a life that resonates to those beliefs, dearie. We experience what we expect to experience, and that's even more true *after* death than before."

"So, what's this got to do with marijuana?"

"Thousands of years ago, the major religions were created as spiritual prisons. They convinced people that God was outside themselves; that they needed priests and ministers to act as inter-mediaries between them and God. They convinced people that God was arbitrary and distant, and that there was a fundamental gap between the way people behaved and how God wanted them to be. Anyone who didn't accept this premise was burnt at the stake or worse. The only reason the Inquisition is now over is that its result was so successful. Virtually everyone today believes that this picture of God is accurate."

"There are alternative religions," Faye pointed out. "The New Age movement, for example."

Norma shook her head. "The New Age movement *started* as a genuine alternative," she said, "but it was quickly infiltrated to bring its adherents back to the One, True Faith. If you ask, you'll find that most New Agers believe they need the help of angels, or channelers, or mediums, or Tarot cards, or *something*, to communicate with God. And you know, from our earlier conversations, that God is to be found *within*—and is readily available to *anyone* who looks there for divinity."

"Then—what's the answer?" Faye asked, baffled.

"*Looking* within. Have you done that heart meditation I suggested to you?"

"Uh..." Faye was embarrassed. "I did once, but I've been so busy, with Robert being arrested and my house being ransacked and delivering medicine to Robert's patients..."

"Hush, hush!" Norma cautioned, holding her palm out. "Those are just distractions, dearie. They are just like TV, newspapers, talk radio and the rest. They are, in fact, game pieces given to you by your opponents, to keep you from discovering your inner connection to God."

Norma paused. "I know you've been trying to figure out why I seemed to disappear in the canyon."

"I think it was because you told me I was on my own, and that saddened me. I could no longer 'tune you in,' like a radio turned to the space between stations."

"Excellent analogy," Norma congratulated her. "Why can you see me now?"

Faye thought. "Is it the pot?"

"Partly," Norma smiled. "It's really the lack of distractions. No lights, no television, no music. The only distractions you *would* have had were all the worries jumbling around in your head—and the hemp helps you focus, helps you look past them for the moment. The result is that your vibrations, your energy, rises in frequency to the point that you can tune me in perfectly. Of course," the woman added, "I had to actually be here. But if your frequency were too low, nothing I could do would have gotten your attention."

"Okay," Faye agreed. "That makes sense."

"Now, at higher frequencies, the mind naturally considers spiritual subjects rather than mundane, lower frequency ones. In time, those who have maintained a high frequency vibration will stumble on the inner God *on their own*. They need no church, no books, no guides, no gurus. All they need is time without distractions."

"Not easy to find in the modern world," Faye remarked, ruefully.

"Which is the value of hemp," Norma continued, "and a few other natural substances with similar effects. It helps create a zone of no distraction even in the midst of the biggest, busiest city." She reached for the joint and took a last hit.

"Now, our opponents in this game, in order to win, must keep as many people from finding their God-connection as possible. It follows that they keep us as *distracted* as possible. They create those big, busy cities. They create laws and economic situations that encourage us to leave the peaceful farms for the cities, where we find poverty or wealth—either of which is *very* distracting. They create an environment in which traditional religions distract us from looking for God within, by filling us with the belief that he is to be found 'up there.' And, they make extinct or illegal, every substance that might help us to find that connection in any way. Hence, laws against marijuana, peyote, psilocybin, and so on."

"So, what can I do? What can *we* do?"

"We've talked about this before. You can quit playing their game. *Become* a hermit. Spend the rest of your life away from distraction. Find that connection and disconnect from that endless cycle of birth and re-birth."

"And if I'm not willing to do that?"

Norma smiled. "You can play the game *knowing* it is a game— and knowing that, to win, you must create times of no distraction so you can discover and maintain that God-connection within.

"Then, not only do you get to break that cycle—you can help others do so, as well."

A Federal Case

Sunday, December 28, 1997

Faye awoke in Chuck and Dave's guest room, surprised, in fact, to feel so rested, given the late hour at which she had returned.

She dropped by Frank's to make sure he was all right. He was, except for his annoyance that the hospital had apparently not made any effort to discover *why* he had left without checking out—not even calling his place to see if he was there.

Arriving home, she saw Dave overseeing the delivery of her new furniture.

"Omigod—did I buy *that?*" she exclaimed when she saw the plush, new sofa being rolled out of the delivery truck.

"Relax, girlfriend," Dave shushed her. "You can afford it. That settlement check was plenty generous."

It was true, she had decided it was time to be generous with herself. She had intentionally selected things that were not bottom-of-the-barrel. Now she had a home she was actually proud to call her own—the first time she'd been able to say that. "Not too bad!" she shouted triumphantly, grinning. And when Grant dropped by, she was very pleased to be able to show it off to him.

"That was fast work," he complimented her.

"Well, I had help," she said. "And, I needed *something* to keep me busy until the arraignment."

"Will you be there?" he asked.

"Oh, yeah," Faye assured him.

"I might be, too," Grant said. "How many charges is he up against?"

Faye replied, "The two murders, and the marijuana."

"Interesting," Grant said, tapping his knee with his thumb. "You know, if we could just get them to drop the Meany murder charge..."

"I'd like them to drop *all* the charges!" Faye cried.

"Well, of course. But the Meany charge is the one that makes all the difference."

"What do you mean?"

"Meany was a congressman, a government employee. Anytime a government employee is murdered, it becomes a federal case. The FBI investigates, and the case is tried in federal court. If that charge was dropped, your boyfriend would have to be tried locally."

"What's the difference?" Faye asked. "I mean, besides having two charges against him instead of three."

"Don't you see? Medical marijuana was voted legal in this state last year, but federal law still prohibits it. If he is tried in federal court, he could be found guilty of the marijuana charge even if he is acquitted of the other two."

"Oh, my." Faye thought furiously. "Do you think that's why they did this to start with? Framed him for Meany's murder, just to jail him for possession of marijuana?"

"It would sure send a loud message to other doctors in the state who were considering prescribing marijuana for their patients."

"It's so—so *crazy!*" Faye exclaimed. "And so unfair, and so unjust, and, and—"

"Well, calm down, Faye," Grant urged her. "There's a way out of this."

"What's that?"

He grinned sheepishly. "Well, as it happens, I have a habit that isn't quite kosher, but it's going to pay off big time!"

Don't Arraignment My Parade

Monday, December 29, 1997

The courtroom was packed. Word had spread about the arrest of Meany's murderer, and the TV news shows and newspapers were well represented. Faye found herself intimidated by the number of people present. She was glad Bitsy had given her permission to sit with her at the defendant's table. Robert sat with five other prisoners waiting for arraignment. Faye was surprised to see so many. "How many congressmen were killed over the holiday?" she asked sarcastically.

"Hey, c'mon! They're here for breaking federal law, not just murder. Some of those guys are probably guilty of helping Mexicans cross the border illegally."

As they waited for the judge to arrive, Faye was surprised to see Grant run up to the wooden barrier that separated them from the benches on which the spectators sat. He had said he might be here, but she didn't expect that he would actually make a contribution, despite his statement the previous evening.

After a minute of Grant's fevered whispering, Bitsy waved the prosecution lawyer over to the defense table. The lawyer, who Bitsy whispered was named William Shears, looked up haughtily and then returned to papers on his desk. Bitsy stood, annoyance all over her face, and said aloud, "I am required to disclose any new evidence I uncover. I've just discovered that the FBI *planted* evidence on the murder scene. If you prefer that I present this information to the press *after* arraignment, I'll be happy to wait."

Shears almost killed himself getting to their table. Faye stifled a laugh.

"What nonsense is this?" the man growled.

Faye instantly knew she wouldn't like him, even if she had only met him socially. He was the kind of person she'd encountered at the garage who would bring a car in for servicing and then blame the mechanic for the original problem.

"This is Grant Taylor, the officer who was first on the scene," Bitsy said, by way of introduction. "He took photos."

"So?" Shears challenged rudely.

"They don't show the murder weapon," Grant offered.

"What?" The prosecutor snatched the photos from Grant's hand before the officer could offer them properly. "These aren't police crime scene photos!"

"I'm not a police photographer, sir," Grant explained. "I just happened to be first on the scene. And I always take my own photos, with a disposable camera. As you can see, the murder weapon is not where the FBI crime scene photos place it."

"How do *you* know where the gun was?" Shears snorted. "You probably just didn't notice it. Not to be rude, sonny, but the FBI investigators have a lot more experience in these things than you local boys."

"*I* know where the gun was supposedly found," Bitsy interjected, "because I was present when your photos were used as the evidence that got my client indicted in the first place. As it happens, our photo here—" and Bitsy pointed at one in which Meany's outstretched arm and hand were plainly visible— "shows that there was no gun near the congressman, as your photo indicates. Therefore, 'evidence' was planted after Officer Taylor took his pictures, but before the FBI photos were taken. Think the papers would get a kick out of getting a copy?"

Shears' face reddened to the point that Faye feared he might have a heart attack on the spot. "These snapshots were obviously taken *after* the FBI removed the gun for analysis," he said.

"Nope," Grant grinned. "Once the FBI moved in, we 'local boys' as you call us, weren't allowed on the premises. And *certainly* not before the congressman's body was removed!"

The clerk of the court stood, and Shears hurried back to his table. "The People of the United States of America versus Doctor Robert Thompson."

A bailiff walked to the jury box and escorted Robert to the defense table; the clerk read the indictment from the grand jury.

"Charges are murder in the first degree, murder in the first degree, and possession of a controlled substance, namely, marijuana."

"How does the defendant plead?" asked the judge perfunctorily.

"Not guilty to all charges, your honor," Robert replied calmly.

"Let me hear from you on bail, counselors," responded the judge, marking the plea that Robert entered on a form.

"Your honor," Shears said, "I beg the court's pardon, but I have just been handed evidence that proves the suspect not guilty of the charge of murdering Congressman Meany. Consequently, we must drop that charge. Since that was the only charge that merited the attention of this court, I request that he be remanded to the Maricopa County Court, State of Arizona, for trial on the other two charges."

"Make it so," the judge said, banging his gavel. Robert was swept away, and Bitsy led Faye away to make room for another defense counsel to deal with the next defendant—but not before Faye saw Shears shoot Bitsy a look of pure, unadulterated hatred.

Powwow

Faye had ridden to the 9th District Court with Bitsy; afterwards, they also rode back to Sun City together.

"That was a good thing, right?" Faye asked.

"Not necessarily," said Bitsy. "I'm still figuring out the ramifications. At least, it means that Robert has a much better shot at being found innocent of the marijuana charge."

"Well, that's good, isn't it? Because they can't possibly find, or even manufacture, evidence that he killed Marian. Because *I* know where that happened, and who did it, even if I can't say anything."

There was an odd chirping sound that Faye didn't recognize. "Just a minute," Bitsy said, and pulled a cellular phone from her purse. Faye had never seen one up close.

"Cunningham," Bitsy announced. There was a pause of perhaps two minutes, punctuated only by the occasional grunt or "Oh, really?" uttered by Bitsy as she steered with her other hand. Finally, she said, "I will present that option to my client," pressed a button, and returned the device to her purse.

"What was that?" Faye asked.

"Something funny," the retired lawyer revealed. "That was Shears. He told me that he would only press for second-degree murder—if Robert would reveal the source of the marijuana he prescribed his patients."

Faye felt her face go red. "But, Robert doesn't *know* where it comes from—Marian supplied it to him, from the members of the Sun City Cannabis Club. And not even Marian knew all the members; one member of each grow group would give her the harvest from their group."

"And Marian is dead," Bitsy continued. "If Robert doesn't reveal some names, the feds are going to suggest that he killed Marian over some kind of drug deal, where she wasn't supplying him with the amount he demanded or something like that."

"Wait—I thought Shears dropped the murder charge, so it isn't a federal case anymore, right? So, how can Shears be making deals?"

"It sounds to me like Shears intends to orchestrate the state's case against Robert. After all, whatever evidence there is, the FBI gathered it."

Faye sighed heavily, her euphoria from the seeming victory in court evaporating. "I always believed the truth would solve any problem."

Bitsy snorted. "We're dealing with people who don't *care* what truth is. They are only looking for a convenient, tidy story that will explain how a headless, handless corpse wound up next to a dead U.S. representative in the house of a woman who's *still* missing. And, if they can manage to discredit a doctor who's been prescribing marijuana for medical purposes—so much the better."

"But Grant told me the reason they wanted to keep this case federal in the first place was to find Robert guilty of the marijuana charge. Why don't they drop *all* the charges now?"

Bitsy's jaw was set. "Someone planted evidence once, that's clear. They can do it again. Remember, the real goal here is to *discourage* Arizona doctors from prescribing marijuana."

"But if he's found innocent of the marijuana charge, won't that have the opposite effect?"

"Yes, if he's found innocent. But, don't you see, that's the one thing the FBI cannot allow!"

"Why do you say that, Bitsy?" Faye asked.

"In federal court, the issue would have been mere possession of marijuana. Now, it's *medical* marijuana that's under attack," the lawyer explained. "The U.S. Supreme Court has always sided with the states when state law conflicts with federal law. If that happens with medical marijuana, drug law enforcement will no longer be able to justify the money spent on extra agents, courts, and jails to hold most of the thousands of marijuana users they arrest each year. And let's face it, Faye," she concluded, "nothing is more vicious than an organization that's budget is about to be cut."

"Then why don't they just drop all charges and be done with it?" suggested Faye.

Bitsy shook her head. "They've made too big a deal of it," she said. "It's going to be embarrassing enough that evidence was planted. I predict they will crucify Robert in the papers, make it seem that he really is guilty of Meany's murder, but that a technical snafu is the reason Robert was remanded to state court. Most people don't know the difference, anyway."

"Then, what can they do? If they can't drop all charges, and they don't want the state court to find him innocent—"

Bitsy gripped the steering wheel so tightly her knuckles turned white. "If Robert dies before the trial, the Feds get everything they wanted," she said.

Faye blanched. "Dies?" she exclaimed. "But he's in perfect health!"

"Think about it. If he goes to trial, I guarantee Robert will be found innocent of both charges. But if he dies *before* it goes to trial...well, the image in the minds of the public will be of a marijuana-crazed murderer who died before he could be convicted. And *that* will set the cause of legalizing marijuana back another ten years."

"You mean someone might *kill* him?" Faye gasped. "But who would do that? Certainly not an FBI agent."

"What, you never heard of Waco? Or Ruby Ridge?"

"But they're turning him over to the county," Faye pointed out.

"Well, who will lose most if this case goes to court?" Bitsy asked. "Not only federal law enforcement. Even the local police aren't going to want to see medical marijuana legalized, no matter what the voters want. After all, they've been thoroughly indoctrinated to believe marijuana is truly dangerous—and the 'War on Drugs' pays a hefty portion of their salaries."

"Marian used to talk about how much money the 'War on Drugs' makes for the politicians."

"All you need is *one* fanatical officer or guard or even janitor in the right place at the right time—and Robert becomes late, as in the *late* Dr. Thompson."

"But, why Robert?" she wailed.

"He may simply be the busiest marijuana-prescribing doctor in the Valley. Or he may have come to the attention of whoever orchestrates these things somehow. Hell, it could even have been your T-shirt web site, Faye. When they couldn't stop it by killing Marvin, maybe they figured they'd just distract you by jailing your boyfriend."

This was exactly the possibility Faye had feared most. This all started *after* the people in the mine had examined her purse; they'd had days to explore her house, where there was no shortage of information regarding the man who was often her overnight guest.

"Do you *really* believe Robert is in danger?"

Bitsy patted Faye's hand as she drove. "I'm afraid I do," she said. "I admit, I've never had a case quite as high-profile as this. I warned Robert that he would do better to get a top criminal lawyer, like that Johnny Cochran fellow but he insisted on keeping *me*. And now, yes, I fear for his safety and I don't know what I can do to protect him."

Faye blew her nose and swallowed hard. "What," she said, "if we busted him out of jail?"

Bitsy took her eyes off the road long enough to stare at her passenger. "Bust him out of FBI headquarters? Are you nuts?"

Faye bit her lip. "It might be possible," she said, "if they were transporting Robert somewhere, like maybe to the courthouse."

"They *will* be transporting him," Bitsy declared.

"Where?" Faye demanded, excitedly.

"Well, to Maricopa County Jail," Bitsy replied. "Now that they've dropped the federal charge, they can't keep him." She paused. "Hmm. Interesting twist—Robert hasn't been indicted at the state level, yet. Technically, I guess, he is still simply under arrest. He'll have to be indicted again, and arraigned again, too, when they set bail."

"Then, we'll have to do it, soon," Faye announced. "We'll have to free Robert, for his own safety."

Bitsy rested a hand on Faye's shoulder. "Faye—I agree with you, but I don't see how you can get away with it," she said, shaking her head. "It's not only risky, it's insane. First of all, *we'd* be breaking the law—aiding and abetting a known criminal, conspiracy after the fact, and so on. Escaping is also illegal. People who escaped before their trials have sometimes been found innocent of the original crime, but sent to prison for the crime of *escaping*. Then there's the danger of being killed in the act. The FBI will shoot to kill if someone tries to capture one of their prisoners and they're *very good* at it. Finally, there's the fact that you'd be condemning Robert to the life of a fugitive, and probably yourself, as well."

"I'm aware of those dangers," Faye admitted. "Now, how much danger do you think Robert is in if he remains in custody?"

Bitsy's shoulders drooped. "He's a dead man," she said flatly. "Grant meant well, but showing up when he did condemned Robert. If we'd stayed in federal court, the worst we'd have had to worry about would be twenty years in federal prison for the marijuana charge."

She shook her head. "I didn't think it through."

"Suppose I can improve the odds?" Faye suggested. "I have a plan that won't make Robert a willing participant in his escape. That will buy us time, at least, until the trial."

"You have a *plan?* Faye, do you have any idea how many people there are in prison who *thought* they had foolproof plans?"

"I appreciate your doubt," Faye smiled, "but I happen to have a secret weapon."

She glanced at Bitsy's purse. "May I use that cell phone of yours? I'd like to call Frank Timmons."

Bait and Switch

Tuesday, December 30, 1997

Faye awoke before her alarm clock went off. She had gotten high the night before on a tasty new strain of hydro, celebrating her new furniture and her home's new look with Chuck and Dave. She had then set up her new computer, installing the software Marvin had given her—miraculously tossed aside in the trashing of her house—and, as the finishing touch, downloading from her web site a set of files to use as a local copy so she could continue to maintain the site with new T-shirt designs, additional pages, and so on.

And now was the big day: The day she would join the ranks of Bonnie Parker, Leona Helmsley, and possibly Hillary Clinton, as a female lawbreaker. However, unlike Bonnie and Leona, but like Hillary, Faye hoped to get away with it.

She took a leisurely shower. Her head was clear and focused. Not being hung over was to her advantage. She donned one of the new outfits she had purchased with Dave—a white silk blouse with frilly front, Navy blue slacks and simple black flats. It made her feel competent and sexy; exactly the effect she wanted.

She realized it would be better if the phone call she had to make was not made from her own home. A pay phone would be too public. And what better place to make it than Marian's? So that's where she drove.

When she turned the corner onto Marian's street, her heart skipped a beat. Marian's car was parked in the driveway. If only her friend were at home, normal as a glass of milk! It couldn't be...Marian had been beheaded, a condition that was almost always fatal.

How did Marian's car get there? Faye wondered. This was the vehicle she and Marian had driven to Wickenburg, and which had been driven away while they were in the mine. *And, how long has it been here?*

In spite of herself, she was trembling as she turned her copy of Marian's house key in the lock.

"Hello?" she called, hopefully, as she entered. "Marian?"

But there was no answer, as she'd known would be the case.

She sat down and cried.

Briefly.

The police had come and gone, she knew. She could smell a trace of stale tobacco smoke, something Marian would never have permitted in her house. She checked the grow room. The door was opened and the room had been cleaned out. Faye didn't know whether it was by whoever had returned the car, or the FBI, and she didn't really care.

Determined, she sat at Marian's desk, and holding the phone with a handkerchief to avoid leaving fingerprints on it, she dialed the number she'd been given.

A male voice answered. "Agent Barrow," he said, in an efficient tone.

"Beware the jabberwock, my son, the jaws that bite, the claws that catch!" Faye said quietly.

Barrow responded in a flat tone. "Beware the jub jub bird, and shun the frumious bandersnatch. What sword should I use?"

"Your vorpal sword," Faye replied.

"Command me," said the voice over the line, and Faye did...in detail. She had notes so she wouldn't forget a single point.

Then, she added, "Do you know of anything that might prevent you from following these directions?"

After a pause, Barrow answered, "I do not."

"Then follow them," Faye directed. "And one more: You are *not* to take orders from anyone but me. No one else may put you under control. Do you understand?"

"Only you may command me," Barrow replied.

"Hang up, then, and forget consciously about this call...but carry out all my instructions."

Instantly, there was a click and the line went dead.

Faye locked the house, and started toward her own car, but hesitated. She'd known that using an automobile registered in her name was the weakest link in her scheme. On the other hand, there was a disadvantage in driving a car she'd never driven before. But Marian had shown her how to work all the Torino's custom gadgets, and if Faye was ever going to need them, this afternoon would be the time.

Taking a deep breath, she glanced in the car. To her surprise, the keys were in the ignition. Whoever had delivered the car here had apparently left them...and, of course, the vehicle's unattractive exterior had protected it from theft.

She transferred the outfit she'd gotten from Robert's closet from her car to Marian's. Then, taking another deep breath, she opened the door and slid behind the wheel.

The engine instantly came to life, purring smoothly as if it had not been sitting idly for, perhaps, most of a week.

Faye adjusted the mirrors and carefully backed into the street. She put the vehicle into gear and tapped the accelerator. It leaped forward as if it were rocket-propelled. *This is going to take some practice*, Faye thought. Her years spent married to a mechanic paid off; she'd helped out by driving hundreds of different cars from

Edwin's garage to a customer's home and it didn't take her long to develop a feel for a new vehicle.

By the time she was to pick up Frank, she was ready.

Faye waved cheerily at Frank's receptionist as she walked to the elevator with the clothes. Fortunately, the woman now recognized her and didn't make her sign in. Once upstairs, Faye rang the bell and the door opened immediately. "Frank!" she exclaimed. "You look wonderful!"

"Thanks," he acknowledged. There was no trace of the gruffness that previously had been a part of his voice. "Let me put these on."

He accepted the clothes from Faye and disappeared into the hallway.

"How are you doing?" she called.

"Really well," came the reply from the open bedroom door, accompanied by the swishing sounds of dressing. "Better than I have in years, actually. I can't explain it." When he emerged from the bedroom, he was dressed in a suit just one shade away from the one Robert would wear today. Faye gave a prayer of thanks that Robert had turned out to be such a clothes horse—and that Frank was his height. Certainly not his girth; Frank was still much thinner than the muscular Robert. But, Frank tightened the belt, leaving the suit just slightly baggy.

"Let's get going," Faye suggested, and they left the apartment and got into Marian's car.

They took Del Webb Boulevard to Grand Avenue, which cut diagonally across the streets directly to downtown Phoenix, while Frank calmly pointed out the things that had changed in the past twenty years. There was plenty of traffic, but nothing at all like the crush of automobiles Faye remembered from San Diego. In a brief recreation of his former grouchy self, Frank snarled, "If they keep building like this, there's gonna be more traffic than the road and highway system can handle. Then, goodbye to driving and hello to road rage." However, the traffic wasn't that heavy and they made good time.

"When does this transfer take place?" Frank asked.

"According to Bitsy, Robert is to be transferred from FBI head-quarters at one o'clock. I have no idea how prompt the FBI is on such things, however."

Frank shrugged. "There's also the question of whether Barrow is gonna be a trustworthy pawn."

Faye nodded. "There it is," she said, indicating the corner building. There was a clot of people jamming the doorway. She saw cameramen and others she assumed were reporters; their trucks were parked at the side of the street, leaving no available spaces. She had planned on staking out the building from a park-ing space, but now she had to drive on around the block. When they returned, there was no change, either to the crowd of reporters or to the available parking. The in-dash clock read four minutes after one.

Her mind flashed back to the last time she watched the minutes pass on an automobile clock: The day Marian had come to her rescue at the supermarket. Then, she'd been fat, alcoholic and despondent. How much had changed, and in such a short time! The realization never ceased to amaze her.

As they approached on the third pass, Frank pointed. "Black Cadillac," he said. "FBI youbetcha!" It was stopped on the corner, in front of the main entrance to the building. A policeman made them wait; another car immediately came to a stop behind her. She put her head out the window and called to the policeman, "What is it?"

The officer strolled closer to her car, which was now completely boxed in. "Just a prisoner transfer," he said conversationally. "You'll see it on the news tonight, I guess."

"Will it take long?" Faye asked impatiently.

"Naw," replied the policeman. "These things just take a moment or two. You'll be on your way in a minute."

As the officer spoke, a man was led from the building, coat pulled over his head in the traditional paparazzi-defying pose. The three TV cameramen were shifting angles, trying, apparently with little success, to catch a glimpse of the alleged murderer. Meanwhile the reporters thrust microphones in the prisoner's face while FBI agents in their trademarked black suits tried to hold them off. For a moment her heart sank when she didn't spot Barrow among them. But then, there he was, running out of the building and around the reporters, opening the door of the Cadillac and getting behind the wheel.

She watched as Robert was placed into the back seat of the vehicle. *So far, so good!* She thought.

And then, another black Cadillac pulled behind the first.

"Looks like they're going to have an escort," Frank remarked.

Shit! She swore to herself. It hadn't occurred to her there would be another car following. Her plan required Barrow to drive without witnesses into the I-10 tunnel. The Maricopa County Jail was just a few miles from there. If the switch didn't take place in the tunnel, it wouldn't happen.

The two Cadillacs pulled out, followed by the three news trucks. Finally, the officer allowed Faye and Frank to proceed. Faye turned to follow the news trucks.

The parade proceeded south on Second Street, then east on Clarendon. That was opposite the direction of the county jail but it avoided the heavy traffic of the business district and, conveniently, would lead to the tunnel that went beneath it. At Seventh Street they turned south.

This wasn't at all what I had in mind, Faye worried internally, unwilling to let Frank know the plan had already gone awry. Why hadn't she foreseen the news trucks, much less the escort vehicle?

"Make sure your seat belt's tight," she warned, as she flipped a toggle switch that Marian had told her would invert the license plate, revealing a phony—but realistic—one behind it.

She made her move. Flooring the accelerator, Marian's car leapt ahead like a Formula One racing car. She passed the news van in front of her, and the next and the next.

Seventh Street fed into the big I-10 tunnel through a feeder tunnel that was just one lane wide. Faye continued on, illegally passing the FBI escort vehicle in the emergency lane just as Barrow and Robert entered the tunnel ahead of them. Jamming on her brakes and expertly twisting the wheel, Faye fishtailed into the escort vehicle. Its driver unprepared, the vehicle nosed into the wall, causing its rear end to swing around and completely block the narrow entrance to the tunnel. A glance at her rearview mirror showed the chain reaction as the news trucks and other cars crashed into the escort vehicle, completely blocking the entrance to the main tunnel.

She also saw agents leap from that vehicle, guns drawn; fortunately, the primary tunnel was curved at this point, and she was out of sight in seconds, probably before they could even identify what kind of car had hit them.

Still in the tunnel, she pulled up behind Barrow's vehicle, and they both pulled into the emergency lane and stopped. She and Frank opened their doors and bolted towards the Cadillac. Faye found the back door unlocked, as expected. She opened it and looked into Robert's astounded face.

"What th'—" he gasped.

"Get out of the vehicle *now*, Dr. Thompson," Barrow urged, as he, too, leapt from the car. "You are in danger. Your friends are here to help."

Robert didn't hesitate. In less than ten seconds, the cuffs were off Robert and on Frank; Frank was in Barrow's car, and Robert was in Marian's.

"Good luck!" Faye wished Frank, and blew him a kiss. She slammed the door and Barrow took off, reentering the flow of traffic.

Back in Marian's front seat, Faye jammed the accelerator to the floor. The vehicle leapt forward, achieving 55 mph in seconds and pushing Robert deep into the cushioned seat.

"What is going on here?" he demanded.

"Buckle up!" Faye ordered. "We aren't out of the woods, yet!"

Driving, as every Phoenician does, ten miles above the speed limit, Faye neither dawdled nor attracted attention as she sped eastward on I-10. She passed Barrow's Cadillac just as it veered onto I-17 South. Once they were out of sight, Faye sped up slightly. She did not intend to return on Grand, with its innumerable traffic lights. Instead, she kept on I-10 as long as she dared. When she saw flashing lights far behind them, she exited onto 75th Avenue and headed north.

There was no traffic on this road that cut like an arrow through the orange groves, and they shot along it past trees and fields. Faye turned left at McDowell, which took her out of line-of-sight of any police cars that might look down 75th as they passed on the highway. Then she headed north again on 99th.

The road was unpaved. Faye took a left at an even less navigable-looking dirt road and drove into an orange grove. She threaded among the trees until the road was completely out of sight, then stopped the car and shut off the engine.

After the sound of the crashes in the tunnel, and the highway noise that had followed, the silence in the grove was a blessing to Faye's grateful ears. There were no sounds at all, even after Faye rolled down her window. They could hear each other's breathing. She removed her seat belt, turned toward Robert, and kissed him. He resisted at first, but quickly melted into her and kissed back.

The deep kiss slowly subsided and their lips reluctantly parted. "I love you," Robert said, "and I want to keep on kissing you. But, please, tell me what just happened!"

Then Faye told Robert the whole story, everything that had transpired since the police had arrested him. She took her time, leaving out nothing. And then she allowed him to digest it all.

Just when she thought he might not understand that she had saved his life, and be angry with her for forcing him into an escape that might well bring them both even more legal troubles than they already had, he smiled shyly. "It's weird," he confessed. "But, somehow, I find being sprung from prison by a sexy woman who can drive one hell of a getaway car, to be very...arousing."

In the privacy of the grove, they made love on a blanket found in Marian's trunk; then again.

Faye found herself thanking Marian for her recently-developed stamina.

And the infinite power of love, for Robert's.

Surprise

It was dark when Faye, cautiously, rounded the corner to Marian's house. Although the car had been displaying the fake license plate Marian had built into the vehicle, Faye was afraid the distinctive vehicle might have been recognized.

But the street was not packed with police cars; it was lit, as usual, by tasteful street lamps just bright enough to hide the stars. Most of the homes were dark, each with just one or two windows modestly lighted—enough to show that there was life behind them. Drapes were drawn across almost every window; a nod to the glaring sun during the day, and to long-habitual propriety at night. Even inhabited homes weren't much brighter than Marian's deserted one.

Quietly, Faye pulled into Marian's driveway. She shut off the headlights and killed the ignition. Without speaking, she and Robert exited the car, walked calmly but purposefully to Faye's waiting Ford, got in, and drove away.

Once out of the neighborhood, Faye and Robert breathed twin sighs of relief.

"I think we did it, Robert," Faye exhaled. "Maybe I should go into business. What do you think of 'JailBusters'?"

Robert laughed explosively, the pent-up tension released like air from a popped balloon. "A dangerous business, don't you think?" He blinked. "How about 'Jailbreaks 'R' Us'?"

Faye's neighborhood was as quiet as Marian's; as, indeed, all of Sun City becomes once the sun goes down and the "I-don't-drive-at-night" crowd settles down for an evening of brain-numbing TV and early bedtimes. Relaxed, she pulled into her driveway.

They walked in a manner that would hopefully not merit a second look from anyone who might, by freak coincidence, happen to look out an undraped window at just that moment.

She turned her key in the lock, let Robert enter, and followed him in, flipping the light switch as she shut the door behind her.

"SURPRISE!!!" came the shouts of half a dozen people, leaping to their feet in her newly-decorated living room.

"Holy shit!" she and Robert cried in unison.

That was followed by a stunned silence as the visitors, which included Chuck, Dave, and Bitsy as well as others she did not know, recognized Robert and realized who he was.

"Omigod," Bitsy breathed at last. "You brought him *here?*"

Following The Leader

"It's an emergency meeting of the Sun City Cannabis Club," Dave explained, as Faye collapsed into a kitchen chair. "I thought it would be fun to combine it with a surprise housewarming party, and a farewell for Marian."

"After all, you're Marian's successor," Chuck explained. "You were going to have to meet these people, anyway."

"And Marian had always said she wanted her wake to be a celebration of her life, not a sad occasion but a joyous one," Dave concluded.

Faye's eyes widened. "You're throwing a *surprise wake?*" she asked incredulously.

Dave smiled weakly. "Aren't they all?"

"You don't have to worry about any of these people," Chuck added. "They are the heads of their grow groups."

"They all have grow rooms like yours," Dave pointed out. "Some of them bigger. Think of it as the Underground Railroad of Pot. By moving at night from one secret grow room to another, we could get Robert across the Mexican border easily, and even into Canada if he prefers, in absolute safety."

"And stoned," Chuck added.

"I am *not* escaping anywhere," Robert announced. "I intend to stand trial." He focused on Faye's face.

"How do you feel?" he asked.

"Much better," she replied. "But, Robert—you're in danger!"

"Only until the trial begins," the doctor pointed out. "According to your analysis, *that's* what the enemy wants to prevent. Once it starts, there's no point in killing me." He sighed. "*Then* I get to go to jail for escaping, even if they find me innocent of dealing marijuana."

One of the guests whom Faye did not know poked his head into the kitchen. "The tape is rewound and ready to go," he said.

"Who was that?" Faye asked, allowing Robert to help her up.

"Cal Martin," Dave answered, obviously relieved that Faye wasn't angry with him. "Come, meet everyone." He led the way back to the living room.

The furniture was new, and even though Faye had picked it out and spent yesterday evening getting used to it, it still seemed like someone else's home. The guests, who had been sitting, rose to their feet.

"Introduce yourselves," Dave suggested.

The guests did so, reaching to shake Faye's hand and then sitting back down.

"It's nice to meet you, Cal," she said, and, "Alice, I'm glad you could come." She had learned the trick of remembering a new name by repeating it after first hearing it long ago, when greeting customers at the garage. Her knack for making them feel like friends had resulted in a repeat business that allowed the enterprise to flourish.

"Now," Dave announced, "for the evening's entertainment, we have the Faye and Robert show!" Someone turned down the room lights, leaving one small lamp burning. Cal pressed the "Play" button on Faye's new video tape recorder.

The TV screen lit up to reveal the logo of the Channel 2 *Six O'clock News*. Faye instantly recognized the face of newsreader Audrey Flowers.

"The Valley was rocked today by the daring prison break of Doctor Robert Thompson, the so-called 'Pot Doctor' who is the alleged assassin of Representative Carvel Meany, and accused of the mutilation death of a Sun City resident. For details, we turn to Channel 2 reporter John Pacer."

The scene changed to the Maricopa County Jail. John Pacer, a young reporter, stood with his back to the brightly-lit building, holding a microphone. "In one of the most fantastic jailbreaks of the last few decades—"

"He's done *no* research on this!" Bitsy cried over Pacer's voice.

"—Doctor Robert Thompson has somehow escaped the FBI *during* his transfer to Maricopa County Jail. Thompson got *into* the FBI vehicle at FBI headquarters—" Here, the image cut to a shot of Robert, coat over head, being escorted into the Cadillac. "—but when the vehicle arrived at Maricopa County Jail, *this* man got out!" The image cut again to a daytime shot of the Cadillac opening its doors and a very befuddled-looking Frank Timmons getting out. Chuck and Dave both gasped, unaware of Frank's involvement.

The close-up of the FBI driver, Desmond Barrow, laying eyes on his passenger was like a scene from an episode of *I Love Lucy*— each man staring at the other as if he had never seen him before.

"It's assumed that the switch somehow took place in the I-10 Tunnel, where a freak hit-and-run accident—now thought to be intentional—separated the FBI car and its escort at the entrance to the—"

The screen abruptly returned to the image of Audrey Flowers. "We interrupt this report for a late-breaking development."

The image returned to Pacer. "—reporting live from the Maricopa County Jail, where FBI agents and sheriff's deputies have been trying to piece together today's daring escape. Apparently the agent who was driving the alleged prisoner is going to make a statement."

The camera swung to the left to reveal Desmond Barrow, who only Faye and Robert recognized, standing in front of a cluster of handheld microphones. Faye crossed her fingers.

"Good evening," the agent said. "I have a statement as to what occurred today when my prisoner, Robert Thompson, escaped."

Barrow took a deep breath. The microphones poised before him pushed slightly closer. "The FBI has determined that Doctor Thompson did not kill Representative Meany. The murder gun was never in Doctor Thompson's possession and his fingerprints were not on it. Neither did he kill the woman, Marian Higgins. There was not enough blood on the scene for her to have been killed there. Her body was brought to the scene, probably by Meany. The only charge remaining is that of possession of marijuana, and *I* placed the evidence in the trunk of Thompson's car on the orders of my superiors. Dr. Thompson has been prescribing marijuana in accordance with Arizona State Law, and the FBI wanted him arrested to serve as warning to other Arizona doctors to not prescribe the substance, even if state law allowed it. Since Dr. Thompson was innocent, I felt I could no longer, in good conscience, keep him prisoner and I took him to a safe house where he will be until his trial. I knew his life would be in danger as long as he was held prisoner, so I freed—"

The screen suddenly went black. A moment later, Audrey Flowers reappeared, flustered. "Well!" she said. "We seem to have lost our feed. But, apparently, we have just learned that a rogue FBI agent was responsible for the escape of the prisoner Robert Thompson today as he was being transported by the agent from FBI headquarters to the Maricopa County Jail..."

She continued to blather on, repeating the same catch phrases over and over, until even she seemed to tire of it; then went on to a story about a drowned child. Cal turned off the TV. Faye's visitors sat in stunned silence.

Finally one of them, Alice, turned to Faye. "So, you were working with this FBI agent to hide Dr. Thompson?"

Faye considered. "Um, yes. But, Alice, the less you people know about this, the better for *all* of us, don't you think?" There was a general assent.

Bitsy stood. "Faye, as you may know, Marian left you executrix of her estate. She also, in her last will and testament, left you her house, goods, *et cetera*. That's official; I was her lawyer."

Faye thumped heavily into a kitchen chair someone had thoughtfully placed behind her. "I—I had no idea," she stammered.

"Unofficially," the semi-retired lawyer went on, "she also let me know that she wanted you to take over leadership of the Sun City Cannabis Club."

Faye blinked. "I thought there *was* no leadership," she said.

Bitsy nodded. "Leadership is probably too strong a word," she said. "Guide might be better. The club needs to have someone to turn to when a person needs advice on growing the plant, or distributing it. It needs someone to locate new potential members, to decide whether a potential member someone else has found is genuine and not a trap. While it's true the Sun City Cannabis Club has no organizational leader, we do need a spiritual leader. That was Marian, and she has passed the job on to you—if you will accept it."

Faye sat, numb. "Do I get to think about it?"

"Of course, Faye!" asserted the woman named Alice. "And you can always change your mind. This is an honor, not a prison sentence."

"And if it were, you could always get your FBI friend to help you escape!" Dave quipped. Everyone laughed but Faye.

Faye stood. "I think we'd all be able to think more clearly after a joint, don't you?" There was instant agreement. She started in the direction of her bedroom.

Robert rose quickly. "I'll get it, darling," he said.

He was entering the hall when Faye called after him, "But you don't know how to open the—"

Dave jumped up and interrupted, "I'll show him." He returned with a joint a minute later, and, winking at Faye, said, "Robert will be right back."

Faye accepted the joint and placed it in a new, ornate ashtray that adorned the new, glass-topped coffee table. "Before we light this," she said, "let's have just a moment of silence to honor the memory of our friend, Marian."

"Amen," someone responded.

Faye closed her eyes and thought, *How odd this all is!* Here she was, mourning the loss of her friend. Here she was, suddenly thrust into a position of responsibility in an organization she hadn't even dreamed existed six months before. Here she was—

Suddenly, there was a violent pounding on the front door, startling Faye out of her meditation. Her guests, shocked, stared at the door. A booming voice cried, "This is the FBI! We have a search warrant. Open the door, or we'll break it down!" Without skipping a beat, the door was thrown open and two black-suited men charged in, guns drawn.

"What are you doing here?" screamed Faye angrily.

"Are you Ms. McRae?" one of the agents demanded. He removed a sheet of official-looking paper from inside his jacket and waved it in her face. "This is a warrant to search the premises for an escaped prisoner."

Intrusion

The agent looked with surprise at the guests. "What's with the crowd?"

Faye answered. "We're friends of Marian Higgins, who died recently. This is a memorial, a wake."

"Well," the agent growled, "all of you stay put. We won't be long." The two men moved together into the hallway.

Another man appeared in the doorway. "Oh, thank God!" Faye cried in spite of herself. "Grant! What's going on?" she asked convincingly. She hated deceiving her friend, but she knew it was the only way.

"I couldn't talk them out of it," the detective confessed. "But at least I convinced them to let me come along as local representation." He grinned. "They *hate* that!"

Faye tried not to hold her breath while waiting for the agents to return. Would they find Robert in the bathroom? How could they *not* find him? She couldn't turn her gaze away from the empty hallway, but could see from the corner of her eye that everyone else's attention was directed there as well.

When the agents returned, they were alone. As they rushed to the kitchen, they fortunately did not hear everyone exhale at the same time.

"Are you having a party with the lights out?" Grant asked, taking in the visitors.

"It's a wake for Marian," Faye explained.

Suddenly, she could tell Grant's attention had been riveted by something on the coffee table. In a flash, Faye knew what it was. The joint was sitting there, in the ashtray. Her mind raced to come up with an excuse, an explanation, some move that would allow her to pocket the thing before the FBI agents saw it.

She heard the door connecting the garage slam and the purposeful steps of the agents striding through the kitchen back toward the living room.

Suddenly, Grant leaned forward, scooped up the joint and pocketed it.

The agents entered the room, glowering.

"No sign of the prisoner?" Grant guessed, sardonically.

"Sorry to have troubled you, ma'am," one of the suited men grumbled as they left. Grant, leaving last, turned at the door and held his right hand to Faye. She automatically extended her own right hand to take it.

"Ms. McRae, we apologize for the intrusion. Have a nice evening."

He left, closing the door behind him.

Faye looked at the joint he'd placed in her palm, then held it up for her guests to see.

"Wow," said Cal. "Looks like we have a friend in high places."

Ignoring him, Faye cried, "Where's Robert?" She ran down the hall, through her bedroom, and into her bath. All the windows were closed. There was no sign of the doctor. Taking a deep breath, she pulled the lever that worked the hidden grow room door. It opened, and there he was, waiting patiently next to the grow unit.

"Are they gone?" he whispered through a beaming smile.

"Yeah, yeah, yeah!" Faye laughed, and led him back to the living room.

The group sat quietly conversing. Faye did her best to keep the topic on Marian and away from Robert's escape. After all, it *was* a wake. They discussed the ways in which Marian had guided the growers of the club. Half afraid the FBI might return, they did not light the joint.

Finally, Faye announced, "This is Marian's memorial. We aren't going to let it end without smoking one in her honor."

Alice quavered, "But the police..."

Faye smiled. "If we let the mere *idea* that police might arrest us to keep us from doing what we know is right, then the dictatorship has already won."

So she lit the joint, took the first hit, and passed it to Bitsy. Dave produced a joint of his own, and passed it to the others. There was ample weed to buzz everyone, a proper toast to Marian's memory.

It's A Date

Monday, February 9, 1998

Bitsy's voice spoke over the phone. "Faye," she said, "the date has been set. It's time to come home."

Faye looked wistfully out the window overlooking the mountains of Pend Oreille County in eastern Washington state. It was as different here from Sun City as it was possible to be—and from San Diego, too, for that matter. In the weeks they'd been registered at this incredibly out-of-the-way bed-and-breakfast, they'd seen the snow fall, huge banks of fog roll through, and, occasionally, sunny days in which the glare of sunshine off snow and ice was sharp and exhilarating.

The downside was the warning not to walk in the woods alone due to possible cougar attack, and the intense cold. Or maybe the latter was an upside—because it gave the couple an excuse to snuggle all the more closely at night.

Not that they needed one.

Faye was glad they were not there as fugitives. A phone call, placed from a phone booth, had facilitated Grant's picking up Robert without knowing that Faye had been involved with his escape. Robert claimed to have escaped from a safe house in which supposedly-crazed FBI Agent Barrow had left him. In Grant's custody, Robert was indicted on the remaining charges and released on bail.

Not trusting the FBI with Robert's safety, Faye had taken him, by circuitous route, to the most out-of-the-way spot she could find on the map: Washington State's Pend Oreille County (which, she discovered after their arrival, was pronounced "Pond O-ray"), an area of several hundred square miles and no cities and few roads. Now had come the call summoning them home.

"One more, thing, Faye," the voice on the line interrupted her reverie. "The prosecution is sure to include three or four lawyers. I heard from a friend that Shears is going to be there, even though the case is now being heard in a county court. Since I no longer have a practice, I don't have anyone to act as my assistant, and I was hoping you'd—"

"Oh, yeah, of course! Anything, anything."

Faye put Robert on the line, and stepped outside to give him some privacy. The broad veranda opened onto a wide expanse of snow-covered lawn and a spectacular mountain view.

In just moments, he joined her. "It's time," he said, smiling. "The date's set, locked in. The trial is this coming Monday."

"Good. I'll start packing."

He took her hand and led her to the big, hanging swing. They sat in it, as they had many times, looking northward up the mountain slope that merged with the low clouds scudding by.

"Faye," he said, "when this is over, and assuming I am found not guilty—let's get married."

She squeezed his hand. "We *are* married, darling."

"I mean, really. Legally."

She turned toward him, studied his countenance. "After all the crap we've been through," she said, "why do you want to bring the *law* into it?"

A confused expression crossed his face. "Don't you want to marry me?"

"As far as I'm concerned, we *are* married, Doctor. As far as our friends are concerned, we're married. What are you looking for, a tax deduction?" she added, giggling.

Robert looked hurt, and Faye immediately regretted her flippant remark. "It seems to me, Robert," she continued, "if we believe government has no place regulating our lives—what right does it have to regulate our *bedrooms?* Look at Chuck and Dave. No one is more married than they are, yet the government won't even *allow* them the option! Don't you see, if we go through the motions of getting a license, and blood tests, and the rest—don't you see, we are buying into the whole idea that the government has a right to be involved!"

Robert nodded reluctantly.

"And look at how that interference has been misused. Sure, now it's gays that aren't allowed to get married. But it wasn't that many years ago a relationship like *ours*—a black man and a white woman—was illegal. It seems to me all those interracial couples that fought to change that law were missing the point. Immoral laws *should* be ignored. Right-thinking people should have realized, back then, that marriage—that most sacred union of people—should *never* have been allowed in the halls of government.

"They should have all, as Nancy Reagan advised, *just said no.*"

"I love you, Faye. I want to shout our commitment to the world."

"Let's just shout it to our friends. Let's have a commitment ceremony of our own, inviting everyone whose opinion we respect. Let's not involve a bunch of mindless bureaucrats and partisan politicians in yet another arena where they don't belong."

"All right," Robert said, puzzled; and then, more strongly, "All *right!*"

"Now that that's settled," Faye said, snuggling into his shoulder. She looked into Robert's eyes, smiled, and said, "Me love you long time."

The Trial Begins

Tuesday, February 10, 1998

"All rise, court is now in session...the Honorable Lila Williams presiding."

Rising with everyone else in the courtroom, Faye looked around her. She had never before attended a trial, let alone assisted at one. Edwin had once gone to court over a traffic ticket, but he had forbidden her to accompany him.

In preparation for Robert's trial, Bitsy and Robert and Faye had gone over and over every scrap of evidence that would be presented. "The prosecution is required to share all the evidence they have with us," Bitsy explained. "It's pretty flimsy. But, if presented strongly enough...well, we've got to have a more compelling explanation."

The courtroom was packed. Many were seniors and Robert's patients, but there were also a substantial number of young people attending in support of Robert.

Just as gratifying was the fact that a great many people present were wearing T-shirts Faye had designed and uploaded to her web site while she and Robert were in exile in Pend Oreille County. *No Just Government Forces Its Citizens To Live In Pain* was one of her less imaginative ones, but quite a few people had apparently liked it enough to have it printed onto T-shirts, pullovers, and Henleys. *A "Democracy" That Doesn't Obey Its Citizens Is A Dictatorship* was another popular slogan. So was *I Vote For Freedom Of Choice*, with a large marijuana leaf graphic. The overwhelming favorite of the day said simply, *Free Doctor Thompson!*

Faye sat between Bitsy and Robert, directly in front of the wooden barrier that separated the legal representatives of the trial from the onlookers. She loved that she could sit next to Robert, and have a part in getting him out of this bizarre situation, for which Faye felt at least partly responsible.

Judge Williams, Faye noted as the woman walked to the bench, was Asian; Faye hoped that the judge's being a minority might provide some degree of consideration for the doctor. She spotted Bitsy's expression of evaluation. She imagined Bitsy trying to assess what demeanor would be most advantageous with this judge. Of course, the FBI lawyers were doing the same. The naïve might think it was all in earnest, but Faye now understood the whole thing was just a show.

The clerk of the court stood. "Case number 103-18871A, the State of Arizona versus Doctor Robert Thompson."

"Are counsel ready to proceed?" the judge asked. The government attorneys and Bitsy stood and affirmed they were. "The prosecution may make its opening argument," Williams instructed.

There were three people sitting at the prosecution's table. All of them, Faye thought, looked as if they'd taken a strong laxative the night before—unsuccessfully. One was Shears, whom Faye recognized from the aborted Federal arraignment. He bore a pallor that evidenced never going outside. *I wonder how he got to the courtroom without being exposed to even a little sun,* Faye thought. Of the remaining two, one was a man, and one was a woman. All three wore severe black suits; Shears rose and strode towards the jury with his hands gripping the lapels of his coat as if it might suddenly try to shake itself off him.

"Your honor; members of the jury," the lawyer began. "My name is William Shears, and along with Denis O'Bell and Darcy Benson, I shall be representing the people of the State of Arizona in the prosecution of Robert Thompson for first-degree murder and possession of a felonious amount of a controlled substance, marijuana.

"Now, I know you have heard the lie that marijuana can be used in treating certain illnesses and Doctor Thompson's lawyers will try to convince you that he has been doling out marijuana for that purpose. However, we will be able to show you, beyond a shadow of a doubt, that under the influence of this dangerous, controlled substance, Doctor Thompson tortured, dismembered, and finally murdered poor old Marian Higgins, a little old lady who never did anyone any harm.

"We will demonstrate that 'Doctor' Thompson tricked her into growing marijuana for him, and when she refused, he killed her in a manner so horrible I fear you will all have nightmares for weeks to come. I trust you will take those nightmares seriously, and find 'Doctor' Thompson guilty of murder in the first degree."

Faye sat stunned as the pompous man strutted to the prosecutors' table. His charges against Robert were so preposterous, she couldn't imagine how the man had made them with a straight face. Yet, he had, and Faye had a dizzy feeling that he might be able to do all he had promised.

From his expression, Robert was as dismayed as she.

Meanwhile, Bitsy rose, stepped out from behind the desk, and brushed out a few imaginary wrinkles from her skirt. She had explained to Faye that every motion that lawyers made in court was theatrical; each designed to convey a certain image.

"Forget law," she had told Faye. "It almost doesn't matter how much law you know. And it sure the hell doesn't matter whether the defendant is guilty! The best actor wins." By straightening her skirt, Faye knew Bitsy was projecting a confidence she didn't really feel. In addition, while the prosecution's table was covered with reports, folders, laptop computers, and more, Bitsy's table was clear except for a simple notepad, suggesting, as Bitsy intended, that she needed nothing but logic to prove Robert's innocence.

Bitsy walked toward the jury box and smiled. Then she nodded toward the judge. "Good morning, your honor. Good morning, ladies and gentlemen of the jury. I am Elizabeth Cunningham, and I will be defending Doctor Thompson against these silly charges. Why do I think they are silly? For two reasons. First, I've known Doctor Thompson for years. When I was diagnosed with breast cancer, it was Doctor Thompson who saved my breast—with the help of a prescription for marijuana, I might add. Yes, other medications were involved. But my cancer was cured, my breast was saved, and, yes, I became his friend for life. It might interest you to know that I am *not* accepting payment, other than one dollar, for representing him.

"Second, I want you to look at the three people at the prosecutor's table. Unless you are a professional juror—" At this, the jury laughed, knowing that at a daily payment of $12, none could *afford* to be a professional juror! "Unless you are a professional juror, you won't realize that William Shears is *not* the county prosecutor. Our county prosecutor is Denis O'Bell. Now, it is not unusual for the county prosecutor to turn a case over to a subordinate for experience. That would be Ms. Benson—Hi, Darcy! That hairstyle suits you so much better than the old one!—But, that leaves a mystery: Who is Mr. Shears?

"Mr. Shears, ladies and gentlemen of the jury, works for the FBI. That's right, the Federal Bureau of Investigation. Now, you might wonder what interest the FBI has in a local murder case. And I'll tell you: None at all. It's the *marijuana* aspect of this case that has the FBI's attention. See, Doctor Thompson *has* been prescribing marijuana—legally, in accordance with the wishes of the voters of this state—to many sick people in Sun City. *And they've been getting better.* The federal government, so much of which is funded by corporations that profit by keeping marijuana illegal, is terrified that word of this might spread. And so, to put it bluntly, they *framed* Doctor Thompson. And so I shall prove.

"Murder case? Piffle. They have no case. Make no mistake, folks—this is about the marijuana. And, by the time I'm done, you *will* return a verdict of not guilty. Thank you."

As Bitsy returned to her seat, Faye stifled an urge to applaud and Robert grinned.

"You may call your first witness," the judge said to the prosecution.

That witness was an FBI agent. He described coming on the scene at Selma's house, seeing the carnage, feeling sick. "A headless, handless body," he said, swallowing hard. "I've seen worse in my career, but not much."

The judge then gave Bitsy the opportunity to cross-examine the witness.

"Tell me, Agent Zembruski," she asked in a friendly manner, "were you the very first person on the scene of the crime?"

"No, I wasn't," the agent replied. He referred to his notebook. "I relieved a local officer, one Grant Taylor, who got there ahead of me."

"So Detective Taylor was there when you arrived. Was anyone else?"

"No."

"Now, did you take photos of the crime scene?"

Faye saw Shears start to rise, then think better of it. But his face was threatening as thunder.

"I did not," Zembruski replied. "They were taken by an FBI photographer who arrived about twenty minutes after I did. My job was to relieve Taylor and to make sure no one contaminated the crime scene before the rest of the investigation team could arrive."

"I see. Did the entire team arrive at once?"

"No, ma'am." He referred again to his notes. "Agent Barrow arrived about five minutes after I did. But everyone else was there in twenty minutes."

"Was Agent Barrow ever alone in the crime room?"

"No, ma'am."

"Are you sure?"

"Of course, I'm sure!"

"Where were you when you were called to the Sun City crime scene, Agent Zembruski?"

"I was on a case in Scottsdale," he replied.

"And, how long did it take you to get to Sun City?"

The agent looked surprised. "About an hour, I'd say. Maybe a little longer."

"And how much water did you drink on your way to Sun City?"

The agent blinked in astonishment. "I—beg pardon?"

"This is a desert. That was a long drive. How much water did you drink on your way to Sun City?" Bitsy repeated.

"Most of a liter bottle, I'd say."

"So, Agent Zembruski. You drank a liter of water in an hour. You replaced Detective Taylor at the crime scene; I understand you doing that immediately because, after all, *you're* FBI and he's local. And then Agent Barrow arrives, five minutes after you do. Are you telling me that you didn't take a moment to use the bathroom after Agent Barrow got there?"

The face of the FBI agent suddenly went hard, as if he'd figured where Bitsy's questions were leading.

"The whole house is considered a crime scene, Counselor. I didn't leave the crime scene."

"But you did use the bathroom, didn't you?" Bitsy prodded.

Shears jumped to his feet. "Objection! It's irrelevant, and she's badgering the witness!"

"It's not irrelevant, your honor," Bitsy said. "We have reason to believe the evidence was tampered with."

The judge looked over her wire-rimmed glasses at Shears. "I'll allow it," she said, and then, to Zembruski, directed, "Answer it."

"Yes, I went to the bathroom. But only for a moment."

"I'm glad you can eliminate a liter of water in a moment," Bitsy muttered, loudly enough to be heard, as she returned to the defense table. "At my age, I need half an hour!

"No more questions, your honor," she added in a louder tone.

There was a trickle of appreciative laughter through the room. Faye realized Bitsy had just won over the hearts of some of the spectators, and perhaps a few of the jurors.

Another witness for the prosecution—they all seemed to be FBI agents—described the time of death for Marian, and how difficult identification had been. The FBI lawyer said, "Then, Agent Maxwell, how *did* you identify the headless body? By the time you found it, it was already starting to decompose. There was no head, ergo no dental records or retina patterns. There were no hands, and so no fingerprints. I happen to know Marian had no living children and, in fact, no living relatives at all, against whom to make a DNA comparison."

"We made a DNA sweep of the Higgins house," the agent explained, "and we found 157 hairs in Ms. Higgins' bed, from two individuals. The DNA of one of the individuals matched the DNA from the body and we were able to determine the body belonged to Marian Higgins."

Bitsy started to waive cross-examination, but then asked, "Who belonged to the other hair?"

"We don't know," Agent Maxwell replied. "It was human hair, but the DNA didn't match anyone we have on file."

When she returned to the table, Bitsy whispered to Faye, "Was Marian sleeping with anyone?"

"No!" Faye replied, also whispering, "at least, not that I know of. And I'm sure she would have told me if she were."

Testimony and cross-examination seemed to take forever. Robert's business card, found in Marian's purse, was offered as evidence—"Exhibit A," the judge called it. Another agent showed photos of Marian's grow room, before the marijuana was removed. "Exhibit B" was the results of Robert's urine test, taken after he'd been arrested, that showed incriminating levels of tetrahydro-cannabinol. Another agent described the opulence of Robert's home, and the fact that *no* marijuana had been found there. Finally, the judge announced a recess. "Court will reconvene tomorrow morning at ten." Robert was led away by the bailiff.

That night, with the details of the days' testimony tumbling in her head, Faye realized two things. One, the prosecution intended to make it appear that Robert's wealth came from selling marijuana rather than doctoring. And two...

Faye knew that Robert wasn't selling the marijuana, but it would be hard to prove that. Instead, clearly, the prosecutors intended to prove that marijuana had no medical benefit and nail him for selling a quack cure. Worse, getting rich from one!

Faye leaped out of bed, ran to her living room, and turned on her computer. The only way they could prove marijuana had no medical benefit would be to present some kind of study, or perhaps a series of studies. Since she knew, by personal experience, that marijuana *did* have medicinal benefits, those studies would have to be flawed. All she had to do was find the flaws.

In less than an hour, she found what she was looking for and her little ink-jet printer began humming. When she ran out of paper, she drove four miles to Glendale, to an all-night computer-and-copy store, and bought more. At four in the morning, when the printouts were complete, she returned to the copy store and had them spiral-bound into a series of books, each with a plastic cover and a title page. When she finally got into bed, she was exhausted but triumphant.

Day 2

Wednesday, February 11, 1998

That morning, Faye took the box of reports with her to the court-house. When Bitsy saw it, she looked askance at Faye.

"I have a feeling we'll need what's in this box," was all Faye would say. She didn't want to admit to the hours she'd spent printing the pages if she were wrong. "We can bring it to the table, can't we?"

"The bailiff will want to search it, but as long as it isn't loaded weapons it will be no problem. But, Faye, if you have any evidence that I should know about..."

"This isn't evidence, I promise," Faye assured her. "Just a rebuttal, in case we need one."

Bitsy gave Faye a questioning look, then grinned and said, "Bring whatever you want, honey."

As the second day of the trial commenced, the FBI prosecutor called a witness who presented a computer list, obtained, he said, from Robert's computer, of patients who had been prescribed marijuana. The prosecution asked that it be accepted as evidence.

"Wait! How did you get this list?" Bitsy asked.

"I already said, I got it from the doc's computer," the agent, a hairy, definitely non-FBI-looking nerd, slurred.

"We heard you, young man," the judge said, making the witness uncomfortable. "Now, sit up straight and tell the court how you *came* to get this list?"

"Oh, yes, ma'am" the youth said, suddenly respectful. "There was a warrant."

"Indeed," Bitsy said. "Did you see this warrant?"

"No, I didn't see it," the young man admitted. "But my boss said there was one."

"Yet this warrant hasn't been introduced as evidence yet, has it? Your honor, did I miss something? Where is this warrant?"

"Counselor, may I see the warrant?" There was a shuffling of papers at the prosecutors' table, and Darcy Benson held up an official-looking sheet of paper.

"Here it is!" she called, cheerily, making no effort to move from the table.

"May I see it?" Judge Williams requested, clearly annoyed. Benson scurried to the judge's bench and handed her the ostensible warrant.

The judge examined the paper closely. Finally, she said, "What is this?"

Benson blushed. "That's the w-warrant to search Dr. Thompson's office," she stammered.

"This warrant was issued to search for a murder weapon or blood," the judge observed. "What were you doing in the defendant's computer?"

"They told me to," the computer expert responded, clearly anxious.

"I am asking Ms. Benson," the judge said, flatly. "Well?"

"Uh—Mr. Shears obtained that warrant." Faye almost laughed out loud at Benson's expression of panic.

"For all we knew," Benson hastily explained to the judge, "Thompson might have killed the victim with some drug before beheading her. We were entitled to look throughout the office, and that's what we did."

"*Mr.* Shears," the judge snapped. "The law protects the doctor-patient relationship with great care. This warrant is for a murder weapon or blood. You should know very well that it entitled you to search for the tools used to perform a decapitation. They would not be found in a computer. Not only is this computer list *not* admissible," and at this, she turned to the jury, "you are to disregard any statements made by this witness regarding the defendant's patients *or* their medications."

Bitsy rose. "Your honor, we appreciate your ruling to keep the doctor's patient list private but we do not deny that Doctor Thompson has prescribed medical marijuana in appropriate cases, in accordance with Arizona state law. In fact, we will be bringing some of Dr. Thompson's patients forward who have been aided by this therapy."

Faye saw Shears glare at Bitsy. It seemed he had expected her to fight the charge.

Shears then called an agent to the stand who'd searched Robert's house. After she assured Shears that no marijuana had been found on the premises, she presented photos of the house, which Shears requested be accepted as evidence. The photos were handed to Bitsy.

"These are in color, Ms. Hood," she said. "And beautifully composed. They look like illustrations in an issue of *Martha Stewart's Living*. Aren't crime scene photos usually done in black and white?"

"The defendant's home was not a crime scene," the agent replied. "We had a warrant to search it, and these photos are the result."

"You *found* these pictures there?" Bitsy asked, incredulously. "Your honor, I cannot see what relevance a set of—of *Home and Garden* shots of the defendant's home are to this case." She frowned. "Unless the prosecution wishes to accuse the defendant of having good taste."

Above the titters of two of the jurors, the judge said, "I agree. I see no point in admitting as evidence, photos that show no evidence. Unless you have another explanation?"

The prosecutors conferred quietly, then Shears said, "Your honor, we withdraw the request."

Bitsy waived cross-examination, and the next witness for the prosecution, Faye was astonished to see, was Vera! She seemed oblivious to the fact that she had been called to the stand by the opposition.

Vera took her seat, and, seeing Faye and Bitsy and Robert seated at the defendant's table, waved to them. "Oh, Doctor!" she cried. "I'm so glad to see you! Hi, girls!"

The judge banged her gavel, which got Vera's attention. "What was that?" she cried.

"That was *me* warning you to be quiet. You are to answer questions you are asked, and otherwise remain silent."

Vera frowned as if she'd been slapped. "If that's what you want, judge. I mean, *your honor.*"

Shears rose and addressed her. "Ms. Daye," he said, "please tell the court how you have been employed for the past four years."

"Oh, I haven't been employed, Mr. Shears."

The lawyer looked startled. "What? But you told me you worked at—"

"I told you I *worked* for Doctor Thompson. I didn't say I was *employed.*"

"They're the same thing!" Shears thundered. "You're honor, this is a hostile witness!"

"I am *not* hostile, and how dare you say such a thing!" Vera cried. "Everyone says I'm one of the nicest people they've ever met!"

The judge looked over at Vera, assessing her. "Just answer the questions."

"They're *not* the same thing, smarty pants," Vera snapped. "I was doing volunteer work. The doctor never paid me, so I was *not* employed."

"She's got you there, counselor," Judge Williams agreed. "This witness doesn't seem hostile to me. Please continue."

"In your time as a *volunteer* for Doctor Thompson's practice, what was your position? Your job there, Ms. Daye?"

"I was his receptionist," Vera replied.

"So you dealt with his patients?"

"Oh, yes. I scheduled their appointments, handled their cancellations, and of course did the billing and books."

"How many patients did the defendant see a day, on average?"

"Well, we tried to see one each fifteen minutes but there were always cancellations. So...say 25 to 30 a day."

"And how much did the defendant charge for one of these visits?"

"Well, it varied. Officially, a first-time visit was $80, while subsequent visits were $60. But he charged less if a patient couldn't afford that much."

"Was that true of many of his patients?"

"No, most of them could pay, between insurance and Medicare." Vera grimaced. "You wouldn't believe the paperwork involved in getting those things billed right!"

"So, the defendant took home about $1800 a day, isn't that right, Ms. Daye?"

"No."

"I'm very good at math, Ms. Daye. Thirty times sixty—I gave him the benefit of the doubt, there, and used the lower figure—is eighteen hundred."

"He didn't take it home, Mr. Lawyer. The rent for the office space alone is over $20,000 a month. The payments on the equipment are almost twice that. Then there's the utilities, and my cab fare, and the bus rental to take the folks to Mexico, and—"

"Wait, Ms. Daye. Did you say Mexico? Why did he take patients to Mexico?"

"So they could buy their prescriptions at reasonable rates."

"Or so they could buy marijuana?"

There was a hush among the spectators.

"No, Mr. Lawyer. They did not buy marijuana in Mexico. In fact, they didn't buy it at all."

"Do you expect us to believe, Ms. Daye—and I remind you, you are under oath—do you expect us to believe that Doctor Thompson *never* sold marijuana to his patients? The defense has already admitted he prescribed it. So, where did they get it, if not from him?"

"Oh, they got it from Doctor Thompson, all right," Vera assured the prosecutor. "But they didn't buy it, because he *gave* it to them."

"Gave it to them?" Shears snorted. "Oh, please. A man who makes $80 in a quarter hour? Of course he charged them. How else could he pay for that immense house of his?"

"Objection!" Bitsy cried. "Leading the witness and asking for—"

"I withdraw the question," Shears sneered. "Forget I said anything."

"Strike that last from the record," Judge Williams instructed the court recorder. "You may cross-examine, Counselor."

Bitsy rose and walked over to Vera. "Vera, Ms. Daye, did you keep all Doctor Thompson's books for him?"

"No, he has an accountant for that. I just do—I mean, did—the basic, day-to-day bookkeeping."

"So, you knew about the rent and utilities and so on, why?"

"Because I paid the bills."

"Did you also make bank deposits?"

"Oh, yes."

"Were all the deposits from the patients and insurance companies?"

"Well, and Medicare."

"Anything else?"

"Well, every four months, Robert received an enormous check from his stock dividends."

There was a stir in the courtroom.

"Was this a very large sum, Ms. Daye?"

Vera giggled. "I'll say! He was very, *very* lucky in the market. If Robert were any other man, he'd have up and quit *years* ago. But, no, he wanted to keep helping sick people. He'd done it all his life and just couldn't stop, even now that he was rich."

She beamed at the doctor. "He's a saint!"

The three members of the prosecution looked nauseous.

After the noon recess—Faye found herself envious of the judicial lifestyle, with court beginning at ten in the morning, taking two hours off for lunch, and leaving at five in the afternoon, much gentler hours than those of a garage mechanic!—the prosecution announced its next witness, Doctor Neil Downs, a professor of psychiatry at Arizona State University.

"Doctor Downs," Shears began. Faye found herself wondering why the county prosecutors had come at all; this was clearly Shears' show. "How much marijuana has been proven to be beneficial in the treatment of disease?"

"Exactly none, Mr. Shears," the professor responded.

"Really? But we have a doctor here who claims medical benefits to his clients. How can that be?"

"Objection!" Bitsy cried. "The witness cannot answer how or why the defendant makes claims."

"I withdraw the question, your honor," Shears said quickly. "Instead, Professor, can you tell me what *evidence* there is for and against the medical uses of marijuana?"

"Certainly, Counselor. In 1992, the National Institute on Drug Abuse issued a seventy-two page report containing sixty-one abstracts under the title, *Harmful Effects of Marijuana.* It includes four reports on immunological, seven on respiratory, four on cardiovascular, and thirteen on reproductive effects of marijuana. As you can tell from the title, none of these studies found any medical benefit to marijuana at all."

"You wouldn't happen to have a copy of this study, would you?"

"I do, Mr. Shears."

"Your honor, I would like to submit this report as evidence proving that there *are no medical benefits* to be found in marijuana."

The judge looked at Bitsy as if expecting her to object, but Bitsy casually acquiesced. "I don't mind at all, your honor."

Faye tugged on Bitsy's sleeve. "*This* is where my box comes in!" she whispered excitedly.

"Bailiff," directed the judge, "mark this as Prosecution Exhibit C." And the report, about half an inch of 8½ inch by 11 inch paper, was presented to the bailiff, who placed it on the evidence table.

Shears' eyes glimmered in triumph. "Thank you, Professor," he said.

Faye pulled on Bitsy's sleeve. "Let me!" she begged in a whisper.

"Let you what?" Bitsy whispered back.

"I can disprove his claim!" Faye returned. "Let *me* question him!"

"You may cross-examine," the judge directed Bitsy. Bitsy rose, but nodded at Faye. "Go ahead, honey," she said, her expression adding, *I hope you know what you're doing!*

Faye's heart leapt in her chest. She had not expected to speak in court! But she remembered Bitsy's speech about appearances in court, and forced herself to focus on what she was doing. *Performing.*

"Professor," Faye nodded in a friendly fashion as she approached the man. "What are the health benefits associated with smoking tobacco?"

The man looked confused. "There aren't any, I suppose. But I am not an expert in that field."

"But, surely you know what everyone knows—what we've all heard on television and radio and newspapers and magazines. The Surgeon General's report, the lawsuits against the tobacco companies, and so on."

"Yes, of course," Downs admitted.

"And yet, *you* smoke," Faye observed. "Oh, please, don't look so startled; I saw you smoking outside during lunch recess. Professor, why shouldn't *you* be arrested for smoking cigarettes?"

The professor puffed himself up like a pigeon. "It is not illegal to smoke tobacco!"

Faye nodded. "No matter the evidence, it isn't illegal. You are exactly right. And, sir, in Arizona, it is not illegal to prescribe nor to ingest marijuana for medical reasons. It doesn't matter whether marijuana is beneficial, any more than it matters that tobacco is not. This is not a court of what's-good-for-you, it's a court of law."

Faye turned around theatrically, and noticed that Bitsy's jaw had dropped. Downs began to rise, but Faye stopped him. "Just a moment, Professor, I'm not through with you. You mentioned that in the NIDA report, there were 61 abstracts. Is that right?"

"That's right."

"Will you please explain to the jury what an 'abstract' is?"

The man coughed. "An abstract is a summary of a longer paper. Perhaps some of the jury are familiar with Cliff's Notes?" Several jury members signified they were by laughing guiltily.

"You said the report was 71 pages long, and contained 61 abstracts," Faye said.

"It's 72 pages long," the professor corrected.

"So that's—what, about a page per abstract? With ten of them running two pages?"

"That's approximately accurate."

"Shorter than the Cliff's Notes Counselor Shears had to read for law school!" Faye quipped, falling into her role and getting a chuckle even from the judge.

"Professor, is there a word for twisting a story in such a way that the storyteller's prejudices influence the reader's understanding of the story?"

The educator seemed unwilling to appear unable to answer a question, even though he must have known where Faye was heading. "Um, bias?" he finally offered.

"That's right, Professor," Faye shouted. "Bias! Tell me, have you ever actually *read* the reports that are abstracted in the NIDA report?"

"Of course I have!" the educator snorted indignantly.

"My guess is that most of the members of the jury have not." Faye returned to the bench and picked up the cardboard box she had brought in that morning. She opened it and began taking out the bound reports she had made early that morning.

"These first four reports," she announced, "are printouts of the *actual immunological studies* to which the NIDA report refers. In spite of what the abstracts in the NIDA report imply, two found *no* harmful effects from even *large* doses of cannabis, that is, marijuana. One was inconclusive, but found significantly more problems in tobacco smokers than in pot smokers. The fourth report was conducted on *in vitro* lab studies; attempts to corroborate it in real life were, for some reason, *never attempted.*"

She handed the reports to the bailiff, and returned to her box. "Then there's the seven reports on respiratory effects, which apply to smoking only, not use of marijuana in tea, or as an herb, or a poultice, or in a cream. The only effect found was a link to bronchitis, but tobacco's was far more serious."

"One moment, Counselor," the judge interrupted. "You cannot introduce evidence until it's your turn. We are still hearing the *prosecution's* case."

Faye blushed. She had been doing so well pretending to be a lawyer, she had forgotten she *wasn't* one. But Bitsy came to her rescue.

"But, your honor," Bitsy said, "This isn't *our* evidence. It's merely the full text of the abstracts the prosecution presented. All sixty-one of them!" The judge grinned, and the prosecution team whispered among themselves as Faye continued to load the bailiff down with bound reports from her box. "Then there's the behavioral reports," she said. "Nine of them. *None* of them found use of marijuana to lead to violence. Several found marijuana users to be more peaceful than an average group of citizens. Then there are these six reports on drug testing, which clearly have nothing to do with marijuana's medical benefits. Oh, and there's—"

"Your honor," Shears interrupted, rising. "We withdraw our request to use the NIDA report as evidence."

The judge gave the prosecution a long, hard look. "It's already been accepted, Counselor. It stays." And so, there on the evidence table, was the slim, bound volume labeled *Harmful Effects of Marijuana*—and a small mountain of reports that proved the opposite.

After the trial had recessed for the day, Faye and Bitsy had dinner together at J. B.'s, a popular Sun City restaurant. Bitsy raised a glass of wine to Faye. "Here's to you, Faye," Bitsy toasted. "You never cease to amaze me. From poor swimmer to accomplished swimmer to ersatz lawyer in just a few months!"

"I was terrified at first," Faye confessed. "But I tried to focus, the way I do when I've been—" and here, her voice dropped to a whisper— "you know, smoking dope—and I found I could, even though I wasn't high! Isn't that amazing?"

Bitsy smiled. "Well, you'd better use that skill tomorrow. I expect Shears will probably put you on the stand tomorrow."

Day 3

Thursday, February 12, 1998

"I solemnly swear to tell the truth, the whole truth, and nothing but the truth. So help me, God." Faye swallowed hard after making the oath, and sat down in the witness' chair—a place she'd never, in all her days, imagined she'd ever be.

And now, here was Faye as the prosecution's last witness. Bitsy had warned her to *seem* cooperative, or they would be able to declare her a "hostile witness," which would allow them to ask leading questions and curtail her answers. Bitsy also warned Faye not to lie, but promised she wouldn't ask any questions about the underground mine—and guaranteed the prosecution would not think of doing such a thing on their own. Shears, perhaps having learned to fear confrontations with Faye, allowed county prosecutor Darcy Benson to handle the questioning.

Faye explained how she had been given papers showing Representative Meany had accepted illegal campaign funds and how she and Marian had gone to Selma's house to confront her with the papers and had found Meany there as well. She described Meany's killing himself in such a way as to imply he had committed suicide out of despondency because he'd been caught.

She told of the chase after Selma into the high country outside Wickenburg, and implied they'd simply lost Selma's trail.

"What became of Marian Higgins?" Benson asked.

"I don't know," Faye answered, truthfully. "I went to sleep. When I awoke, she was gone—" *if by 'gone' you mean dead*, Faye interjected to herself, "and I don't know exactly *what* happened to her. It took me three days to get out of the canyon. Marian may have gotten lost or been taken, I don't know. I just know that, when Robert came to get me, he told me Marian was dead."

Darcy Benson looked Faye in the eye. "Ms. McRae," the lawyer began, "were you, of your own knowledge, aware that Marian Higgins was growing marijuana in her home?"

Faye took a deep breath. "I did know that," she admitted.

"How did you know that?"

"I stumbled on her grow room once."

"When was that?"

"It was last Thanksgiving."

"Did you report it to the police?"

"No."

"Why not, Ms. McRae?"

"Because she wasn't breaking the law. She was growing the marijuana for Rob—for Doctor Thompson to distribute to his patients who needed it."

"Growing marijuana is illegal, Ms. McRae."

"Prescribing it is not, Ms. Benson. State law allows it. A prescription is useless if it can't be filled."

"Are you aware that the federal government *grows* marijuana for medical purposes, Ms. McRae?"

"I am," Faye replied, tartly. "Are you aware that only six people have access to it?"

"What?" Darcy gaped. "What sense would that—"

"Objection!" called Shears from the prosecution's table. "The witness is not an expert on marijuana."

"You could have fooled me," the judge said wryly. "Sustained."

Ms. Benson smiled. "I understand you and the defendant are close friends. Is that true?"

"It is," Faye said, smiling nervously at Robert.

"In fact, I gather you are *very* close friends."

"We are," Faye agreed.

"Has Doctor Thompson asked you to marry him?"

Faye blushed slightly. "Yes, he has," she admitted.

"More than once?"

"Yes," Faye agreed, still smiling.

"Tell me, Ms. McRae, are you aware that a wife cannot be made to testify against her husband?"

"Huh?" The prosecutor's statement had been so unexpected Faye wasn't sure what she'd said, but Bitsy was.

"Objection!" she cried, leaping to her feet. "Irrelevant, immaterial!"

"Overruled," the judge announced. "Ms. McRae, you may answer the question."

"What question?" Faye asked.

"I asked, are you aware that a wife cannot be made to testify against her husband in a court of law? Even in murder cases?"

"I—" Faye hesitated. After behaving as a lawyer for the defendant yesterday, Faye didn't want to seem ignorant now. "Yes, of course," she said. "What does it matter?"

"What does it matter, indeed?" Benson mused. "Tell me, Ms. McRae, how long have you known Doctor Thompson?"

Faye thought. "Something like four months," she said. She grinned. "It seems like forever, though."

"In that time," Benson asked, speaking with great care, "did *Doctor Thompson* ever ask you to grow marijuana?"

"No!" Faye replied with vehemence. "No one has *ever* asked me to grow marijuana."

Darcy Benson must have been a good lawyer in her own right, because she seemed to hear something in Faye's voice that caused her to cock her head. "That's nice, Ms. McRae," she replied. "But do you grow it anyway?"

Faye's face felt like it was about to explode. She knew it had turned furiously red, so red that even the spectators in the back of the courtroom must be able to see it. What was she going to say?

She must have paused longer than she thought, because the judge prodded her. "Answer the question, please, Ms. McRae."

"I'll repeat the question, Ms. McRae, in case you didn't hear me the first time. *Do you grow marijuana?*"

The room swirled around her. Why didn't Bitsy object? Wasn't there something about the Fifth Amendment, about not having to incriminate oneself?

"Oh, *enough* of this!" a voice cried from the back of the courtroom, as one of the spectators rose from her seat.

"Order! Order in my courtroom!" Judge Williams demanded, pounding her gavel.

"Your honor," the woman continued, unfazed. "*I* am Marian Higgins, the woman Robert is supposed to have murdered!"

And Faye, seeing that it was so, screamed.

New Evidence

Marian made her way to the wooden gate, where one of the two bailiffs blocked her way. Judge Williams ordered him aside. The other saw to Faye, offering her water but Faye brushed the bailiff's arm aside and ran to the gate. She and Marian embraced.

"Marian?" Robert whispered, and stood up. The bailiff was quick to block him, and the judge did not interfere.

"Hello, Robert, darling," Marian waved.

"*Where have you been?*" Faye demanded, angrily.

"Order! Order!" Judge Williams pounded her gavel. "Counsel, in my chambers *now!*"

Bitsy threw a dazed expression over her shoulder, then followed the judge and Shears through the same door from which the judge emerged at the beginning of each session. The other two members of the prosecution team followed.

Faye considered accompanying them, but couldn't tear herself away from Marian. "Where have you *been?*" she again demanded.

"I promise I'll explain it all later, darling," her friend vowed. "For now, let's just say I got lost near Wickenburg."

The judge, the prosecution, and Bitsy emerged from the judge's chambers and resumed their customary positions. Shears remained standing. "Your honor," he requested with quiet dignity, "in the light of this new and unexpected evidence, I request a recess in order to match a hair sample of this person with the other samples found in the Higgins' bed."

"How long will you need, Mr. Shears?"

"It should be ready by morning."

"Counsel?" the judge nodded at Bitsy.

"The defense has no objections, your honor," Bitsy agreed.

"Court is adjourned until tomorrow morning at ten," Williams announced. "Bailiff, instruct the jurors..."

The moment the judge had left the courtroom, the bailiff came for Robert—but Faye noticed he now treated the doctor with a little more deference than he had that morning or the day before.

As the courtroom was clearing, Denis O'Bell approached Bitsy. "Just when were you planning to disclose this witness?"

"Believe me, Mr. O'Bell," Bitsy replied. "I'm as surprised as you are. I can't wait to find out where she's been. I don't need a lab test to tell me it's really her. Marian has been a personal friend for years, so you better start figuring out how you're going to handle this."

Marian, still on the spectator side of the gate but close at hand, added, sweetly, "And, Mr. O'Bell—I suggest you check Selma Graves' *own* bed for DNA that matches the body you found—and also hair samples that match Representative Meany. Or did you already do that?"

O'Bell's startled expression showed that he had not.

Faye turned to face Marian, but only saw her friend's back as she scurried to the courtroom exit. "Marian!" she called, but either her friend couldn't hear over the hubbub of exiting spectators, or she was ignoring her.

"Oh, and Mr. O'Bell," Bitsy added. "About the marijuana charge—tomorrow, I am going to show my client's billing records, bank accounts, and statements from his stock brokerage. It will be clear that he has made a lot of money from the stock market, and a mere pittance from his patients. More of them receive treatment, and medical marijuana, at no charge, than Vera implied. What do you think that will do to your theory that Robert was making a fortune selling marijuana to sick people?"

O'Bell's jaw dropped, and he whirled and stared at Shears with hatred. He stood nose to nose with the FBI lawyer, growling, "We have to talk!" He grabbed the federal prosecutor's arm and literally dragged him away.

Faye giggled. "A lover's quarrel, don't you think?"

That night, Faye was unable to contact Marian. She did not answer her home phone, and when Faye drove to her house it was as deserted as it had been the night Faye used Marian's telephone to call Desmond Barrow.

Trembling in the dark, Faye realized that, if anyone checked Marian's telephone records, *Marian* could be implicated in the murders and Robert's escape.

Faye could only hope that hadn't happened.

Council of Counsels

Thursday, February 12, 1998

In the morning, Faye was awakened by the ringing of her telephone. "Yes, hello?" She was somewhat confused and not fully awake.

"This is Bitsy, Faye. I'll pick you up in twenty minutes. O'Bell wants to talk."

Faye was ready in fifteen. When Bitsy arrived and Faye had climbed into her car, Faye asked, "What's going on? What does O'Bell want to talk about?"

"I don't know, but I can guess. I think he's fired Shears, and wants to make a deal."

At the courthouse, they were led to a conference room where they found Robert waiting for them, unguarded. Less than a minute after she and Bitsy arrived, the two county prosecutors, O'Bell and Benson, entered the room. O'Bell looked angry, Benson embarrassed.

"Good morning, Counselor, Dr. Thompson, Ms. McRae," O'Bell said. The fact that he included Robert in his greeting showed a distinct change in the prosecutor's attitude.

"Good morning, folks," Bitsy returned easily. "What's up?"

O'Bell compressed his lips, then spoke. "As you knew, that was Marian Higgins who showed up last afternoon."

"Where has she been all this time?" Faye blurted.

"Hiding out, apparently," Benson supplied. "She corroborated your story of confronting Graves regarding illegal campaign funds, and following Graves into the high country. She said she got separated from you, stripped to soak in one of the springs in the area, and when she left the water, her clothes were gone and Graves' were left in their place, so she wore them. When she got back home, she was so tired she slept in them, which is how Graves' hair wound up in Higgins' bed."

"But then, when she heard on the news that someone wearing *her* clothes had been found dismembered in the Graves house, she panicked and went into hiding," O'Bell finished.

"She told you all that?" Faye prodded, thinking that it wasn't like Marian to panic—or not to include Faye in her plans.

Benson nodded, wryly. "But not until she got immunity from the charge of growing marijuana in her home."

"Which *Shears* gave, thinking he'd be able to get evidence to use against Dr. Thompson," O'Bell added. "He's no longer on the team, by the way, except for one last task."

"So," Robert said, breaking a stoic silence, "where does this leave me?"

"Well, cleared of the charge of murder, obviously," O'Bell replied. "You knew Higgins; there's no evidence you knew Graves."

Benson said, "We now think that it was Meany who murdered Graves in the Wickenburg canyons, brought her mutilated body back to her house, and then killed himself. When the FBI *finally* analyzed the hair and skin cells from *her* bed, they found both Graves' and Meany's hair there—obviously, the two had been having an affair. So, there's no mystery other than where Meany left the head and hands, and searchers are combing the Wickenburg canyon area right now, looking for them."

Faye resisted the urge to suggest looking for a mine complex with an entrance beneath a windmill.

"That still leaves the possession charge," Bitsy remarked, calmly.

"Yes, well..." O'Bell shifted uneasily in his seat. "That was Shears' baby. He insisted on trying that charge. But when I got back to my office, last night, I found a videotape that had been mailed to me, no return address.

"Remember the FBI agent who abducted you, Dr. Thompson?"

"Er, yes, of course," the doctor replied, clearing his throat.

"You may not be aware of this, but when Agent Kingman arrived at Maricopa County Jail, he announced on live TV that he had hidden you in a safe place, and some other crazy things. His whole ranting was not shown on live TV, but the cameras never stopped rolling, or whatever video cameras do when they're on. Well, this videotape *does* contain the *entire* speech—and, in it, the agent claimed *he* had planted the marijuana in the trunk of your car, under orders from his superior."

"One of the cameramen must have leaked it to us." Darcy Benson added.

"That was the same agent who was left alone in the Graves house while Zembruski took a whiz," O'Bell continued. "Good call there, Counselor. Obviously it was Barrow who planted your late husband's revolver, Ms. McRae." He took a sip of his coffee. "If the trial were continuing, I would have to drop the possession charge, anyway. But now, well...we will be dropping everything."

"So, I'm free to go?" Robert asked.

"Almost," Benson assured him. "There's only the formality of dropping the charges in court."

Case Dismissed

"All rise."

The increasingly familiar ritual was conducted but before the judge could direct the prosecution to continue, Shears rose. Faye was surprised to see him, but this was apparently that last task O'Bell had mentioned. Shears was a changed man, humble, penitent. "Your honor," he began, "the state wishes to drop all charges against Dr. Robert Thompson. New evidence has turned up proving his innocence."

"Indeed," the judge said, dryly. "Very well. But first, I want to say something for the record." The judge glanced at the court reporter, who was busily transcribing into her little machine. The reporter looked up and nodded.

The judge glared at the prosecution and said, "This has been the most poorly organized, researched, and presented case I have heard in my twelve years on the bench. I find the idea that hairs found on the murder scene were not analyzed to be so ludicrous that I am tempted to slap a contempt-of-court on the entire prosecution team for mere stupidity.

"It's obvious what really happened here. The FBI wanted to tie the murder of a congressman and prescribing marijuana together in federal court, where medical marijuana would be considered illegal. When that didn't work out they had *you*, Mr. Shears, continue with the remaining murder case, still trying to tie it to medical marijuana. In order to maintain this course, Mr. Shears, you neglected to produce all available evidence—the congressman's hair in the murder scene bed—for no other reason than to bias it against the defendant.

"I am disgusted and sickened by the lengths you've taken to prevent the defendant, a doctor, from continuing his practice in accordance with the laws of the State of Arizona. I never want to see you in my court again. I hope I've made myself clear, sir."

She had. Shears was red in the face and having trouble swallowing. *No wonder*, Faye thought. *He's choking on crow!*

The judge slammed her gavel. "Case dismissed!"

Smoke-In

To her amazement, Faye detected the unmistakable aroma of marijuana. She turned to see who was smoking it, amazed that anyone would have the gall.

The judge spotted the smoker before she did. "You, in the grey suit!" she cried, smashing her gavel against its anvil. "I said case dismissed, not start smoking! What are you doing? Stand and address me!"

Faye turned, and spotted tall, bony, Frank Timmons in the back of the courtroom. He rose slowly, painfully—so painfully, that Faye knew he was exaggerating his stiffness for the occasion. "I'm takin' my medicine, your honor!" he announced.

The judge appeared flabbergasted. "Sir, smoking is not allowed in this courtroom at any time!"

"I'm in pain, and I'm taking my medicine! You just said it was okay."

The judge considered. "Taking medicine is all right, but it is not all right to smoke in any Arizona State courtroom. The law does not specify what may not be smoked. If you need to smoke, now, go outside and do it."

With that, there was a mass exodus as the gallery raced for the doors of the courtroom. The judge began to pound her gavel again, but no one could hear over the confusion. The bailiff, trying to preserve protocol, called, "All rise!" which Faye, Robert, Bitsy, and the three prosecutors all did. The judge left through the door to her chambers.

"You're free to go, sir," the other bailiff told Robert.

Faye threw herself into his arms and they kissed. "Let's go!" she whispered, and led the doctor through the wooden gates into the land of the free. The courtroom was still emptying and Robert and Faye were forced to join the mob as it raced from the room.

"Congratulations, doc!" one of the spectators called, but other than that, they were mostly ignored by the people who, Faye had thought, were there because of their interest in Robert. They found themselves outside on the steps of the building, blinking in the glare of the Arizona sun. Below, on the courthouse steps and on the broad walkway and on the lawn on either side—was a crowd of people, hundreds of them...all smoking.

All smoking weed, Faye realized, to her amazement and joy.

Marian was standing next to her, inhaling deeply of the hand-rolled joint she held in her fingers. "I haven't been in a smoke-in since the sixties!" she exclaimed. "Doesn't it feel great to have a voice!"

Faye's rough estimate was 400 people, most of them senior citizens but certainly not all of them, standing and sitting around the court-house steps, all smoking, all filling the air with the pungent scent of burning weed. Police officers had, at first, begun frantically demanding to see people's prescriptions for marijuana. But, when the people they asked were actually able to produce such documents, they gave up and kept busy keeping traffic in front of the courthouse from stopping and staring at the unusual sight.

And then, quietly at first, a murmur arose from the crowd that began to build into song. It was not a tune that Faye had ever associated with pot smoking, and in fact was not a song that she knew well. But she knew the title, and she now understood its significance. She and Robert joined in, his *basso profundo* enabling her to follow the lyrics when she wasn't sure.

> *"We shall overcome*
> *We shall overcome*
> *We shall overcome some day*
> *Oh, deep in my heart*
> *I do believe*
> *We shall overcome some day."*

Tears welled up in Faye's eyes and when she looked at Robert, she found he was crying. Marian passed her joint to Faye, who took a hit, handing it to Robert.

> *"We'll walk hand in hand*
> *We'll walk hand in hand*
> *We'll walk hand in hand some day*
> *Oh, deep in my heart*
> *I do believe*
> *We shall overcome some day."*

Four hundred people, most of them strangers to one another. And yet, all of them bonded through this ritual, so long suppressed by a government that had sold out to the corporate interests of powerful pharmaceutical, prison, lumber, chemical, oil and law enforcement lobbies that most people had been convinced this essential, earthy right would never be recovered. Now, today, in one state at least, the people's voice had been heard and at least a small sliver of this basic freedom had been recognized.

> *"We shall all be free*
> *We shall all be free*
> *We shall all be free some day*
> *Oh, deep in my heart*
> *I do believe*
> *We shall overcome some day."*

Marian squeezed Faye's hand. "Follow me, darlings," she said. "I know I owe you an explanation."

Back From The Graves

Robert, surrounded by grateful patients and well-wishers, gave Faye a look of desperation. She waved back at him, calling, "We'll catch up with you later." He tossed back a grateful grin as Marian led Faye away from the crowd into a nearby coffee shop. They ordered coffee and scones, and then sat at a small table. Faye found herself growing frustrated.

"What—how—why—?" was all she could sputter.

"Shhh," Marian warned, her forefinger to her lips. "I know you're upset, but I had a good reason."

Faye's voice dropped to a whisper. "They cut your head off!"

"Obviously, they did not," Marian replied primly.

"Then, how did you get away? And who's body was that? Was it really Selma's? Wearing the sweatshirt I gave you?"

Marian shook her head. "It was quite an adventure, darling."

"The last I saw you was when you shot the lights out in that room."

"The Great Room, as I've been thinking of it. Yes, and the moment they went out, I edged my way towards the tunnel we came in by. I found the wall, and then I felt for what I hoped would be the right tunnel."

"You kept your balance and found the right hall in the dark? Marian, you're amazing!"

Marian grimaced. "I wish. No, I did not find the right tunnel. I wound up in a different one, lined with small chambers or rooms. I held my breath and ducked into one. After a time, the commotion outside seemed to be over. Emergency lights had come on. It was dim, but I could see the tunnel was empty. I could even see down to the Great Room and heard voices from there, so I crept a little ways closer until I could make out what they were saying...and who to."

Marian stopped to catch her breath, and Faye gently shook the older woman's shoulders. "Well, who was it? Don't keep me in suspense!"

"It was Selma Graves, darling."

Faye caught her breath.

"The same voices that talked to us were giving her a royal ass-chewing. I mean, they were laying it on and she sounded like a teenager caught with a beer."

"But they were her friends!" Faye exclaimed. "They must have been, why else would she have come there?"

Marian shook her head. "Apparently not. More like her superiors—and she had really screwed up by leading us there. So the big argument was, should they have her killed on the spot, or have her look for me?"

"I knew then that they had captured *you*. But I figured, as long as one of us was free, there was a chance of freeing the other."

Faye smiled reluctantly and squeezed Marian's hand.

"Anyway, they finally decided to send her out to find me. The moment Selma left the chamber, I simply followed her. The elevator wasn't at the bottom of the shaft; she had to wait for it."

"What happened when you caught up to her?"

"Well, darling, as I said, the elevator was still coming down. The bulb in the cage was casting a very dim bit of light to the floor of the tunnel, but it was enough for her to spot me when she heard my footsteps. She turned and pulled out her pistol. Before she could draw a bead on me, I kicked the gun from her hand. Then she threw herself on me, scratching and clawing like a cat! Really, she was snarling and everything!"

"But how did you behead her?"

"Me? Oh, darling, I'm not that cold! When I kicked her gun, it landed just at the edge of the shaft and she dove for it. I tried to warn her that the cage was almost there but she wouldn't listen. Then the elevator came down and clipped her head off at the neck. She'd been reaching for the gun, and her hands got chopped off, too."

Faye gasped. "Oh, my God! No!"

Marian nodded. "It was gruesome. I knew I didn't have much time to try and gain an advantage. So I pulled off Selma's blouse and slacks, bloody as they were, stripped off my clothes, and put them on her." She shook her head. "I *hated* giving up my beautiful, embroidered sweatshirt, darling. But what else could I do?"

Faye reached and squeezed her hand. "I'll get you another."

"My clothes weren't a perfect fit, but I knew they would fool anyone into thinking it was me—after all, when a person's head is missing, one doesn't pay that much attention to the outfit."

"But, why, Marian?"

"Why? Why, to let them think *I* was the one who was dead! That way, they'd stop looking for *me*. I rode the elevator back up, ran to my car and left to get help."

"Who would you get?" Faye asked helplessly. "Who would even believe you?"

"That's easy, darling. I sent Norma to help you."

"But why did you pretend to be dead? I mean, why didn't you let me know?"

Marian patted her hand. "Do you remember how old I am?"

"Not exactly," Faye hedged.

"C'mon, think about it," Marian suggested.

"I—well, I know you had a son who was old enough to join the Army in the Second World War," Faye admitted. "So, depending how old you were when you had him..."

"I'm 92, darling," Marian whispered softly.

Faye inspected her friend's clear skin, bright eyes, and lustrous hair. "Now I remember," Faye sighed. "Not possible."

"But it is," Marian insisted, "if you eat right, exercise, and do the other things I taught you. Especially, keeping your mind free of resentments, anger and fear. *Those* are the things that age a person."

She sighed. "But it isn't easy being 92 in a world that sees you as being 60 or 65. And so, as my mentor, Norma, once had to do, I planned to start a new life, with new identification that indicated I was my *apparent* age, instead of my actual age."

"And leave all your friends?" Faye challenged. "Without saying a word?"

"Darling...try to understand. If I were 92 years old and died, you wouldn't be surprised, would you? You wouldn't be upset that I was leaving you!"

"But then you wouldn't have a choice," Faye pointed out. "You had a choice."

"True, Faye, but, it *had* to be done sooner or later. And, here, fate had handed me the perfect opportunity. I wasn't looking for it, but with Selma wearing my clothes and having conveniently lost her head and her hands, all clipped off neatly by the elevator—making it difficult to prove it wasn't me—I took advantage of the situation. But then..." Marian took a sip of her coffee.

"Then what?" Faye prompted.

"I drove home. I knew you were safe with Norma, and I was so exhausted by the time I got there, I just collapsed into bed, still wearing Selma's clothes, of course. In the morning, I walked over to your house and found it had been trashed. I realized this was no coincidence—they had gotten your purse, with your address on it, and mine as well. It seemed likely that someone was setting us up for something. So, I felt, the decision had been made for me. I hitchhiked out of town, and hid at a friend's house, who could make new IDs for me. I wasn't going to come back to Sun City—until I learned that Robert was being framed for my murder. That's when I realized Marian Higgins would have to be resurrected."

Faye took a bite of her scone, washed it down with coffee. "But, Marian...you could have told *me*."

Marian reached for Faye's hand and squeezed it. "I never had a chance," she replied. "Your phone was surely being bugged, and then you disappeared the day after Robert did. I figured you were together, but I didn't know where."

"Oh." Faye sat back in the uncomfortable metal chair. The inside of the coffee shop was decorated to resemble an outdoor courtyard, and the chairs were more decorative than anything else.

"I'm still going to leave and start a new life," Marian reminded her. "The people in that mine know where I live, and I don't like that. I don't want to play that game, as Norma might have put it, so I'm getting out of here. You should probably do the same," she added.

"I've thought of it," Faye admitted. "But I have a better plan. I'm still working on the details...I'll let you know if it works out."

Marian smiled. "You're a brave girl. And, as long as you're here, I will still be able to contact you every now and then, with new T-shirt designs and to check on the progress of the club. And, some-day, I might pop up when you least expect it! But, for now, it's goodbye to Sun City for me."

"But you love Sun City!" Faye exclaimed. "Don't you?"

"I'm tired of it," Marian admitted. "I'm ready for some new horizons. Maybe Tahiti—or Iceland!"

Faye frowned. "There's one thing you haven't explained," she said. "You said you sent Norma to help me. How did you do that, exactly?"

Marian grinned. "Telepathy, darling. Be patient and that'll come to you, too."

A Quiet Night

That night, Faye and Robert eagerly anticipated a quiet night alone. Faye was acutely aware it would be their first time together at Robert's house. As they entered, Robert embraced Faye. "It's so good to be home," he said. "Good for both of us." Faye kissed him gratefully.

Her attention was caught by a large, ornate clock hanging on the living room wall. "Say, it's about time for the news," she said. "Where's your TV? It'll be fun to watch the smoke-in again."

Robert led her to a media den she had missed on her earlier, unguided tour. He picked up the remote control and clicked it. Almost immediately the TV screen flashed to life, showing the flashy graphics of the *Channel 2 Evening News.*

And then there was the face of Audrey Flowers. "Channel 2, always there first, bringing you the news of this evening, February 12, 1998. In our top story, Unocal Vice President John J. Maresca testified today before the House of Representatives that until a single, unified, friendly government is in place in Afghanistan the trans-Afghani pipeline will not be built. With a pipeline through Afghanistan, the Caspian basin could produce 20 percent of all the non-OPEC oil in the world by 2010. A consortium of American oil companies, including former President Bush's own Zapata Oil Company, stand to make billions of dollars from the pipeline if it can be built..."

Faye and Robert waited through the political news patiently. Faye was a little disappointed that the wonderful demonstration at the courthouse hadn't been considered headline news but on reflection, she realized it probably wasn't *that* significant...certainly in comparison to the former President's oil profits. Still, as the stories came and went without mention of either the dismissal of Robert's case or the smoke-in at the courthouse, she began to sense a sinking feeling in the pit of her stomach. "Let's check the other channels," she suggested. Robert already had his remote control in hand and Faye realized he had been considering the same thing.

But it was the same story on all the channels, just in a different sequence. Another station was going over Channel 2's top story about the pipeline as they switched to it; Robert quickly clicked passed. He even checked CNN's Headline News, and then its non-headline counterpart, to no avail.

Faye sat, slumped. "They didn't cover it," she said. "I can't believe it. They simply ignored us. Pretended it never happened."

"Since the case was dismissed," Robert added, "there won't even be a verdict to act as precedent for future medical marijuana trials."

"And now no one knows about it," Faye wailed. "Other doctors heard on TV how you were arrested for prescribing pot to your patients, and none of them have heard the case was dismissed. Now they'll hesitate to prescribe it to their own patients, no matter how badly the patients need it. It isn't fair!"

Robert chuckled sadly. "Who told you the world was fair, dear?"

Faye abruptly rose to her feet. "Well, I can do something about it," she said. "I have a voice. Marian gave it to me. I'm going to design a T-shirt that spreads the word. People have to know!"

Robert reached for her. "Do you have to do it right now?"

She took his hand but did not let him pull her onto his lap. "Yeah, right now," she said. "You understand, don't you?"

The doctor smiled regretfully. "I do, honey pie. I would expect nothing less from you." He rose, and kissed her, and walked her to the door.

The house was just as lovely as the first time Faye had been here, getting clothes for Robert to wear in court. Beautiful, tasteful, complete...and all Robert, through and through. "You love your home, don't you?" she asked after they had exchanged a final kiss at the door.

The doctor laughed, then corrected her. "Our home," he said.

"As mine is yours," Faye agreed.

At home, Faye unlocked the door—after making sure it was still locked, a new habit she might never lose—turned on the lights and went straight to her new computer, but was stopped before she could turn it on by the ringing of the phone. Bless his heart, Faye thought, smiling. Robert is calling to make sure I got home safely, just as she had done when Robert left her house in the evening. She picked up the phone and said, "Hello, Dar—" but was interrupted by a woman's voice.

"Beware the jabberwock, my son, the jaws that bite, the claws that catch."

"Beware the jub jub bird," Faye replied, "and shun the frumious bandersnatch. What sword shall I use?"

"Your vorpal sword!" the voice on the line replied.

"Command me," said Faye.

Continuance

· · · · · · · ·

Heavier Than Air

Faye drove south on 99th Avenue beneath a dark gray, starless sky. Edwin's gun, which had been returned a second time by Grant that afternoon after the trial, was tucked securely in her waistband. It was fully loaded. She hadn't yet decided if she would use it. She wasn't, in fact, sure she *could* use it. With all the skills Marian had taught her and all that she had learned on her own since Edwin's death, sharp shooting still wasn't one of them—and her humiliation at the gun range was still well within memory.

The road hummed beneath the car. The last time Faye had driven this road, she'd been springing Robert from the clutches of the FBI. Now, she was speeding toward the clutches of...who? She wasn't sure. The voice she'd heard on the phone was vaguely familiar. In fact, she felt as if she'd heard it recently. But she could not quite place it.

She had been startled beyond imagining when she received the phone call, so startled she'd almost blown the chance to meet this link in the mind control chain. She wondered if this was the *last* person in the chain. She could only hope so.

Frank had *told* Robert and her that the woman who controlled him had a voice he didn't recognize. Later, it seemed that it had been Selma. But that had been a loose end. After all, when Frank's grandson had been murdered, Frank didn't know Selma. But he certainly knew her later, working for her as he did at Meany's re-election campaign headquarters. And yet he had never expanded on his story.

And, of course, the question of who was *Selma's* controller was an open one. It might have been one of the mysterious voices in the mine. But it might not. And tonight's phone call suggested there might be yet someone else involved.

But the nerve of that woman! Not only had she ordered Faye to come to her, presumably to die—but she demanded Faye bring her a snack! It was sitting on the seat beside her. Faye had fumed the whole time she prepared it. And that now frightened her.

What if Faye *were* under mind control, even now? She had no idea what it felt like. Maybe it felt just like this, fuming because one was following orders, but following them nonetheless. If so, then what would happen if the woman who called her ordered her to kill herself? Would she do it? She might be angry, or sad, or even neutral—but wind up just as dead. Just to be safe, she had smoked a joint—the first from her *very own crop,* which was a treat!—while she made the sandwiches. She wasn't certain that marijuana provided a defense from this mind control business, but if it did, she wanted all the protection she could get.

As instructed, Faye turned right on Glendale Avenue. It was dark, except for a bright blue light that flashed once or twice a minute. *That's Glendale Airport,* Faye thought. A municipal airport, it wouldn't be open at this hour and there would be no traffic.

A huge, black, mass suddenly loomed in front of her, blanking out the dim glow of the sky and even the flashing blue light from the airport. She jammed on the brakes. The 1940 Ford screeched to a halt. The shapeless form ahead of her seemed to absorb the beams from her headlights like a sponge absorbs water. What was it?

And then she saw a pillar of blue flame erupt, glow for thirty seconds, and extinguish; with a chill, she knew what was blocking her way:

Channel 2's hot-air balloon.

Audrey Flowers' balloon.

Her eyes adjusting, she could make out the Channel 2 logo dimly in the darkness, with the motto, "A Fresh Perspective."

Faye turned off the ignition but left the headlights on, removed her keys and exited the car, carrying the snack she'd prepared. Her loose blouse, chosen for the purpose, hid the butt of Edwin's gun. She used that focusing power of the buzz she now felt to concentrate on presenting a neutral countenance. All she knew about the way mind-controlled victims felt was that they seemed devoid of emotion or expression. Duplicating that effect might provide her only hope of survival.

She reached the basket of the balloon, dwarfed by the huge orb that was half inflated. A fan as tall as she was blew air into the balloon, and every few seconds the burner would blast, warming the cool night air and making the balloon bob upwards with less and less effort.

She found the newswoman on the other side of the basket, controlling the blast from the burner. Faye stood quietly, not sure what to say or do.

Flowers turned, picked up a large flashlight and aimed it at Faye. "It's you. You're here."

"Yes," Faye said, in a neutral tone. She was relieved to hear that her voice didn't quaver. Thanks to the pot, she was able to focus past her fear and concentrate on the job at hand.

Flowers asked, "Did you bring the food as I commanded?"

Faye held the bag out at arms' length, and Flowers took it, opened it and peered inside with the aid of her flashlight. "What kind of sandwiches are these?" she asked.

"Tuna salad," Faye replied, "with fat-free mayonnaise."

"And you even included a brownie!" Flowers marveled. "Well, that was nice. I will enjoy it." She switched the light off, and gazed at Faye's silhouette. "After I've...killed you. How do you feel about that?"

"I feel...nothing," Faye lied.

Flowers nodded absently. "That's what he said would happen, but it still seems pretty amazing to me. Don't you hate me?"

"No." Faye was intensely curious, however, to know who "he" was. *Patience, my girl! Patience,* she thought to herself. It was beginning to look as if Flowers was not Selma's handler at all, perhaps she had nothing to do with Mickey Timmons' death, either. Flowers behaved as though she'd never tried the mind control trick before and did not seem to be in a trance.

In fact, Flowers seemed damned interested in this entire process, thought Faye.

"I got a call today," Flowers said chattily, as the balloon continued to fill with hot air. "It was quite a surprise, the man who got me my first radio job, and of course my present position at Channel 2. I hadn't heard from him in years, but he told me that it was time for me to return the favor to him. And then he gave me the code to control you, and your phone number. Frankly, I didn't think it would work. I mean, mind control! But here you are. Amazing."

Faye couldn't believe Flowers was telling her all this, but as the woman chattered on, Faye began to understand what was happening. First, Flowers had been placed at the TV station by someone in the plot, someone related to Marvin's global elite, perhaps, for no other reason than to be able to pull in a "favor" now and then.

Second, Flowers didn't seem to have a compunction against murdering Faye, but was nervous about actually doing it—and, as a result, was chattering away. Flowers wouldn't see the harm in revealing this information, of course, because Faye soon would be dead, according to the plan.

"We're just about there," Flowers announced, as the bag finally broke free of gravity and, still tethered, floated ponderously in the night air. The newswoman started to break down the ground gear, then suddenly realized she had a willing slave present. "Here, you—unplug that fan from the inverter and roll it to the truck." Faye did exactly that, then waited at the truck for further instructions.

"Well, don't just stand there like a dummy!" Flowers cried after a minute. "Put the fan into the back of the truck!" Faye complied.

"Come over here!" Flowers called, and Faye did so. The anchorperson stared at her in the night. "Of course," she marveled. "I have to tell you *exactly* what to do!"

Suddenly, Faye realized that the voices in the mine had never been certain whether her discovering Marian's corpse—or, as she now knew, *Selma's* corpse—had triggered the psychotic break necessary for mind control to succeed. They wouldn't risk a direct confrontation so they called in their favor with Flowers. If Faye had been successfully conditioned, if she were a "rabbit" as the voices had called it, she would obey Flowers' every command, up to and including the last to kill herself. In that case, Flowers would probably be groomed to replace Selma. If, on the other hand, Faye fought back, or even simply disobeyed, the voices would know for certain that marijuana formed an effective prophylaxis against their mind control tricks. And if Faye killed Audrey in the process, it wouldn't be a great loss to them. Ambitious people without brains or scruples were certainly an easily-obtained commodity.

Flowers went around the four sides of the basket with her flashlight, explaining all the while how the ropes were to be fastened to the balloon, what knot to use, the history of that knot, and why it was better in this situation than either of the other two commonly-used alternatives. Faye began to wish the woman would just shut up.

Still enjoying the power she thought she had over Faye, Flowers ordered her to tie up the remaining two sides. Faye did so.

Then, the bag fully inflated and with the basket straining at the anchor ropes, Flowers ordered Faye to get into the basket, and then to help her into it.

Flowers cast off the ropes, and the basket rose smoothly into the air. Faye had never ridden in a hot air balloon before, and hadn't known what to expect. She didn't think it would be a violent takeoff, but in fact she had felt almost nothing. Rising into the night, she couldn't even tell they were gaining altitude. Particularly surprising was the fact that she felt no wind, not even the slight breeze that had been blowing on the ground.

Flowers looked over the side of the basket and said, "Look at that! Gary's right on time!"

Faye chose to hear Flowers' remark as an order, and joined the newswoman in looking over the side. She saw twin cones of yellow, far below, faintly illuminating the road. When Faye stood upright once more, she saw Flowers' face suffused with an eerie green glow. It took Faye a moment to realize that Flowers was speaking into a cellular phone, and that its display was providing the illumination.

"Gary," Flowers said, "you've got a fix on my transponder?" There was a brief pause, then she said, "Good. I'd hate for my chase vehicle to lose me in the night." She pressed a button and the phone darkened. As they continued to rise, Faye and Flowers were left in an intense dark, becoming faintly lit, by a constellation created by the city lights of Phoenix clustering at the horizon.

Faye decided this had gone far enough. "You've never killed anyone before, have you?"

Flowers suddenly stopped chattering. When she spoke again, it was with a grim tone. "You aren't really under control, are you?"

"No," Faye admitted.

The balloon continued to rise, silent except for the automatic blasts of the burner.

There was a pause, a slight sound, and then Faye felt something cold and hard being pressed against her temple. "You almost had me for a moment. But let me clarify things for you. I owe my friend many things, not only my career but also for putting a stop to my sonofabitch stepfather visiting me in my room at night.

"If he says he wants you dead, it's the least I can do. Now, I think we're high enough and far enough from the airport that no one will connect your body with my flight.

"Step out of the basket, lady."

"And if I refuse?"

"I'll blow a hole in your skull and dump you out myself."

Faye's hand slapped the barrel of the gun away from her temple; the weapon flew silently into the night. "A bit of advice," she observed mildly. "Never let the person you intend to shoot get within arm's reach of your gun—especially if she knows kung fu."

Faye found Flower's hand in the dark—it wasn't far from where it had been when it held the gun. She grabbed it, twisted it the wrong way, and forced Flowers to drop to her knees in front of her.

A piercing pain in her shin caused her to let go of Flowers' hand. "Ow!" she cried, jerking back into the side of the basket. Flowers had bitten her. The newswoman quickly regained her feet, punching Faye in the chin. Faye's head was knocked back but she moved forward and slammed her knee into Flowers' midsection. The woman doubled over and Faye thumped her on the back of the neck with both fists. Flowers wavered, falling back into the far side of the basket, groaning.

"You don't have to do this!" Faye cried. "We don't have to be enemies. The *real* enemy is the person who told you to do this! Together, we can stop him!"

Audrey Flowers was an ambitious, unscrupulous woman whose only loyalty seemed to be to herself, her career and the mysterious man who had made it all possible, yet Faye was reluctant to kill the newswoman. It didn't seem as if it would solve any of her problems. Faye wanted to get out of this game. It would not help her to kill Audrey, because then she would have to kill the next threat, and the next, and the one after that—until, finally, inevitably, she failed and they killed *her*.

There *had* to be a better way.

She had to have something, *something* that she could use to barter for her freedom. Money, certainly, would not do the trick. Merely promising to keep quiet about the mine didn't seem like it would be effective, either. Barrow had warned her that it would have been cleared out by the time she could tell authorities it was there. Besides, it seemed likely that the authorities *did* know about it—or that the voices there *were*, in fact, authorities of some sort...at some level.

One person swearing she'd discovered a hidden base of the global elite, the people responsible for wars and famine and, for all she knew, the heartbreak of psoriasis, was only going to make her seem crazy. In fact, the more she continued to consider, the more she realized that it wasn't her knowing about their base that made her a threat to them at all.

Perhaps she could figure out the answer by looking back further. When had the killing started? That was with Marvin, and she was pretty sure it had been related to the web site. Even Robert's arrest had seemed to be aimed at keeping her from keeping the web site actively supplied with new T-shirt designs, though the laptop Robert had gotten her had enabled her to keep it up nonetheless.

Flowers, still groaning, struggled to rise; Faye kicked her in the head and she slumped back onto the floor of the basket. Faye continued her search for a solution. What was the T-shirt that had triggered the interest of the Elite? Almost certainly, the one with the list of Meany's illegal campaign contributors, though another popular one had been the one with the latitude and longitude of Meany's Mexican marijuana farm.

Maybe it *was* that the T-shirts really gave her a voice. If the global elite monopolized the media, as Marvin had proven—that included TV, radio, records, greeting cards, every way that people had of communicating to a large segment of the population—they would guard that monopoly jealously.

With a sudden flash of insight, Faye could imagine how the Internet must have been an unexpected blow to the elite. They would *have* to shut it down, or find a way to limit its freedom. Claiming it was somehow a threat to the well being of children, or a potential tool of terrorism, might serve their purpose. Until then, Faye's website not only was an unfettered voice for truth—it was an example to others what could be done.

No wonder they were willing to kill her to shut it down!

But Faye was unwilling to let them get away with this scheme. All she had to do was to become a bigger threat to them dead than alive.

She lifted her blouse and pulled the huge pistol from her waistband.

It's weight surprised her every time she lifted it, and this was no exception. Edwin had said she couldn't hit a bull in the ass with a bass fiddle. She intended to prove him wrong. Directly over her, occluding most of the sky, was the Channel 2 news balloon. She pointed the gun straight up and pulled the trigger. Six times.

Six times there was an explosive sound; six times a yellow flash of fire. She knew those bullets were tearing through the delicate fabric that kept the light, hot air in and the heavy, cool air out.

When the gun was empty she let it fall into the night. She never wanted to see it again.

The shots had deafened her, but as her hearing returned she heard Audrey Flowers struggling to her feet, and then the sound of the propane heater on full blast. It was no use. The balloon did not drop like a rock, but it was definitely losing altitude.

"She's coming down fast, you crazy bitch!" the newswoman whimpered, banging on the side of the propane heater as if to make it burn hotter.

They drifted north; and the buttes of the Cave Creek area were close enough to blot out large sections that would otherwise be neatly lit by streetlights. Audrey began throwing things out of the basket, but there wasn't enough to help. The balloon itself now seemed smaller from Faye's point of view, though she knew it was just becoming taller and thinner. And, more to the point, less buoyant.

The propane burner couldn't keep up. Faye realized they would not clear the next butte.

"*Listen* to me, Audrey! I have a message for your boss! I hope you take cues well, but I want you to repeat it word for word."

"You bitch, I don't have to listen to you!" the newswoman cried, cowering.

"This is important!" Faye insisted. "Your friend will *really want* to know this!"

That stopped the newswoman, at least for a moment. "What is it?"

Faye swallowed hard. "The message has two parts. First, since your boss and his friends started messing with me, they've lost Selma Graves, Carvel Meany, several soldiers in their underground base, the usefulness of that underground base, and the usefulness of FBI Agent Desmond Barrow. I've lost one friend, but since my friends and I don't fear death, that's not an issue.

"So here's a warning. Mess with me, and you're asking for more trouble than you can handle." That last was a bluff, of course, but Faye said it with conviction.

"Second, when I die, whenever that may be and whatever the cause, I have programmed instructions that will cause information to be made public that would prove *very embarrassing* to your bosses. That includes the exact location of Meany's marijuana farm and his connections to alcohol and drug interests. Exactly *which* individuals at those companies made those donations. And then there are the photos I took of the soldiers in the underground base before my friend shot the lights out."

At this, Flowers laughed, though it wasn't a merry sound. "A fat lot of good that will do. People like me will never broadcast it. Newspapers will never print it. You're no threat at all."

"Thanks to you, I've learned my lesson about TV and newspapers," Faye admitted. "No, when I fail to input a certain password one day to my web site, all that information will be made public *there*. And I get thousands and thousands of hits every day. You thought people started asking questions before? Try facing the wrath of a truly informed public!"

There was a sudden lurch and a snapping sound as a corner of the basket hit the pinnacle of a butte. Faye hadn't seen it coming. Flowers screamed. The butte receded-and again they were drifting downward. The basket seemed to be hanging from three corners; the fourth angled toward the ground like a teapot about to pour.

"It sounds like you're offering a deal," Flowers suggested, her voice shaking.

"Sure, if you want to call it that," Faye agreed. "Leave me alone or my proof goes public."

And now, looming ahead in the darkness was another butte. Faye estimated they would pass no more than ten feet over it.

There was no more than a five-second window. Using the flexibility and strength she'd learned from Marian, she lifted herself and sat on the rim of the basket; then, grabbing the rim with her hands, did a backward roll into the night.

She came down on the butte's rocky surface and skidded a few feet on the loose gravel before coming to a stop. With the loss of weight, the balloon sprang higher into the air, then again resumed its hasty descent. Faye quickly lost sight of it and Audrey's screams faded with it into the darkness.

On the desert floor below the butte, Faye could see what looked like a campfire. Around it were the figures of men. *An Indian tribe?* she wondered. *Well, whatever...*

She half-climbed, half-slid down the butte and walked towards the campfire. The men around it were not dancing as she thought Indians might, just sitting and standing and, apparently, drinking from cans of something. *Oh, oh,* Faye thought. Had she dropped, literally, from the frying pan into the fire? Who *were* these men, and what might they do to her?

Still, she needed their help. "Hello!" she called. Several turned to look at her, and, shocked, she realized that they were all naked.

But they didn't seem to mind her intrusion. "Hi!" one of them, a very heavy man with a moustache and beard responded. "You seem to be out late without a light."

"I just fell out of a hot air balloon," she confessed, feeling foolish.

"Oh, sure," said the man.

"Say, look at this!" another man interrupted. "She's banged up and bleeding. Hang on a minute." He ducked into a pup tent and returned with a first aid kit. "Did you really fall out of a balloon?"

"I did," Faye said ruefully. "I wouldn't kid about a thing like that."

"My name is Sandy," the man told her, "and I have a certification in first aid from the Red Cross so you're in good hands."

"I appreciate your kindness," she told Sandy, as he applied ointment to her scratches. "But, I have to ask. Why are you all undressed?"

"We're ANDES," the heavy man watching over Sandy's shoulder explained.

"Andies?" Faye replied. "You mean, you're all named Andy? What does that have to—"

"No, no!" the heavy man laughed good-naturedly. "ANDES. The Arizona Nude Dudes."

"We're a gay men's nudist club," Sandy added.

"Really!" Faye cried, relieved. "Do you know my friends Chuck and Dave from Sun City? They're gay," she added.

"No," said the big man. "Can't say we do. But, you know, all gay men don't know each other. It's not like there's a central membership list, or anything."

"No, of course not," Faye agreed, embarrassed.

"But that doesn't mean we can't walk you out of here and give you a ride back home," the big man continued.

"In the morning," Sandy clarified. "It's about two miles to the road from here, and we were just about to hit the sack. You're welcome to use my sleeping bag," he added. "I have an extra blanket, and I'll just lay out by the fire."

A Fond Farewell

Saturday, February 14, 1998

"Happy Valentine's Day, darling!" Marian cried cheerfully, as she hugged Faye at Faye's front door.

"Happy Valentine's to you, too," Faye replied, giving her friend a hearty hug back. "Who's that in the car with you?" Faye could see that someone was in Marian's car, but could not make out who it was.

"I'll tell you in a minute. First, though, how are you doing? The bruises look like they're coming along nicely."

"I have a great doctor," Faye grinned. "And, yes, I'm actually feeling pretty good. At least, no one tried to kill me yesterday,"

"That's always a good sign," Marian agreed.

"So, who's your friend?"

"Well, darling, that's kind of what I came to tell you about. You know, I want to make a clean break."

"I know, Marian," Faye said understandingly. "I'm just so grateful you showed up when you did."

"It's amazing, sometimes, how things work out. But it's really time for me to move on. You're more than capable of taking over the Sun City operation for me. There are other places for me to go, other people for me to help. It's a big world filled with slaves, and I can free the largest number of them by staying in a spot just long enough to get a club going, and then moving on."

Faye's heart sank. "You're really leaving?"

Marian nodded with regret. "I'm afraid so, darling. And as far as most people are concerned, I'm just going to drop out of sight."

"I hope you'll at least send a postcard now and then," Faye begged.

"Better than that, I'll send e-mail," the older woman grinned. "For the time being, at least, it's harder to trace."

"Send e-mail? *You?*" Faye laughed. "But you're the one who swore she'd never touch a computer!"

"Well, I have someone to do that for me," Marian admitted. "I want you to meet him, and I want you to promise not to scream or make any unusual sounds or expressions. You never know who's watching."

Faye stared at Marian. "What is he, a Martian? A former president? You can't be serious."

"I'm very serious. Promise." Faye promised, and Marian led her through her front door and to Marian's car. When Faye had a good look at Marian's passenger, it took all her willpower not to scream.

Or laugh.

It was Marvin.

Or, more precisely, it was Marvin, with his perennial five-o'clock shadow, wearing a blonde woman's wig and a dress.

"Oh, my God," Faye breathed softly. "You, too? How can you be alive?"

"How could I *not* be?" the author challenged. "As paranoid as I am, did ya think I wouldn't have a fuckin' *bomb shelter?*"

"You mean—?"

"Of course. The moment that truck hit my house, I dove into the shelter and sealed the hatch. I spent the next two weeks in there, laughin' my ass off. Free at last, I kept sayin'. God almighty, I'm free at last!"

"So you were—"

Marvin nodded. "Hiding out while you were in that mine."

"When I got home, and slept in my bed that night," Marian explained, "I had no idea Marvin was sleeping in my guest room. I almost had a heart attack the next morning when I found him there. In fact, that was one of the reasons I decided this was really the time to make my exit. I figured we could pull two vanishing acts for the price of one."

"Doodlebug put me in a motel, after that, 'cause she figgered the cops would be checkin' out her house—and she was right."

Faye stepped back and said, critically, "So...what's with the dress?"

Marvin frowned grumpily, and Marian replied, "It's just until we get out of town. I didn't want anyone to recognize him."

"You could probably get better fashion sense from Dave," Faye suggested.

"No!" Marian warned. "No one must know, Faye. We're sharing this secret with you, only."

"I finally did read your book, Marvin," Faye told him. "I thought it was brilliant. Disturbing, but brilliant."

"Thanks!" Marvin grinned, something Faye had rarely seen him do. "Doodlebug told me what you been through, the deal you made with those bastards," he said. "You have real balls, Pixie. But you need *real* evidence, stuff to nail those guys."

"I don't know how to get that kind of evidence," Faye admitted. "And I don't want to spend my golden years playing Nancy Drew. I'd really rather get really good at growing pot, getting it to people who need it, and maybe putting a new T-shirt on-line every now and then, just to keep interest in the web site going strong."

"That's fine," Marvin assured her. "But just be aware, I e-mailed you copies of info I dug up that's really hot. There are pictures, affidavits, secret reports, everything. Some funny stuff going on in Florida regarding elections—too soon to see where it's going but they're about to remove several thousand Democratic voters from the roles. Somethin's goin' down with the next election, seems to me. Anyway, you keep this info, you drop a hint if, you have to, that you got it. Keep it on your mirrored web sites, trig-gered to display if you don't log in, like you tol' Flowers—and you'll stay safe."

Faye leaned over and gave him a kiss on his bristly cheek. "Thanks for that," she said. "You're right, that's just what I need for insurance. I don't know if the answer to the world's problems is exposing the elite—I think Marian's suggestion, to ignore them, is a better solution."

Marvin thumped his fist on the car window frame. "With the right leader, we could overthrow the mothers!"

Faye shook her head. "We will never find peace through a leader," she smiled. "But someday, we *will* find it when we stop relying on leaders and create our *own* peace. We will never become informed listening to media that tells us what it wants us to hear but we *will* become informed when each of us makes it our business to learn.

"And we will never find God through religion, but each of us *will* find God within ourselves...when we decide to look."

A New Acolyte

Wednesday, April 20, 1998

Faye looked in on her babies, as she called them. In their womb of light, nutrients, and moisture, they were growing like, well, weeds. There were three crops growing at once; each couple of months she harvested one and recycled the others.

Realizing she was nearly out of plant food, she closed the door to her secret grow room and drove to Home Depot, mentally ticking off her day's schedule: Deliver prescriptions to two of Robert's patients; look in on Vera, who had broken a toe the week before and was still uncomfortable; dress for a date at a comedy club in Tempe with Robert. Oh, yes, and add a new T-shirt design Marian had sent her to the web site. She was wearing the design, a simple one: "God Doesn't Take Sides."

She had no idea where Marian and Marvin were living, except that there were high mountains nearby—she could tell that much from the photo they had attached. Faye suspected it might actually be Pend Oreille County, or somewhere near there. But it didn't matter. Marian was as near as Faye's computer keyboard, and that was surprisingly satisfying because, in addition to that, she knew where to find Marian in her heart.

She hadn't seen Norma since that night before Robert's pre-trial hearing, but she had sensed the woman's presence several times. Sometimes she wondered if Norma were, in fact, a ghost or spirit. Then she remembered she had seen her eat and drink. Whichever it was, Faye would never think about death the same way again. After all those years of thinking one was either dead or alive, in the way that a light is either on or off, she had developed an entirely new way of looking at it.

Life and death were more like a dimmer switch, she thought, as she walked past the electrical fixtures in the lighting section. A person could range from being fully conscious, as Norma was, and as Faye aspired to be, to states where one was breathing but not thinking at all. Paradoxically, it seemed to her that a spirit like Norma was far more alive than any number of people who were, oh, say, passionately involved in crusades for or against abortion or gay marriage or this war or that election simply because their favorite pundits had taken a stand and it was easier to become caught up in the sound bites than to think for oneself.

Faye found the plant food she was looking for, but, lost in thought, she nearly crashed into another shopper. Faye began to apologize, then recognized the woman. "Michelle!" she cried. "Michelle Worthington!"

"Oh, my!" the woman replied. "Faye McRae! I read about you around Christmastime, in the papers. How are you doing? Did it work out okay? I know your doctor friend went to trial for murder, but I don't recall hearing how that worked out."

"It worked out fine," Faye assured her, and gave her a quick rundown of the official version of the story. There was no point, she thought, of including the facts that Michelle's husband and son had both been murdered. If the opportunity ever came up, she might be able to feed Michelle information in a way that would enable Michelle to come to those conclusions on her own. Besides, she looked terrible. Michelle had put on weight, and the unflattering muumuu she was wearing didn't help any.

Instead, Faye asked Michelle how she was holding up. "Barely," the woman confessed. "I'm so tired I don't know what to do. Look at me; I've put on twenty-five pounds since Brian's death." She grinned ruefully. "Sometimes, a half gallon of Rocky Road is all that gets me through the day."

Faye hugged the woman. "Please, give me a call if you ever need to talk," she said. "You still have my number?"

"I do," Michelle replied.

"All right, then. You be well, dear. And call me."

"I will." She started to roll away, but her too-long dress became entangled with the rear wheel of her basket, and Faye took a moment to help her untangle it.

They parted, with Faye feeling as if she should, somehow, do more. Michelle reminded her of herself before Marian saved her.

On her way to the cash register, Faye passed a shelving section and, on impulse, added some five-foot metal posts, brackets, and shelves to her basket. She'd been thinking a few shelves would make a nice addition to her living room. She'd been thinking of displaying the photo of Marian and Marvin. No one would know it had been taken recently.

She allowed the cashier to ring up her items and paid in cash, then wheeled her cart into the parking lot. One of those booming cars was nearby, playing rap music that not even pot could help Faye appreciate. The pavement vibrated with the over-amplified bass beat.

The sound was coming from a red convertible. Faye was annoyed to see that the driver wasn't even looking where she was going— she was reading the display of a cellular phone, and trying to dial it. Neither hand was on the wheel, yet the vehicle was in motion.

Instinctively, Faye looked ahead to make sure the convertible wasn't about to hit anything. Instead, she spotted a forklift about thirty feet from her, trundling across the pavement with a load of building supplies headed to a customer's truck. To Faye's horror, she realized that the load was positioned directly in front of the forklift operator, obscuring his view. The two vehicles were on a collision course. But what froze Faye's heart in mid-beat was the realization that Michelle Worthington was standing at the spot at which the two vehicles were about to collide—and her dress, again, seemed to be caught in the faulty wheel of her shopping cart.

Michelle couldn't move, and was shouting and waving one hand in a "Stop!" motion, but she couldn't be heard by either driver. In a moment she would be crushed unless someone did something.

Faye acted without thinking. She grabbed one of the shelving posts and hurled it like a javelin at the forklift. Faye didn't wait for the makeshift javelin to complete its journey before she hurled the second one at the convertible. The sound of the first metal post clanging into the metal frame of the forklift caused the operator to stop to investigate. The second post bounced off the convertible's hood, making enough of an impact for the driver to look up, spot Michelle, and jam on her brakes.

Faye sprinted the distance separating them and helped Michelle extricate her skirt from the wheel of her basket.

"You saved my life!" Michelle cried, close to tears.

"I'm so glad I was here to help a friend." After taking a moment to lambaste the driver of the convertible for not looking where she was going, Faye helped Michelle push her basket to her own car.

When they had reached it, Michelle sighed heavily. "I feel so worthless," she said, hiding her eyes. "I couldn't have done what you just did. Throw? Run? Look at me! I'm nothing but a fat pig."

"You don't have to be," Faye pointed out. "You could watch what you eat and exercise. I used to be much heavier than you, but with the right food and activity, I shaped up. I feel better, better than I have in forty years."

"I wouldn't even know where to begin," Michelle complained. "I've always been overweight, but the depression since Kenny's and Brian's deaths has just been so overwhelming..."

Faye gave her a hug, patting her back. "I know, I know," she said. "Remember, I've been there, too. But, if you *want* to turn things around—well, I'd love to help you."

"You? Would help me?"

Faye smiled. "Call it paying it forward," she said. "The woman who helped me turn my life around is...is gone, now. The best way to pay her back is to help someone else as she helped me."

Michelle found a handkerchief in her purse and blew her nose noisily. "I would be so grateful!" she said.

"You'd have to work," Faye warned. "Changing your life takes real effort and dedication."

"To be like you?" Michelle said, in awe. "It would be so worth it, if it's possible!"

"It is possible," Faye promised. "Give me a call when you get home, and we'll talk about setting up a schedule for working out."

"Working out? You mean, at a gym?"

"Exactly. Don't worry. We'll make it happen!"

Michelle got into her car and started the engine. Faye stepped back to give her room to back out of her parking space, but Michelle rolled down her window. "Faye—you're an angel, a real angel!" she said.

"Darling, we all are," Faye responded, smiling.

She turned on her heel and sashayed away.

"When one smokes marijuana,
one's eyes become bloodshot,
one's appetite increases,
one's mouth becomes dry,
and one becomes mildly euphoric.
To eliminate the redness, use eye drops.
To eliminate the increase in appetite,
have a healthy, nutritious snack.
To eliminate the dryness of the mouth,
drink some pure, cool water.
To eliminate the mild euphoria,
scrutinize the government."

Molly Dowd, née Marian Higgins,
at the Government Complicity Protest,
on the Site of the former World Trade Center
September 11, 2006

"A little patience and we shall see
the reign of witches pass over,
their spells dissolve,
and the people,
recovering their true sight,
restore their government
to it's true principles.
It is true that in the meantime
we are suffering deeply in spirit,
and incurring the horrors of a war
and long oppressions
of enormous public debt ...
If the game runs sometimes
against us at home
we must have patience till luck turns,
and then we shall have
an opportunity of winning back
the principles we have lost,
for this is a game
where principles are at stake.
Better luck, therefore, to us all;
and health happiness, & friendly
salutations to yourself."

Thomas Jefferson, 1798,
after passage of the Sedition Act.